Excuse Me for Asking

Also by Janis Arnold

Daughters of Memory

JANIS ARNOLD

EXCUSE ME
for ASKING

A NOVEL

ALGONQUIN BOOKS OF CHAPEL HILL

1994

Published by
ALGONQUIN BOOKS OF CHAPEL HILL
Post Office Box 2225
Chapel Hill, North Carolina 27515-2225

a division of
WORKMAN PUBLISHING COMPANY, INC.
708 Broadway
New York, New York 10003

This is a work of fiction. Names, characters, places, and incidents
are either the product of the author's imagination or are used
fictitiously. Any resemblance to actual events or locales or persons,
living or dead, is entirely coincidental.

LIBRARY OF CONGRESS CATALOGING-IN-PUBLICATION DATA

Arnold, Janis
  Excuse me for asking : a novel / by Janis Arnold.—1st ed.
    p. cm.
  ISBN 1-56512-057-4
  1. City and town life—Texas—Fiction. 2. Friendship—Texas—
Fiction. 3. Family—Texas—Fiction. 4. Women—Texas—Fiction.
I.Title.
  PS3551.R4847E95 1994
  813'.54—dc20

                                                94-25655
                                                CIP

10 9 8 7 6 5 4 3 2 1
FIRST EDITION

Many thanks to my editor Robert A. Rubin, whose talents and assistance were invaluable to me during the writing of this book.

I am deeply grateful to Joyce Armstrong Carroll and Edward E. Wilson, whose enthusiasm and encouragement inspired me in countless ways.

I also want to thank: Verna Alvis and the late Dr. Milton E. Alvis, for all that they taught me about life and love; Gary and Liz Baird, for friendship, laughter, and shared addictions; my son's pediatrician, Dr. Henry Lipsitt, for answering my questions; and my husband, Steve, for his endless patience, as well as for the scenes from his memories that have made their way into my books.

once again,
for Steve and Will,
with love

Excuse Me for Asking

PROLOGUE

VERONA

First thing I did that September of 1951, the day my daughter was born, was get up and look out the window of my bathroom. From my bathroom I could see the French doors that lead out from our den to what's now the patio that our house is sort of U-shaped around. However, at that time, it was just a backyard planted with St. Augustine grass. The patio didn't get put in until the year Julia turned eight.

From out the window I noticed Hattie already had two loads of washing out hanging in the sun. Julia was over two weeks overdue and I was sick to death of the wait. I knew if I had to go waddling around as big as the side of a barn much longer I would go stark raving mad. Summer in Texas is no time to be pregnant. I stared out the bathroom window. *Going to be hot again today,* I told myself. *Get yourself here,* I said to the child inside me, *we might as well get this show on the road.* I'd taken to talking to her already. Already she wasn't listening to me. Staring out the window, I kept looking to see a red Ford truck parked in our driveway. Not that a red truck in our driveway was likely, but sometimes I scared the daylights out of myself with the thought that it was sitting there, in broad daylight, for all the world to see.

Butch was on the bus he caught every morning at 7:20 to ride up to school. And Tom, who had been out of the house as usual before sunup, wouldn't be home for coffee before 9:30 at the earliest. So when I turned from the window and started down the hall and sensed someone in the bedroom with me, I screamed out loud. It scared me so bad I'm surprised I didn't go into labor right then and there.

"Calm down, it's me," said Tom.

"What are you doing home?"

"I thought I ought to stick around the house today. I'm the one who is going to drive you to the hospital."

JULIA WAS BORN two weeks and one day past her due date. She weighed eight pounds exactly, was twenty-one inches long, and had my eyes and no hair to speak of. Her father said to me, "Verona you have just produced the most beautiful baby in the world." Butch took on over her much as you might have expected a ten-year-old to take on over a new puppy. Hattie, our housekeeper, allowed as how Julia did have a pair of lungs on her. She was a pretty child, no denying that. But every old hen thinks her chick is the fairest, I reminded myself. I wasn't going to fall into that trap.

TOM

Verona explained to me that Julia was pretty from the minute she was born because, unlike the other babies in the nursery, she was a caesarean birth and did not arrive all wrinkled and compressed. She definitely was not your typical red squalling infant. She had these big brown eyes that she opened right up and stared straight into my eyes with. She was so solemn and watchful. "Gonna be tall," said my mother. "Like all my grandkids."

"She's got my eyes," Verona said. They were similar, but

Julia's eyes aren't Verona's. Verona has eyes so dark you can't read them. Julia's eyes I can read like books. My daughter's eyes are richer and softer than her mother's.

I held Julia and whispered in her ear, "This is your daddy, sweetheart, whatever you want in this world Daddy is going to get it for you." I'm not a religious man, but the day my daughter was born I found myself praying to God. *Thank You for being so good to me,* I said.

Butch was in the hospital with us. They have a rule about who goes on the maternity floor. No children under fourteen. Butch, who was ten and tall for his age, didn't get questioned but once. One of the battle-ax nurses said something the night we brought Verona in. "How old is that child?" she asked.

"My son is fourteen years old," I said to her.

"Daddy, suppose she finds out you are lying," Butch whispered to me. "I can wait downstairs."

"The hell you will."

The battle-ax met my stare and wilted. It certainly wasn't like Butch was going to be running up and down the halls disturbing the tranquillity of the new mothers.

"Want to hold your baby sister?" I asked Butch.

BUTCH

"Sure, Dad," I said. Julia was the first baby I ever held but I don't remember feeling nervous. I put my little finger in her fist, I sort of pried her fingers open and then, once she had my finger inside her tiny baby fist and was gripping onto it for all she was worth, I looked at her and noticed she was looking right back at me. Julia acted like she knew me already.

"Wow," I said to my dad.

"Wow is right," he said. "We got ourselves a keeper here."

SUSIE

"Don't worry about my little sister, you are going to love her," Butch said to me the night he took me home to meet his parents. Julia was out on a date—she was sixteen at the time—so I didn't meet her until the next day when I had Sunday lunch with the Salwell family.

I cannot remember exactly what I expected, but I can tell you it was not the Julia Salwell I got to meet. First off, she looks nothing like her brother. My husband, Butch, has sandy brown hair and hazel eyes and is tall and slightly portly. He has ruddy red skin which freckles easily.

The only way Julia resembles Butch is the two of them are both tall. Other than that you'd never take them to be related. Julia has an olive complexion, huge brown eyes, and thick straight brown hair, with legs so long that the first thing you think when you see her is she could be a model.

But the big difference between Julia and Butch is the way they act. Butch bends over backwards not to make waves—he is overwhelmingly kind and considerate. Julia runs around looking for something or someone to stir up. She appears to be averse to tranquillity. Not that she's a bad person, but she *is* different.

The night my first son was born one of the things I remember Butch saying is, "This one doesn't have the grip Julia had."

"He's got your eyes, Butch, sky blue, just look at them."

"Yeah. You know, Susie, Julia had the biggest, brownest eyes."

I thought at the time Butch kept on comparing our baby to

Julia because Julia was the only baby Butch had ever been around. But two years later when we had the second one, Eugene got compared to Julia as well.

"Look, Eugene's got the same little chin Thomas has," my mother noticed.

"Eugene has got his daddy's eyes," I pointed out.

"Cute kid," Butch said.

"Is that all you can say?" I teased him. Butch isn't a talker.

"Well, you know, I think Julia's head was barely wobbly at all," he said.

ROBIN

The first time I saw Julia, she was wearing her brother's shirt and a pair of cutoff jeans. She wasn't wearing any makeup, although there were bottles and tubes of Clinique cosmetics all around the counter near the sink, and the cigarette butts in the ashtray beside her bed had bright lipstick smears on them. *She's gorgeous,* I thought, and I felt this sinking sensation. Flashy gorgeous girls and I don't have the first thing in common. I figured she was going to hate me.

Julia covered the receiver of the phone with her hand. "Hi, that's your bed under the pile of clothes. You can just shove them anywhere. I'll be off in a minute."

I made five trips up and down the stairs, tiptoeing in and out of the room, stacking my belongings in a neat little pile off to one side of the door. Each time I walked back into the room, she rolled her eyes at me as if she expected me to share her chagrin at whoever she was in the process of giving hell to.

Several minutes after my last trip she was finally off the phone. "Don't you just hate mothers?" she asked me. The two girls from down the hall who had taken pity on me and helped me with the last several loads were just walking out the door. I didn't know what to say to her. *If I had one I might,* I guess I could have answered.

This was the first—definitely not the last—time that something Julia said left me speechless. The next thing she said was on the same order. "God, you must be smart," she said, staring at the books spilling out of one of the boxes that had split open when I dropped it on the cement floor. "It never occurred to me to bring books to college!"

AUNT KATE

After Robin left for college all I heard was Julia this and Julia that. From the sound of things the two of them spent all the time out in Julia's car driving around. "Don't you girls ever study?" I asked Robin.

"After 9:00. We have to be in the dorm by 9:00 P.M."

"Robin Tilton, you are always in bed by 10:00."

"Not now that I am in college," she told me.

I couldn't wait to meet this Julia.

PART I

JULIA

Undoubtedly, it was a dream that woke me up. I have this love-hate thing with dreams. They're not all frightening. Some, such as the dream I had when I was maybe ten years old, I like. I remember going to bed mad as anything at Verona and dreaming during the night that she was a wizarded old box turtle with scars on her back. Somehow or another she'd gotten herself stuck upside down and her scabby legs were frantically clawing the air. I saw her and smiled, taking my time before I reached down and picked her up by her shell and sat her back on her feet. "Get on your way and see that you don't get yourself in this fix again. You can't count on me always being around to bail you out," I said to her. In my dream, I could have taken a bat and squashed her flat. But I didn't. I am not, at heart, a vindictive person.

The dream that woke me up had something to do with my mother. Now that I'm out of college and on my own, she's trying to take over my life again. I sat up in bed and listened to the echo of her voice in the room around me. Yesterday, on the phone, when Verona called me to make sure I was coming home for the weekend, right from the first *hello Julia this is your mother,* I could feel myself starting to get angry. My stomach sort of clutches in on itself and I feel itchy, like I've gotten myself into the poison ivy. Likely as not, I'll catch myself tossing my head from one side to the other.

"What time can I expect you Friday evening?" Mother asked me. Maybe I'm wrong, but it seems to me that every time she calls to ask me questions like this, she has her pen poised to note down my answer: *10:00 A.M. Thursday morning. Julia says no but means yes.*

"I'm not coming home this weekend, Mother."

Dead silence. I hate her silences, mainly because I can never outlast them. "I am not coming home for the weekend. I have stuff to do here, Mother," I said.

"Your father will be disappointed, and I'd thought maybe you and I could do some shopping," she said to me. The part about my father was a crock. My father would be down at the coast fishing if he had his way.

"Put him on the phone, I'll tell him why I can't come," I said.

This was a Thursday, the day after my 6:00 P.M. Wednesday evening session with Helen, my therapist. "You don't have to explain everything you do, you're a grown woman now." Those were Helen's words. I repeated them to myself but I had a hard time living by them.

"Julia, it's after lunch, you know good and well your daddy is laying down taking his nap."

That might have been the truth. Daddy did like to lie down after lunch. "Sorry, Mom, you're on your own, don't count on me, I have tons to do myself," I said.

I hung up before she said another word and started getting the material together for the "Mystery Man Mr. Watts" presentation I had scheduled at 2:00. That is my job right now—I teach little kids all about electricity. I have three talks I do, one for the preschoolers, one for grades one and two, and one for the third- and fourth-graders. As for the older children, someone who presumably understands electricity a lot better than I do takes over.

This is my best job to date although if I don't start getting more sleep I don't know how on earth I am going to hang on to it. Getting up at seven in the morning when you've tossed and turned half the night is no picnic.

I only lasted a week as a management trainee for Foley's. Actually, since the first day was entirely given over to orientation, you could say I only lasted three working days. Thursday of that first week I left for lunch and didn't go back. They had me down in linens counting sheets so I could "learn the merchandise," when the thought occurred to me that I hadn't gone to college for four years to count sheets. Not that I didn't learn something from that job. I learned that enjoying shopping and working in a store aren't anywhere close to the same thing.

After my brief sojourn at Foley's I found a job working for an insurance company, where I was employed for almost two months. Sallie, my boss (Data Processing Supervisor was her title), told me the first week I was there that she would be grooming me to take over her position when she made vice-president. "Julia, you remind me of my daughter," she said to me. I don't see how, I met her daughter and we are nothing alike.

Looking back, I think I was flattered by the idea that I could become a supervisor and have an office with people running in and out of it asking me questions, because I remember feeling sort of excited by her words. What I did at that job was read insurance policies and rate them according to a numerical system I must say I never entirely understood. After I put the numbers on the little sheets I attached to the front of the folders, I passed them on to the keypunch department.

My title was Coding Clerk; there were four of us coding clerks. Our desks were shoved together into a square so we could confer. Tammy, who had been with the company for three years, was the expert. All you had to do was call out the first paragraph of a policy and she'd let fly back at you a string of numbers. I don't know how she did that. I guess I'm not cut out to work with numbers. I couldn't seem to remember them from one day to the next. My last day on the job I don't know whose voice it was that I heard—it wasn't mine, that's for sure—but someone or something was telling me it was time for a career change. *Julia this job is not for you.* I picked up my purse and walked into Sallie's office. "Sallie," I said to her, "no offense, but I'm just not cut out for the insurance business."

"Sit down, Julia, let's talk about this," she said to me.

I sat down in the chair across from her desk.

"Have you already had your donut?" she asked.

One of the perks of the insurance job was donuts and coffee or soft drinks in the morning. After over a month of gobbling down free donuts I couldn't button half of my skirts. I tried to explain to Sallie that I could not envision myself supervising something I hadn't come close to catching on to after two months of doing it day in and day out, but I don't think she understood what I was saying to her. Eventually the only thing left for me to do was stand up and say, "Well, I really have to go. Thank you so much for everything."

Her jaw dropped. "You're leaving now?" she asked me.

"That's the way I am—once I make a decision, I like to act on it," I told her.

"Julia, what on earth will you do? What about your living expenses?"

That is when it dawned on me that Sallie was worried about me. Somehow I had never gotten around to telling her my parents were subsidizing me until I got on my feet and right then did not appear to be the time to get into that subject. "Don't worry, Sallie, I'll find a job that suits me better," I assured her.

"You be sure and use me for a reference," Sallie told me. She followed me all the way down the hall as I left. "I could never live with myself if I thought you were somewhere out in Houston trying to find work and having a hard time doing so," she said. I was at the door to the parking lot by then. She looked like she was fixing to cry.

"Don't worry, Sallie. I'll be fine," I reassured her. She hugged me once more and that was it, I was unemployed again.

"How is this going to look on your resume?" my former roommate Robin asked me when I told her what had happened. Ever since our freshman year at Texas Tech Robin has been the one of the two of us concerned with the rules. She gets that from growing up with her aunt Kate, the librarian, who is nice but a stickler.

Short little employment stints don't look bad if you don't write them down. When I filled out the application for my present job, under the space for previous employment, I wrote none. Which was true. I didn't have any experience remotely similar to the job I applied for. "Things like this have a way of coming back to haunt a person," Robin told me when I admitted to her what I had done.

"I'll cross that bridge when I come to it," I said to her. I reminded her of a boy we both knew who flunked out of Tech twice before he enrolled at ACC in Abilene. And he lied his head off on his application. He acted like he'd never been to college a day before in his life. Last I heard he was a semester away from a degree (finally), and expected to graduate cum laude with no one the wiser.

PROBABLY IT *WAS* a dream that woke me up.

I hate it, those nights when for no reason whatsoever I

awaken from a sound sleep and sit straight up in bed as wide-eyed as if it were the middle of the day. There's nothing worse than being wide awake when everyone else in the world is sound asleep.

The dream more than likely had something to do with food. Food is another thing I have a love-hate relationship with. I wish I was one of those people who eats when they're hungry but I'm not. I eat when I'm anxious. Like last night. This is what happened. I was supposed to meet Robin at Chorizo Pete's after work, but I called the school where she is teaching and talked to her during her lunch break. "Robin, I'm going to Cypress Springs tomorrow night so let's skip Chorizo Pete's," I said to her.

"Fine, do you want me to pick up something for us to eat on the way home?" she asked me.

"No, I'm not going to eat tonight, I'm going to vedge out. I'll call you when I get back Saturday or Sunday."

"Sure, have a good weekend," she said to me.

We're not roommates any longer although we do have apartments only one door apart. I thought it would be just the same between me and Robin but it isn't. Working is different from college. It is not nearly as much fun as college was. You can't just skip class and take the two points off your next test grade. Back in college, I didn't worry about how I'd feel the next day if I couldn't sleep. Actually, I didn't have a problem sleeping when I was in college.

I watch Mother like a hawk, trying to figure out how she does it. I hate the way she gets me to jump when she says froggy. That's why I have a therapist. One of the reasons anyway. I'm trying to figure out how Mother controls me so

I can stop letting her do it. The other reason I am seeing Helen is to figure out what I want to do with my life. Actually, I first went to Helen for vocational counseling. This was after I quit my insurance job and was depressed because it didn't look like I was ever going to have any fun again. "Go back to school and get your teaching license," my father said to me.

I might have been tempted if I hadn't known what Robin was going through. "You don't call it a teaching license, it's a certificate," I told my father.

"You never should have majored in English," my mother said to me. "I tried to tell you to take subjects you could do something with."

The thing was my mother was irritated at my father for continuing to pay my rent. She thought if I couldn't hold a job, I ought to move back home until I could.

I HAD TO take the bus home from work yesterday because my car was in the shop for new tires among other things. Daddy came down to Houston early yesterday morning and went with me to take it to the shop, which isn't but four blocks from where I live. I could have done it myself but he wanted to talk to the mechanic. "Who do you think took T-Birdie in when I lived in Lubbock?" I asked him.

"No one, I took care of your car every time you limped home for a vacation," he said. That is sort of true. I've gotten so used to Daddy looking after my car that I don't pay much attention to it. One time I pulled up to a station for gas and turned off the radio and rolled down the windows before I shut off the engine. I was appalled at how loud a clattering sound I was making.

"Check under the hood," I told the man who walked out from inside the Exxon station.

"Honey, I can already tell you you need oil in that bird," he said to me. I drive a Thunderbird, which I have had for six years. Daddy originally bought it for Mother. She only drove it about a week before she got tired of getting in and out of the front seat. Mother is a little portly and station wagons fit her better. Daddy offered to buy me a new car for graduation but I said, no, T-Birdie and I have a special relationship and I don't want a new car.

Gus, the Exxon man, was right. I was low on oil. He put in several quarts and sold me a case for the trunk. But I think gas station attendants who call their customers Honey ought to stop and listen to themselves. It sounds so common.

Daddy ran me on into work after we left my car but he couldn't hang around all day to cart me home. "Don't worry, I'll take the bus," I said to him.

"Well, be sure you sit up front next to the driver and watch your purse," he said to me.

"I always do," I said. I hadn't actually ridden the bus before but I didn't say that to him. He really would have worried.

The bus let me off at the Stop and Go on the corner of San Felipe and Chimney Rock. I hadn't planned to, but I went inside the store and walked over to the candy section. I bought a package of candy bars—six Milky Ways. I don't believe I had eaten a candy bar since high school. Robin and I never bought them. It wasn't on purpose, it was just that it never occurred to us to go out and get candy.

I put the candy on the coffee table in front of the couch and turned on the television. That's another thing that is different. I've started watching TV again. I sat down with a can of Dr. Pepper and a large glass of crushed ice. One habit I picked up in college is that I now drink my Dr. Peppers with crushed ice. We had an ice machine in the basement of the dorm. Since I've been in my apartment I've been using Mother's electric ice crusher.

The next thing I knew the candy bars were gone. All six of them. I barely remembered eating them. What happened afterwards was pure old reflex. This wave of nausea gripped me. A force strong as human hands grabbed onto my shoulders and shook me back and forth. I shut my eyes so I couldn't see the room start to spin. My whole body started to feel clammy and my stomach felt like it was turning itself inside out. I barely made it to the bathroom before my knees folded in on me. I knew I had to throw up so I put my finger down my throat. I think I cried a little, but maybe not. Maybe I imagined that part.

While I was there, on the tile floor, I noticed a spiderweb running from the back of the toilet to the corner of the bathtub. I could see the remains of the spider's last meal trapped in it. When I got the washcloth and the Comet to the bathroom, I wiped off the web, which was so fragile that I couldn't find a trace of it on the cloth once I'd gathered it up.

I HAD AN aunt, my mother's sister. I never saw her much, despite the fact that she has a daughter almost exactly my age. Back when my grandparents were alive Aunt Hilda and her three kids used to come for several weeks during the summer. They'd stay with my grandparents out on their farm. After Grandma and Grandpa were dead and buried, Aunt Hilda and Mother exchanged phone calls on each other's birthdays and sterile Christmas presents and that was it. We never saw them anymore.

I can't say as I miss my cousins. It's been years since I've been around them. However I do remember one summer, I couldn't have been over fourteen or so, when Aunt Hilda was telling me and Sumter (that's Aunt Hilda's daughter who is named after her grandmother on her father's side) about how she kept from putting on too many pounds. This was probably the fifth of July since on the Fourth we'd had the family reunion and every one of the grownups had eaten themselves silly. Aunt Hilda told us sometimes she just put her finger down her throat and made herself throw up. Aunt Hilda didn't act embarrassed even when her daughter and I screeched at her, "You do not!"

At the time Aunt Hilda was talking I thought to myself I could never ever do that, make myself throw up. But it wasn't too long after that conversation that I found myself with my own finger down my throat. Maybe it was Aunt Hilda who got me started. One thing that has occurred to me to wonder about: does Sumter do it too? If it weren't for the fact that I've never let anyone know about this habit I have, I'd call her up and ask her.

I haven't seen my cousin since before we graduated from high school. Even when it would have been easy to do so, I didn't make the effort. For instance, Robin and I were in San Antonio (which is where Aunt Hilda and her husband and their kids live) last February for our friend Marie's wedding. I didn't call Sumter to say "Hi what are you doing?" For all I know she's been in Houston and not called me. I heard from my mother, who learned it from Aunt Hilda during one of their twice-yearly phone calls, that Sumter had graduated summa cum laude from University of Texas and was coming home to live with her parents while she attended graduate school at Trinity. I am sure Sumter hasn't changed. If Mother and Aunt Hilda had gotten along, I'd probably keep up with her. But since they didn't, it never seemed like the thing for me to do either.

Marie, who went to college with Robin and me, got married last February after she spent all summer in school so she could graduate a semester early because both Donnie—that's the guy she married—and her parents thought it would be better if he married a college graduate. Not that she'll be looking for a job. Marie married Donnie for his money first of all and his looks second, and made no bones about it. She thought maybe she'd fall in love with him on the honeymoon.

"Have you mentioned to Donnie that you don't love him yet?" I asked Marie the day she showed up at the dorm flashing her two-carat diamond ring.

"Julia, don't be asinine," she said. "What kind of thing would that be to say to the man I plan to spend my life with?"

I didn't dare so much as meet Robin's eyes. I grabbed her by the arm, said, "Time to go, we gotta hit the books," and got us out of Marie and Kathy's room. Once we were back down the hall, in our own room, with the stereo belting out Janis Joplin for all she was worth, we started laughing and didn't stop until we were both limp.

I can't believe Marie went ahead and married a guy she wasn't in love with. That's all I could think about at her wedding last year. Money isn't everything. Doubtless she knows that by now.

VERONA

Julia was a difficult birth and a difficult child and I cannot say that she has gotten easier to any appreciable extent despite the fact that she is now twenty-three years old. I expect her to show up Friday night around dinnertime even though she told me not to look for her this weekend. She'll walk in the door, stumbling all over herself carrying in a basket of dirty laundry piled so high you'd never in a million years guess I spent a good four or five hours the previous Saturday doing her washing and ironing for her. I told her that I've a good mind to quit doing it, especially in light of the fact that Julia has this thing about 100 percent cotton. She won't wear anything else despite the fact that fabrics with even a hint of synthetic in them are infinitely easier to launder.

"She'd quit buying all these cotton shirts and slacks if she was the one ironing them," I mentioned to Essie as I was putting away the four cans of spray starch which I'll go through in less than a month keeping up with Julia. Essie is my housekeeper. When the children were younger I had Essie coming in every day of the week. Now she comes on Mondays and Fridays—Mondays to pick up after Julia, Fridays to get us in shape for the weekend. "You don't feel like coming in on Saturdays for a while, do you Essie?" I asked her. I knew I hadn't a prayer. Essie does not work for anyone on Saturdays. She has her five days filled and her Social Security has come in now and she's set. My guess is she's probably better off than half of those of us who pay her to clean.

I picked up the phone and called Susie, Butch's wife. "I'm getting the meat out to thaw, I need to know how many steaks to take out of the freezer," I said to her. Susie and Butch have been married for seven years. We'd about given up, his father and I had. Butch was twenty-seven years old when he finally married. There wasn't a person his age or reasonably younger not yet spoken for. Not out here in Cypress Springs, there wasn't.

By the time he brought Susie home, Tom and I had gotten so used to Butch being single we didn't even ask him "isn't there some girl you'd like to call up for a date?" any longer. And then he comes into the house one night, I'd say this was in late fall or early winter because I seem to remember I was wearing this rose-colored wool skirt and sweater set that I dearly loved. I still have that outfit although it has gone so out of style I wouldn't consider putting it on. Anyway, in walks Butch, just as his father and I are watching the news on the television, and says, "There is someone I want you to meet." Why his words made me think of Julia I couldn't tell you, but they did. She was out on a date that night.

Back when she was in high school, every time Julia went out on a date I'd get this sort of dull, dread-filled feeling in the pit of my stomach the minute she left the house. I could never relax because she couldn't be counted on to return home at the time we'd agreed upon. This was a big problem we had with her the year she turned sixteen. She wasn't old enough to be trusted. Well, she may have been old enough, but she wasn't responsible enough, not by a long shot.

It didn't matter what cock-and-bull story Julia came in with, I'd see clear through it and Tom would start making excuses for her. Not that she couldn't make plenty of them for herself.

"Well, now, sweetheart, let me and your mother talk, I can see how that might have happened just the way you say it did." Tom fell for whatever line Julia dreamed up time after blessed time.

There I sat, one eye on the clock, thinking about what I was going to say to Julia when she dragged in the front door. And instead it was Butch who was standing by the kitchen door grinning from ear to ear. Since he was a little boy Butch has been the one of my children with the sunny disposition.

He is all smiles. When I think of Butch that's what comes to mind, how he was the happiest, sweetest little boy. Of course he is all grown up now; I didn't have long enough with him before Julia came along and complicated things.

"HER NAME IS Susie. She's waiting out in the car."

This was the first I'd heard of someone named Susie. "Butch, the house is a wreck, why didn't you tell me you wanted to bring company over?" I asked him.

"Mother, the house looks fine," Butch said to me. "Come meet Susie."

Tom was halfway out the door as I stood there in the middle of my kitchen wishing I had at least put the dinner dishes in the dishwasher. Butch went right with him, leaving me to bring up the rear. "About time you brought someone home," I heard Tom say as the door slammed shut in my face. I felt awkward and I wondered what kind of background this Susie came from that she would be a part of a situation with such a potential for embarrassing someone who she hoped was going to be her mother-in-law.

DESPITE MY INITIAL fears, Susie is exactly the sort I would have picked for Butch to marry. I've said that to more than one person. I am not afraid to admit I am wrong when it is a fact staring me in the face. And I was wrong when I told Butch I didn't think Susie was the person for him.

Susie doesn't stand on ceremony—she's the kind of person who isn't too proud to wade right in and do what needs to be done. Plain down-to-earth-practical—that's Susie for you. Lots of Houston folks think they're better than those of us who still live out in what they call the boonies. Julia, for one, I suspect of getting too big for her own britches by virtue of the fact that she has been living in Houston since this past August. "Mother, what on earth would I do if I moved back to the boonies?" she said to me when I dared to mention that if she couldn't find a job and pay her own rent it looked like to me she'd be better off living at home rather than expecting her father and me to pick up the slack for her.

Susie, to her credit, has never once tried to pull that "I'm from Houston and I know more than you do" stuff on me. For example, at the church dinner last Sunday, there was Susie back in the kitchen, washing up the cups and saucers. They'd piled up in the sink and on the counter, and she noticed them sitting there needing to be washed. Before I picked up the towel and dried for her, I went over and checked and sure enough, Susie's name was nowhere to be found on the kitchen cleanup committee. But Ruth Schwartz and Duwayne Elliot, who had written their own names on the kitchen cleanup sheet when it went around last Sunday morning after Sunday school, were, as usual, out front in the fellowship hall flapping their gums. Neither one of them had so much as darkened the door to the kitchen.

I like to think Butch married Susie because, in some ways, she takes after me. We do have some things in common I am sure. Used to be it was a given that on Friday night Susie and Butch would take their supper with us. That's the night Tom likes to fix steaks on the charcoal grill outside. I usually bake potatoes and we have a big salad, which is why I need to know how many to plan for. It isn't like I'm fixing a casserole that can feed from eight to twelve.

"I think we're going to the game, Verona," Susie said to me this particular time when I called.

"Whatever for?" I asked her.

"The kids like to see the high school team play basketball and so does Butch."

They didn't have any business dragging those boys—barely out of diapers the youngest one is—out in the night air. "I thought I noticed Eugene had a runny nose," I mentioned to Susie. "If you think he's fixing to come down with something, we'll be glad to keep him here for you."

Susie laughed. "Eugene's had a runny nose since he started nursery school. It's gotten to where we wouldn't recognize him without it."

That was another thing. In my day, you kept your children at home with you until they were in first grade. It was a mother's duty. But Susie has had her two enrolled in this little school that Dawn Sullivan started in her garage since before they were out of diapers. No wonder they've been sick—I could have told her that. But I bit my tongue before I said the first word. Susie is entirely too casual with both Thomas and Eugene but I know my place and far be it from me to interfere. I have seen more than one woman ruin a relationship with her son's wife doing that very thing.

"Well, I'll tell you what," I said to Susie, "I think I'll just go ahead and put your names in the pot. That way, if you change your mind, there'll be plenty to eat."

TOM

Julia's home every weekend. She tells her mother she's staying in Houston, she's got things to do, for us not to expect to see her. "She'll be here, you mark my words," Verona will get off the phone saying to me. And come Friday night, ten to one, I'll hear Julia's car pulling in over the cattle guard. The backseat of the car will be filled up with dirty clothes, which Julia will drag inside the house and dump in a heap in front of the washing machine. "Don't touch my clothes, Mother, I'm going to do them tomorrow," she'll say to Verona. Next morning I'll hear the washing machine going before six in the morning. When I go in to get my first cup of coffee, Verona will have the ironing board set up in the middle of the kitchen and she'll be hard at it.

Julia gets up somewhere between nine and ten, about the time I come in for midmorning coffee, and says to her mother, "I told you to leave those clothes alone," before she starts mixing up her muffins. This is their standard weekend routine.

This Saturday it was obvious to me Julia had not slept well. There were circles under her eyes and she wasn't able to sit still for five seconds. When Verona laid her iron up on the metal pan it rests on and announced she would be back in a minute, I went over to Julia, who was standing at the kitchen sink staring out the window. We both knew from past experience Verona would be in the bathroom for a good ten minutes. She had taken her cup of coffee and the *Reader's Digest* with her.

"What's wrong, sweetheart?" I asked my little girl.

"Daddy, you are wearing your boots again," she said to me. "Didn't the doctor tell you that's what makes the arthritis in your knees act up?"

"Your car running okay?"

"Just great. The mechanic said you told him to put it on your credit card. Thanks, Daddy."

"That's what daddys are for. You been having dreams again?" I asked her. Since she was little, Julia has had nightmares. I've never known what to do about them.

"No," she said. "Well, yes."

I hugged her around the shoulders. It surprises me to find

her shoulders on a level with mine. I don't think of her as grown up the way she is. "Remember, honey, you wake up scared, you just yell your head off. I'll come running."

"Thanks, Daddy," she said and leaned her head on my shoulder. We stayed that way until we heard Verona coming back down the hall. Right before Verona came back in the room I said one more thing.

"I don't like the idea of you living alone, honey. Why don't you get Robin to move in with you? Tell her your daddy said so, don't worry about the rent, I'll take care of that. You girls save your money for your old age."

"Daddy, you say the same thing every weekend. Robin and I both *like* having our own places."

Later on that morning, she was still on my mind. Butch and I were back in the south pasture. "Soon as it dries up some we've got to get the tractor back in here, mow this field," I said to my son.

"Right, Dad." He took out the little notebook he always carries in his shirt pocket and wrote it down. Butch is that way. Tell him something once, that's all you need to do.

"Julia has been having those dreams again," I told her brother. "I don't like the idea of her living by herself."

"Susie went down to Julia's apartment last week, Dad. Helped her hang some curtains. She says Julia is doing fine. You worry too much."

Butch is right.

ROBIN

"Hi, that's your bed. Under the pile of clothes. Just shove them anywhere. I'll be off in a minute." It surprises me to remember that those are the first words Julia Salwell ever spoke to me. Actually she sort of mouthed them in my direction. At the same time she was waving her right hand, the one holding the lighted cigarette with lipstick smeared on the filter end of it, back and forth in a theatrical movement I immediately characterized as fake. She's trying to look cool, she isn't smoking that cigarette, I thought, as a shaft of genuine fear pierced me. Whether it was fake or not, the truth is Julia looked unbelievably sure of herself.

First impressions are so important—that is one of the little bits of wisdom Aunt Kate sent me off to college with. Aunt Kate was completely right, and dead wrong. In some cases first impressions turn out to be totally misleading. My first impression of Julia was *Oh, no: a society-type rich kid who is going to spend the next year acting like she is too good to live in the same room with me.*

The only part of my first impression I was correct about, as it turned out, was the rich part. Not that knowing Julia has money required any great intuition. Anyone who looks at Julia can tell that she is rich. I don't know what it is about Julia, but there is *something* 100 percent intangible but nevertheless a very real part of her, which signals "money." I've walked into department stores with Julia when she has on old jeans which I know good and well are cheap since I was with her when she bought them at Target, and flipflops so worn out they look like she got them at the Goodwill, and watched it happen. What she's got on doesn't make one iota of difference. The sales ladies fall all over themselves to wait on her.

The day I first laid eyes on Julia she was piled up in the middle of one of the beds in the room, dressed in her brother's shirt, had her thick brown hair pulled back in a ponytail, and wore these totally ridiculous pink fluffy scuffs on her feet. All the while I was moving in she continued talking into the phone that hung on the wall right at the head of her bed. At the time I assumed she already had this large social circle. It never occurred to me that she was talking to her mother. Or that she would do so at least once, sometimes twice a day, for the next four years. Julia didn't look like that kind of person at all.

I put my purse and the two suitcases I had lugged up the three flights of stairs with me down by the door and walked back downstairs. If I'd had anywhere to go that was private I'd have gone to wherever that was and shut the door behind me and cried my eyes out.

While I hadn't expected fireworks and a marching band, this wasn't the reception I'd hoped for either. The drive out to Lubbock with Cindy hadn't been any picnic and then, to top off that dismal nine hours, my new roommate couldn't get off the phone long enough to introduce herself. I trudged downstairs wishing I had stayed at home and enrolled at University of Houston. If I still hated Tech by Christmas I wasn't going to be too proud to transfer to somewhere I might like better. Like back home with Aunt Kate.

Cindy, the senior from Houston who had given me a ride out to Lubbock, couldn't wait to get me and my stuff out of her car so she could get on over to her dorm room and call Bill, her fiancé of three days, and tell him how desolate she was without him. She did everything but get behind me and push to get me up and down the stairs as fast as possible.

The two of us, assisted by two girls from down the hall, made five trips upstairs and back down and each time I walked into the room Julia waved at me and went right on talking. I nodded back at her, trying to act like I was feeling competent enough to live over the slight of being the next thing to ignored. The ashtray on the floor beside Julia's bed was filled with cigarette butts, it looked as if that was all she'd been doing for days. Smoking and talking. And changing her clothes and tossing them over on my bed.

There really wasn't any way I could have avoided overhearing her half of the conversation. Even if I had gone in my closet (thankfully, it was empty so I didn't have to clear Julia's possessions out of it), and shut the door behind me, I'd have been able to hear every word she said.

"Mother, you know good and well that is nonsense."

I could hear squawking sounds from the phone all the way across the room.

"Look, my roommate has just walked in the door, I have to go."

"Squawk, squawk, squawk."

"Well, if you don't like what he is doing, you can talk to Daddy about it. There isn't any reason for you to call and tell me. What can I do about whether Daddy was at the coast for four days last week? *Remember,* Mother, I'm way out in Lubbock."

"Squawk, squawk, squawk."

"Well, tell Butch then, don't tell me!" Crash. Julia ended the conversation by slamming down the receiver and hanging up on her mother. I was shocked at the time. I'd never in my life hung up on anyone.

Julia hadn't actually spoken to me yet. More than anything, I felt like crying. I was in a strange place with a self-assured person and I didn't know the first rule about how I was supposed to behave. It could have gone that way. I could have cried and our friendship would have been doomed before we'd known each other twenty minutes.

Instead, I looked around the room and saw my books and ordered possessions. Each cardboard box had a typed inventory affixed to it, courtesy of my aunt Kate. Even my wardrobe was labeled and inventoried. My possessions were surrounded by Julia's flamboyant clutter. Strangely enough, I found myself wanting to smile, maybe even laugh. Julia and I didn't fit together, not at all. At that point a flutter of optimism I hadn't been aware I possessed raised its rather tentative head. Julia didn't know who I'd been before. It hit me that she had started right in talking to me as if she expected me to agree with her, as if she thought I saw the world the same way she did. "It never occurred to me to bring books to college," she had said.

"What did it occur to you to bring to college? Besides clothes, that is?" I asked her. I remember thinking, *I won't be normal either, then. I won't say hi, I'm Robin, glad to meet you. I'll act like she does.* She stared at me for a long moment, her eyes narrowed as if she were evaluating me. Once I got to know her mother it was easy to see what Julia had been doing that day we first met—she was scrutinizing me and the words I had spoken, looking for any barb my words might contain. But then, and this still seems slightly miraculous to me, she smiled back.

She stood up and stretched. "Besides clothes, I've got cigarettes," she said. "And the keys to my car. I must say you took your own sweet time getting here. I was beginning to think you'd chickened out. Shove those books out of the doorway. There's nothing under your bed—put them there. Let's go to Mr. BB's and eat hamburgers and talk!" Julia didn't wait for a response from me, she kicked off her pink slippers and bounced down from her mattress to the floor, her hand snaking back and forth in an attempt to snare two shoes that were mates. "They can't have gone far. I wore my tennies this morning," she muttered to the dust and accumulation she was disturbing. "You know the cafeteria here is the pits—unless you've got on a dress they won't even let you in the door!" She looked down at her own cutoffs with an approving nod. "Have you ever heard of anything so ridiculous? Let them keep their food. You know everything they cook here is loaded with saltpeter, and besides, I'd rather eat out."

First I ought to unpack. And then I need to take a bath and wash my hair, I feel so grimy. Besides, shouldn't we eat in the cafeteria since the meals for the entire semester are already paid for? And what is saltpeter? I've never heard of it. I didn't say any of that. That's what I was thinking. Instead I grabbed my purse and followed Julia down the hall.

As I walked out to her car, I kept replaying those first bantering words I had spoken to Julia. I hadn't sounded all that dumb, after all, I thought. Maybe I was going to hold my own in college. Maybe I'd even have friends. It looked like my roommate and I were going to hit it off. I couldn't have looked nearly as good as Julia did, though. I'm sure I looked the way I felt, as if I'd been beaten. I'd driven almost the entire nine hours it takes to get from Houston out to Lubbock because Cindy, whose car I was in, had been in the backseat most of the way sleeping off a hangover.

"Lucky you, driving out to school with a friend," Julia said to me. "My parents brought me. I thought they'd never get on that plane and get out of here. They acted like I couldn't find the way out to Lubbock all by myself. My daddy is such a worrywart! There isn't a single person from Cypress Springs currently enrolled at Tech so I couldn't get anyone from home to come along. Of course that is one of the reasons I picked Tech—no one out here here knows me." I wondered if she noticed the inconsistency in her words. It struck me as strange, hearing her say what she did. I wondered about that stuff about no one knowing her; it sounded as if she was reinventing herself too.

"I might as well have been alone, Cindy slept the whole way," I said. "I hated the drive out here."

"It was long," Julia agreed.

"And lonely," I told her. I'd stopped in Temple for gas—this was about three hours out of Houston—and heard the first sounds Cindy had spoken since she'd picked me up at my aunt's early that morning. "Get me a Coke when you're inside paying for the gas," she'd said to me. When I came back out to the car with her Coke, she raised up from the backseat, took the can I offered her and said, "Thanks," before she disappeared from sight again. I heard several gulping sounds, followed by a belch, and that was it for another five or so hours. I might as well have been alone on the moon, which is what my first look at West Texas suggested to me.

The second time I stopped the car Cindy and I were on the Houston side of the little town of Post, which is not an hour's drive from Lubbock. By then, the landscape, the barren sameness of it, had really gotten to me. There were no landmarks to plot your course by. It has always been important to me, on the few occasions when I've traveled, to know exactly where I am. At any given point I am aware of how to get back to where I've come from. The fact that two-lane paved roads in the desert all look the same worried me. Driving to Lubbock the first time, I understood why they'd once called this part of the country a Dust Bowl. For miles and miles, all I saw was arid-looking farmland peppered with plants. The poor things looked to be wedged into the earth, gripping the soil for all they were worth because there was no water to be seen. Well, no real water. No lakes. No rivers. Not even any smallish ponds. The trees, what few of them there were, looked as if they were petrified in place. Even their green leaves, which they did have, looked brittle, almost artificial. Some of the fields were in the process of being irrigated with water pumped through these huge metal arms that moved slowly around in circles. Mostly it looked like the water dried up before it reached the plants; certainly the water from the metal arms didn't linger long enough to pool up on the ground.

I saw the pumps of more than a few oil wells. The wells, scattered here and there in no discernable pattern, bobbed up and down, keeping time to some invisibly set rhythm. Oil wells are not warm and welcoming. They reminded me of machines monitoring the body rhythms of patients in an intensive care ward. As I drove Cindy's car I'd slide past deserted houses, occasionally an occupied one. West Texas towns, few and far between, look like stage sets for 1920s hard times movies. I began to get a little crazy.

There was one totally weird moment. During the part of the drive right before we got to Post, the land around me appeared to be completely and totally uninhabited. I could see no evidence of human habitation. There wasn't even litter beside the road. The road was paved. Someone human did that. *Maybe that was years ago,* came the thought. A good thirty minutes had passed without so much as a pickup truck going in the other direction. The emptiness began to spook me. I don't think of myself as prone to dramatics—certainly I don't normally go hysterical over solitude—but after driving and driving all that time through a part of Texas that is only bearable if you're into starkness, and as good as traveling alone for all the company Cindy had been, I started to have these wild fantasies. I told myself maybe I had gotten caught in some kind of time warp where I was doomed to drive forever and ever, never to arrive at my destination. Maybe I even had a dead body in the backseat with me. Wouldn't that have been a kick? I imagined the headlines, *Elderly college freshman, who graduated from Lamar High School forty years ago, discovered in vintage car in West Texas. Her companion, a body in the backseat, shriveled and dried beyond recognition. Gray-headed blue-eyed girl, who cannot recall her name, says she realized she must have taken a wrong turn but kept going thinking sooner or later she'd get to somewhere where she could ask directions.*

I craned my neck over toward the center of the car so I could see myself in the rearview mirror. I didn't look all that old, thank goodness. "West Texas gives me the creeps," I said out loud, trying to shake my mood. "Why would people live out here?" I raised my voice and turned my head toward the backseat and repeated my question. It was time Cindy woke up, hangover or no hangover.

"Don't know any better, that's my guess," came the words from the backseat. "Pull over. If you don't, I'm gonna pop," she said. She must have been awake for some time. She sounded human again.

I stood by the driver's side of the car, jubilant beyond reason that I wasn't alone in the barren landscape any longer. As I stood stretching and listening to the hissing sound of Cindy relieving herself beside the car, I noticed the sun wasn't as searing hot as it had been. Off in the distance I spotted a normal-looking house surrounded by a white picket fence. It had green shutters on the windows and five or six large shade trees scattered about. I could see children's play equipment in the yard. "Mama Mildred's" read the sign beside the dirt road leading up to the house. The car was parked directly under the sign.

"I'll drive the rest of the way," Cindy said, so I walked over to the passenger side of the car. The puddle was draining toward some weeds that had grown up between cracks in the asphalt. *Weeds will grow on anything, anywhere,* I thought. I supposed Mama Mildred also found something to sustain her.

I'm glad it was Cindy who drove the last hour into Lubbock. Once she got to talking to me, I did start to feel better. Cindy obviously had survived her freshman year. "Don't you hate it, the dry sameness of the landscape out here?" I asked her.

"Don't even see it anymore. What I hate is the way I feel after I spend a Saturday night drinking cheap red wine," she said to me.

"So why do you do it?" I asked her. One thing I wasn't going to do was drink my way through college.

"Who knows? Seemed like the thing to do at the time," Cindy replied. Then she put her hand out in front of her and studied her engagement ring. It was a beautiful ring. Diamonds encircled a round sapphire that had been Bill's mother's. I'd already admired it earlier that day. "I miss my sweetie," Cindy said. Without waiting for me to reply, she asked me to reach around in the back in her purse and find her some more aspirin. She'd already had no telling how many but I figured she knew what she was doing. I almost gagged as I watched her swallow three of them dry. I'd never seen anyone do that before. However, I hadn't met Julia yet. Julia also likes cheap red wine, and can take a handful of pills without so much as a sip of liquid to wash them down.

AFTER WE'D ORDERED steak sandwiches at the window of Mr. BB's on Fourth Street, we sat in Julia's car waiting for them. Julia swore to me these sandwiches were going to be the best I'd ever eaten. "It won't matter what they taste like, I'm so hungry," I replied. "And I've got a headache. You don't have any aspirin in the car, do you?" I asked her.

She reached under the front seat and pulled out a fistful of bottles and several little metal tins. "Bufferin? Excedrin? Bayer? Take your pick."

"How come you keep your medicine in your car?"

"Because if my mother sees me taking aspirin she assumes I have a hangover. It's easier this way."

"Oh."

"Why did you choose Tech?" she asked me.

"Tech was the only school that offered me a scholarship," I admitted.

"Well, shit, I knew you were smart. That's *good*. Smart people don't have to spend all that much time studying. The main reason I dropped out of rush was I found out if you pledge you have to spend your entire first year going to study hall so your big sisters can help you make your grades. Forget *that* nonsense, is what I said to that. I didn't come to college to have someone telling me when to study. If I'd wanted that I could have stayed home with my mother!"

I laughed at her words. It didn't seem to me there was a person alive who could convince Julia to do something she didn't feel like doing. Somehow or another Julia and I had skipped the initial awkward stage I thought all friendships had to weather. I think this was mainly because Julia treats everyone she meets as if she has known them forever. Julia told me she liked me the first time I stuck my head in the door. I had immediate cause to be thankful for that fact because I soon saw Julia around people she took a dislike to. Julia is a straightforward person and she never bothered to fake it with the girls in the dorm she didn't care for—like Cheryl Sanders, this girl who lived across the hall from us. Julia couldn't stand her.

"What's so awful about Cheryl?" I asked Julia later that night after Cheryl popped in to introduce herself. "She's a creep," Julia replied. "Her parents brought her to school yesterday, and I knew when I saw her hanging on to her mommy and daddy out in the parking lot that she was going to turn out to be one." For the entirety of our freshman year, Cheryl was lucky to get the time of day from Julia. Even when Julia had mono and Cheryl brought Julia notes from her Economics classes for two weeks straight, Cheryl was fortunate to hear more than a "Thank you tons, Cheryl," and "Could you shut the door as you leave?" from Julia.

"You ought to be nicer to Cheryl," I said to Julia one day, although normally I do not tell other people how I think they ought to act. But it got to the point where I felt sorry for Cheryl. "I know I ought to be," Julia said. "But I don't like her."

By November, Julia and I had become best friends. For me, that was the greatest thing about college. "You two are so different," Marie from down the hall used to say to us. "It amazes me how you get along so well." In some ways Marie was right. Julia and I were different, particularly the parts of each of us it is easy for observers to see. But, in other ways, Julia and I had a lot in common. For instance, neither one of us had an old high school gang we couldn't wait to get home to every holiday. Julia had her brother and her father and mother. I had my aunt. Both of us acted as if what we had was enough.

Not that we weren't honest with each other. "I want a boyfriend who'll turn into a great husband," Julia said to me one night when we were fooling around with the Ouija board she'd brought to college with her. We spent lots of time pushing it back and forth trying to make it tell us our futures. "The two of us will have lots of kids, all of whom I will love equally. Only maybe I'll have a career first."

"Will you move back to your hometown?" I asked.

"When hell freezes over. The man I marry is going to want to live somewhere exciting like Paris."

"Have you ever been to Paris?"

"No, I've never been out of Texas."

"Me either," I admitted.

"So we're both saving Paris for marriage," she said and grinned at me. "You have to save something for marriage and heaven knows my virginity is long gone!" She said that to shock me, I realized that. It worked of course. I was shocked and awed. But the more I got to know Julia the more I realized she was nowhere near as carefree as she strove to appear.

Julia acted like she was fast. I'm sure most of the girls we went to college with would never have believed she didn't sleep with any of the guys she went out with. She acted so blasé about sex. Acted isn't the right word. She talked so matter-of-factly about sex. For example, there was a time when this girl down on two finally got her period after having been worried sick for weeks. Julia went to a bakery and bought Beverly a big cake, which she stuck candles all over. She invited half the dorm in to celebrate with Beverly. "I'd be big as the side of a barn if I bought a cake every time I'd been worried about being late," I heard her say to someone. It was like she wanted to create this impression of herself as someone way too sophisticated to have spent her life in the little town with the population of 3,358 that she actually came from.

"What about you, Robin?" she asked me. "Do you want to get married?"

"Someday, I really do want to get married someday, Julia, but for now I'd settle for dating someone fun." I wasn't a total wallflower, but my social life never caused any of the other girls any great pangs of envy.

Julia and I *were* perceived by most of the girls in the dorm as total opposites. Everyone thought she'd sleep with a guy at the drop of a hat. And the truth is that she went through four years of college without once going to bed with any of her dates. Everyone thought I was a studious goody two-shoes. The truth there was that I spent the majority of my junior year hopping into bed with my art history teacher. If it hadn't been for Julia I don't know how I would have gotten through that period in my life. My first big love affair. I acted like a gullible jerk the entire time Zeke and I were dating. The rejection I felt when I realized I was simply the coed of the semester I can recall as if it were yesterday. I cried for days. It was Julia who got me through it.

"What do you need with a balding creep who thinks he is God's gift to virgins?" she asked me. "You've got better things in your future, I can see them coming." And then she'd haul out her Ouija board and have it tell me how rich and famous and adored I was going to be. "One of those days Zeke is going to be begging for the privilege of taking you out, you wait and see! He'll come to his senses and realize what a jerk he is, but it will be too late, you'll have seen clear through him," Julia said. "Now wash your face, we've got stuff to do, we're going to a movie. And out to dinner, my treat," she'd say. She held my hand and bullied and coddled me until I finally got it back together. By college graduation I would have bet my life on the fact that Julia and I had a lifelong friendship that would only get better as time went on.

JULIA

It helps to have rules to live by. Like the matter of my pictures. Where I put my pictures matters to me. On the refrigerator I like to tape up snapshots of people I know. But I have this rule, no dead people. It is okay to have dead people in frames in your house but not on the refrigerator.

When Mother called—this was back during my last summer out in Lubbock—and said that Aunt Hilda had died, the first thing I did was go straight to the refrigerator. There were two pictures of Aunt Hilda and her family taped to the front of the freezer door. Their Christmas card pictures from the past two years. I took them both down and peeled the tape off the backs of them before I put them in the top left-hand drawer of my desk. This is where I put things I am not sure what to do with. It had been years since I had seen my aunt when she died.

Rules are important. However, I make it a point to make my own rules. Other people's rules are apt to be worthless. My rule about pictures is don't put them out if you don't want to look at them.

I didn't go home to Cypress Springs for Aunt Hilda's funeral because I was in the middle of summer school and I was devoting myself to passing the last three classes I needed to graduate. "She'll understand if you don't come home," Daddy had said to me on the phone. I didn't think Aunt Hilda would understand. I didn't think *she'd* think at all. Funerals are for the living. They are the last thing dead people have on their minds. I was surprised Aunt Hilda was getting buried in Mother's family plot. It appeared to me she had gone a long way from her roots. But I suppose when all is said and done, blood does turn out to be thicker than water. And Aunt Hilda had to be buried somewhere.

NOT TWO WEEKS after Aunt Hilda's funeral, when Butch called me to say Daddy was down in the emergency room with his heart, I regretted the way I'd been so callous about Aunt Hilda. Maybe if I had left Aunt Hilda on the refrigerator Daddy wouldn't have had his attack. I was standing in the kitchen part of my one-room apartment as I listened to Butch talk. I'd pulled the cord of the telephone as far out as it would go so I could get over to the refrigerator. There were seventeen pictures on it at that time. Daddy was in seven of them.

"Thank God you were at home by the phone and Mother had the presence of mind to call you first thing," I said to Butch when he phoned me the second time in not much over an hour to say Daddy was out of surgery and was doing fine, I was not to worry. That was easy enough to say, and I knew for certain Butch wouldn't lie to me, but I also knew I'd never rest easy unless I flew home to see for myself that Daddy was alive and recuperating.

"Susie would have called High Sullivan to go get Daddy if I hadn't been around to make the phone call," Butch said to me. High, who owns Cypress Springs' one and only dry cleaning establishment, also owns and operates the Cypress Springs Rescue Service. The rescue service consists of High, who has had some emergency medical training but is in no way, shape, or form a medical doctor, and his ambulance. Emergency phone calls are what High Sullivan gets off on. He dearly loves to barrel down the highway with the siren going full blast from his long black hearse. Other than emergencies, High's ambulance is mostly used for parades and funeral processions.

I've never understood how someone could want to do the job High does. That's the thing. With Daddy it was a heart attack. No blood at least. Lots of times the emergency will be a car wreck out on the highway or someone with gunshot wounds. I can imagine what that entails. High's son, Laser, who would have been in my class all the way through school had he not been held back in first grade, has been right there beside his daddy since he graduated high school. What kind of a life can he possibly have? Bundling up people's clothes and cleaning and pressing them. Washing and waxing the black hearse once a week. Waiting for a phone call so he can hop in it with his daddy and rush off to officiate at somebody's heart-stopping nightmare. I hate to say this, but what Laser and his father do is too gross to think about. Only I suppose someone has to do it.

As events transpired, Mother called Butch, Butch called High, who was out the door before Butch so much as finished saying to him, *Daddy's laying in his front yard clutching his chest, Mother says it looks to her like it is his heart,* and Daddy arrived at Memorial City Hospital in record time.

I was living all by myself out in Lubbock at the time of what we all later took to calling "Daddy's spell." Not by choice—I just didn't have anyone to room with. Once it became apparent to me I was either enrolling myself in summer school or I'd be back out in Lubbock the coming fall, I discovered I didn't know a soul who hadn't graduated already or wasn't set with a roommate for the summer. It was just as well. Living by myself forced me to buckle down and pass Speech (which I had put off for years—most of the people in the class were freshmen, sophomores at the most) and Chemistry, which I had failed twice before. I also had to take Journalism that summer, and it turned out to be the worst. All that typing.

Despite the fact that I was only weeks away from the end of summer school, I caught the first plane I could get to Houston. "You don't need to come home, Julia," Mother said

to me, "your daddy is going to be up and out of the hospital
before you know it. You stay where you are, finish those
classes, and then come home as planned."

"I'll be there on the next plane, Mother. Send Butch to
Hobby Airport for me in two or three hours. I'm leaving for
the airport the minute I hang up this phone." I had not called
to check on reservations, but that didn't worry me. I figured I
could wait for the first plane I could get out of Lubbock sitting
in the airport lobby as well as I could sit in my apartment and
wait. I arrived in Houston before nine o'clock that same
evening. Once I was on the plane I wished I'd called Robin to
come pick me up. She would have done that for me. And then
Butch wouldn't have had to leave Daddy. It wasn't that I
thought Mother would deliberately neglect Daddy, but she
can't be counted on. In a crisis Mother is nothing but a
hindrance and will, if you let her, make things one hundred
times worse. And I was sure, as late as it was getting to be, that
Susie would be at home with their two little boys.

Once I got to the hospital, I insisted on talking to the
doctor myself. I sat down in Daddy's room in the only
comfortable chair there was to sit in and said, "I will not leave
here until I personally speak to the doctor. Mother, you can
frown at me all you like, but that is the way it is."

I felt better the minute after I said that because I could see
the grin tugging at Daddy's mouth. He wasn't so bad off he
couldn't smile that I was there holding his hand and patting
it. That was the thing.

"Julia, if you are going to be stubborn, you can count on
sitting in that chair all night long. The doctor will not be in
before seven o'clock in the morning." This was Mother
talking to me thinking I would get up and go on home with
her like she wanted me to.

Butch took Mother home with him, where she slept in his and Susie's guest room. The two of them were back in the hospital by seven o'clock Saturday morning. Still, the doctor had come and gone by the time they walked in the door carrying a box of Shipley's donuts. I had heard with my own ears that Daddy had a small, almost minuscule, rip in the arterial wall, which had been fully repaired. The doctor said as tough an old goat as Daddy appeared to be, he should be up and out of the hospital within ten days.

I reported this to Mother and Butch, and Mother said she could have told me the same thing the night before. "That is to a word verbatim to what the doctor said last night," she said. "If you had listened to me, Julia, you wouldn't have had to spend the the night sitting up in a plastic fake leather chair." Which is when I pointed out the rollaway folded up over in the corner that the nurses had brought in for me.

Daddy was sitting up in bed and talking, although it was obvious he had been through the wringer and needed his rest. I hated the thought of going back to school and leaving him to Mother's mercies.

Daddy read my mind—I swear he does that to me all the time. "Julia, you get on back out to Tech and finish your courses. No point in going this far and quitting right at the end."

He had a point, but I still might not have gone had not Mother chimed in, "Let her alone, Tom. I never finished my college degree and I can't see the lack of one has ever harmed me in the least."

IT WAS ON into the next fall before Daddy told me about the birds he saw right before he had the spell that scared us all so bad. I'd gone down to the coast with him—this was after I had moved into my apartment in Houston but before I had found my second job. After I discovered that the retailing profession was not my calling, it actually took me a week or so to get to job hunting again. Daddy had been fussing about needing to winterize his house down in Port Aransas and Mother's only answer to him was to say there never had been a freeze before Thanksgiving that she could remember and the house could wait, she was up to her eyebrows in the church fall bazaar. "I'll take you down there, Daddy," I said. He could drive himself anywhere he wanted to go, but the Port A house is one of those that is up on stilts and he wasn't supposed to be hopping up and down doing manual labor yet.

"Julia, you hate the coast," Daddy said to me.

That was true. I'd hated that place for years but neither one of us, me or Daddy, wanted to get into that.

"Well, it's not like we'll be going fishing, Daddy."

"I'd thought I might take a quick spin out in the *Darlin' Vessel* before winter sets in," Daddy said. Mother winced when he said the name of his boat. Truthfully, the first time I heard what he had named his new boat I thought the name sounded silly myself. But I never let on to Daddy.

He sounded so wistful when he talked about his boat that my heart went out to him. "Okay, I give in," I said. "I suppose I can call your doctor and see if boat riding is on your list of allowed activities."

WE WERE OUT in the boat all the last morning we were at the coast. Around eleven we came in and sat out on the deck of the house. The deck, which is as long as the house itself and every bit as wide, is always tree-shaded and cool. It is, of course, up on stilts the same as the house. Daddy's furniture out there is wrought-iron metal and has wonderful thick cushions on all the chaises and chairs. When I'm at the coast that is where I like to be—out on the deck in the middle of the trees. I don't care a thing for the water. Salt water is wearing.

The day was gorgeous, one of those crisp bright late October days where it seems like there can't be a thing bad in the world. I was drinking a Dr. Pepper, Daddy was swigging on a beer he'd found in the refrigerator. I didn't say a word to him when he walked out through the sliding glass doors with it in his hand. I wasn't about to turn into his nursemaid.

I was sitting on the deck with my feet up on the railing, looking out at the place where the water and the sky come together, but Daddy was looking up, higher up, and off to one side, at the boat-tailed grackles lined up like so many gossips on the telephone wire leading into his house. "Damn birds give me the creeps," he said. He hauled off and threw his beer can at them. It was almost full and sprayed foamy liquid out as it spiraled upward. The birds scattered without the can ever coming close to them.

"Never have been able to stand birds," he said.

"You didn't like Aunt Hilda's Tweety?" I asked.

Aunt Hilda had this little green parakeet that had the run of her house—she talked to it like it was human. Silly thing would sit on her shoulder while she was on the phone and chirp into the mouthpiece along with Aunt Hilda. Neither one of them ever said a word that made sense. I thought that mean thought about Aunt Hilda before I remembered she was dead. "Sorry, Aunt Hilda, hope I didn't hurt your feelings," I whispered to the air around me. I felt my face screwing up in an apology. Aunt Hilda hadn't been a bad person. I had no idea why she and Mother never managed to get along.

It is true what my father said about birds. The time he and Mother and Butch and I drove into Houston to see *The Birds* it was Mother who insisted we see that movie. She has seen every Alfred Hitchcock ever made. Butch and I were scared, Daddy was grossed out, and Mother thought the movie was one of the best ones Alfred Hitchcock ever made. Halfway through the movie Daddy went out in the lobby and bought himself a hotdog and didn't come back in the theater. After the show was over, we found him out there sitting on a bench, scowling. "Last time you pick the movie, Verona," he said to Mother.

"I saw birds right before I had my attack, Julia, just like I saw them today. Lined up on the wire leading into the house."

Daddy had broken out in this sweat and he looked sick all over again. "Daddy, don't," I said. "Don't get yourself all worked up."

He kicked over the chair he'd been sitting in, knocking it toward the deck railing, and scowled once more at the place where the birds had been. Then he turned and went inside the house. "Time for my nap," he said. Twice while he was sleeping I went to the door of his bedroom and looked in to make sure he was okay.

We drove on home that afternoon. It's a nice drive, takes about two and a half hours.

DANNY, MY HIGH school boyfriend whom I had not dated in over four years, was there when we pulled up in front of my parents' house. I had intended to let Daddy out and drive on down to my apartment in Houston. We'd had a good time together and I hated to go inside and risk Mother spoiling it for me. But when I saw Danny's pickup parked in front of the white picket fence next to the front sidewalk, I turned off the engine of my car and put the keys in the pocket of my jeans.

"You coming in the house?" Daddy asked me. Neither one of us acted like we had seen Danny's truck. I thought about whether I really wanted to go inside. I had not seen Danny in over a year. Last time our paths had crossed he had been dating Sissy Sanders, but I knew from my sister-in-law, Susie, it hadn't lasted long. I could have told Danny that Sissy wasn't his type. Sissy chews bubblegum and paints her fingernails while she's having a conversation with anyone just about anywhere. A person who will do her nails in public won't last long with Danny Clark. I remember telling Robin that, months before Susie told me she'd heard they weren't dating any longer.

"Why not?" I said. "Might as well see what Danny has been up to."

Daddy opened the front gate for me. He was pleased that I was coming in, I could tell. He had always liked Danny. Everyone likes Danny.

They'd been eating brownies, I could tell that from the plate of chocolate crumbs on the table. Danny looked exactly the same as the last time I saw him. He had on jeans and a plaid shirt that I recognized as one I gave him back when we were dating.

"Do you always wear the shirt I gave you when you come out to visit my mother?" I asked him.

"Only when I hope she's been making brownies," he said.

We both stood there and grinned at each other while my parents watched us like they were trying to read something into the fact that we were being civil. I don't understand why they'd expect any less. Danny and I have never had any animosity between us. We simply drifted apart.

"What have you been up to?" I asked him.

"Farming with my dad," he answered. "And getting ready to build myself a house."

That was a surprise. I hadn't heard a thing about Danny building a house. He is an only child and had been living at home for the past year. His parents live in this huge two-story house that was built by his grandfather. He couldn't possibly need a house of his own. "Where?" I asked, although it didn't really matter to me.

"On some land we have in the family, there's an old house that was built no telling how long ago. You know the place I'm talking about? Lightning caught the old house on fire years ago so I'm going to have the part that's still standing taken down. But the well has water and the old pump works. And the oak trees are some of the prettiest in this part of the country." Both Mother and Daddy nodded that they knew the place he was talking about. So did I.

"Near one of your family's rice wells," I said before I thought.

"Yeah, that's the place I'm talking about," he said and he gave me another big smile.

It wasn't at all difficult for me to realize that Danny was thinking about the exact same thing I was thinking about. The numerous rice wells located in the rice fields around Cypress Springs were everybody's swimming pools of choice as teenagers. They're actually just large dirt-bottom holes in the ground dug as holding tanks for irrigation water. They're about the size of your average pool, I suppose, except the only deep part is right under the big metal pipe where the water gushes out when the pump is running. For large parts of the year, the rice wells are empty muddy holes with hard packed sand and dirt sides, but during the hot summer when the farmers are irrigating, the wells are filled with clear, icy cold water.

Except for the times when we swam in the high school pool for gym class, most of us did all of our swimming at the rice wells. In the summer the water was fantastically cold and adult supervision was nonexistent. Which of course was the real attraction the wells had for Danny and me. We'd spent lots of time at that particular well back when we were in high school. But I didn't want to think about rice wells or houses Danny might build any longer. What did rice wells matter to me? These days I had a nice pool outside my own apartment door if I wanted to go swimming.

I started toward the door. "I have to get on home now, see you later," I said as I walked out the door. Danny reached out and put his hand on my arm. "Don't run off, Julia. It's been a coon's age."

I looked at the hand on my arm. It was his left hand. The hell of it was guys don't wear engagement rings so I still didn't know why Danny was thinking about a location to build himself a house on. "I have to get on home, I'm tired," I said again.

"Meet you up in town, I'll buy you a hamburger—split an order of onion rings."

"French fries," I said. It was a reflex response. One thing we always argued over was whether to order onion rings or french fries. Usually we ended up getting both.

"Done!" he said. "See you at the Tastee Freez in ten minutes."

It seemed to me as if Danny had tricked me into doing something I didn't want to do. I felt funny as I was driving away from my parents' house. Looking in my rearview mirror, I saw Danny's truck behind me all the way to town but when it got to the place where I should have turned to go to the Tastee Freez I kept on driving. If he was engaged to Sissy Sanders or anyone else, the news could keep.

ROBIN

"Why ever did you tell Danny you'd meet him at the Tastee Freez and instead drive straight into Houston?" I asked Julia. She'd been waiting on me when I got home from work. We had keys to each other's apartments so I was never surprised to find her piled up in the middle of my bed sound asleep. Nine times out of ten, when I arrived home from school, I found Julia there waiting on me. Julia never could stand to be by herself.

Julia sighed. "I looked like hell, I didn't even wash my hair after we came in from the boat this morning."

Julia did not look like hell. She looked great. Julia looks fantastic even when she thinks she's at her worst, but when she feels ugly there is no convincing her otherwise. Julia gets these ideas in her head, and it is as if they are set in cement. The first few times I heard Julia put herself down I assumed she was fishing for compliments. But once I got to know her I realized Julia really and truly doesn't have an inflated sense of who she is. When she says she's ugly or stupid, she's telling the truth as she sees it. I can't understand it, the way she fools herself, because it seems to me all she'd have to do is look in the mirror to set herself straight. But arguing with Julia is an exercise in futility. It didn't take me long to learn to ignore the things she says that don't make sense. Doubtless I have my own blind spots as well.

"Your dad okay?" I asked her.

"Fine," she said. "Let's go to the Cellar Door and get something to eat, I'm starving."

"We could eat here, I have half a roast in the refrigerator. Aunt Kate insisted I bring it home with me," I said.

"Come on, Robin, I want to go somewhere," Julia said. Actually, I didn't want to stay home and eat another roast beef sandwich myself, but I had all this work I needed to do. Besides, it seemed like Julia and I were forever eating out. Even when we had groceries falling out of the refrigerator, we'd pick up and go out to eat. Up until I met Julia I doubt I'd eaten out more than once a month in my entire life. Aunt Kate and I were in the habit of eating regular balanced meals that were so predictable as to become almost invisible. I'd never want to go back to that. However, since taking up with Julia, I had to admit there were times when I longed for something green to eat. How she managed to survive on the diet she did is one of life's mysteries.

"Julia, I've got a stack of papers I ought to grade. Two sets of unit tests." Not that I *wanted* to grade them. I already knew they were dismal.

"These them?" she asked. When I nodded, she picked the papers up and flipped through them before she tossed them in the trash can. Then she grabbed up a half-full can of Dr. Pepper sitting on the bedside table and threw that in as well. "Tomorrow morning tell your class the tests got Dr. Pepper spilled all over them at the hands of your sloppy roommate and they get to take it over. Say you'll pass it out to them in ten minutes. The *same* test you unavoidably couldn't grade. Only let them quick pull out their books and study while you check roll. They'll love you. I guarantee it."

"You win, let's go to the Cellar Door," I said as I picked up a comb and ran it through my hair. "Give me a minute to change my clothes."

"That's all you're getting, one minute, then I'm dragging

you out of this apartment, dressed or not," Julia said. "I'm starving. Except for several Dr. Peppers I haven't had a thing to eat today."

The Cellar Door was a restaurant on Old Spanish Trail, and we were regulars there. "Hi, Julia. Hi, Robin," the manager greeted us when we walked in. People always called us Julia and Robin. Never Robin and Julia.

There was a young couple with a baby sitting in our booth, the one next to the kitchen door. They'd eaten all their food and were sitting talking while the father fed the baby a bottle. Julia was ahead of me in line. As soon as she had her tray with her baked potato and fudge pie and iced tea assembled, she walked over to their table. "Don't you want to move to a clean table?" she asked the couple.

"Why?" the mother wanted to know.

"This table is drafty. And noisy. Not good for a baby. Besides," and here she flashed a big smile, "my roommate and I always sit in this exact booth when we have something really heavy to talk about."

"We will be happy to move," the dad said and Julia rewarded him with another big smile. The mother didn't look as pleased.

"Thanks so much," Julia said. "You know what it's like, boyfriend probs," she intoned solemnly and rolled her eyes at them both as she helped clear away their dishes. The busboy appeared at her elbow to wipe off the table. How she managed to create this sense of camaraderie between herself and some guy who was feeding his son beats me, but she did it. Even the busboy didn't act the least bit surprised that, with only one table in the entire restaurant occupied, Julia decided it was the one she had to have.

I grinned across the table at her. Life in Julia's orbit was addictive. Why just walk into a restaurant and sit down when you could walk in and create a scene and then sit down?

"Did your dad get his house winterized?" I asked her. In spite of my addiction to Julia's breezy lifestyle, I found the only way I could operate was by being methodical. A to B to C. That's me. Comes from being raised by an aunt who knew the Dewey Decimal System better than she knew the names of any of the current television series.

"No, Daddy got away for a while, which was what he wanted. Mother was starting to get to him."

"What did you do for four days then?"

"Nothing. Rode in the boat. Ate. Slept. Got in the car and came home. I think Daddy would have had a better time without me."

"Sure he would have."

I couldn't even begin to imagine why she'd have said that. Her dad absolutely adores Julia. I think that's been one of the problems Julia has had with her mom. Both Butch and Tom are so crazy about Julia that Verona has felt left out. Still, the way Verona is, it is no wonder that she gets left out. Every time I'd catch myself wishing I'd had a dad or a brother like Julia does, I'd remind myself that at the least I'd had my aunt instead of her mother.

"What did you do all week?" Julia asked me.

"Educated the young," I said. That was a phrase I'd picked up from one of the coaches who taught four English classes. "Lord, I'm tired," he'd say. "I've been educating the young," he'd call out as he walked into the lounge, slapping the grammar book against his thigh. "It's a tough job but someone has to do it." All year long I'd been watching him. Bob Adams. Probably close to forty. Divorced. No kids. No discipline problems either. He never took any papers home with him. When I walked by his room his classes seemed to be scribbling industriously. I couldn't figure out when he graded their work. Or wrote out his lesson plans. Most of the time, Bob was standing in the doorway watching his students work. His room, located next door to the lounge, was a stopoff point for many of the teachers. They'd walk by, talk to Bob for a minute or two and then go on into the lounge for coffee. I'd gotten into the habit of visiting with Bob as well.

Both Bob and I taught freshmen and juniors. "Did your class do well on the unit on *Great Expectations*?" I asked him back in October. "I don't think my kids understood half of it." Actually I was feeling massively depressed at the time I asked him that question. I'd spent two days grading their essays and realized that, except for the papers of three of my students, nothing I thought I'd been teaching for the first four weeks of school seemed to have gotten across.

"Yeah, they ate up *Great Expectations*," Bob said. "We knocked it out in about seven days. Working days. Took the weekends off," he said and winked.

"I'd love to see some of your quizzes," I suggested. That was as close as I could let myself come to asking outright.

"Sure, sometime we'll compare notes," he agreed but that was the last I heard anything about *Great Expectations* from Bob Adams.

Mrs. Harmon, the department chair, also taught *Great Expectations*. She'd shown me her plans and quizzes. In detail. She kept each of the units she taught in a fireproof box. In case the building ever caught fire she didn't relish the thought of losing a lifetime's worth of preparations. She'd taught *Great Expectations* for thirty-seven years, she told me. Every year the kids got dumber. And this year's crew was impossible. No way they could understand real literature. But, she counseled, don't lower your standards. Teach it anyway. That's what she did.

"How does Bob do it?" I asked. "He said his kids loved the book."

"So would yours if you used Classic Comics," she sniffed.

It was difficult to know what to think. Mrs. Harmon didn't have discipline problems either.

"Besides educating the young what did you do?" Julia asked.

"That about sums up my week," I said.

I didn't want to tell Julia about Saturday. I wasn't even letting myself think about it. I have a very constricted history. I was raised by an aunt who is compassionate but plodding. I'm more or less the same way myself. Messiness makes me nervous.

Julia doesn't tolerate reticence willingly, however. "You're bound to have done something, Robin. Come on, give!" she demanded.

"Nothing. I did nothing. My life is a big fat zip," I said. And then I surprised us both by starting to cry.

"Well, shit, Robin, excuse me for asking. What you need is a drink. Let's go to the Red Barn, this is Tuesday, two for one until midnight."

We went on over there.

Even after several drinks, I didn't talk about Saturday. Julia can carry on all she wants about her screwy mother, I didn't feel like bringing mine up. Not after what Aunt Kate had said. And the things I feared she had been too polite to say. Some questions you wonder why on earth you ever asked. "Tell me about my parents," I had said to Aunt Kate. She had coughed and blushed and coughed again.

The two of us were in the process of lifting the window air conditioner out of Aunt Kate's bedroom window preparatory to storing it in the garage. We'd done this for years, since I'd been old enough to hold up my end of the unwieldy rectangular box. Most people just tape around the air conditioners and leave them in the windows. Some people also put plastic all over the outside. Aunt Kate says it is best to take the units out entirely and shut and lock your windows securely.

"Why do you ask about your parents?" Aunt Kate said. She had smoothed her face out, but you could hear the frown in her voice. Over the years I'd gotten used to Aunt Kate getting uneasy when the subject of family came up.

"Idle curiosity, don't tell me if you don't want to," I said to her. Already I was backpedaling the same way I always had in the past.

"Your mother was sixteen years younger than me. She was a cute baby," Aunt Kate said. "She married your father after a whirlwind romance."

I'd heard all that before.

"So, what was she like?"

"Headstrong. Just like my mother, your grandmother. You've got her eyes."

"And she died in a car accident?"

"Actually, I believe she was on a motorcycle. I'm a bit fuzzy on the details."

Aunt Kate was never fuzzy on details. I don't know why that thought had never struck me before.

"What about my father?"

"Robin, he was an impetuous young man. He was driving the motorcycle."

"And he died as well?"

I was going through the motions, traveling the familiar landscape of a conversation she and I had had before.

"I, well, perhaps, he was only injured."

Right then Aunt Kate changed the script. I felt a coldness settle somewhere in the center of my body. I could feel it happening inside me. If he didn't die, where had he been for the past twenty or so years? "I really don't want to know this," I said to my aunt.

"Just as well, there isn't much I can tell you, as I said the details are fuzzy."

What kind of a conversation would that have been to relay to Julia? If it had happened to her, she'd never rest until her aunt told her every single fact there was to tell. But Julia isn't a big coward.

JULIA

By the time I got out to my parents' house Saturday, Mother had forgotten all about how she absolutely had to have me there for the weekend so I could get my room cleaned out before she let the painters have at it. She didn't mention it and I didn't either. I did look through my closet. There wasn't anything in there I couldn't live without.

Butch and Susie were over Saturday night with their two boys. Mother doesn't rest easy unless she manages to badger them into eating at least one meal at her house on the weekend. And heaven help them if they try to go anywhere after church except home with her to sit down to the roast or ham she has cooking in the oven. "I don't know how you put up with it, Susie, living right down the road from her. Doesn't she drive you crazy?"

Susie just shrugged. She is incredibly easygoing—she'd have to be to marry into this family. I know Mother calls up to their house sometimes three and four times a day to get either Butch or Susie to do something for her. Or to make them listen to her complain.

All the time I was talking to Susie or Mother I kept getting these pictures of Robin in her apartment dressing for her date with Thad. Robin, who had complained all year long about not having a prayer of meeting anyone at the high school where she teaches English, was fixing to go out with the father of a student. He'd come in for a conference one day, driving an expensive car and flashing a Rolex watch on his arm, to talk about how his son wasn't going to get into UT if he failed her class. Robin says she and Thad talked about the kid for five minutes, agreed to get him a tutor to help with his essays and papers, which had been the pits, and spent the rest of the hour talking about other stuff. "What other stuff?" I asked her.

"I don't know, just stuff," she said back to me with this syrupy expression on her face. I could tell she was snowed even though she said to me, "Thad is just a friend, that's all. But we do have so much in common."

"Like what?"

"I don't know yet," she giggled. It bothered me, Robin giggling about some geezer old enough to be her father.

About seven o'clock I couldn't stand it any longer. I went to the phone and called her. "Are you dressed yet?" I asked.

"Yeah. At least a dozen times," she laughed.

"So what are you wearing?"

"My blue Lanz dress. And your white linen blazer."

"What shoes?"

"Red flats?"

"How about those white little spool heels you got on sale at Foley's?"

"You're right! I forgot all about them!"

"What time do you think you'll be home? Call me no matter how late it is!"

"Julia, I can't do that. Suppose it's midnight. Or later. Your folks will have a fit."

"You aren't planning on sleeping with him, are you?"

"No, for heaven's sake. You're beginning to sound like my aunt!" Robin laughed.

"I know," I groaned. "I wish I was there. So I could see what he looks like. How old is this guy anyway, Robin?" I demanded. I couldn't believe I hadn't asked that question two days ago when I first heard Robin was planning to go out with him. He had a seventeen-year-old son. For all I knew he could be thirty-five. Or forty. My God, think about it! He'd almost have to be forty!

"Forty-eight."

"You are shitting me, my *father* is fifty-seven, only nine years older than that."

"So?"

"Robin, he's too old."

"We're not getting married, Julia. We're only going out to dinner," Robin laughed. I could tell she was so excited. That was the thing.

After dinner I told Mother I'd do the dishes but before I could so much as shake a stick at them, she was in the kitchen, doing them herself. She's always been like that, she'll ask you to do something for her and then shove you out of the way. She did it this time as I was scraping the plates into the sink.

"Julia, be careful! You'll clog up the septic tank."

"Mother, nothing is going down the sink."

"Move over, I can do it faster myself," she said, pushing me aside. If I had a dime for every time Mother has said that to me, et cetera, et cetera. I didn't even argue with her, I just left the room. Butch and Daddy had run over to the barn to check on a cow. They'd taken Thomas, the oldest of the kids, with them. Susie was pulling out of the driveway with Eugene in the car with her. It was by this time after eight and Eugene is one kid who does not do well if he is up much past his bedtime. He gets sort of cranky and whiny. Susie's lucky, I said that to her as she was leaving. Because Eugene gave her an excuse to get on home.

I didn't feel like wondering what Robin was talking about with Thad any longer so I picked up the phone and without thinking twice about it dialed Danny's number. Although this was the first time I'd called him in years, the number came to me like it was my own. As I listened to the phone ringing (I hate the sound of the Cypress Springs phone system, the rings are these totally obnoxious growling sounds right up against your ear), I told myself if either of his parents answered I was going to hang up. It was Danny himself who answered.

"What are you doing?" I asked. I hadn't thought over what I was going to say to him. I hadn't even planned out that I was going to call him. Stuff sneaks up on me like this all the time.

"Just fixing to walk out the door," he said.

"Oh. I'm at my parents'," I said back to him.

There was this pause while he waited for me to say what I was calling him about. Since I had no idea what I was doing talking to him on the phone, I couldn't very well do that.

"Do you want me to come over?" Danny asked me.

"How about I meet you?" I suggested. I didn't want to see the smirk on Mother's face I knew would be there the minute she saw me walking out and getting in the truck with Danny.

"Where?"

"Wherever." I knew as well as if I could hear her that if I was to phone Robin and tell her what I was up to, she'd say to me, *Julia, I hope you know what you are getting into.* I didn't. I didn't want to know, that is the truth. I like surprises. And I hate the feeling that everything and everyone around me is all planned out and predictable.

"I'd say Tastee Freez but the last time you agreed to meet me there I got stood up," Danny said to me. Fortunately he did not appear to be holding a grudge.

"The rice well, then," I told him.

THAT WAS A mistake, meeting Danny at the rice well. Right off the bat it started us off on the wrong foot because Danny and I have this history. This is the way it is: we started dating when I was in the ninth grade and he was in the tenth. I wouldn't go so far as to say that Danny was the only guy I ever dated, but he was certainly the first and only one I ever got serious about despite an unfortunate interlude with a guy named Tillman Salinas. But that was after Danny and I broke up. My rebound relationship, I suppose you could call it.

Danny and I went to homecoming his sophomore year on our first date. That sort of set the tone for us. He was on the football team and I was a cheerleader and everyone said how good we looked together. Thing is, we have the same coloring and we're both tall. I suppose that's it as much as anything else.

My parents have always liked Danny, he's super polite to grownups. Ditto all the teachers at the school were snowed by him. I, on the other hand, didn't always get the adult seal of approval. Danny's mother, for one, always thought I was a smart ass. Of course, she thought she'd taken pains to conceal her true feelings, but Cypress Springs is entirely too small a town for that kind of thing to remain hidden. *Julia Salwell is too smart for her own good,* this is just one of the things that Danny's mother has said which has gotten back to me. And, *There is such a thing as too cute, Julia.* She said that to my face.

The dates Danny and I went on were the same as everyone else's in Cypress Springs, I would suppose. You go to the games—football in the fall, basketball in the winter; come springtime you can go to the track meets, but not everyone does that. And like to no one ever went to the baseball games. One year they barely had enough guys go out to make up a team. Afterwards we'd go to the Tastee Freez with the rest of the kids in town. There isn't anywhere else. Most people, me included, weren't allowed to car date into Houston until they were sixteen. And then you had to be in by twelve and could only go into Houston one night on the weekend—Friday or Saturday, never both. I think the mothers sat up in the beauty shop and agreed on the rules; they sure enough were all singing the same tune about what we could and couldn't do.

Except, of course, for the fast kids. There were some of them. They went dancing in the bars in the little hick towns around Cypress Springs. The ones I am talking about had live bands and served beer to anyone who looked close to eighteen. "Bohemian beer joints," Mother always called them. "You better not let me hear you've been over to any of those Bohemian beer joints," she used to say to me.

Contrary to what Danny's mother probably thinks, Danny and I never did go anyplace like that. The only time I ended up in New Caney or Roundtop, I was nineteen or twenty and went with some kids I met at Tech.

The other thing we usually did on dates was go out to the rice wells. Everyone did it but no one talked that much about it. At least the girls didn't. I heard that the guys were always bragging, spouting off such things as "got her boobs last night" in the locker room, but you have to take that kind of thing with a grain of salt. Even as a teenager I was smarter than to try to live my life based on what someone else might or might not say about what I was up to. "You don't want the teachers up at the school talking about you, Julia," my mother used to say to me.

"Mother, as far as I am concerned if what I'm wearing or doing is all they can find to talk about, then they're hard up, that's all I've got to say," I used to say right back to her.

Danny and I would take something to drink out there with us sometimes. Sometimes we wouldn't. Sometimes we'd just go. We'd swim if it was hot. We always ended up making out on the bank next to the tank of water. Danny kept an old quilt in the back of his pickup for us to spread on the ground. If it was cold we'd make out in the front of the truck. We'd run the heater from time to time to keep it from getting too freezing inside. That was one of the jokes around school: "I saw your car at the rice well but the windows were too steamed up for me to see in." Of course, Danny and I went to one of his daddy's wells—usually the same one, the one his father never seemed to drive by. In all the time we went parking, we never saw anyone else out where we were. Like I said, Danny on purpose chose a remote spot. And he didn't go talking about where we'd been the Saturday night before every Monday morning, either. In this respect we were unlike some of the other kids who, the things you'd hear in school, were always getting caught.

"You ready to go home?" Danny would ask me after the game or the movie or the hamburger which was the ostensible reason for our date.

"Not really," I'd say.

"Well, how about we go somewhere and talk?"

"Sure."

Talking meant making out. For over a year that is all it meant. The first time we went ahead and did it . . . I couldn't tell you to this day why events transpired the way they did. Like a lot of other things that have happened to me in my life, going all the way with Danny Clark sort of crept up on me and took me unawares.

It was homecoming of Danny's senior year, so I guess we had been going together almost two years to the day. Most of that period of time we went steady. We sort of drifted into that as well, because once we'd gone out together less than a handful of times no one else would ask me out for fear of hurting Danny's feelings. Not that I was helpless. If there had been anyone else interesting I would have dumped Danny fast enough. But there wasn't. Cypress Springs is limited in that respect.

Homecoming night Danny's senior year, despite the fact that it was November, the temperature was hotter than all get-out. I wore a wool suit to the dance after the game because, like everyone else, I'd had my homecoming outfit picked out down to the last accessory for weeks. Friday mornings getting my car loaded to leave the house invariably felt as complicated as if I was packing to go away for a week. I'd have to put on my school clothes, make sure I had my outfit for the pep rally as well as my uniform for the game, not to mention getting together whatever I was going to wear to the dance afterwards if it was a home game. If we had an out-of-town game, I just wore my cheerleading skirt and sweater home.

That particular night I was sweating like a pig, but so was everyone else. Danny was the last person out of the locker room. He stalked out the door in a vile mood. Cypress Springs had lost the game and their record for the year was six losses, two wins. Not what you want to have to look back to as your high school record.

First thing Danny said to me when he stepped out of the boys' side of the gym was, "I'm not going to the dance."

"You have to! You are one of the co-captains," I reminded him. As if he didn't know that fact himself.

We went, but he wouldn't dance more than once or twice the whole night. He just stood around in his blue suit scowling at the world in general. At that time, it was traditional that the cheerleaders were in charge of sponsoring the homecoming reception. Which meant that in addition to wrapping the goal posts, which we did for every home game, we'd also decorated the rec room and gotten the refreshments together. We were also supposed to do cleanup, but we'd agreed in advance to meet up there on Saturday morning and take care of that because no one wanted to do it Friday night after everyone else left. There is a limit, you know.

When Danny and I pulled up to the rice well, it was eleven-thirty. Normally I'd have had to be home by midnight, but my curfew had been extended until one so that we could get a hamburger in Houston after the reception. The seniors were all going to Two-Kay's on Westheimer. I wanted to go, too, because Danny was a senior and we were going steady and it wouldn't be fair to him if he missed out on it because the girl he was dating was a junior. That is how I had put it to my mother. Mother didn't see the sense of it, but Daddy said to her that if everyone else was going to go, he didn't see the harm of me going along. Only of course we didn't actually go to Houston. Some of the kids did, but Danny and I didn't.

I was absolutely burning up, that I do remember. I got out of Danny's truck and walked over to the well and reached down and stuck my hand in the icy cold water. Doesn't matter what time of year it is, well water is always as cold as if it has ice cubes in it. "God, this feels good," I said to Danny.

I don't know why once I started taking off my clothes I didn't at least stop when I got down to my underwear. Our pattern was I'd kick off my shoes and shimmy out of my hose myself and Danny and I would negotiate the rest of my clothes off piece by piece. Sometimes we were in the cab of the truck, sometimes the back of it. Most often, unless the mosquitoes were all over the place or it was colder than kraut, we put the quilt over on the bank beside the well and stretched out on it. Danny always switched the pump on because we enjoyed the sound of the rushing water.

I love to watch the stars out in the country. Lying on my back, looking straight up, I feel like I am a part of the universe in a way I never can be when surrounded by city sounds or other people. Some of those times back in high school, out in the middle of one of the Clark rice fields, where there wasn't a human person around for miles and miles other than me and Danny, we would lie on our backs and listen to the gushing of the water running and I would feel the most peaceful I'd ever known how to be. The dark star-filled nights could be counted on to lull me into a complacent "at one with the world" state time after time.

I'd never ever taken off my panties with Danny before. But this time it was different. I was different. I can't blame Danny for what happened, it was me. I stood over by the well in the moonlight, which was bright as day, and stripped down to nothing. I didn't say a word as I was doing it, either. Danny watched me all the while, speechless, his hands clasped in front of him like he was holding himself motionless so as not to break the spell. I couldn't see his face but somehow I knew the beads of sweat were breaking out around his hairline and nose. "I'm going for a swim," I said right before I cannonballed out into the middle of the well. I didn't even worry about how I was going to explain my hair to Mother. I figured as hot as it was I could tell her I had dunked it in the water fountain at school and she wouldn't be able to prove any different.

I'll say this. Danny forgot all about how depressed he was because Cypress Springs had blown the football game. We made love on the quilt after the swim. It wasn't that big a deal, I have to say that. I'd read *True Confession* magazine for years and was expecting excruciating pain followed by wild abandoned passion—neither of which I experienced. But at least Danny got to use the rubber that had been in his wallet so long you couldn't tell any longer what color the foil package had started out being. I wondered how many of those things he had stashed away in the toes of his boots in his closet at his house. Afterwards, Danny was solicitous. Once his breathing slowed down, that is. "Are you okay, Julia?" he asked me.

"Great," I replied.

"Huh, I mean really okay?" he repeated. I could tell he wanted me to give him some details, like did I see fireworks or did the earth move or were my legs so gone to jelly it would be hours before I could stand on them without wobbling.

"Really, I'm okay, Danny," I said, and that is the sum total of what I said on the subject. I felt a little disappointed, but all in all generally peaceful and I didn't want to get into talking and analyzing that feeling away. I could tell my mellow mood wasn't all that strong when I felt myself getting irritated at Danny's solicitousness.

I wasn't about to ask Danny did he still respect me? What the hell would that have told me anyway? I didn't have all that much respect for either one of us at that point. We both seemed too damned predictable—I'd been thinking that for the last couple of months. Danny was worse than I was, always doing what people expected—even making love. He and I might not talk about what we had done around school but everyone in their right mind at least suspected that people who'd gone together as long as we had were screwing. It didn't bother me I wasn't a virgin any longer. I didn't even care that I hadn't experienced earth-shattering fireworks. But I hated to think we were like every other couple in Cypress Springs, Texas. Dating through high school, exchanging class rings, going off to college and maybe (but more than likely not) graduating, and finally getting married, and raising three or four kids who were destined to turn out just like us.

"I love you," Danny told me, pulling me over so my head rested on his chest. I felt like crying right then. I wished I didn't know Danny so well. There wasn't any mystery at all left for us, that is how I felt at that moment.

"I love you, too," I replied. What else could I have said? I'd just slept with him for heaven's sake. What good would it have done for me to say, *Danny you're dull and I'm afraid that's all I'll ever be if I stick with you? So, please, would you give me back my virginity?*

After the first time, Danny and I made love just about every weekend for the next year or so until my senior year when I broke up with him. That wasn't planned either, it sort of just happened. I know some people live planned-out lives, but I've never understood how they do it. How on earth do they figure out what they'll be wanting five years from now, much less take aim for whatever they've decided upon and go for it?

Danny was a freshman at A&M and he didn't come home to Cypress Springs every weekend. He'd said he would, but it seemed like there was always some reason he couldn't get away. He had to study. Or they had a home game and he wanted to see the Aggies play. When he did come home, we didn't hit it off the way we had. He talked college. I talked high school. The only thing we had in common was what we did at the rice well every Friday and Saturday night before he drove me home.

The night we broke up was the night he'd driven from College Station to Cypress Springs to take me to homecoming my senior year. Homecoming. Seems like it was always the beginning or the end for us. We went to the game. Cypress Springs won—not that it really mattered to me. I was runner-up for homecoming queen. The fact that I hadn't won didn't surprise me. What surprised me was that I had even been nominated. I never was one of those people everybody just loves to death, if you know what I mean. I imagine I got nominated because I'd been a cheerleader so long my name just came up. The winner was a girl named Lydia Carson, who had been runner-up for Most Beautiful and had also won Most Likely to Succeed Girl. Mother said the fact that Lydia won homecoming queen over me showed that finally the football players were starting to develop some maturity and prefer substance over splash. Daddy told her if she couldn't say anything any nicer than that she ought to keep her mouth shut. I don't think I'd ever heard him tell Mother to shut up before. "Don't worry, Daddy," I said. "I don't listen to what Mother says, anyway."

Danny and I hung around the reception as long as we needed to and then went straight to the rice well, where of course we made love. Thing is, once you start that kind of thing, you can't just say *I'm waiting until I get married* anymore. It no longer holds water. As the saying goes, what's one more slice off the cut loaf? I don't suppose that night was any different from the ones that had come before it, but there was this air about Danny. He didn't even inquire *would you like to go home?* or *could we go somewhere and talk?* He just drove out to the rice well and shut off the engine of the truck and reached for me. He was acting like we were married and had been for some time, for heaven's sake. There was no *will she–won't she?* element of suspense to us any longer. I knew it hadn't been there in months. But that night it really grated on me.

After we were dressed and sitting up in the cab of the truck sharing a sort of lukewarm beer, I said to Danny, "What do you think, I mean about us going steady? Don't you think maybe we're flogging a dead horse here?" Frankly, this was another one of those times that I had no earthly idea what I was fixing to say until the words were already out there. And I didn't stop with one sentence. As I heard myself going on and on about there being no romance left and maybe we ought to quit trying to flog a dead horse (I must have used that phrase about the horse three or four times), I wasn't looking at Danny. I didn't want us to break up but I did want us to. I guess what I really wanted was some fireworks. I felt so damn dull.

Danny touched his senior ring, which was hanging from a chain around my neck. "We've been going steady for almost three years now, Julia. I've always expected we'd get married after I finish college."

He sat there, staring at me with his soft eyes, so patiently—like a spaniel would stare at you, hoping you'd smile at him and rough up the fur around his ears. A little touch and he'd wiggle all over himself with joy. I sort of shuddered. I didn't want to marry Danny. I didn't want to marry anybody. What I wanted was to get out of Cypress Springs and find some excitement.

"You're bound to have met somebody you'd like to date," I said to Danny. For sure I hadn't met anyone new. Everyone who lived in Cypress Springs I'd known since birth. "I know good and well you have. Hell, for all I know you've been dating your head off."

"No, I haven't, Julia. There isn't anyone I want to go out with if I can't be with you." Every single word he uttered to me was so predictable. All over Cypress Springs that night, from one rice well to the next, Cypress Springs boys were saying those words to Cypress Springs girls. *If I can't have you I don't want anyone.*

"Well, I don't see the sense of either one of us going off to college and not taking advantage of the experience. Think what we might be missing, Danny."

"I don't see that I'm missing anything. I'm at college to get an education, not a girlfriend. I already have a girlfriend."

"Well, it is time you opened up your eyes and looked around you then, because you aren't going to have one much longer," I said. Truthfully, I did not care in the least what I was saying to him at that point. It was as if, having started the fire, I was determined to keep tossing gasoline on it until this particular blaze was beyond putting out. Sort of a ritual burning of the bridges.

"I don't believe what you're saying, Julia," Danny said. His eyes looked hurt but I convinced myself that was because I was chipping away at the habit of us. Danny is a very conventional, tradition-bound sort of person. I was making him think. That's what I was doing.

"I mean it when I say you ought to date other people, Danny. That, in a nutshell, is what I am saying. So should I. Four years from now if we still think we're in love we can always get married. Right now is our one chance to get out in the world and find out what is there for us." I handed him his senior ring, which I had unhooked from the chain around my neck.

He shook his head disbelievingly at me. "Is there someone else?" he asked.

Although the answer was a resounding no, I lied to him. "There might be," I replied.

"Oh," he said. That's all he said. He started up his truck and drove straight to my house. When he pulled up out front, he switched off the engine, got out, walked me up to my front door, said, "Call me if you change your mind," in this grief-stricken voice. Then he walked off. *He's being dramatic,* that's all it is, is the thought that occurred to me. But, part of me was already busy screaming at the rest of me, *Julia you ought to have your head examined. You have most of your senior year in high school left and Cypress Springs is a mighty small town. Who the hell is going to ask you out?* However, mostly I felt this amazing freedom starting to well up inside me. Maybe no one else would ever ask me out, but I didn't care. At least I wasn't still weighted down by Danny's metal ring with the red stone in it dragging down on my neck.

I may not have had any plans about what I wanted, but I knew enough to know what I didn't want. Getting stuck living the same kind of life my parents had wasn't what I wanted. And a person didn't have to have twenty-twenty vision to realize that was the direction Danny Clark was headed in. Well, thanks but no thanks. That is exactly how I felt the night that I was a senior in high school and he was a college freshman and I broke up with him.

And now here I was, over four years later, driving out to Danny's father's rice well near where Danny was fixing to build himself a house. But some things were different, I thought to myself. I mean, at the least, I was driving my own car, which meant I could leave when I wanted to. I wasn't in Danny's truck, I was getting myself to the rice well under my own steam.

Thinking about Danny and me and Cypress Springs took my mind off Robin and her date, the man old enough to be her father, whom, I could tell, even if Robin couldn't, she was already infatuated with.

Danny was at the well when I drove up. His truck was parked under the oak trees in the regular place. I could see the shadow of him, leaning against the left front bumper. He was smoking a cigarette. That was new. Back when he'd been playing football, his body was a temple. At least his lungs used to be. I wondered if he was also still drinking beer. Or had he gone on to what my daddy called the hard stuff?

"How can you stand living back at home?" That was the first thing I said to Danny.

"Hi, Julia, I've missed you," he said to me.

"Doesn't your mother drive you crazy?"

"You still smell the same." By now his arms were around me and he was sniffing my hair. Danny has always had this thing about how I smell.

"I heard you're engaged."

"You heard wrong."

It was only because Cypress Springs is such a dull little town that I heard this voice, which had to be coming from somewhere inside me, say, *Thank God.* Other than that, I had no reason to be particularly interested in whether or not Danny Clark was engaged and fixing to build himself a house or not.

R O B I N

I hadn't been home from my date fifteen minutes before the telephone rang. I wasn't surprised that it was Julia on the phone. "I'm calling to see if you are in love," she said. "No," I informed her. I wasn't in love. I wasn't even in *like* any longer. In addition to being rich, self-centered, and impressed with his own money, Thad also had let it slip that he had a wife who lived in London most of the time because they didn't get along. Thad was the first person I'd dated who wasn't a college student—well, the first person other than Zeke. If he was any indication, it didn't look to me like my romantic life post-college was going to be much of an improvement. I don't know what it was about me, but I never seemed to be the type that attracted guys.

"Well, shit, Robin," Julia said. "If I'd known Thad wasn't going to turn out to be the love of your life, I never would have gone out with Danny!" she said.

"You *what*?" I shrieked. I was soaking in a bathtub full of bubbles. Actually, I'd had to scrounge to get myself a bubblebath together. I'd used dishwashing liquid since I was all out of bath oil beads. Julia and I had finished off the Gallo the night before. Instead of wine in my wine glass I was sipping flat Dr. Pepper. I almost knocked the glass over when she told me she'd been out with Danny.

"Don't dare drop the receiver in the bathtub," Julia said to me. "You'll fry yourself. It is all your fault," she said. "If you hadn't gone all gaga over this Thad I never would have called Danny up and agreed to meet him at the rice well."

"The rice well?"

"We only talked."

I had no idea whether I ought to believe her or not. Unlike me, it usually isn't hard for Julia to lie to anyone anywhere. She says that lying is a skill she learned so as to live with her mother. Since I couldn't see her face I wasn't sure if she was grinning or not. Although Julia will lie to me she usually gives her lie away by the big smile on her face. "Sure, you and Danny only talked," I said.

"Robin, you've got a very suspicious nature," she said. Then she laughed, which didn't really prove anything either. "See you tomorrow, Robin, sleep tight," she said before she hung up.

It took me forever to get to sleep. Much as I love Julia I can't say I wasn't jealous of her right then. Of course it was because I didn't have any old boyfriend who was still in love with me to call up on the phone. And she did.

JULIA

Danny called me early the Sunday morning after we met at the rice well the night Robin went out with Thad. More times than I can count I've wished I'd never picked up the phone and called him that night. "Julia, I want to talk to you, there are some things I should have said to you last night." I'd left, shall we say, abruptly the night before. The last thing I said to him was, "Danny, if you think I'm falling right back into the same old rut you and I were in before, you're full of shit." It wasn't what you might call a romantic ending to the perfect evening. Of course, we hadn't had the perfect evening, either.

But we had made love, which made me angry. For a while that night it was like we belonged together, the easy way we fell into our old patterns. You ever hear of imprinting? That's what Danny Clark did to me. First time I stuck my neck out of the egg, I saw Danny. And ever after, try though I did, when it came to men, it was Danny I seemed to be looking for.

"I'm on my way back to Houston," I said to him the next morning on the phone. "I don't live in Cypress Springs with my parents, I made a mistake calling you last night, and I don't think we should see each other for a while." I should have said forever but something stopped me. I also should have told him that I was engaged to a French guy from Paris. Unfortunately, early learning dies hard.

PART II

VERONA

Julia left a catalog from the University of Houston behind the last time she was here for the weekend. She's thinking of going to graduate school, she says. I had to laugh. The idea of Julia in graduate school! Julia, who barely got her college degree, even talking about going back to school should have been enough to have had our entire family rolling on the floor in stitches. "What on earth do you want any more schooling for?" I asked her. "By the time I was your age I was married with a baby on the way and a husband in the war."

"Mother, I'm not you," she informs me. As if I was confused on that fact.

"I don't see the sense of it, myself," I said. Although of course I suspected that Julia was interested in college because it was less demanding on her than a job was turning out to be. And she certainly wasn't awash in boyfriends, either. She is going to have to go somewhere to meet someone eligible if she keeps on wasting time the way she has been doing. Heaven knows I hope she doesn't think she can wait to marry until she's approaching thirty, the way her brother did. It is different for a woman, which Julia may learn the hard way someday if she doesn't pay attention to what I've been trying to tell her.

"I'm not sure what I'll take, I'm considering several fields," she replied. She had the catalog out on the dining room table and was scribbling down who-knows-what in one of her notebooks. She also had her reading glasses on, which she always pulls out and perches on her nose when she is trying to impress someone with her studious nature. This is aimed at her father, most likely. I certainly am not likely to fall for the charade. "You know, Daddy, I think maybe I should get an advanced degree so I would know more. I might want to work with underprivileged children," she said.

Tom fell right in with Julia. "Honey, that is a *good idea*," he says to her. "You'd be a wonderful teacher." He's got it in his head that Julia should be teaching up at the grade school because of how it was drummed into him that teaching is the only acceptable profession for a young woman. Tom has been beside himself ever since Julia graduated from Texas Tech last summer and rented herself an apartment down in Houston. "And where did she get the money for that apartment, I ask you?" I said to him. If Tom would ever learn to put his money where his mouth is regarding his daughter, he'd sleep better nights. "She'd be at home living under our roof if you'd quit covering her overdrawn checks at the bank. Have you ever considered that fact?" I asked him.

Looking through the catalog it was amazing to me the number of subjects there were to study. Real estate, interior design, textiles and clothing, the list went on and on. Although I don't think Julia has any business back in school, leafing through that book I could see how she'd be tempted. Some of those subjects did sound interesting. And, as far as I could tell, neither she nor her best friend, Robin, had so much as the hint of a boyfriend between the two of them. I wondered if this could be the influence of Robin, who seems nice enough but was raised by an old maid aunt.

One thing for sure, I raised my children a sight different from the way I was raised. And not just in material ways, although that of course is one of the differences which first comes to mind. Julia and Butch never woke up to a Christmas morning where the only things in their stockings were an apple, an orange, and a new Sunday school dress their mother had sewn for them. Not that there couldn't have been more for Hilda and me. My parents ran the general store that was located on the road to Wallford for years and years. We may have lived dirt poor, but there was money in the bank. We weren't destitute, despite the fact that my father acted like every quarter he parted with was going to be the one the lack of which was likely to send him to the poorhouse.

Some of my earliest memories are of playing on the splintery hardwood floor in the back of the store while my mother waited on customers. Our store burned to the ground one year the day after Easter. I was twelve or thirteen and my sister, Hilda, was two years older. Up until that time, I'd have to guess Hilda and I had both spent more time in the store than in our house, which was located about twenty yards back behind the store. Once the store burned to the ground, Daddy never got around to building a new one. He could have spent the money and built the store up again. But he did the same thing with his insurance money he did with every dime he ever got his hands on, he bought himself another little piece of land.

I said to Hilda later on, once I got used to the store being gone, that I liked not having it there in front of our house so well that if I'd have thought of it I'd have put a torch to it myself. Hilda gave that nervous little giggle of hers. "Hush, Verona," she said, "someone might hear you."

The blessing was, once the store was reduced to cinders and rubble, Hilda and I weren't stuck working there every afternoon after school and all summer long, which meant we could hire ourselves out to some of the farmers' families who lived close around us. Mostly Hilda babysat and house-cleaned. But I realized I could make twice as much money when I could convince one of the farmers to let me drive a tractor and pull a plow. One summer, the summer before Hilda had to marry Johnnie Wayne Walters, I made close to two hundred dollars. That was a fortune in those days. Daddy made us put half of the money we earned into a savings account for our futures, one tenth went to the church, the rest we got to keep. Hilda and I, for the first times in our lives, were able to attend school wearing store-bought clothes. Later on, once the church awarded me a scholarship to Baylor University, I sat down and figured out that I'd gotten my 10 percent back and then some, which wasn't a bad deal, I decided. Hilda, who married the year she was seventeen, never got a dime back from the church.

After Hilda married Johnnie Wayne, he joined the army and got himself sent out to California for basic training. Hilda surprised us all. She loaded up his old Chevrolet sedan with all her clothes and their wedding presents and drove out to California to join him. "You could stay here, have the baby," Mother said, the night before she left. "I hate to think of you way off in California. You'll be all by yourself and pregnant."

"Johnnie Wayne is my husband. My place is with him," Hilda said.

"Your father saying so don't necessarily make it so. Your husband is more than likely going to be sent overseas, then where will you be?" Mother asked her.

"Johnnie Wayne says there will be some money for me to live on, his pay from the army. And I won't be the only army wife in California. I'll wait till he comes back and then we'll go where he's sent. I wouldn't feel right, Mother, living under Daddy's roof now that I am a married woman."

My head was spinning the entire time Mother and Hilda were talking. I couldn't for the life of me figure out how I missed hearing that conversation, the one Mother alluded to which had gone on between Hilda and Daddy. Or why, since I hadn't overheard it, Hilda had neglected to tell me about what Daddy had said. Up until Hilda and Johnnie Wayne got serious, Hilda never kept the first secret from me. But marriage changed her. It appeared to bring out an independent streak I had never before seen in my sister.

Millie Harwell, who was always close to Hilda, being that they came within four hours of having the exact same birthday, is the one who told me what had happened. I don't hold a grudge, but it galls me to this day to think that it was Millie from down the road who was the one to tell me the truth about my own flesh and blood. In a nutshell it boiled down to the fact that Daddy told Hilda Johnnie Wayne would never amount to much and, since she had gotten herself in a fix to where she had no choice but to be marrying him, she had better be prepared for a lifetime of doing without. She was not to expect her father to take care of her, nor could she look to her mother for financial support. "You made your bed, now lie in it," he said.

There never was a thing wrong with Johnnie Wayne except he came from a Methodist family and Daddy always was suspicious of Methodists. Johnnie Wayne's father was a plumber, and if he didn't make a lot of money, he made enough to pay his bills and give his children some advantages, which certainly should have been enough for Daddy. Daddy was a hard man, however. He carried on more or less the same way with me when I got engaged to Tom. Talking about how I should finish the education people in our community had sacrificed to give me. And he had a few words to say about the Salwells, who were not regular churchgoers and were Methodists to boot. "Yes, Daddy, I expect you're right," I said. "I'll pray on it," I told him. Once you told Daddy you were praying on something, that was a signal to him to let up on it, it was out of his hands. Hilda could have learned a thing or two from me. I didn't tell Daddy everything I was doing or thinking because, to be blunt about it, it was none of his business. But Hilda always was honest to a fault so she went ahead and told Daddy that her marriage to Johnnie Wayne wasn't strictly speaking optional since there was a baby on the way. She never should have done that. Mother had told her to keep her mouth shut. So had I. But Hilda couldn't stand lying, even when to do so all she'd have had to do is keep her lips clamped tight. "I'm pregnant, Daddy, and Johnnie Wayne and I are in love." Millie says this is what Hilda said to Daddy, and then that was all she wrote, there was no reasoning with Daddy after that. Hilda never did come home again, except to visit. And when they did come to town, like as not they'd stay over at Johnnie Wayne's parents instead of with Mother and Daddy.

"You might as well let bygones be bygones," I said to my sister. By this time she'd been married over ten years, and I'd been married to Tom six years myself.

"I have," she replied. "I don't hold any hard feelings toward Daddy, but I like staying with Johnnie Wayne's family." It made me glad I'd married Tom and stayed home where I belonged, the way I saw Hilda and Johnnie Wayne gradually getting more and more distant from us all. Came the time when Hilda and I had to work hard to have a conversation, we were so different. She was so different, I should say. This came as a result of living all over the country the way she and Johnnie Wayne did. It irks me no end, the way some people change themselves from who they started out to be.

Millie Harwell who runs the beauty shop and my sister, Hilda, remained friends until the day my sister died, despite the fact Hilda and Johnnie Wayne never did come back to Cypress Springs to live. Somehow or another Millie managed to keep up, I suppose. I don't see how, she didn't see Hilda all that much, either. Johnnie Wayne stayed in the service for no telling how many years, and even the time he was overseas for over one entire year, Hilda didn't come home. She stayed put on the base he'd shipped out of. Eventually they settled in San Antonio, Johnnie Wayne and Hilda and their children.

While he was in the service Johnnie Wayne started going by J.W., but no one in Cypress Springs ever could remember he liked to be called by his initials. J.W. went to college on the GI bill and became a pharmacist. Later on he bought his own drugstore. Unfortunately Daddy was dead by then so he didn't get to eat his own words, the ones about Hilda having to spend her life doing without. Hilda did right well, despite Daddy's dire predictions. Hilda got her high school diploma by mail and then went on to earn a college degree herself. I know all her kids did well in school. One of them, Sumter, who was the one closest in age to Julia, was valedictorian of her high school class. All of this I learned from Millie at the beauty shop, who got it from my mother or Hilda herself. Hilda never told the first thing to me. Like I said, because of how different Hilda and I became, it got to where we couldn't seem to carry on a decent conversation.

When our parents died, I called Hilda the minute I heard the news. Both times she said to me, "Make whatever funeral arrangements you want to, Verona. You are the one who is there on the spot." For Daddy's funeral she didn't stay in town twenty-four hours. "You could spend some time with Mother," I told my sister when I heard she was driving back to San Antonio the morning after the funeral. "Help her adjust. She's never in her life lived alone. This is going to be hard for her."

"Mother's going home with me for a few weeks," Hilda told me. That was the first I'd heard of Mother going home with Hilda.

"Whatever for?" I asked.

"She's never been to San Antonio. She'd like to see it."

"Mother," I said. "I didn't know you'd been wanting to go see San Antonio."

"Well, I think it will be nice," she said. "I've always been curious about the places your sister has gotten herself off to." She spoke so softly, I don't think she'd ever her entire life raised her voice. And she wasn't in the habit of saying what it was she did want. I thought at the time maybe she was just going home with Hilda because Hilda wanted her to do it. Later on, though—years later, when Mother herself passed on—I found the entire bottom three drawers of her dresser were filled with mementoes from Hilda and her family. For every place Hilda had lived Mother had a map, and at least one of those books that tells all about the state and the cities in it. Hilda had lived in seven different cities and Mother had a box for each city. She had the pictures and letters Hilda and the kids had sent all pasted into notebooks. It was as if Mother had made herself a storybook for every place Hilda had lived.

I was all alone cleaning out Mother's house. I'd been thinking to myself that it defied comprehension that I had once lived in this tiny *poor* little place. Hilda had been into town for the funeral. She was gone three days later. "You have to stay and help me clean out the house. How will I know what you want otherwise?" I said to Hilda.

"There isn't anything in their house that I want."

"But how can you know until you look?" I asked her.

"I know," she said.

I couldn't *not* look, so I went through the closets, all four of them. And the kitchen. And in the end I had to conclude that Hilda was right. Mother hadn't *had* anything to speak of. The only surprise was the books of Hilda's life. I was tempted to burn them right then and there without saying a word to my sister. It would have served her right. But I did the correct thing. I called Hilda from Mother's house. "Mother saved every letter you and the kids ever wrote her. She's got them all here, with the pictures you sent, organized into books. Storybooks of your life, Hilda." I felt so angry with my sister. That my mother had done this for her and Hilda hadn't even been the one to find it. Nothing there for her, she'd said. And in reality there was something. And I'd been the one to find it. There was nothing for me to find for myself, however. "Hilda, I hope you realize if it wasn't for me being willing to do the hard work of cleaning out this house you would have never known of these books. I hope you realize that fact."

"Oh, I didn't know she'd done that. I would like the books, could you send them?" Hilda's voice was soft, like Mother's. Either I'd never noticed before how much Hilda sounded like Mother or, with Mother gone, Hilda had appropriated her voice. That was likely.

"I'll take them to my house," I said. "The next time you're here you can get them. All Mother's hard work, I wouldn't dare trust them to the mail."

Hilda didn't even have to come and get them though. Millie, who along with her husband was going to spend

Thanksgiving in San Antonio with Hilda and Johnnie Wayne, took them to her. I didn't get to see Hilda's face when she looked at them for the first time.

Even though I never went anywhere you'd have thought Mother could have made at least one book for me.

It is so easy to get lost in the past. Events, like people, do have a way of running together. I start in talking to Julia and find myself somehow or another in a conversation with my sister. Julia has always gotten irritated no end with me when I call her Hilda. It isn't intentional. It is simply one of those things that happens.

Not that there aren't some similarities. Julia, like Hilda, has always had a bee in her bonnet to go somewhere. Anywhere. First it was off to Texas Tech. Her grades were good enough, thanks to me, that she could have gotten into Rice University right down the road in Houston. It seemed to me that Rice was a good school, small enough to where it was likely the teachers could keep up with the students. And, failing that, I'd have been able to get down there and see to it that Julia was at least doing her homework.

Mr. Fields, who was the assistant principal when Julia was in high school, told me himself, "Julia has excellent test scores and her grades are right up there. She could get into just about any school in Texas."

"I'm thinking about Rice University," I said to him.

"Certainly Rice would more than likely be thrilled to have her."

Then Julia up and decided on Texas Tech. "What on earth is she thinking of?" I asked Butch. "You'd better talk some sense into her, do you have any idea where Lubbock, Texas, is?"

"Mother, it's not the moon, she'll be fine at Texas Tech if that's where she wants to go."

"Who is going to get after her the first time she doesn't turn in her homework is what I would like to know. Butch, Julia isn't like you. She isn't the first bit responsible."

Susie, who hadn't been in the family two years at that time, sided with Butch and Julia. "She may surprise you, Verona," she said.

"That will be the day." I wasn't surprised by what she got up to during her college years. It is a well-known fact that Julia barely graduated from college. She made it out by the skin of her teeth. She had to take some of her science courses the third time. This from a young lady who had made the highest grade ever recorded on her high school biology exams. She simply did not apply herself once she got out from under my thumb. And now I learn that she expects to enroll herself in graduate school. And Tom and Butch are sure to say to her, *Well, Julia dear, that is just so wonderful.*

I never expected this. People used to *listen* to me. After Tom and I married we lived, for the first year, in an old frame house we rented just outside of College Station while he finished up at A&M. It was tiny, two bedrooms, one bath, and had a small, inconvenient kitchen. The yard was fenced because the house itself was located on some land the owner ran cattle on.

The minute I suspected I was pregnant I told Tom we were going to have to get ourselves our own house built back in Cypress Springs. I wasn't bringing a child into that tacky little farmhouse we were living in. It wasn't like we didn't already have the place we wanted to build on in mind. We owned, in both our names, two hundred acres his parents had given us as a wedding present. And there was a spot, sort of up on a hill, where Tom and I thought our house should go. In the middle of a semicircular cluster of oak trees which looked to have been planted years ago as a setting for a two-story colonial mansion.

That isn't what we built. We built a sprawling brick ranch-style house. I was torn, I admit, between ranch and colonial. But Tom's parents' house was colonial and I didn't want to build a house that looked like I was trying to copy them. The other thing that influenced my decision was the fact that, not five hundred yards behind our home site, sat three frame houses which were used off and on for hired hands and their families. These houses were situated near a barn and corral, and while our house wouldn't overlook them, I'd never lose sight of the fact they were there. When I was showing my house plans to Millie, right before I had definitely told Tom we were going with ranch style rather than colonial, something Millie said while she was rolling my hair hit me wrong. "Go for the colonial, Verona, then you can do the grande dame bit up right. You've already got the slave cabins back behind it."

"The very idea!" I said to her. Millie has the worst excuse for a sense of humor. That remark was, plain and simple, in poor taste. As if I, or any civilized person, would support the idea of slavery.

We had planned to take out a mortgage for the money to build the house. Certainly there was no reason why we should not have done so. But Gram, Tom's grandmother on his father's side, got wind of what we were doing and like to have had a fit. "Salwells don't borrow from the bank to build their houses. They don't mortgage their land. You should remember that it wasn't that long ago when the banks failed and those who had a mortgage on their homes like as not lost them! What you do is save your money until you can pay cash." Tom, like everyone else in his family, was so in the habit of listening to her that I had the devil's own time convincing him to go on up to the bank with me and at least talk to the bank president. "No offense, honey," I said to him, "but your grandmother is old. She isn't at all up on the way things are done now."

There wasn't any problem borrowing the money, but we didn't actually need to do so. Once Gram realized we were serious about having our house built before our first child was born, she insisted on giving us the money herself. "No call to go throwing money away, that is what you will be doing. What do you think interest is? Money thrown away, that is all in the world interest money you pay to the bank is."

Not that Gram wrote out a check and gave us free rein. Far from it. She had something to say about near every decision we made. "Why do you want three bathrooms?" she wanted to know.

I tried to be sensible with her. "Tom and I plan a large family, two boys, two girls. So we need a master bath as well as one for the girls and one for the boys." If I had thought of it, I'd also have had a half bath put in off the utility room, but it took several years of living in my house before I realized how convenient that would have been. And necessary. A bathroom off the utility room is an absolute necessity when you are living with a farmer for a husband and a little boy who takes right after him.

"One bathroom is all you need. Haven't you ever heard of taking turns?" Gram asked me.

I just ignored that. As I mentioned to Millie later, the woman had grown up in a house without indoor plumbing. She lived with an outhouse up until after she herself married.

So it was ingrained with her, the idea that one bathroom would do. For her, the simple fact of being able to use the facilities without stepping out in the cold or heat of the day was a luxury. But I didn't plan to let her limited aspirations throw a pall on my dream house.

"Brick? Do you realize you are adding two thousand dollars to the cost of this house? What is wrong with frame, I would like to know? You can brick the house yourself when you're spending money you've earned!"

"I don't like frame houses. They're spindly-looking and always need painting," I said. "I read an article in the *Good Housekeeping* magazine which plainly states that it is wisest to build the house you want right from the start. It is much better than to go into a brand-new house already thinking of the changes you are going to want to make."

"I am sure that *Good Housekeeping* magazine is full of advice for young whippersnappers who are still wet behind the ears," she said to me. Gram did have a tongue on her.

"Look, Gram, Tom and I do appreciate your generosity," I said. I didn't bow down to her the way the rest of the family did, but I was polite. "If you'd rather not pay for the entire house we've got our hearts set on, then I'm sure the bank will loan us the extra money we need."

By the time I was seven months pregnant we were moving into the house, all of which was paid for by Gram. She unbent at the housewarming and said to me, "Well, it is a nice house, young lady. I hope you enjoy it."

"I plan to," I assured her and everyone else who complimented us on our taste. The house was perfect, it truly was. Not that, over the years, we didn't make alterations to the basic plan. But I've never regretted that I decided on ranch style rather than colonial. That *might* have been pretentious. And, you know, I have decided that in a two-story house all you seem to do is run up and down those stairs. Who needs that?

IT WASN'T TOM who checked me into Methodist Hospital in 1941 to have my baby. Tom was on his way to Hawaii four days after our housewarming. I'll never believe he didn't know that was coming and keep it from me. I'm sure he thought he was being considerate. I have never been one to keep up with world news and so it is understandable that I wouldn't have had the first clue what was coming. And it would have been just like Tom to decide not to tell me until after we had moved into our new house.

"Why you?" I asked. "You have a baby on the way. And a brand-new house that we've barely gotten the drapes hung in. This is not a good time for you to go over to fight in some place that to be perfectly honest I have never even heard the name of before."

"Verona, you knew all the time I was drilling at A&M that they'd send me somewhere after I finished. Be thankful you're in the house. Your mother will help with the baby. So will mine, for that matter. I'll be back before you know it!"

Famous last words. Tom was gone over a year. But at least he did come back. His best friend, Charlie, never did get home. I suppose, in a perverse sort of way, Cypress Springs is lucky there weren't but the two men from Cypress Springs at Pearl Harbor. It was a devastating time for all of us, those of us who were left back home to cope as well as the men who had to go. Many of the wives found themselves in a situation similar to my own, all alone in an unfamiliar house trying to take care of a brand-new baby. Despite the fact we weren't sent anywhere, we certainly did not find ourselves lolling about in any bed of roses.

The day after I had Butch, Tom's mother came down to see me, bringing a letter from my husband. "I stopped by the post office to get your mail, Verona," she said as she handed it to me. I grabbed that letter and clutched it to me like it had my husband himself inside the envelope. At least he was still alive even if he wasn't by my side where I wanted him to be. By then we had all heard Charlie Sullivan was not going to be coming home. Tom and Charlie had been best friends since they were little boys. They'd gone all through school together, they'd roomed together at Texas A&M before Tom and I got married and moved into that house outside of town. Charlie was best man in our wedding. Charlie and Tom used to have identical rings. These were two-carat diamond rings their families had given them as graduation-from-college presents. Tom had his made into an engagement ring for me. I never did hear what happened to Charlie's ring. I don't know whether he had it with him and it got sent back or if it got lost. Maybe he left it home with his family. This isn't the kind of thing you just up and ask people even if you *are* wondering.

"If the baby is a boy, I would like to name him Charles Sullivan Salwell," Tom wrote. "After my best friend, Charlie."

Poor Tom, way off on an island having to watch his best friend pass on. I know it was terrible for him, every bit as terrible as it was for me, having to go into the hospital and give birth, which it is obvious I had never done before. When it came time to put down the name on the birth certificate, I wished I'd never had that letter from Tom. I didn't want to name my first-born Charles, I wanted to name him Tom Junior. After thinking it over very carefully that is what I did.

The way I explained my decision to Tom was to say that Butch was the spitting image of his own daddy from day one and it would have been just plain wrong to name him anything else. "We'll name the next one Charlie," I promised Tom in the letter I wrote him that night from the hospital.

I hadn't been totally truthful with my husband. Butch, when he was born, wasn't the spitting image of anybody. He was a red wrinkled little baby who looked like what he was, a new baby. The real reason I named Butch after his daddy was this feeling I couldn't shake. Off and on ever since Mr. and Mrs. Sullivan got the telegram from the government, I'd get this terrible thought. At times it got so strong that I was really and truly afraid I was having a premonition. I'd shiver from head to toe inside myself every time I had the thought, but I couldn't stop having it. The thought was this: *Tom himself isn't home yet. And if he doesn't get back then there would never ever as long as I lived be another baby to name Tom Junior.* You can see why I couldn't have written those words to Tom. And why it was equally impossible for me to name Butch Charlie.

Butch had seven teeth and was walking all over the place before his daddy saw him for the first time. "What do you think of your son?" I asked my husband.

I can't remember what Tom said back to me. Something noncommittal I am sure. He came home wounded, and a much quieter man than the one he'd been when he left. It took him months to unwind, to settle back in. I blamed the war. It seemed as if my perfect dream life had become tarnished by a war somewhere that had nothing whatsoever to do with me. Tom came home different. I suppose maybe I should have left the house alone while he was gone. But, then again, he'd been gone a year. Life goes on, I said to him, he couldn't expect us to stand still until he got back. I had had the white picket fence put in while he was gone. And I did have the entire house carpeted. And there was some furniture I bought. Other than that, things were the way they'd been when he left. "What do you think of the carpet?" I asked him. "I had it done when Butch started crawling all over the place. Hardwood floors are the worst on baby knees."

"He isn't crawling now."

"Well, he was. You should have seen it. Butch was the cutest little thing. He first took to crawling with his legs stiff and straight up from the ground. So he looked like a little London Bridge waddling from one end of the house to the other. That is what led me to decide I had to carpet the house. Because it seemed to me the only reason for a child to crawl without his knees touching the floor was because the floor was just too hard on the poor soft baby knees." Tom didn't say a word, he simply stood there and stared at me. I was forced to say something else just to break the silence. "Do you like the fence, at least?" I asked him.

"A fence is a fence, I suppose," he replied. I don't think, for all he said he felt superfluous, that it mattered to him what the house looked like. It was as if he didn't *care*. One time he said to me, "Verona there are things more important than houses." As if I had to be told something so obvious. The other thing I noticed about Tom was the nightmares. Night after night I'd have to wake Tom up. "Quit that shouting, Tom, you'll wake the dead. There are no airplanes here. You are at home in your own bed."

He didn't believe it though. It was like, once he went to sleep, he went somewhere else. He took to sleeping with a loaded gun under the bed.

"For heaven's sake," I said to him. "We've got an impressionable child in the house. My daddy never even owned a gun," I said to Tom. Most things I was able to discuss calmly and reason with him about. But the gun wasn't one of those things. Tom Salwell slept with a loaded gun in his bedroom from the day he returned from the Pacific. This over my most strenuous objections. And when he went somewhere in his truck you better believe he carried a weapon in his glovebox as well.

Have you ever dropped something? Say, three buttons? Two fall together on one side of you and one is way across the room by itself. You find yourself thinking how on earth can this be, the buttons were all three right here in my hand and I didn't do a thing to them but catch my hand against the fabric of the cushion, which caused my hand to open and the buttons to fall. So why did two drop right below where they started out and one get itself so far across the room I've had to search for an hour to turn it up?

That's the way of life it seems to me. I started out with a husband I'd known from the cradle, so to speak, and the two of us married and moved into a house we built not three miles as the crow flies from where we both grew up. You'd think there weren't any surprises in store for us, wouldn't you?

Be careful what you ask for, you're likely to get it. Whoever first said that spoke the truth, I suppose. I can't in all honesty say that fact has not been borne out in my own life. I asked for a loving husband, children, a nice house. That's *all* I ever really asked for. I didn't want a job. Certainly when Julia talks about how maybe she should have a career, she might as well be talking a foreign language as far as I am concerned. I wanted to marry someone wonderful and have myself a rich, full life—like you see in the magazines.

I suppose I have the things I always said I wanted, but this house is empty. It never did fill up right. What am I trying to say? I built it straight out of a magazine. Maybe if there had been four children. And no war. Tom, when he would sit down to a meal, he never smiled and looked out lovingly at his wife and the table she'd so beautifully set. Butch seemed to go from the hospital delivery room straight off to college, he was in and out of the house so fast. I remember the first premonition I had that it was happening. Butch was about three years old. He was wearing the red cowboy boots his Aunt Hilda had sent him from Colorado, the ones Julia wore years later. "I go work with Daddy," he told me one day. He'd put his own boots on and was rummaging around in the closet looking for his straw hat.

"You're too little," I said to him. "Little boys have to stay home with their mommies."

"I go to work with Daddy!" he said and stomped that boot on the floor right in front of my face.

Tom laughed and said, "Why not? He can go with me this morning." I watched Butch walk out to the truck with his daddy and realized that there wasn't a thing for me to do inside the house. Hattie was in the kitchen doing the breakfast dishes. After that, she'd be out hanging the laundry. What was I supposed to do? I'm not too proud to admit I went inside and bawled my eyes out. After that I got in my car and drove out to my mother's.

"What did you do when your kids left home?" I asked her.

She smiled like she thought I was making a joke.

"Your son is far from leaving home," she said to me. She never did understand what I wanted to know from her—which was, why on earth wasn't there more to life than a nice husband, a brand-new house with three bathrooms, and a child who wasn't going to stay mine long enough for me to shake a stick at?

I made my adjustments, I just didn't make a world-class production out of the fact that I was having to do it. Julia is prone to do just that—Sarah Bernhardt I should have named her. By the time Julia was three years old she was doing much more than stomping a boot-clad foot in my face. When she was not yet four, she left home. Just up and left. I had no earthly idea she'd do such a thing. "I don't like you, I'm going to find my daddy!" she stormed at me. "Your daddy is over at Grandma's working cows today, you're stuck with me," I remember saying to her and thinking no more of it. She stormed into her room, slamming her door behind her. I got busy around the house and I guess it was an hour, maybe two, before it occurred to me I hadn't heard so much as a peep from the direction of her room. She's fallen asleep in her room, I thought, and tiptoed down the hall to check on her. Her door was open and she was nowhere to be found. I started right in, looking high and low and was just starting to panic when Tom walked in the back door, Julia in his arms.

"What on earth?" I asked.

"I found her out on the highway, halfway to Mother's house. She told me she was mad at you and she was coming to see me," he said.

I was speechless. Julia had left the house and gotten herself out on the highway. If she was halfway to Tom's parents' house then she had to have been a good two miles down the road. It gave me the shivers to think what might have happened to her. Just as I was fixing to lay down the law good to her, Tom let out a positively indecent whoop of laughter. "Honey, you do beat all," he said and gave her a kiss and an affectionate pat on the backside as he sat her down.

"But you don't do that again, you could have gotten lost. Or hurt. And then Daddy would have been very, very sad."

"Very, very sad, my hind leg. That child needs a good spanking. Do you realize what might have happened to her?" I said.

Julia was in the den, turning on the television set. We never allowed Butch to turn on the television set himself when he was four years of age. I worried about electricity shocking him. I'd told Julia not to turn it on so many times I'd lost count. "She doesn't mind me worth shooting," I said to Tom. "And you laughing at what she does the way you do undermines my authority."

"I talked to her in the truck coming home, Verona. She won't get out on the road again without one of us with her, she promised me. But you have to admire her spunk!"

I sometimes think it is lucky I didn't have but the two kids. Another one like Julia would have been enough to send me to the funny farm for sure.

I HAD JUST started selling home cosmetics when it first dawned on me I might be pregnant with her. Actually, it first dawned on Hattie. I was coming out of the bathroom one morning as she was going in my room to do up the bed. Butch was off at school—he was nine years old by that time—and Tom, true to his lifelong custom, had left the house to see to what he needed to see to that day long before eight o'clock in the morning. Many was the morning he was gone before seven. Usually Butch rode the bus to school. There really wasn't any reason for me to get up at the crack of dawn. They got their own breakfast, the two of them did, while I slept late. Then, once Hattie came in to work, she and I had something together before we got our day going. It wasn't the life I had envisioned, but it satisfied me. As I said, I had made my accommodations.

I said to Hattie, "I believe the fish we had last night might have been off, I have just had an upset stomach."

Hattie lifted her eyebrows at me and replied, "It does not seem to have upset any other stomachs in this house. I bet you five cents Charlie is fixing to put in his appearance."

As soon as she said the words I knew she was right. I waited until the doctor confirmed my pregnancy, of course, before I said anything to anyone other than Hattie, but from that morning, once Hattie and I exchanged looks, I knew a baby was on the way. And I also knew, in the way women know things, that this one would be the last. Having long since reconciled myself to one child rather than the four I had envisioned, it took some doing to get my mind settled to the idea of even two. Once you've made some of life's compromises, you expect them to stay made. At least I did. The truth is, at that point in my life, it was extremely difficult to think of starting over with diapers again.

Not that it was Julia's fault, of course. But it is an unfortunate fact that my life certainly went haywire after she put in her appearance. She didn't affect the rest of the family in a like fashion. Not a one of them came close to understanding what I was going through. It was me that had all the changes to deal with. And I am not talking simply about the fact that I was the one who waddled around fat and pregnant for nine long months. It was me who had every single thing in her life go topsy-turvy for what seemed like an eternity. The worst part was when Hattie, who, granted, was long years past her sixtieth birthday, decided she had postponed retirement as long as she cared to.

"But what will I do without you?" I asked her. By this time, Julia was nine months old and past the colic, which like to have done us in, me and Hattie both. Hattie, who had worked for me for years, let me know in no uncertain fashion that blood is indeed thicker than water and there was no blood tie between the two of us. "I never in my life thought you'd run out on me at this juncture," I said to her.

"Miss Verona, you know as well as I do, what you need to do is to get someone younger in here, someone who can keep up with that child," Hattie said to me. "I'm too old."

Hattie was right. Once Julia started crawling, Hattie couldn't keep up with her. But, my heavenly days, I was a lot younger than Hattie was and I didn't feel like I was coping all that well myself. So, regardless of how old she felt, the time Hattie picked to desert ship was not in my best interests. At least that is the way I saw it. Hattie, whom up until that time I had felt to be my best friend, left my employ without much more than a backward glance. Thereafter, when she and her daughter were out for a Sunday spin, she might drop by and say hello. That was it. Quite an eye-opener the entire experience turned out to be. I will say this, Hattie did find me Essie before she left me high and dry with barely so much as a backward glance. Because I told her, if you think you're leaving me here helpless, you better think again. There has to be someone here to help me out or I *will* go crazy.

Either I had forgotten what it was like to have a baby around or Butch must have been a picnic compared to Julia. The thing was, she was so active. I don't remember having to watch Butch every single minute the way Julia needed to be watched. From the minute she started crawling, which was at seven months if you can believe that, Julia was either asleep or into something. "My first one, Sally, was the same way,"

Tom's mother said, and laughed as she said it. I thought to myself, *I'll bet Sally was grown and gone before her mother got to where she could laugh about how she had been.* That was the way I felt with Julia, I can tell you that. There were days I despaired I would ever again know a moment's peace.

And it wasn't as if, from the minute I learned I was expecting her, I had not taken every precaution. The minute I first suspected I was pregnant, I gave up my evening cocktails completely. I didn't need to be told twice that the alcohol I consumed would go straight to the baby. Julia has recently gotten into her head that I drank and smoked when my kids were on the way. Nothing could be farther from the truth. With Butch, I hadn't yet developed the habit. And with Julia, I realized it was the cocktail habit, as much as anything, that had led to the predicament I was in. I certainly didn't want any repeat of what happened with Wiley Sutton. Some people will make the same mistake over and over. Not me. One mistake is all it took. I learned my lesson.

What happened was this. Tom was gone from home. His daddy and mother were thinking of buying this land out in Colorado, and they'd been after him and after him to come look at it. Butch, who was in second grade, had a few days off from school, some holiday or another, and went with his daddy, which left me and Hattie at home rattling around in the house all alone. Then Hattie up and decided as there wasn't much for us to do she would go down to Houston and spend several days with her married daughter and her grandchildren.

I was bored. That is the truth of the matter. I took to having my first drink without even waiting for five o'clock to come around. The second night Hattie was gone, I guess it had to have been after eight o'clock and was just getting dark when the phone rang and it was Wiley Sutton from down the road wanting to borrow one of Tom's cattle prods for the next day. I said to Wiley, sure, come on and get it. I didn't think twice about saying that to Wiley.

What happened next I will never if I live to be a hundred years of age understand. It started, I expect, while we were out in the barn back behind the house looking high and low for the cattle prods. Finally I gave up. "Tom must keep them in the house, Wiley, you'll have to see if you can't find them yourself." The garage is where I meant, of course. Wiley followed me into the garage where, sure enough, he found several of them on a shelf. "Well, come inside the house, you might as well have a drink before you go on home," I said to him. Wiley, who was about five years younger than I am, was not married at that time. As the saying goes, one thing led to another and the next thing you know we were laying on the couch, the two of us, both undressed and he was on top of me. This was a completely unplanned development. But Wiley started in talking about how he had always been so attracted to me and, let's face it, I'd been an old married woman for so long that I was flattered to think I was still able to command that kind of masculine attention. Certainly for years and years Tom had taken me totally for granted. I couldn't even remember when the last time was my husband had said the first admiring word about how I looked to me. And when Tom did compliment me, likely as not he'd say something like "Nice dress, is it new?" when whatever I had on was something I'd had for ages.

Of course it didn't last, Wiley's mad passion. "Oh, Verona, I, uh, well when did you say you expect Tom to get on home?" Wiley asked me this as he was in the process of scrambling all over the place looking for his clothes. The way he was carrying on, it appeared as if he thought someone was fixing to walk in the door and start shooting at him. This must have been two or three o'clock the next morning. We'd fallen asleep, and if it wasn't for the fact that that couch is darned uncomfortable who knows how long it would have been before either one of us woke up?

Wiley got himself dressed and left my house, all the while stumbling over both his words and his feet. I wasn't flustered in the least. Wiley was acting ridiculous enough for both of us. "Look here, we have made a mistake, I should have fixed you coffee like I offered to instead of letting you into the sipping whiskey, Wiley. But we will just put this entire night out of our minds. That is the only thing to do." To tell you the truth, I think I must still have been a little looped myself at that point because I remember giggling at how nervous he was. "Relax, Tom and Butch are out in Colorado for another two days, we'll just forget the entire thing ever happened."

"I hope no one drove past and saw my truck," Wiley said.

"No one saw your truck, now get on home," I said to him. Wiley certainly wasn't then, and never had been, my type.

"Uh, Verona, the thing is, I mean, except for you are married, I would like to see you again," Wiley said to me. He just couldn't leave it alone. I was somewhat flattered—I had forgotten the heady feeling you get when some man you don't know well at all gives you the eye. Even if it is in point of fact only Wiley Sutton, five years younger than you are, who the main thing you remember about him is the two of you used to ride the same school bus and growing up from junior high on he had a perpetual case of acne. "Well, I am an old married woman, Wiley, so let's just sort of forget we ever opened this can of worms; remember now, mum's the word. I won't tell if you don't," I said to him as I sort of gave him a shove out the back door. And damned if I didn't give out another ridiculous-sounding giggle. It was then and there that I should have given up my evening cocktails.

The next few times I ran into Wiley he blushed just looking at me—actually past me, heaven knows he couldn't meet my eyes—and I remember I smiled nicely at him, all the while thinking to myself at least it is good to know that I am not totally over the hill, that someone still finds me attractive. But of course I realized the entire while that I would remain entirely faithful to my husband. Actually I considered that I had been. That night with Wiley wasn't really being unfaithful, it was just this one tiny forgivable little slip.

I barely gave the night with Wiley another thought. It was like a dream I had had. Real when I was dreaming it. And vivid the next morning. But after a week or two there just wasn't anything left but a smoky, not-quite-solid memory. Nothing to back it up, if you know what I mean. At this late date I sometimes wonder if I really did sleep with Wiley Sutton. It is equally plausible to me that I dreamt the entire episode.

When Hattie and I first started looking back and forth at each other and speculating with our raised eyebrows, I was thrilled, that fact I clearly remember. My first reaction was sheer delight—Butch was finally, after almost ten years, going to have a brother or a sister. It was all I could do to wait until I had seen the doctor to tell Tom. I didn't want to raise his hopes simply to dash them, so as it happened I was almost three months along before I told my husband. But from the first I had been doing everything possible to give Julia a good beginning. I ate right. No alcohol. No caffeine. Well, not over a cup or two of coffee a day. I did watch it.

The first little twinge I had which hinted to me maybe this pregnancy wouldn't be as great a blessing as my first occurred as I was standing in the bathroom, staring out the window at the driveway that leads from around our house to the garage. From the master bath you can see the entire back of our house. I had told Tom our big news when he came in from out back that past night. He'd walked in and, before he even took off his boots, I said, "The doctor called, we're having a baby!"

Tom came close to causing me to miscarry, the way he picked me up in his arms and squeezed me so tight. You'd have thought I'd just handed the man a check for a million dollars. It had been a great evening, start to finish. We were both still sort of caught up in the rosy glow from the night before the next morning. Tom was shaving and I was standing behind him in the bathroom, looking out the window, not expecting to see anything, of course, just sort of idly gazing out, thinking over how glad I was we were having the second child. The smell of shaving cream is the thing I remember. Medicated and slightly tart. Tom started naming off months out loud. How long before the baby came is what he was figuring. Mid-September, in the doctor's opinion, I had already mentioned that to him.

Standing there in my own bathroom, looking at nothing and half-listening to my husband, I saw something which surely wasn't there. It was parked in the middle of our driveway behind the garage doors, which, of course, at that time of the day were closed. It was Wiley Sutton's red Ford truck parked right off my kitchen porch. I blinked but the blamed thing didn't go away. My stomach lurched and I reached forward and clutched the towel bar under the window, hoping I wasn't fixing to throw up. I must have moaned aloud because Tom turned real quick-like and said to me, "Verona, sit down before you fall down!" *You'd look pale too if you'd just seen a ghost,* are the words I almost said to him. But fortunately I collected myself before I let them slip out. Otherwise, what on earth would I have said to Tom to explain about the ghost vehicle I was seeing?

"Do you see anything out there, in the driveway?" I did go ahead and ask him that question. That was stupid of me, of course, but I was in such a panic, I couldn't think. And I had to know. The sight I saw was so real that I couldn't believe it wasn't there.

"There's nothing out in our backyard, honey, let's get you on back up in the bed."

Before I let him lead me out of the bathroom I turned and looked again just to be sure. The minute I looked out there, I could tell Tom was right, there wasn't any truck in our driveway. But it had been so real not minutes before. The thought occurred to me that maybe Wiley had pulled in our driveway, stopped, thought better of it, and driven away. After Tom left for work I went out and checked for tire tracks. There were plenty of those, of course. They had come from my car and Hattie's as well as Tom's own truck. Hattie walked outside to see what I was doing. "What are you looking for?" she asked me.

"I thought I saw a strange car in our driveway this morning," I said to her. I purposely didn't say Wiley Sutton's red Ford truck to see what Hattie would say back to me. If there had been a truck, she almost had to have seen it. At the least she would have heard it drive in over the cattle guard. She'd been in the kitchen fixing our breakfast with all the windows wide open. Although it was late February, we hadn't had any winter to speak of that year and already the days were getting back up in the eighties. The first thing Hattie liked to do when she came in every morning about 6:30 or

7:00 A.M. was to crank open the kitchen windows. Hattie enjoyed filling the house with morning air. Around noon, she'd start shutting windows and pulling down blinds, to keep the afternoon heat out. Neither she nor Tom liked to run the air conditioner if they could get away without doing it. Me, on the other hand, I'd just as soon have the air that is going to be swirling around in my house be filtered twelve months out of the year. Why else have the central system?

"Wasn't any strange cars or trucks in your yard this morning or any other morning that I am aware of," she said to me. Hattie gave me one of her long level looks. One of those looks, there were several ways in which they could be taken. Like maybe she knew something more than she was saying and maybe she did not. But, whatever the case, her message to me was that it would be in my best interests not to go talking about ghost cars or trucks. Of course she was right. Wiley Sutton's red truck had absolutely no reason to be parked out back of our house. Therefore it was plain as the nose on your face that I had not seen it there.

After Julia was born, I was relieved that Tom and his family and I had never been on social terms with the Suttons. It wasn't as if I thought of Wiley Sutton from one month to the next, to be sure, but I was, on the occasions when our paths crossed in town, relieved that I didn't run into him any more often than I did.

AUNT KATE

When Robin told me her roommate was from the little town of Cypress Springs, Texas, the first thing I wondered was, "Where on earth is Cypress Springs, Texas?" I had to look it up on the map to discover that it is northwest of here, approximately one hour's drive out of Houston. That sounds just fine, a girl from a small town will be a good person for Robin to be roommates with, I remember thinking. I had it in my mind that, being from a small town, Julia would be quiet, studious, and conservative. I had to laugh at myself later. Why did I ever think someone from a small town would necessarily turn out to be quiet and conservative? My own mother, who grew up in the little town of Larned, Kansas, was as far from conservative as you'd ever want to see.

Mother was born on a farm where, to get electricity for the lights in the house, her father had five or six windmills connected to a generator, which then was hooked up to car batteries in which the energy was stored. Underneath all those windmills sat a shed full of car batteries filled with stored-up electricity. Wires ran from the windmills to a generator, into the batteries in the shed, and then on into the house they lived in. I've wondered, in light of recent information about the hazardous effects of living under or close to power lines, if all those batteries storing up electricity in the little shed right behind the house didn't somehow or another affect Mother's mind. She was a live wire, that is how everyone who knew her always described her. Perhaps the electricity took its toll.

Aurora Jane Jamison was the name she started out life with. Her brothers ordered a kit and put themselves together a Ford Model T. Aurora stole that car and abandoned it the same night about ten miles from the house, where she'd driven out to a cornfield to meet Patrick Larson, the barnstormer who had flown into town the day before to give flying demonstrations. Mother was the first person from Larned, and the only person in her family, to go up in the plane with him. "How was it, Aurora?" her father asked her when she was back on the ground. "Thrilling beyond belief," she is said to have replied.

The next day, when Patrick flew off for the next stop on his tour, my mother went with him. They flew around the country, landing in farm fields and camping out near towns, making money giving the people of the central plains their first-ever airplane rides. They did this for two years before they finally lit in the little town of Mission, Texas. Only twice during that time did they made it back through Larned for Mother to visit with her family. Not that she was lonesome for them, she once told me. Mother said no one in her family ever was much on family ties. Certainly she never talked about the family she'd left behind with any nostalgia that I could hear. Actually, I can't recall her ever talking about her parents at all.

Eventually, Mother and Patrick, my father, moved into a boarding house in Mission, planning to settle down. Patrick had in mind that he would be able to earn a living as an air taxi pilot once the new wore off plane demonstration rides and the South Texas market for them dried up. I learned most of these facts from a feature story that was written about Mother when she opened her boarding house. I never saw the article at the time, as I would have been six years old when it was first printed. I found it, tucked away in Mother's top dresser drawer, when I was packing to move her to the nursing home. "Do you want this?" I asked her. "Put it in my bag, Katherine, and quit your fussing," she said to me.

I read it before I packed it for her. They married in Enid, Oklahoma, sometime during those two years when they were, to quote Mother as the newspaper clipping did, "seeing the world from the air, the only way to see it." Once Mother learned she was pregnant with me, she and Patrick decided they needed to quit their gallivanting and establish a home base. Mother was quoted as saying she was the one of the two of them who had the hardest time with the idea that they were going to have to settle down and stick to one place in order to raise a family. "Once you fly in the air," she said, "it is hard to settle back to walking on the ground." She didn't come right out and say she wished she'd never gotten pregnant in the first place but, reading between the lines, it was obvious that is exactly what she wished. Some women are maternal. Nesters. Mother, through no fault of her own, didn't seem to have that bent. It is tempting to think that had my father lived, he would have turned out to have been more paternal than Mother was maternal. But, based on what I do know of him, it seems more realistic to think that he and my mother were cut of the same cloth. I doubt he would have taken the responsibilities of parenthood any more seriously than she did.

I don't have a thing beyond the vaguest memories of my father. He died when I was so young. The plane he was in crashed to the ground as it was coming in to land. Mother was there, waiting for my father, and saw it burst into flames. She had to be restrained from rushing into the conflagration in a futile attempt to save him. I know these details from the newspaper clipping. She never talked to me about my father. By the time I was old enough for conversations, she was already married to the second of her four, perhaps five, husbands.

I do have vivid memories of Mother. She worked in a ladies' ready-to-wear store for a period of time. Not that she fit in. Even I, at six years of age, could see that. The ladies who worked there all wore sedate, business-looking clothes. Mother dressed as if she were on her way to a party. She wore makeup, lots of it, and so much perfume you could smell her coming even when there was a strong wind blowing in the other direction. I was in grade school at the time Mother worked for Brimmer's Mercantile Company; I had to walk three blocks from the school to the store every afternoon. I sat in the back of the store, doing my homework and being quiet as a mouse until Mother got off work at six. I remember squirming with embarrassment day after day as I sat there. Mother was louder than the other women. Different. I wished she would act like everyone else.

Mother didn't have it in her. Perhaps it was all the electricity she grew up under. I never met her brothers, my uncles, but from what I heard, they didn't turn out resoundingly normal either. Neither of them ever married—one worked as a sailor for a shipping line, the other went west to make his fortune as a blackjack dealer. Mother lost track of both of them after her parents died.

Mother and I lived in a huge, decrepit old house. We were boarders there when my father died. When Mother got her insurance money, the house was up for sale, so she bought it. Gradually we lost most of the boarders. Mother wouldn't cook—she'd buy bags of food and tell the men coming in hungry at night and expecting a meal that there was food in the kitchen, the least they could do was cook it themselves. Naturally, that went over like a lead balloon. I believe this is what led to the job at the Mercantile Company. She worked there until her second marriage, which was to a man who had some connection to the railroad. He traveled. I'm not sure what happened to him—I think Mother more or less ran him off. Later on, she had other husbands. Between her husbands, she had other jobs. By the time I was in high school, I had gotten it down to a science, how to live with Mother and act as if she and I had only the most cursory of connections. The truth is, plain and simple, I was embarrassed by my mother.

I was sixteen when Mother had my sister, Sandra. I left home when I was eighteen. I really didn't have the opportunity to know my sister. I recall her as a cute little kid who grew up fast. She'd have had to do that. With Mother the way she was, her daughters had to as good as raise themselves. The times I was around Sandra as she grew older, it pained me to see she was turning out just like my mother.

Once, I think Sandra was about thirteen at the time, Mother called and insisted I come to Mission. She had some government papers she couldn't make heads or tails of. She'd thrown no telling how many away but they kept coming. She wouldn't mail them, nothing would do but I had to get in my car and drive down there and read them in her presence. So she could mutter and carry on all around the room as I tried to concentrate. She had the idea that, once I had trained as a librarian, anything with print on it fell within my bailiwick and I should be able to explain it to her.

I drove the six hours it takes to get from Houston to Mission the first chance I had. This was the time the government caught up with her. I can't for the life of me figure out how she had existed all the years she had without paying property tax, but apparently she had done so. It took over three years and a certified tax attorney to get that snafu straightened out. I turned everything over to the expert. "Please, don't tell me one thing about what she has done," I said to him. "I do not want to know." The only advice I was able to give him was that, in dealing with Mother, it helped to be able to ignore her histrionics.

Before I left the valley that Monday morning, I also refereed two arguments between Mother and Sandra, over, first of all, what time Sandra was supposed to be in the house on a school night and, secondly, which one of them left the cap off the lipstick. That is correct. They got into a blazing row over which one of them was using their lipstick and not replacing its top. The two of them used the same lipsticks! "You work this out, I've got to get back to Houston," I said and left. There wasn't any way I could come close to making order out of the chaos they lived in. And I got a splitting headache just from thinking about trying.

When I first heard that Sandra had run off with some boy named Kyle whom she hadn't known for longer than two weeks, I knew she wasn't doing a thing other than following in her own mother's footsteps. I felt sorry for my baby sister. And for her child, once I heard there was one on the way. But I didn't feel as if there was anything I could do for them.

I'd only seen Robin a time or two before Sandra was killed and it became clear I was the one who was going to have to step in and take charge of things. I had no earthly idea what I was going to do with a child to raise. Driving down to Mission I had enough sense to be scared. I may not know how to raise a child, I told the road ahead of me, but I know how *not* to raise one. I promised myself Robin wasn't going to grow up embarrassed by me. Or by any of her other relatives' memories.

My goal was to give her a nice, normal childhood. A life where she could come home from school knowing that dinner would be cooked and on the table. A life where her aunt could be counted on to make the cookies for the school parties and show up with them when she'd promised they'd be there. One where the people who lived in the house with her didn't disappear overnight without so much as a good-bye in her direction. In my zeal to give her a normal childhood, I went overboard in keeping the past from Robin. In doing so I imbued it with mystery rather than sordid shabbiness. Initially, it never occurred to me I should have been telling her more about our family. However, by the time Robin was eight or ten, I sensed she wanted to know more than she knew. But it was so hard for me to decide what to tell her. I didn't want her embarrassed the way I had been. My error was on the side of caution. I made a mystery out of a poor muddled nothing little story. I can see that now.

I wish I had said to Robin, back when she was a child: *Your parents and your grandmother were sad people. Sad little people who tried to make some excitement for themselves and failed. This is what I know. They weren't bad people, just misguided.* Then I could have gone on to tell her the entire story.

PART III

At least once a week I feel like taking Julia and shaking her and saying, "Why do you keep aggravating her? You know how your mother is going to react, so why do you keep provoking her?"

I met Julia when she was sixteen years old and by the time I had known her for fifteen minutes I'd recognized that her relationship with Verona was star-crossed. Butch had taken me over for Sunday lunch, which was roast and rice and gravy, several vegetables, and a Jell-O salad. Also, Verona's pride and joy, her homemade rolls. Verona and Tom and Butch and I ate the lunch. Periodically, throughout the meal, Verona asked either Butch and Tom if they didn't think she should check on Julia—"Make sure she is still alive back there," is how she phrased it.

"She's fine, Mother," Butch said. "Let her alone."

"When you were sixteen, you no more slept through church and Sunday dinner than the man in the moon," she said.

"Julia'll get up when she's ready to, Verona, let her be. She's not hurting anyone sleeping late," Tom said. They appeared to take turns responding to Verona.

"It is the height of rudeness for Julia to be laying up in bed like she's sick or something, particularly when we have company. I wish you'd go on in there and speak to her."

"Mother, Susie isn't exactly a guest, she is going to be my

wife," Butch said. This is how he chose to inform his parents that we'd gotten engaged several days earlier.

Tom immediately broke into a grin and stood up so fast his chair fell to the floor with a loud crash. "Well, it's about time, son," he said as he pounded Butch on the back enthusiastically. "She's such a pretty thing, I can see what you were waiting for. Welcome to the family, sweetheart," he said to me. I was smiling at them both, feeling all warm and accepted, when Verona burst into tears. "You could have told me first," she said and left the room.

Butch looked at his dad. Tom shrugged. "Give her time, she'll come around. Butch always has been his mama's pride and joy," he said to me; then he followed his wife down the hall.

"It's not too late to change your mind," Butch told me.

"Nothing doing," I assured him. "I'm sure once your mother gets to know me we'll get along great."

We were alone in the dining room, still Butch leaned over and whispered in my ear. "Not many people get along with my mother," he said.

About ten minutes later, Verona reappeared. She looked fine to me—if she'd been back in her room sobbing her heart out you couldn't tell it by looking at her. Tom and Julia were right behind her. Julia had on cutoffs and a T-shirt and was barefoot. She was also braless. "Hi, Sis," she said and grinned across the room at me. "Don't let it bother you that you started out right off the bat making Mother cry. I do that all the time."

How was I going to reply to that? I moved closer to Butch, who put his arm around my shoulders in a comforting way. "Susie, this is my little sister, Julia," he said. "The one I told you you're going to love. Now, Julia, you be nice," he admonished.

"Julia, do you want anything to eat or should I clear away the lunch?" Verona asked.

"I am not eating if you fixed the same thing you fix every Sunday," Julia said as she looked over the food on the table and made a face. "You know I don't like red meat," she said.

Tom and Butch looked bemused, as well they might have, given that the family business was raising beef cattle. "Since when," Tom asked Julia, "did you stop liking red meat?"

Julia shrugged her shoulders, causing her breasts to jiggle under the thin T-shirt she wore.

"Don't eat, then," Verona said huffily. "It's no skin off my nose." She began clearing the table.

"I've decided to become a vegetarian," Julia said. "Eating flesh is cannibalistic."

Not a member of her family responded to her words. Butch and Tom exchanged another look and Verona went right on bustling around the table. She acted like she hadn't heard her.

In my family, the kids cleared the table and did the dishes. If I had been at home, I'd have started gathering up plates without thinking. But I was feeling ill at ease at the Salwells'. "Can I help you?" I asked Verona.

"No," she said. "I don't like people underfoot in my kitchen. Julia, get back in the bedroom and don't come out until you put some clothes on."

Fifteen minutes later we all sat down in the living room and ate pound cake mounded with fresh strawberries and whipped cream. We sipped our coffee and visited as if nothing was amiss. Julia wore Bermuda shorts, a starched and ironed button-down-collar shirt, and loafers. Her hair was pulled back in a ponytail. "Don't get up, Mother," she said after we had finished our dessert. "I'll put these things in the dishwasher for you. Then I'm going over to Yvonne's to study."

That's the way it's been ever since I've been a part of this family. Just when I am on the verge of deciding neither Verona nor Julia is normal, they'll sit down with each other and act perfectly decent and I'll admonish myself about overreacting. Just because people are different from the way I am doesn't make them abnormal.

Butch and I had been married four months when we announced our first child was on his way. Once again, Butch reported the news in an offhand fashion at the Sunday dinner table. "By the way, Dad, how do you feel about some little tyke calling you Grandpa?" he asked his father.

It took Tom a minute. He sat there, chewing on his roll and looking at Butch. Then his head snapped over to me and his eyes fastened around the middle of my body. He stared intently, as if he were checking to see if I could have sprouted a basketball belly in the four days since I had last seen him. When Tom's eyes slid back up, they met mine. I smiled at him. Whereupon he actually blushed before he looked back over to Butch. "Well, if that don't beat all," he said and stood up and began to pound his son on the back. Butch jumped up and they hugged each other. They looked exactly the way athletes do when they've won a game. Totally self-absorbed and self-congratulatory. Tom thrust out his hand to shake hands with Butch. "Proud of you, my boy," he boomed.

Verona sat quietly while this was transpiring. "When did you say it is due?" she asked me in a low-pitched voice. Butch and I did not have a long engagement before our church wedding, so by this time I suppose I'd known Verona less than half a year. However, I had known her long enough to where I could tell when she was upset about something. Her reaction wasn't entirely a surprise to me. When I'd told my mother she and Daddy were going to be having a seventh grandchild, I'd said to her, "I don't think Verona is going to like this."

"Susie," my mother said, "Verona may have a little difficulty at first, the first grandchild is something of a shock. I don't think it comes natural to any woman to imagine herself as a grandmother. She'll come around, see if she doesn't."

"You'll have to wait awhile to see your grandchild, Mother, our baby isn't due for almost six months yet," Butch said in response to Verona's question. He had a big grin on his face. Butch and his daddy are so much alike.

"Well, I hope this child isn't early, you know how people talk, Butch," Verona said. Each of her words was clipped and icy. "Since Susie is from Houston she may not be aware of how things are out here in Cypress Springs."

Butch was so used to Verona's way of saying things he didn't even get his feelings hurt. I know because I asked him about it later.

"Didn't it bother you, what she said about hoping the baby isn't early?" I asked him.

"No, that's Mother for you. You'll get to where you don't listen to that kind of stuff either," he assured me.

Julia's reaction was guarded as well. She looked at us—actually she stared at Butch with a wounded look in her eyes and took sneaking little glances at me. You didn't have to be a mind reader to see that she wasn't jumping for joy at the idea she was fixing to become an aunt. "I guess you'll need me to get my stuff out of my room at your house," she said to Butch in a hurt little voice.

"Nonsense, Julia, your room is your room," Butch said. "The baby can have the bedroom on the other side of ours." That was fine with me, but I told Butch later I wished we had talked it over beforehand so I could have felt I was part of the decision-making process before he'd gone and announced where the nursery was going to be.

He was so sweet. "Susie, if you want the baby's room to be the bedroom Julia has been using, I'll tell her. She can switch, she won't mind in the least. Just as long as she has a bedroom at our house, she doesn't care which room it is."

When I first met Butch it had surprised me to learn that his sister, who lived at home with her parents, also had a room at his house. He told me Julia frequently used the room. "She's here, not every night, of course, but once or twice a week. Julia and my mother sometimes get into these arguments. Julia has a room here when she needs it. That won't change."

"Oh," I said. To be perfectly honest, the room didn't look very lived-in when I first saw the house. Julia kept some clothes there. In the bathroom she had some toiletries and some makeup. That was it. To me, who had grown up sharing a room with my sister while my brothers slept three to a room, it looked like the Salwells simply had a lot more bedrooms than they had people to sleep in them. So Julia had two. No big deal.

We'd been married about a week when Julia arrived to spend the first night with us. We weren't expecting her. It was after ten o'clock at night and the news was on. I was sitting on the couch and Butch had stepped into the kitchen to get something to drink. I heard her car, but I was still mentally living in the city and hearing a car at ten o'clock at night was not surprising to me. I didn't pay any attention to it.

"That's Julia," Butch said.

"How can you tell?" I asked him. In the distance I could hear a car, which was getting louder as it approached our house. It certainly wasn't loud enough to where you'd expect to be able to identify the engine noise.

"Julia has glass packs on her car. That is one of the reasons Mother didn't like it, it sounded like a hot rod to her." Julia's car was a Ford Tom had ordered for Verona and that Verona had driven a week before deciding she didn't like it. So they gave it to Julia, making her one of the few sixteen-year-olds I'd ever known with a car, much less a brand-new Thunderbird.

Butch walked out to meet her. Her car had come to a screeching, dust-scattering halt right outside our garage. I started to go with Butch, but for some reason stopped and leaned against the back door frame. Standing on the back porch, I could see them but I couldn't hear their words. Butch was so intent on getting to Julia that I don't think he realized I hadn't come any farther than the back door.

As soon as I saw him put his arms around her, I knew she was crying. Her entire body was heaving with her sobs. I didn't know what to do. I felt trapped. I didn't want to go back in the house and look uncaring, but neither did I want to go down the sidewalk to where they stood and look like I was intruding. I stood at the door feeling awkward. When they walked into the light, I noticed Julia's eyes were swollen and blazing with anger. She'd also been slapped. You could see the hand print on her face.

"I'm not going back there, I am not," she said and glared at me.

"You don't have to," I said, not absolutely sure at the time she was referring to her own house. However, I couldn't imagine where else she could have been talking about.

"I'm going to bed and if she calls I will not talk to her, do you hear me?" she said.

Butch hugged his sister, "Don't worry, she won't call you. You go on in and get some sleep, I'll talk to her in the morning. Go on, get to bed, you've got school in the morning."

Julia walked into the house, through the kitchen, and down the hall without another word. I stood to one side of the back door with my mouth open. Within minutes, I heard the shower going in the bathroom. The sound of running water continued for a solid thirty minutes while Butch and I pattered back and forth around the house in our bedtime preparations. "Do you think she's okay? Should I check?" I finally asked him. If anyone in my house had ever stayed in the shower that long, using up the entire contents of the hot water heater, there would have been the devil to pay. I was thinking perhaps Julia had passed out in there. "She's been in the bathroom for thirty minutes," I said to Butch as we pulled down the bedspread in our bedroom.

"Julia loves the bathroom. I had the largest hot water heater I could get put in for that very reason. Don't worry, she'll be fine in the morning," Butch said to me.

"Butch, I don't want to sound like I'm meddling, but did you see her face? Someone hit Julia," I said.

We were in bed, whispering as if someone could hear us. I felt self-conscious even though it was now my house too and I had a perfect right to be there.

His arm tightened on my shoulders and I sensed his grimace. "I know," he said. "I told you she and Mother don't always see eye to eye."

THOMAS WAS BORN on December twenty-fourth at 10:04 in the evening. He was actually about two weeks late and it got to the point where we were wondering if maybe he wasn't going to wait until the new year to make his appearance. But

Thomas, like most babies, came in his own good time. We named him after his daddy and his grandfather. Butch wasn't so sure about that, but I said, *Why not?* Thomas is a great name and I loved the idea of my son being part of a long line of Salwell men. It did tickle Tom, the fact that his first grandson was named after him. He went out the next morning and bought this little tricycle that is a miniature of a John Deere tractor and came into the hospital room carrying it. The nurses told me they'd never seen anything like it. You should have seen the smile on Tom's face. That's what I wish I had a picture of.

Verona frowned at her husband. "What on earth are you coming in here wagging that thing for?" she said to Tom. "The very idea! If nothing else, you should worry about the germs. This is a hospital!"

"It is Christmas Day," she kept reminding us all. She had the turkey and dressing home cooking in a slow oven and proceeded to get her feelings hurt because everyone decided they'd just as soon eat in the hospital cafeteria with me. Butch whispered in my ear not to worry, he'd told her not to cook anything in the first place because he would be staying at the hospital. And Tom and Julia had said the same thing to her.

Poor Verona. I remember that dress she had on, red silk. She made such a fuss of getting a felt pad on her lap before she sat down with Thomas. And then it was not ten seconds before she was up again putting him back in the bassinet. "Can't be too careful of the dress," she said. Because it was silk and she didn't want it stained, she went on to explain to me. The way she said it, it sounded like Verona thought it was my fault she had decided to put on a silk dress to come down to the hospital. She'd bought it for Christmas and then had gone out and bought one for Julia just like it. "I thought it would be fun to dress as mother-daughter look-alikes," she said to Julia when she pulled it out of the box. I was there the day this happened and I knew before I even looked over at Julia's face she wasn't going to want to dress like her mother. Julia was sixteen years old, for heaven's sake—way too old for that sort of thing even if she had been in the habit of doing it when she was a child.

"Mother, that dress is awful, I wouldn't be caught dead in it," Julia said. Verona acted like she never heard her, she kept on talking and then darned if she didn't walk down the hall and hang the dress up in Julia's closet. Later on, I admit, I walked down there and looked in the closet myself. Which is when I first noticed that fully half the clothes in there had the tags still on them. I couldn't believe my eyes. Why on earth did Verona go on buying things Julia wouldn't even try on?

FROM THE START, Thomas was an easy baby. Slept well. Took his bottle with no fuss. Loved to be carried around. Verona didn't care for that a bit. "That baby's never going to learn to sleep by himself, the way you carry him around all the time," she said to me.

She was wrong, of course. Thomas never had to learn how to sleep. He was born a good sleeper. Still is. The hard thing with Thomas, in later years, became getting him up in time for him to get to school before they'd started serving lunch. Getting him to sleep was never a problem.

Verona loved to give advice, but she rarely stayed on a single subject long enough to notice whether or not you actually took it. Which was a blessing, I suppose. Contrary to what Mother said, I don't think Verona ever took to becoming a grandmother. At least I've never noticed her being overly affectionate toward any of the grandchildren, much less doting.

Julia, on the other hand, surprised me. After Thomas was born, and later on when Eugene appeared, she spent hours playing with them—particularly once they got to the walking-around stage. You couldn't have asked for a better playmate. Both of my boys grew up thinking there was no one more wonderful than their Aunt Julia. Between Julia and Tom and my family the boys had plenty of people to make over them. So if Verona never unbent very much, or for very long, it didn't deprive them.

Julia and I got to be friends after Thomas was born. Lots of times, those first months, she'd come over and the kitchen would be a wreck and the laundry would be piled up, spilling out the utility room door, and she'd bustle around washing dirty clothes and folding clean ones and doing the dishes so fast I used to call her white lightning. It was a side of Julia I hadn't suspected, that she could be efficient and helpful and matter-of-fact about it to boot. I'll never be as close to her as her brother is, of course, but that is as it should be. I'm glad that, by the time the next year rolled around and she was a senior in high school and should have been having the time of her life, we had gotten to the point where she trusted me enough to come to me when she did get herself into trouble. Otherwise, as impulsive as she is, no telling what she'd have done.

JULIA

This is how it happened. I was a senior in high school and all caught up in applying to different colleges. Frankly, all I could think about was getting off to school. I was sick and tired of my mother, I was sick and tired of hearing about how wonderful Susie and the new baby were, and I had had it with high school. My dad was never home and Butch was so caught up in his new family he barely knew I was alive.

To top it off, I had broken up with Danny. I won't even try to say I didn't regret it, because there I was, stuck in the middle of my senior year in high school, with no one to date. Not that there'd ever been that great a selection, but when you're a senior, what the hell, three-fourths of the male population is younger than you are. So you can imagine where that left me. Sitting home high and dry most Saturday nights.

Which is how I came to go out with Tillman Salinas in the first place. His sister Yvonne and I were cheerleaders and were, I suppose you could say, friends of a sort. We did things together all the time anyway. But actually Yvonne and I didn't have all that much in common. I know this will sound snobbish and it certainly isn't the way I mean to sound, but she comes from this real low-rent family. Her father up and left her mother when she was a baby and Mrs. Salinas had to work at the dry cleaners for years and years to support her family. Not taking in the clothes and working the cash register—she worked in the back, cleaning and pressing. Of course, there is nothing in the world wrong with that and what her mother did had nothing to do with the fact that Yvonne and I didn't really have a very solid friendship. Truthfully, I don't know why Yvonne and I weren't better friends.

There were four Salinas children. Yvonne was the youngest. She had a sister two years older than she is and two brothers—Lester, who is about five years older than I am and went in the army straight out of high school, and Tillman, who is four years older than I am. Tillman never went off to school or the army or any other thing, he stayed at home and worked for ranchers around the area. At first he took whatever jobs were available, but it was apparent even back then that Tillman wasn't without ambition. By the time I went out with him, he was working on his pilot's license so he could do what he does now, own his own plane, which he rents out with himself as the pilot. Mainly he does crop dusting. Actually, I believe he does quite well with his crop dusting business.

Tillman Salinas will always give me the creeps, but I don't think he's a bad person or anything like that. It's just that what went on left a bad taste in my mouth. And I have to say he has been very good to his mother. As soon as he started making any money, he insisted she quit that job and let him take care of the bills. Word is, he takes care of his mother to this day. I know they both still live in the house he grew up in, over one block off Main Street, but I did hear Tillman bought the house and now they own it. As I said, I think he's done quite well. He married briefly but it didn't last. I have no idea what happened there. He isn't a bad person, it's just that he wasn't the one for me.

It all started this way. It was early March, almost Easter, and Yvonne and I were in my car. We were always in my car—Yvonne didn't have one. We'd stayed late at school making posters for the senior play, which was coming up in April. Both of us had signed up for the stage crew, not because we had any interest in Cypress Springs dramatics but because it got us out of study hall.

"It's almost Friday night and no date as usual. You want to do something?" I said to Yvonne.

"Actually, Peter Crawford asked me to go to a movie tomorrow night," she said.

"Well, shit," I remember saying, and then I had to floor-board my car fast because I was in the process of crossing the railroad tracks against the flashing light and a train, coming a little faster than it had appeared, started sounding its horn at me.

"My brother said he thinks you're real cute, he just learned the other day you and Danny Clark broke up. You want me to fix you up?" Yvonne asked me.

"Why not?" I said back to her. I didn't have but half my mind on what we were talking about by that time. I was already rehearsing in my head what I was going to say to my daddy who I was sure would hear I'd pulled out on the railroad tracks in front of the train before I so much as got home good. I was right there, he and Mother were waiting for me that night at the supper table. I had to do everything but promise to stop and put my ear to the ground every time I came to the tracks to get them to let me keep my car keys. That's what we were into when Tillman called and asked did I want to take in a movie with Yvonne and Peter the next night. "Sure," I said to him and hung up the phone before Mother could start quizzing me down about who it was. "Have to study," I told my parents and got the hell out of the kitchen.

All in all, I had a horrible senior year. I only went out with Tillman a total of maybe eight or nine times. Had it not been for my family, primarily my mother, I doubt I would have gone out with him more than once. We had absolutely nothing to talk about. However, Mother threw a fit when she found out I was dating him. She objected to him because he was older than me and hadn't gone to college, and had a poor mother and no father. Of course she didn't say it that way but I knew how her mind worked. So, in order to prove to her I was more open-minded than she was, I kept accepting when he called to ask me to go somewhere. Daddy said to her, "Verona, Tillman seems like a nice enough boy to me, you just don't want your baby dating anyone." Even Butch said he thought it was okay.

Little did they know. First off, Tillman had so little to say for himself he could barely put together a sentence. Second, he never picked me up he didn't smell of Pearl beer and Winston cigarettes. Third, since I started drinking with him to loosen up the second time we went out together, we started sleeping together as well. Don't ask me how that happened. It didn't make sense at the time and I can't explain it at this late date. Why I slept with some guy I didn't even half like I will never on earth be able to fathom. Unfortunately I did. That really complicated matters because Tillman started telling Yvonne how wonderful he thought I was and Yvonne started carrying on like she thought I was fixing to become her sister-in-law.

Finally it got to where I couldn't stand it. Tillman started talking about my senior prom and just assumed he'd be taking me. Mother had bought me this gorgeous dress but except for wanting to wear it I had no desire to go to my senior prom. Who was going to be there except all the kids I'd known my entire life and was sick to death of?

It's a good thing school was almost out for good before I broke up with Tillman because Yvonne told it all over the place that I'd dumped her brother because I thought I was too good for him and lots of people started treating me like I was a real creep. I could have pointed out to her that if I'd thought that I was better than Tillman I'd have never gone out with him in the first place, but I didn't even bother. One thing I've learned from Verona is that there's no point in arguing with someone who thinks they know what they are talking about even if you are dead sure you are right and she is wrong.

Besides, two weeks before prom night and three and one half weeks before graduation I had something else to think about. I am referring to the fact that, by that time, I had swiped my mother's old wedding band out of her jewelry box and crammed it on my finger and driven down to Houston, to see a doctor. There, using the name of Jane Smythe, I learned that I was approximately two and one half months pregnant.

I had to tell Susie. I sure couldn't tell Mother or Daddy or Butch. Susie tried to talk me out of taking the Tuesday special out to California for an abortion. First she suggested I have the baby and give it up for adoption. When I told her I was going off to college in September and had no intention of being seven months pregnant at the time, she sort of blinked at me. "Oh, Julia," she said and I swear there were tears in her eyes.

Susie is a real nice person—sweet. And it bothers her that some people, me among them, aren't as good as she is. Not that she'd ever say anything remotely like that, of course. I know as far as Susie herself is concerned she'd just as soon shoot herself as have an abortion. I'm not in favor of them myself. But the thought of staying home and having a kid just freaked me out, it really did. I guess I wasn't subtle, but I came right out and said to Susie, "I'm not having this kid and if you don't find me the money I'll get rid of it all by myself." She turned real pale right about then. That's how she looked to me. Pale and sick. God knows how I looked to her. Finally Susie said to me she'd talk it over with Butch and they'd decide what to do. I had to agree to let her tell Butch, which I hated, but I didn't have all that many options as it was.

Next thing it was Butch trying to talk some sense into me. "It is not a baby," I said to him. "It is a bunch of tissue. That is what the doctor told me. I am going to have an abortion, Butch, and that is all there is to it. It is a simple procedure. People do it all the time. All I need from you is the money to pay for it."

THIS IS HOW you do it. First you find a doctor to do the test and write a prescription. Which is illegible but presumably says you need an abortion. Then you get together over five hundred dollars. For the fee and the plane fare out there and back. Plus another one hundred and fifty if you're chicken and take someone with you. Then you get up early on Tuesday and go to Hobby Airport and catch the plane to L.A. There are lots of women on the plane, and you wonder to yourself which ones are pregnant but you don't know for sure until you look around and see which ones get on the clinic bus with you. Some of the women are alone. A couple of them obviously are with their mothers. Two women are accompanied by men. One of the couples wears matching wedding bands. Your sister-in-law sticks to you like glue, but the two of you don't look at each other. You give your paper plus the manila envelope the doctor in Houston gave you to the receptionist. As you hand it to her you wish you'd looked inside to see if it says anything bad about you. She directs you to room four, where you are given a gown and told to wait. Susie starts to come with you but the nurse shakes her head at her. "She'll be fine, you wait out here," she is told.

You sit on the table like you're waiting for an examination. The feeling of dread is the same. It surprises you when the doctor is a woman, it never occurred to you a woman would do this.

She takes your hand and looks right straight in your eyes and says, "Julia, are you sure?" It annoys you she knows your name when all you know of her is the laminated nametag on her white coat which reads Dr. J. Smith. Smith with an *I*. You wish you were still calling yourself Jane Smythe.

"What does the *J* stand for?" you ask.

She smiles down her nose at you. "June," she says.

"Your mother would have done better to name you Summer," you tell her. "More class." It doesn't bother you that you are rude, in fact you hardly notice it. You do notice that her shoes are cheap, so you figure she isn't the one getting rich at this.

Because she keeps on standing there giving you a liquid look, you glare at her and tell her to go ahead and get it over with, of course you're sure, you wouldn't have flown all the way out to California from Texas if you hadn't been sure.

"Do you want something? For the pain?"

"You're damn straight I do." You don't sound like yourself at all, but she doesn't know that. She probably thinks to herself you're one tough cookie, you must have done this once or twice a year since, since what? you ask yourself. When the nurse gives you a shot you don't look. You shut your eyes and look bored and pretend to take a nap. But even if you don't see what she does, you hear the vacuuming sound. And you feel your baby being pulled out of you. And you tell yourself you had no choice.

The return flight leaves about 5:00 P.M. This puts you back in Houston in the evening. As you file off the plane you and your sister-in-law are still avoiding each other's eyes. Until you see your father. That's when the two of you exchange startled looks. At first you think your father is at the airport because he knows, but then you realize he isn't there on your account at all, he is seeing someone off. A woman. Just as it hits you that the woman, whom you've never seen before in your life, is probably your father's mistress, he feels you staring and his eyes meet yours. He looks away but not before you see the shame start in his eyes and travel down his entire body. For a minute, you forget why you're at the airport yourself. But then you remember.

And that night when you are pretending to be asleep in Susie and Butch's guest room, the room which has been your room ever since Butch first built the house, you cry silently into the pillow. And you have no earthly idea if it is sorrow for your poor betrayed mother you are feeling or if you are grieving for the bunch of tissue that might have looked like you.

THAT NIGHT, THE night after the California trip, was the first night I ever had one of my dreams at Butch's house. I have no idea what time of night it was that the icy coldness from my dream awakened me—way past midnight, I'm sure it was that late. It had taken forever for me to fall asleep, but once I finally slept it was, as the saying goes, the sleep of the dead.

And then, maybe several hours after I had fallen asleep, I wasn't asleep any longer. I was awake, and I felt as if something was hovering all around me. I said to myself, "Julia, you are afraid, but it is only a dream you are having." This is the way a person feels the day after, having committed the worst act in the world, she prepares to face the rest of her life. I heard my voice say these words: *for some acts there is no forgiveness*. I didn't even think of crying. Stones don't weep.

I recalled the first pair of roller skates I ever had. I must have been about eight years old. On Christmas morning I was out on the front sidewalk trying to learn how to stay upright on them. I wasn't going anywhere. I'd stand up, put one foot in front of me, and the other would slide back out from under me. Butch and Daddy were taking turns holding me up while I wobbled back and forth from the front gate to the front porch. Finally I thought I had it. "I can do it," I said. I shook off their arms and took off on my own. Both my feet seemed to fly away as if pulled skyward by a magnetic force. I landed hard on my face. When they pulled me up I was crying. I was bleeding from a cut lip. I had chipped one of my front teeth as well. "Daddy, fix it," I said. "Fix it now." He had his handkerchief out and was mopping up the blood and tears but they kept coming. It scared me. The sight of blood always has made me sick to my stomach. "Fix it NOW!" I screamed. By this time Butch had run into the kitchen and reappeared with an ice pack, which they were trying to hold on my lip, but I was crying so hard I wouldn't let it stay put. "Daddy, help me," I cried over and over.

"Julia, you'll be okay. The bleeding will stop in a minute. It will help if you quit crying and leave this ice pack on your face."

"No, it's too cold. Make it stop bleeding, Daddy."

"Honey, I wish there was something else I could do, but I don't know of another thing there is to do. Some things even Daddy can't fix."

Awake in Butch's guest room, I kept my eyes shut tight. "Julia, you are dreaming. Roll over and go back to sleep," I said out loud. My voice sounded like Verona's to me. Although I wanted nothing so much as to curl back into the covers and sleep again, I opened my eyes and looked around the room. The moonlight seeping in from around the curtains lit up the guest room in my brother's house. I knew I was alone and as soon as I looked around and saw where I was, I remembered what had happened. All of it. Whatever I'd been dreaming about evaporated in the air around me. I didn't expect any different. For years I'd had the habit of waking scared from a dream I couldn't recall the first thing about.

When I saw the eyes staring at me, I blinked and ducked my head. Once and again. And again. To clear it. Every time I dared to look, the eyes from my dream looked right back at me. I felt myself shudder. I didn't want to scream. *Julia, you're at Butch's, there isn't anything in the room with you.* I kept trying to tell myself that, but I was entirely too scared to believe it.

I don't know how long I was like that. Scared to scream. Scared to move. Probably it didn't last ten seconds, but it felt like a very long time. The same way the dream felt like a very long dream.

With my eyes closed, I felt my way to the bathroom. From far off, maybe as far away as Houston, I heard the echo of thunder. It is hard, when you hear thunder, to know if it is or is not gunshots that you are hearing. Thunder, that was thunder I heard. The sound wasn't close, it came from far away. I was in the second bathroom at Butch's house, the bathroom that I always used. I knew the room well but, in the middle of the night, straight from my dream, the bathroom confused me. It was all wrong. The thing that was wrong was there was no window. So, even as I was telling myself, *Julia, you are awake and it was only a dream you were having, it wasn't real, it was a dream,* even as I said that to myself, I kept feeling worse and worse.

I don't know why, but when I wake up from a dream, I have to go to the bathroom and turn on the water to run in the sink. I twist both the faucets hard, turning them as far on as they will go, to make the water come out so fast it splashes up from the bottom of the sink and out onto the floor. With the water running, I can turn and pull back the curtains and look out the window into the night. And then, with the sound of water running behind me and the look of the night in front of me, the night empty of anything other than the moon and the stars and the multitude of dark, shaded tree forms, then I can begin to relax. Once I finally get up the nerve to look, there is nothing there. *Nothing to be afraid of, Julia, go back to sleep.* I always say that to myself once I finally quit shaking and open my eyes and look out the window.

But there is no window in the bathroom at my brother's house. This was the first time I had noticed that Butch had built a house without a window in the bathroom. I ran my hands up and down and all over the wall where the window belonged and felt only cool ceramic tile. I looked at the pink tile with its stripe of burgundy border running parallel to the floor in three different lines and wondered why it was that I hadn't realized before how much I hated the color pink, which is the exact same color of watered-down blood. I turned off the water in the sink and pulled a towel from the towel bar. I didn't realize I had been sick until I saw that the water I was mopping up had vomit floating on top of it.

I guess that is what woke my brother up. The sound of the water. Or maybe I made some noise when I threw up but I don't think so. I think the vomit, like the terror, came without a sound.

"Julia, open the door," I heard him say.

"Butch, is that you?"

"Yes, let me in."

I opened the door and let him put his arms around me. I let him pat my back as I cried. I listened to Butch tell me it was going to be okay, I was going to be okay. And for the first time in my life, once I had run to my brother, I didn't feel safe. Butch was there and nothing was wrong except there was no window in the bathroom and I should have felt safe but I didn't.

"Daddy was at the airport when we got off the plane, Butch," I said.

"I know, Susie told me you saw him."

"He had someone with him."

"Yeah, that's what Susie said."

"She was a woman."

Butch was silent for a very long time. I thought maybe he wasn't going to say anything else to me. Finally he spoke. "Marla's Daddy's friend, Julia. You know how Mother is," he said and then he stopped talking again. I heard him sigh and the sighing sound that came from my brother was sad for me to hear. Right then, he sounded older than Daddy and tired to the bone.

"It's okay, Butch, I understand," I said. He didn't really need to say anything else to me to explain it. I knew what he meant about how Mother was. Who could blame Daddy? "Does Daddy love Marla more than he loves me, do you think?" I asked Butch. I was prepared to hear that he did.

Butch made the warm little chuckle of an inside laugh sound from deep in his chest that both he and Daddy sometimes make. "Daddy loves you more than anybody else in the whole wide world Julia. You know that. Marla's only a friend. She's not you. You'll always be his only Julia."

After Butch said that I felt better and I went back to bed and this time I did sleep. When I woke up it was because I wasn't tired anymore, not because I was scared to sleep any longer because of the dreams I had been having.

IT NEVER RAINS, it pours. That is one of the expressions you hear every time you turn around in Cypress Springs. I always think of a box of salt when I hear it. The round blue box with the little girl and her umbrella and the salt pouring out under her arm.

It was Mrs. Grossman who told me about what happened to Julie Garcia. I should have expected it. I don't know if she knows it or not, but Julie and I have this shared destiny. She was born not two weeks after I was. And her parents, for some unfathomable reason, wanted to name her after me. Her father worked out on our place for my father. They lived in one of the little frame houses back on the farm. There are maybe six or seven of those houses scattered around back there. The Garcias lived in one for years and years up until they had it stuffed full of their six children. If the house had not burned to the ground while they were in town one day, doubtless they'd live there still. Behind us, the Salwells, there would be the Garcias. Like shadows.

This is what happened when Julie was born. Mr. Garcia told Daddy they were going to name her Julia but my mother told Daddy to tell them it wouldn't be a good idea to have two Julias so close to the same age so they should call her Julie.

Julie and I went all through school together. Up until junior high we were in the same class every year because

Cypress Springs is so small there is never more than one of each grade at the elementary level.

We acted like we didn't know each other at school. We never played together at home, either, although it would seem natural that we would have done so, but my mother wouldn't allow it. *It wouldn't look right,* is what she said.

Twice a year my mother took all my old clothes to the Garcia house for Julie. Later on the clothes were for her sisters as well. Mother was always buying things, good stuff on sale, for the Garcia kids. She thought it made them like her, but it didn't. They only hated her for it. They hated me as well.

I don't know if Julie knows this, but every time something bad happens to me, something worse happens to her. I hope she doesn't know it, but I'm resigned to the fact that she probably does.

This is why I wasn't surprised at what I learned later on that day—the day after Susie and I got back from California—as I was sitting at the soda fountain in the City Pharmacy. It was an unusual day. I had slept until noon and then once I woke up, I dressed and got in my car and left. From the way Butch and Susie hung around me I could tell they wanted me to stay there with them, but I figured I might as well get on home to Mother.

I started driving home, but the closer I got to the house the more I knew I didn't want to go there. I drove maybe ten miles past our house to this little town of Slidell. Once I got to the stop sign that signals both that you're in Slidell and that you're fixing to leave it, I had no earthly idea why I had come. Slidell is a pointless place. It has a store or two and a post office station in one side of the feed store. Maybe ten or twelve houses that are occupied, no telling how many others scattered about in various stages of disintegration. No school.

The children, what few there are of them, get bussed over to Roundtop. I'd never known a person from Slidell. Drive through, you'll usually see one or two residents sitting on a bench in front of the store looking old whether they are or not. They'll be just sitting. It always looked like they were waiting for something to me. *Gonna be a long wait,* I could have told them. That fact is obvious.

That afternoon, I found myself wondering about Slidell. I'd never even thought about it before, but that day when I kept on driving past our house and turned up in Slidell, I started thinking about that pointless little town. Why was it there in the first place? I asked myself. And for what reason did the few people who were left in Slidell huddle there together, in the middle of nowhere, as it was. They had nothing to do other than to sit around and wait. I couldn't, for the life of me, come up with a single reason to stay in Slidell.

There used to be a lot more to Slidell, judging from the deserted buildings I saw. One had been a cotton gin. I recognized it because it was the twin of the one which operated in Cypress Springs. If it got to where the place I was living was dead all around me, I know good and well I'd have the sense to get out myself. No matter if I had been born there in the house built on the spot where my great-grandfather once lived. Life's for the living, everyone knows that.

I turned my car around in the parking lot of what had to be the town gathering place—there were two trucks parked in front of this plate glass window so dusty you could barely see there were lights on inside the building—and drove on back toward Cypress Springs. And when it got to the place where I should have turned up into the road leading to our house, I kept on going. By that time it had occurred to me it wasn't but about one-thirty in the afternoon and I knew if I got home that early Mother would wonder why I hadn't been in school.

Cypress Springs looked almost as bad as Slidell when I pulled up. There probably weren't more than a dozen cars and trucks parked around the town square. I went to the drugstore and sat down on a stool at the soda fountain. I was the only customer to come in since lunch. Mrs. Grossman told me that kind of thing liked to never happen. "I'm hungry, can you fix me a hamburger?" I asked Mrs. Grossman.

"Coming right up," she said to me and she took one of the meat patties out of the refrigerator and peeled the waxed paper off of it. "Julia, my word in heaven, why aren't you in school? And where are your shoes?"

That was the first I realized I wasn't wearing any. "I guess I left my shoes at Butch's. I stayed home with a bug," I told her. I laughed out loud at the idea of calling a fetus a bug. Mrs. Grossman looked at me funny then, as if she couldn't tell what I was finding so humorous. I wasn't about to tell her.

"Well, you run on over to the back wall and get yourself some of those flipflops, it is hot as the very devil outside today, you'll burn your feet on the pavement."

Once she mentioned the hot pavement I noticed the bottoms of my feet were sort of stinging so I did like she said. "Put these on my mother's bill, Mrs. Grossman."

Mother had told me I was not to go charging things at the drugstore anymore without specific permission from her, and I knew she had said the same thing to Mrs. Grossman. But both Mrs. Grossman and I knew Mother never looked at the bill when it came to the house, so there didn't seem to be much point in me running across the street to the bank and getting some money to pay three dollars for the shoes and about that much for the food I was fixing to eat. So we let it ride.

I had eaten maybe two bites of my hamburger when the phone rang. From the first "oh my goodness" I could tell something bad had happened. "Julia, honey, you better brace yourself for some bad news," Mrs. Grossman said to me. My first thought was *Oh, my gosh, I hope nothing bad has happened to Daddy or Butch.* But as soon as Mrs. Grossman said to me, "It is Julie Garcia," I wasn't surprised, not the least little bit.

"Where was she hurt?"

"In a car wreck down in Houston. They are quite sure she's going to live, that's what Mr. Grossman just told me, but there has been some injury to her back."

Poor Julie. She wasn't even out of the hospital in time for graduation. I have no idea what plans she had for herself after high school, if any, but I know coming home in a wheelchair, riding in a lift-operated van her daddy got with the settlement from the accident, couldn't have been what she had envisioned for herself. I didn't have the heart to go see her. But Mother did. She came home saying that if it wasn't for the fact Julie couldn't walk, you'd never know there was a thing different about her.

I started several letters to Julie. I felt the need to tell her that I was sorry. But every time I got out a fresh sheet of paper, the words *Dear Julie, I am sorry I brought this on you* would appear. I'd rip up the paper and start over until finally I realized it was pointless. There wasn't anything I could say or do for Julie Garcia that would change what had happened to her. There wasn't any use for me to keep on trying.

ROBIN

When we were still out in Lubbock Julia and I sometimes talked about how much fun we were going to have once we got out of school. We watched the movie *Valley of the Dolls* four or five times, imagining ourselves as career girls in New York City. We'd wear full-length mink coats over our knock-your-eyes-out fantastic wardrobes and file or type a bit before lunch; after lunch we'd talk on the phone. We weren't going to be the character who got cancer and died. Nor did we identify with the one who got hooked on pills. Significantly, the character we both identified with was the one who got dumped by the worldly love of her life yet managed to end up the movie looking great and with a consolation Mr. Right at her side. Barbara Parkins. Julia even looked a little bit like her.

Julia and I both majored in English, although I, who still had my feet on the ground even when I fantasized about this wonderful future in store for us, minored in education so I'd be able to get a teaching job. *If all else fails, I can teach,* I figured. Half of the females in every education class I took said that out loud. The rest of them probably had the same thought in their heads, but had more sense than to announce it to the world at large. The men in my education classes were all going to be coaches. They jocked into class late wearing their coaches' shorts and tennis shoes, laughing loudly at least several times a day at jokes only those of them who sat in the last row of the room were able to catch. I don't think they thought they'd ever have to grow up, so they didn't give their futures a thought. The elementary education majors went around gushing about how much fun teaching was going to be and were too much in love with their future classes to concern themselves with thoughts about what their future pay scales were apt to enable them to buy for themselves. They only intended to teach until they had their first babies anyway. Those of us in secondary ed were more serious—we talked salaries every so often as well as graduate degrees.

Except, of course, for the coaches, who only talked athletic teams and statistics.

Julia called all education majors wimps and weenies. "I couldn't sit in class with those wimps and weenies without barfing my head off," she'd tell me when I suggested she go ahead and get a teaching certificate. I'd lived too long with my practical aunt not to think at least semirealistically about what I wanted to do after graduation. I also worried about what Julia was going to do. "What about after graduation? You have to do something," I'd say to Julia. Particularly our senior year, I kept forgetting we were going to have these glamorous careers complete with fur coats and launched into talking about what kind of a teaching job I was likely to find and whether I'd get an apartment in Houston or live at my aunt's. It never seemed real to me that I would go anywhere except back to Houston. I don't think it ever seriously occurred to Julia to do anything other than go back home either. Although we talked off and on about living in New York or Boston—both of us thought Boston sounded neat— neither of us made the first move, no matter how tentative, in that direction.

Our fur coats were equally nebulous. As far as I was concerned, I realized what they cost and privately doubted I'd ever have one. Julia never concerned herself with cost, but she too repudiated the idea. One day when there was snow on the ground outside, Julia and I sat in the library where we'd gone to work on our term papers. Whenever we studied, we made ourselves work for one hour and thirty minutes and then gave ourselves a break, fifteen minutes time off for good behavior. Julia was our timekeeper, which meant we frequently got more time off. This particular day we sat in the front of the library near the glass walls and leafed through magazines picking out fur coats we liked, until we noticed an ad featuring a baby seal with big sad eyes. "How terrible," Julia said after she had skimmed the text. "Did you know that they club the babies to death? All so some bitch of a woman can have a fur coat! Half the time when my mother wears her coat to Houston she has to run the air conditioning in her car so she doesn't sweat like a mule before she gets where she is going! That's disgusting. What the hell do people need with fur coats?" She burst into tears and threw the magazine across the room. The next day she sent a check off to Seal Watch. And never, in all the time I've known her, has she had so much as a fur collar on any piece of clothing she has owned.

JULIA AND I had more dates our freshman year than all the other three years we were in college combined. I'm not sure when the big switchover happened—one minute every girl in our dorm, us included, was passing around old flames and classmates right and left, the next minute all the boys and girls were paired off. "Everyone who isn't engaged or pinned or thinks she will be this semester, stand up," Julia whispered at an all-dorm meeting early in our senior year. Of course no one did. "See what I mean," Julia whispered to me. "They're all sheep. They only came to college to get a man. You and I have more integrity."

"Julia," I whispered back, "the only person who heard what you said is me, and I didn't stand up either."

"You don't count. I wasn't talking about you or me. The point is *they* have no integrity. They wouldn't have understood if they had heard me. Because they don't want to understand. Besides, haven't you ever heard of the cosmic consciousness? Where all of us know everything there is to know? They know what they're doing. They wouldn't dare to stand up because they're all settling. Even the ones who aren't engaged wouldn't stand up because they want to be. See?

"Not really," I said. Julia was taking philosophy that semester and not a word of what she was reading made sense to me. I don't think she actually understood it all that well herself, although she'd just made an A on the first quiz. "How did you do that?" I had asked when she came waltzing into our room waving her blue book at me.

Her reply was typical Julia. "Tell you my secret, Robin, I just read the questions, decided what the answer ought to be, and wrote down the opposite. If it made too much sense I went back and threw in a little more bullshit. It worked like a charm!"

"One thing about us, Robin, *we're* not settling," Julia kept on whispering to me, even though the dorm mother was frowning in our direction. I never was sure exactly what Julia meant by *settling* when she talked about not doing it. But whatever it was, settling was something she was dead set against. We read a poem that semester that said, "Do not go gentle into that good night. Rage, rage against the dying of the light." I know that these words are supposed to be about death but I think of Julia when I hear them. She raged, raged, against whatever was expected of her. Always. And if I could have, I'd have been just like her. I wasn't the only one either—lots of the girls in our dorm liked Julia tremendously. She was flashy, and could be obnoxious, but it didn't seem to matter. Most of the time she made us smile.

Julia decided, our senior year, to become a hippie. She took to wearing frayed jeans and sandals, even when it was below freezing. Her mother mailed her a clipping about pneumonia and frostbite, complete with photographs. Two girls from down the hall wrote off for information about the Peace Corps. Julia called and got her own packet of information. "Do you want me to get you one too?" she asked, her hand over the telephone receiver.

I shook my head no. I didn't want to learn a foreign language and go live as some poor natives did. I couldn't see Julia doing it either. She went so far as to call and make an appointment for an interview. Then I happened to strike up a conversation with a girl, Sammie Rae, who was in one of my senior English classes and had been in the Peace Corps for six months in Brazil. She was a Tech graduate who was back in Lubbock taking graduate-level classes while she decided what to do with her life. As soon as I met her I made her come back to the dorm with me so she could give Julia the straight poop on the Peace Corps.

"Why did you come home early?" Julia asked her.

"I was sick the entire time I was there. I got some kind of intestinal worms. No matter what I ate, I couldn't keep anything down. I barfed my head off every single day for weeks on end. I got skinny as a rail."

I thought maybe I might have made a mistake. One thing Julia worried about pretty consistently was getting fat. She might sign up for Brazil simply to get some of those worms.

"Couldn't they give you something?"

"Yeah, but I think the treatment they give you is sort of like arsenic, it kills the worms, but if you get them repeatedly it is dangerous for you to keep taking the medicine over and over."

"Maybe you were just highly susceptible," Julia said. "Did anyone else get worms?"

"There weren't that many people from the Peace Corps in the village where I was sent. The other two people didn't get worms. But one of them got these awful sores between her legs from where they chafed together. We had to walk everywhere we went and sometimes her legs were so bad they'd bleed. I heard she was going to get sent home too because she was flirting with infection so severe it might turn into blood poisoning."

Julia sort of shuddered at that. "Don't you think you could have gone somewhere else?" she asked. "Somewhere like maybe a desert place? One where they don't have worms."

"Maybe so. But you know what? I was glad to come home when they finally said to me, 'Give it up, Sammie Rae, you're too anemic, we've got to ship you back to the States.' Because what we were doing isn't a drop in the bucket. All I was was one more peasant scrabbling in the earth. I wasn't going to change anything. I was supposed to be teaching the Brazilians things like rotation of crops and what plants give you more nutrition for your effort. But I wasn't making a dent. As far as I could tell, none of us were."

"Oh," Julia said.

The next day she tossed her Peace Corps folder in the trash can.

During your senior year in college, there are all sorts of recruiters on campus. I wished, as I read the lists for the types of graduates they were looking for, that I had paid more attention to recruiters back when I was a freshman. The only people looking for teachers were the school districts and the Peace Corps. If I'd been an engineer, or a business major, there would have been more options open to me.

"Are you going to make any appointments for interviews?" I asked Julia. I hadn't seen one advertisement asking for straight English majors. Well, none other than those from a couple of the law schools that had sent people to recruit students.

That was the first Julia had heard of recruiters. "What *was* Barbara Parkins in *Valley of the Dolls*?" she asked me.

"I think you'd have called her an executive secretary," I replied. I'd been thinking about Barbara Parkins also. There weren't any New York City companies in Lubbock, Texas, recruiting for executive secretaries the year Julia and I were seniors.

I graduated in May. Julia had to go to summer school and take ten hours to finish her degree. Moving back to Houston was a bittersweet experience for me. I was glad to get my degree and happy that I wasn't going to live in West Texas the rest of my life, but I hated the idea that college was over. Most of all, I missed Julia and all the fun we'd had in the dorm. Life right after college seemed flat, like a soft drink that's been uncapped and forgotten. Heavy, full-strength syrup, no fizz.

Ostensibly, I came home for the summer to chart a course for the next part of my life. Although I was always more practical than Julia, I didn't get any awards for foresight and planning. "I think I'm going to apply to teach out in Colorado," I told Aunt Kate. I'd never been there before, but it seemed more accessible to me than Boston or New York. Aunt Kate had surprised me with a car for graduation, something I'd never in a million years expected. I thought, *With a car I can go anywhere I want to go*. But I was still left having to figure out where that was.

"We have a book on the educational requirements for teachers in all fifty states at the library," Aunt Kate said to me. "It's in the reference collection so I can't circulate it, but I'll bring it home tonight if you like. As long as it goes back first thing in the morning there won't be a problem."

"Aunt Kate, I already have a teaching certificate," I reminded her.

"Your certificate is for Texas," she said. "All states have their own individual licensing requirements." That is the first I'd heard of each of the fifty states expecting to license their own teachers.

I sent off for job applications to several Colorado school districts while I started working at the library in a job Aunt Kate found for me. When the applications from Colorado arrived I didn't bother to open the envelopes, as I'd already taken a job with the Houston Independent School District for the coming year.

"Robin," Aunt Kate said to me one night over dinner. This must have been about a Tuesday, we were eating hot roast beef sandwiches from Sunday's leftover roast. "You don't seem too excited about the idea of teaching next year."

"It'll be okay, I guess," I mumbled. It embarrassed me that I had spent four years and no telling how much of Aunt Kate's hard-earned money and I still didn't know what I wanted to do with my life. "I'm just nervous, Aunt Kate. Student teaching was easy. I always knew the real teacher was right there to bail me out. This time I'll be on my own." I was trying not to even think about all the horrible things I had heard that high school kids did to inexperienced teachers. The only thing I could actually recall from all my education classes was the hoarse voice of one of the coaches telling us the cardinal rule for teachers, whatever their subject matter, was never to smile before Thanksgiving. "If you smile," he said, "the little turkeys will have your number and it will be all over." Every single time I thought of myself standing up in front of a class, I got a heavy feeling in the pit of my stomach. I doubted I'd be able to smile even if that turned out to be part of my job description.

"Robin, have you thought of graduate school? We could certainly afford that if you'd like an advanced degree," Aunt Kate said. Beside her plate at the table I saw that she'd brought home three college catalogs from the library. "Why don't you look through these, see if something doesn't appeal to you?" she said to me, pushing the books across the table to me.

"No, Aunt Kate," I said. "I want to teach next year. Going back to college would just be postponing the inevitable. It is time I did something real."

Aunt Kate hasn't ever been the type to push. "If that's what you want," she said to me and walked across the kitchen to stack the catalogs on the kitchen cabinet next to the back door. That's where we put things we wanted to remember to take with us the next time we left the house. Our lives were full of all these little rules and routines. Sometimes, like now, I thought of all of Aunt Kate's mannerisms and habits as persnickety and they irritated me. *Leave the books on the table until you finish eating, you won't forget them if you try,* I thought. I looked down at my plate, ashamed of myself. Aunt Kate was so good to me, I hated it when I thought mean things about her.

Julia came to visit for Fourth of July weekend but she still wasn't finished; she had one more course to take— Journalism. "I've heard it's a lot easier if you take it from the UT extension service," she said. "I think I might sign up with them and finish that way."

"Will you still get your degree in August?" I asked her.

"I doubt it. Hell, I doubt I'd ever finish that correspondence course, I'm going back to Lubbock and take the damn journalism course and get it over with." That was the most practical thing I could recall ever hearing Julia say.

"*Valley of the Dolls* was at the drive-in out on Fiftieth Street, I went to see it one more time, to check on Barbara," she said.

"How was she?"

"Same as ever, although I hate it that she wears that fur coat. You know how she got her job, Robin? She went through an employment agency. That's what I'm going to do. As soon as I get my degree I'm going to sign up with an agency. I looked in the yellow pages. There are tons of them right here in Houston."

I hadn't gotten around to telling Julia I'd signed a teaching contract for the coming year. I was afraid she'd decide that I was one of the wimps and weenies after all. I could hear her voice going on and on about how she and I *had more sense than to settle.* Yet here I was, living with my aunt, and fixing to sink into a job that felt like a trap.

"I've decided to get an apartment down here," she said. "I thought maybe you could get one next door to me. I'd die before I moved back in with Mother, but it will be fun to live in Houston. That way I can have a fabulous career and still keep my eye on things at home."

I felt disoriented for a minute or two. If Julia even remembered the things we'd both said about living somewhere exciting like Boston or New York, I couldn't tell it. "I've got a contract for a teaching job here next year," I admitted. She didn't even raise an eyebrow.

OUR NEW UNFURNISHED apartments (unfurnished in my case to save forty dollars a month, in Julia's case because she thought apartment furniture was dreck) were located in a complex called Twin Fountains. It was a huge complex with pools and fountains scattered all over the place. Julia and I were on the second floor of Building J, overlooking one of the pools. The pool was barely large enough to make it out of the wading pool category but would be great for sunbathing, Julia said. She, who was in the habit of sunbathing on the dorm roof in the hot Lubbock sun equipped with only a spray bottle of water, pronounced herself pleased to finally live near some real water. I, who hesitated to appear out the door without a hat on when the sun was shining due to my tendency to sunburn and freckle, was glad to see that when Julia got a phone call I was going to be able to put my head out the door and yell for her rather than have to climb up two flights of stairs to the dorm roof to go get her.

I had been teaching almost a month when Julia took her first job, which didn't pan out as either of us had envisioned. The position Snelling and Snelling found her cost her a month's salary, despite the fact she didn't work at Foley's longer than three and one-half days. Julia said she'd be damned if she'd pay them another cent beyond the 50 percent of her first month's salary they'd already gotten, but after she received several collection letters her dad went in and talked to someone and ended up paying the rest of the bill for her. "Think of this as a learning experience, Julia," he said when she told him if she'd known he was going to throw his money away she'd never have shown him the letters in the first place. She went to a different employment agency to find her second job, the one with the insurance company. That one worked out, sort of. At least she lasted long enough to pay off the agency and still make some money. Her third job, and the last one she had, Aunt Kate found for her. I think Julia was reluctant to quit work at the electric utility because she didn't want to make my aunt feel bad. She worked there for almost six months—eons for her. Toward the end, she started collecting college catalogs and talking advanced degree as if graduate school were some magic place she was going to fly away to. Somehow I never could envision her back in school. I don't think she could either. College wasn't what Julia was looking for. Julia, for all her talk, was like me. She wanted to settle.

I SHOULD HAVE suspected Julia was going to end up with Danny. She said it had been a mistake, the way they'd gotten so serious in high school. And that she was over him long before she broke up with him. But she still had pictures of him she kept in a desk drawer. And sometimes, all through college, when it was cold outside, she'd pull out his high school letter jacket and wear it to class.

"Julia, no one wears those things, they're so high school," Marie from down the hall said to her the first time she saw Julia with the jacket on.

"*I'm* wearing it," Julia replied, as if that was all the justification her choice of wearing apparel required. Even after several people in one of her classes made a big deal over never having heard of Cypress Springs, Julia kept on wearing the jacket from time to time. Probably this was as much out of sheer perversity as for any other reason. However, it was Danny's jacket. She also had a high school letter jacket of her own from her cheerleading days. She never wore that one.

Julia, once she was living in Houston, ran into Danny from time to time. Cypress Springs is such a small town it is surprising she didn't see him more than once or twice during the four years she was out in Lubbock. "I can't believe I ever dated him," she said to me once when we were freshmen or sophomores.

"Why? What's wrong with him?" I asked.

"He's dull. He fits Cypress Springs perfectly," I remember her saying. Dull people settle in little towns, that is the way she saw it. Julia didn't want to become a dull person in a small town. At the same time, she couldn't cut herself off from her family. Every time her mother redecorated the house, she had a fit. The new colors were wrong. She didn't like the carpet Verona replaced the old carpet with. When that carpet was ripped up and the floors underneath refinished, Julia thought wood floors made the house too cold. Her mother cooked with too much salt and grease. After her father's heart problems it was insensitive of Verona to serve fried food. It proved she didn't love her husband. It wasn't so much what Julia said about them, it was the way she kept on saying something. One thing right after another. Thinking back, it should have been obvious to me Julia never expected to move away from home. No matter how mad they made her, the bonds were too strong.

I saw Julia and me as close, so close we had few if any secrets from each other. When she went out with Danny a time or two I wasn't surprised. Although she'd said she'd never date him again, I'd always thought maybe she would. The fact that they were dating didn't make me feel uneasy. It never occurred to me that if Julia went back to Danny she'd quit being friends with me. However, it did bother me, once Julia and Danny started dating again, that there wasn't anyone in love with me. I felt sort of lonely about that fact, particularly once Julia came home with an engagement ring.

"Look at this," she said to me. She'd walked into my apartment and switched on the lights without a minute's hesitation, despite the fact that it was past midnight and it was obvious I was sound asleep. I hadn't left the door unlocked. Julia and I had keys to each other's apartments. Generally, when we were both home, we hung out in the same one.

She threw off her clothes, grabbed one of my T-shirts and pulled it over her head to sleep in, and hopped into bed with me. "Move over," she said, shoving me toward one side. I had a twin bed so there wasn't much space for me to move over to.

"Get in the other bed," I mumbled. "You're drunk," I added. I could smell the wine on her breath. And her clothes reeked of cigarettes. "Where have you been?" I asked. I still hadn't opened my eyes more than a slit. I'd been in bed since ten, long enough to have fallen into a deep sleep. "Julia, hell, if I wake up, I'll never go back to sleep, let's talk in the morning."

She was wired. "Don't you want to see my engagement ring?" she asked.

"Your what?" I shrieked and sat straight up. "Well, shit," I said, sounding just like her.

"Is that all you can say?" she asked.

"It's gorgeous, Julia, congratulations. I mean, I think Danny is wonderful, I really do! And you'll be a beautiful bride. Let's celebrate, I'll get the wine," I said. We kept gallon jugs of cheap red wine in both the refrigerators.

"To holy matrimony," she said offering the first toast to herself. She laughed and threw back her head and drained her glass.

As long as I kept my mind fixed on Julia's future life I was fine, but once I started imagining myself living in Houston in an apartment without Julia there to keep the wimps and weenies at bay, I got a little teary-eyed. After my second glass of wine, I said, "But, Julia, I'm going to miss you. I'm glad you're getting married, but I don't want to lose you."

"Don't worry, we'll always be best friends," she promised me.

Julia said she had decided to go whole hog and be a June bride, which meant that she had less than six weeks to plan her wedding. The way she described her plans to me that night, I thought she'd have plenty of time to get the wedding preparations together. "You're going to be my maid of honor and Susie will be matron of honor. That's it, I don't need a huge wedding party," she said. "Danny can have Josh Winter as his best man and his cousin will be groomsman. We'll get married the last Saturday in June and have the reception at the church fellowship hall. Punch and cake, flowers all around, what's to plan?"

"Sounds simple enough to me," I agreed.

"Robin, I don't know why I never thought of this before, I'm going to fix you up with Josh. The two of you will be perfect together. Who knows, maybe we can make it a double wedding!" She'd had no telling how much wine by this time. She fell back on the bed laughing like she'd said something hilariously funny. I didn't laugh with her, but she didn't notice.

VERONA AND JULIA started right in on the wedding plans, which got more complicated by the minute. Julia quit her job the week after she got engaged because she said between her mother and Danny calling her ten and twelve times a day, she couldn't concentrate on anything but the damn wedding anyway.

Her mother, her sister-in-law, and I went with her to pick out her wedding dress. Julia and Verona got into it for the first time that day before we even arrived at the bridal department at Sakowitz. On the escalator on the way up to the third floor, Julia mentioned she thought we might as well pick out the bridesmaid dresses. "Kill two birds with one stone while we're here," is how she put it. She was wearing jeans with ripped-out knees, a yellow Texas Tech sweatshirt that she'd cut the sleeves out of, and her sandals. Her mother called the clothes she was wearing her ridiculous hippie garb. Julia almost never dressed like that except when she was going to be around Verona.

"Julia," Verona said, "it is traditional to have all your attendants with you when you choose their dresses. We'll have to make another trip to do bridesmaid dresses. Getting your dress chosen will be accomplishment enough for today."

"Both of my attendants are here with me," Julia said. She had been first on the escalator and thus was in front of the rest of us, she didn't notice Verona stop dead in her tracks and plant her feet on the floor as she stepped off the stairs. With her hands on her hips and her chin jutting out, Verona looked ready to do battle. Susie and I, as we reached the top of the escalator, had to sort of squeeze ourselves around Verona to get off the escalator without bumping into her. We stood a little ways away from Verona, reluctant to keep walking without her, but not wanting to let Julia get too far ahead of us either.

"Julia!" Verona said.

"Hurry up, Mother, let's get this over with."

"What do you mean to say they're both here?"

Julia frowned at her mother. She'd already forgotten what she'd just said. "Uh?" she asked.

"You will have at least six attendants, Julia."

"Mother, get real, there aren't six people I want to ask. Robin's maid of honor and Susie's matron of honor and that's that!"

"We'll see about what is what, young lady. The very idea, you aren't going to be satisfied with some dippy little wedding."

Julia acted like she hadn't heard her mother. She walked on into the bridal department and buttonholed the first person she encountered. "I need a wedding dress. Soon, in two months, so don't go bringing out stuff it takes six months to get. And nothing fancy, I don't like clothes all gooped up."

"Yes, ma'am."

By then Verona had caught up with Julia and was looking a little frantic. She started talking about afternoon versus evening weddings and empire style versus princess or natural waistline. The saleslady kept trying to listen to Verona while she kept up with Julia, who had walked over to a dress rack and was shoving dresses back and forth.

"Why don't I show you to a dressing room and bring some things back for you to try on? After you've tried on several styles, we'll have more to go on," she said, and successfully shepherded all four of us down a hall to a large room equipped with several couches, three-sided mirrors, and a telephone. One entire wall was mirrored. You couldn't turn around without encountering your reflection and that of everyone else in the room with you as well. All those mirrors made it seem as if we were more than four people, none of us entirely comfortable together. While we waited for the saleslady to return, Julia picked up the telephone and informed us it worked.

"Anyone you want to call?" she asked me. "Now's your chance."

"No," I said, trying not to grin at her. Julia was obviously in a mood, and I didn't want to encourage her. I was afraid Verona would pitch a fit if Julia didn't get a little more serious about this shopping expedition. Susie sat down on a couch and looked through bride's magazines, acting the entire time as if she were perfectly at ease. She probably was, she'd been around the two of them a lot more than I had. Susie is the closest thing to unflappable I've ever seen, anyway. Julia and Verona's squabbling didn't seem to bother her.

Julia tried on four dresses and chose the second one she put on. Verona wanted to keep looking, but Julia announced her mind was made up and refused to let the saleslady bring anything else back to the dressing room. Next, Verona and the saleswoman got into a complicated discussion dealing with what kind of a hat and veil should go with the dress. Julia ignored them and let Verona make the choice entirely on her own. We'd been in the store all told about thirty minutes by this time, and Julia's outfit, except for the shoes, was taken care of. Verona looked at her watch and frowned. I felt sorry for her. It was obvious she wanted a more elaborate shopping trip than she was getting. I knew she had planned to shop for two hours before we went upstairs to the Sky Terrace for lunch. I think it was the time as much as anything that caused her to give in on the question of attendants and let the saleslady bring dresses for Susie and me to look at. She made one last feeble stab at creating a more satisfactory wedding party. "Don't you think you ought to at least ask several of your cousins to be in the wedding, Julia? Sumter, for one, will be so hurt not to be included."

"Mother, I haven't seen Sumter in years, why the hell should she want to be in my wedding?"

"What about Yvonne, your best friend from high school?" Verona persisted. She was actually a little pitiful, standing there trying to think up who Julia might be overlooking.

"Yvonne hates me, I'm not even going to send her an invitation."

Verona looked at the saleslady apologetically. "I'll never understand these girls today," she said. "Julia has more friends than she can shake a stick at."

The saleswoman nodded sympathetically. "What colors had you thought of using?" she asked. She fixed her eyes somewhere in the space between Julia and Verona—she never did act like she could figure out who was in charge.

Julia said she really didn't care what color dresses Susie and I wore as long as they weren't green, she hated green. And no yellow, she specified. Otherwise it didn't matter to her.

The saleswoman left and returned with a sliding cart filled with a veritable rainbow of dresses. She'd learned her lesson, no more of this let's try on a few for size and style and go from there. Verona's eyes lit up, this was more what she'd had in mind. Susie and I stood there, staring at the rack of dresses, I felt reluctant to approach them. Julia lit a cigarette and put her feet up on the couch. "I'm out of this, your turn now," she said to Susie and me. As Verona started sliding dresses back and forth on the rack, pulling out first one and then another to examine it more closely, Julia asked the saleswoman to get her a Dr. Pepper with crushed ice and two Bayer aspirin.

While the saleswoman was out of the room Verona and Julia got into another little spat. "Julia, I think pink. A pale, pale pink, isn't this dress absolutely gorgeous?" Verona said.

"Mother, you aren't going to be wearing the dresses, Susie and Robin are. Let them decide what they want."

"Julia, I've never heard anything so ridiculous, this is your wedding!"

"Susie, Robin," Julia said, ignoring her mother. "Grab something so we can get out of here."

Susie and I exchanged a look as we started sifting through

the dresses. There were so many of them and they were all so different. "What about this one?" Susie asked. "It's the same general style as Julia's dress so they'd look good together. What do you think of the color?"

I wasn't sure who she was asking but it was me who was going to be wearing the dress so I finally spoke up. "I really don't care for orange," I said.

"You're right," said Susie, "it is orange."

By that time the saleslady was back in the room with us. "That dress also comes in teal and lime," she said.

"Maybe teal," Verona said. "Is the teal the same shade as the one here?"

Thirty minutes later, the four of us were standing outside the Sky Terrace waiting for them to start serving lunch. Susie and I, Julia's only attendants, were slated to wear dresses very similar in style to Julia's in a pale, pale teal. Our headgear consisted of tiny pillbox hats covered in the same fabric as our dresses. Our shoes, two-inch heels, would be dyed to match.

The only thing I remember about the rest of the day is at lunch I ordered Julia's favorite item from the menu, the hot roast beef sandwich and twice-baked potato. Sakowitz's hot roast beef sandwich had Aunt Kate's beat all to hell. I doubted that they used McCormick gravy mix from a package the way she did.

IT DIDN'T SEEM like any time at all had elapsed before I found myself in Butch and Susie's guest room getting dressed for the wedding itself. Julia had moved out of her apartment the last week of May, but I didn't really have to start missing her immediately because she stayed with me almost every night up until the night of the rehearsal dinner. The day before the wedding, we both went out to Cypress Springs. It seemed as if Julia turned into a different person when she hit the city limits.

Maybe it was because she was doing all these things that really didn't matter to her. She had mounds of wedding presents to open. Verona had borrowed no telling how many tables from the church to display Julia and Danny's gifts, which filled the entire living room of her house. "What on earth will you do with three electric skillets?" I asked Julia. She also had four irons. And enough of her silver pattern to feed twenty-four people without stopping to wash a fork.

"Mother will have the time of her life next week exchanging everything," she said. "I'm not worried about it." She wasn't worried about the wedding gifts, but she was worried about something. She acted more brittle with every hour that passed.

One thing that had really bothered me for the past weeks was the way she kept saying things like you and Josh are going to have to get together. "Come on, Danny," she'd say, "talk to Josh. I think he and Robin will make a great pair." Then she'd giggle. I didn't think she was trying to insult me, but the way she kept trying to come up with someone for me to fall in love with made it sound like she thought that, without her efforts, I'd never meet, much less have a date with, a man.

I should have said something to her about the way she kept pushing me and Josh Winter together, but I was afraid that one little thing would be the push she needed to set her off so I kept my mouth shut. Time enough to say something later, I thought. After the wedding is over and things have settled down, we'll talk. But, of course, there wasn't any later.

Julia and Danny's wedding passed in a whirlwind of activity. The reception only lasted about two hours. Since it was held at the church there wasn't any liquor served, which irritated Julia no end. "I can't believe Mother thought she could have this reception without champagne. Let's go somewhere and drink," she said to Danny. "Josh and Robin can go with us, this place is getting to me!"

By that time Josh and I weren't even looking at each other. I think he was as mortified as I was. "Julia, you have to stay to toss your bouquet, then you're supposed to rush off on your honeymoon," I said to her. I didn't say a word about going anywhere with them after the reception—neither did Josh, although he was right there and had heard what she said as clearly as I had. The way she scowled at me made me glad I hadn't said anything more than what I did say. Julia didn't like anyone telling her what she had to do.

I was the one who caught the bouquet. She aimed it straight at me. "You're next!" she said loud enough for the entire town to hear. "All we have to do is find you a man!"

After those words of hers, I couldn't get away from the First Methodist Church in Cypress Springs fast enough. I wanted to crawl into a hole and die. People laughed. It sounded like nervous laughter to me. I'm sure they weren't all staring at me either, but I was too embarrassed to look anyone in the eye. All of us tossed rice and waved good-bye and watched Julia and Danny drive away. As soon as I decently could after they left, I found my purse and told Verona I was going to be leaving. She didn't act like she heard my good-bye. "I don't think the photographer got the picture of Julia with her cousins," she was saying to no one in particular. "If he missed that shot, I am going to be so put out with him."

Susie, bless her heart, gave me a big hug. She hadn't missed much. "Don't let it bother you, Robin. Julia was thoughtless, but she didn't mean to hurt your feelings," she said.

I was embarrassed to be so transparent. "My feelings aren't hurt, I'm just tired. We were up until all hours last night," I said.

Susie gave me another hug. So did Butch. "See you soon," they both said as they walked me out to my car. Butch checked to make sure my doors were locked and reminded me to be careful driving home. His solicitousness brought a lump to my throat. Julia didn't know how good she had it, I thought. Driving home, I did cry some. Later on, in the next months, it didn't really surprise me that Julia and I seemed to have lost something. She was married, I wasn't. That seemed to be the crux of the matter.

The few times we talked it was like we had to struggle to come up with things to say to each other. Gradually we got to where we barely talked on the phone at all. At first I kept thinking she'd change back into herself. That didn't happen. As time went on, I made myself stop remembering Julia's wedding and how I'd been so mortified I'd felt like all the world's wimps and weenies rolled into one. Mostly I simply missed Julia.

PART IV

JULIA

Although Danny and I habitually went to his parents' on Christmas Eve, mine on Christmas Day, mine on New Year's Eve, and his on New Year's Day, the holidays that came right after my daughter, Gracie, was born were, in a word, screwed. Danny's mother had died the March before, and his father had chosen to buy a house in Galveston. For the first holiday since we'd married, there weren't two sets of grandparents for Danny and me to alternate our time between.

"Look, Julia," Danny said, "don't you think it is time we start creating our own traditions rather than relying on what one of our families has always done? Robert is almost two. Why don't we have everyone here on Christmas and New Year's?"

"If I invite Mother over she'll never leave, she'll drive me stark raving mad."

"You exaggerate."

Despite the fact Danny and I had been married almost three years he still didn't know me well enough to know when all I was doing was reciting the bald-faced truth. Mother will drive me mad. It's the only goal she has left in life.

We did have my folks over on Christmas Eve. I cooked a ham and a pot of beans, rolls I made from scratch, and a congealed vegetable salad. Susie made the dessert. All Mother did was show up. "This is the meal you're supposed to fix on

New Year's *Day*, Julia," my mother said to me. "Black-eyed peas are what you eat to make sure you have good luck."

"So fill up on salad and put the rest of your plate in the freezer for a week. It'll keep," I said to her.

That's what I mean about driving me nuts. There I was with two kids, no household help, and all she could say about the meal I'd managed to pull together was that it was a week before its time. Susie helped me clean up. "Mother pisses me off so bad. This is the last time I let Danny talk me into inviting her over to my house," I said.

"Julia, the meal was delicious. Don't worry about what Verona says."

"Who's worried, Susie? There is a difference between worried and pissed off. And I'm pissed off."

I TRIED TO call Robin on New Year's Day. I sent Danny and Robert over to Mother and Daddy's to eat lunch and watch the games with them and I stayed home and slept. I had just survived the most depressing holiday of my life. Gracie wasn't six weeks old yet and I was nursing her, which meant I was still morbidly obese. Although I gained all the weight the doctor told me to and nursed both my kids for six months, I hated with a purple passion that I had to stay fat to get them off to a good start. Fat is such a turnoff. "You're not fat, Julia," Danny said to me. Sure I wasn't. The only thing I could fit into were those elastic-waist pants and some "one size fits all" sweaters that looked like they belonged to your typical bag lady.

When the only number I had for Robin rang twice before I got a recording saying, *The number you have reached is no longer a working number,* I felt like crying. All day long I had been thinking of Robin. I reached under the bed and pulled out my wedding album and there, on the second page, was the picture of Robin and me taken the day I made one of the biggest mistakes of my life.

The rehearsal dinner was held at the Lakeside Country Club, which is halfway to Houston. Since Danny was an only child, his parents went all out for what turned out to be the last big party they had occasion to put on. They served prime rib, twice-baked potatoes, something green, and iced tea. Except before we got to the dinner part of the evening, there was an open bar anchored by plates of munchies scattered throughout the room. There must have been a hundred people at the dinner, talking nonstop, giving every indication they were having a great time. With all of those people talking, smoking, and drinking, it was easy to lose sight of the event for which we were gathered. Robin and I both were drinking Tom Collins highballs like they were going to be declared obsolete the next day.

"Julia," she'd whispered to me, "you've had too many." Robin herself was feeling no pain by that time. "My lips are numb," she had informed me.

I had had about six or seven drinks by then. I looked across the room and saw Danny talking to his best friend, Josh Winter. They're both tall and have dark hair and because of the smoky haze in the room and the fact they both were wearing dark suits I felt as if I was seeing double.

"Let's go to the bathroom and smoke a cigarette," I had said to Robin. "I need to clear my head."

Generally, whenever I had a drink I'd have a cigarette, cigarettes go great with booze. But I was never what you'd called hooked. The minute I decided to marry Danny, I took up cigarettes again with a vengeance. At the time of my wedding I was smoking Benson & Hedges. The long ones that sort of show off a great manicure. But I didn't smoke in public. I've always hated it when Mother does that.

Robin and I locked the restroom door and hoisted ourselves up on the countertops and lit our cigarettes. I smoked mine. Robin held a lighted cigarette in her hand to keep me company.

"You remember Marie, from college?" I asked Robin. "She called me today. She and Donnie have two kids now. And three houses. The one in Dallas, which is their main residence. Their Colorado house for summer excursions and skiing in the winter. And one in Florida where they go after skiing to thaw out."

"Cute," Robin said.

"Almost too cute," I said, which made her laugh. I'd told her earlier in the day how Danny's mother always said that to me. "Marie said she hoped I'd be every bit as happy as she is."

"That's nice. I hope she is. Happy, I mean."

"Yeah. Me, too. I guess. Oh, shit, who the hell knows who is happy and who isn't?" That's when I started crying. It was the booze. Booze always makes me nuts.

I didn't have to tell Robin why I was locked in the bathroom drunk and crying on the night before my wedding. We both knew I didn't love Danny any more than Marie loved Donnie when she'd married him. Robin knew I'd said I would never settle for that.

ROBIN

Going back to school in September always made me miss Julia. Even though I hadn't seen or heard from her for what seemed like eons, I was thinking of her as I pulled into the parking lot of the high school where I had been teaching for five years. I had the backseat of my car loaded with teacher's manuals and files I'd taken to work on over the summer. I hadn't done the first thing with those materials and I was feeling guilty as all get-out about my lackadaisical approach to my job. Julia would have said to me, *What the hell—they don't pay you enough for you to work your butt off all summer long.* I thought of her as I loaded my arms with everything I could possibly carry. I didn't want to have to make two trips just to unload my car. I was hoping somehow or another I could race upstairs to my classroom, dust off my desk, and rush around like a mad hatter and somehow make up for all the time I had lost. I didn't have an excuse in the world for everything I hadn't gotten done. It wasn't like I had done anything else all summer long. I had spent one week at the beach. That was my summer vacation.

I was in such a rut it scared me to think about it. And because I was working so hard not to think about how predictable and—well, yes, *boring*—how boring my life had turned out to be, I was in a terrible mood.

"Buck up and quit feeling sorry for yourself, Robin," I said. I closed the car door with a swift hip movement and turned toward the building. *God, I don't want to be here,* I thought. My arms were piled so high with books and file folders that I was balancing the entire stack with my chin pressed against the topmost file. Next thing I knew I had stumbled over one of the potholes and ended up in a heap on the pavement. Just as I was dusting myself off and congratulating myself that at least the whole world hadn't witnessed me falling flat on my rear end, the side door creaked opened. "Need any help?" someone called out.

I didn't recognize the voice. "Nope," I replied without looking up. "I'm just fine." He came out anyway and started helping me gather up my scattered papers. "This is what I get for trying to do things in such a hurry," I muttered, still without taking my eyes off the ground. *Why me?* I wondered. Stupid things like this never happened to Julia.

We were inside the building outside the teacher's lounge before I actually looked at the man. And then it was only because he introduced himself to me and politeness dictated that I at the least make eye contact. "I'm T. J. Damron, Ruth Harmon's replacement," he said.

"I'm Robin Tilton, your next-door neighbor," I replied. I was still feeling surly when I looked at him. I'm sure my jaw dropped when I saw his face. "My gracious good heavens, what did you say your name is?" I said. I can't believe I actually used the words "my gracious good heavens"—I had never in my life used that expression before. I'd never even heard anyone say something so gothic. In addition to talking to myself, I had also spent the summer reading through everything on the library shelves: no telling what irreparable damage I had done. "You are the double of my best friend's brother, I swear you are," I said. "Do you have relatives in Cypress Springs?"

T. J. Damron, like most of the world, had no idea where Cypress Springs, Texas, was, but I noticed my friend Crystal looking at me funny. It wasn't until later on in the day that it hit me what was bothering her. Crystal considered herself my best friend. I suppose by that time she was. Julia, whom I had not seen or heard from in years, no longer qualified. But right at the moment when I first saw T. J., and thought for a minute there that he *was* Butch Salwell, it took me back. And for that little bit of time I forgot how things had changed between me and Julia.

IT HAD BEEN four years since Julia married Danny. And it was almost that long since I'd seen her. I now was spending the entire first meeting of the English department staring out the window and wondering what was going on in Julia's life. *Was she still with Danny?* Of course she was, she and Danny were perfect together! *Did she have kids?* Somehow it was hard for me to see Julia with kids. *Did Butch and Susie have any more?* Probably—the two of them were great parents. I imagined they had a cute little girl and maybe another boy by this time. *Was Verona still a witch?* Doubtless, but at least with Verona around life never became monotonous. *Did Tom still dote on Julia?* I smiled. I'd have given my eyeteeth for a dad like Julia had. *Why had Julia married Danny and cut me off without so much as a word? Why hadn't she at least returned my last phone calls?* To those questions, I had no answer.

That afternoon when I got home from work the first thing I did was pick up the telephone. I called information and got Julia and Danny's phone number. I guess I'd probably done that about once a month for the past year or two. I really did want to talk to Julia. I imagined myself saying to her, "You are not going to believe this, but there is a double of your brother teaching next door to me." "No shit," Julia would say back to me. That was as far as I got. In the end I didn't dial their number. Instead I went over to the University Club and worked out. I took an aerobics class and then, because I didn't want to go home, I hopped on one of the stationary bicycles in front of the big-screen television set.

There was a news report on the exotic pets people were buying that I got so interested in I forgot to pedal. Aunt Kate was on a Far Eastern tour right about then, and I wondered if she'd seen any of those animals. I started thinking about pets. Maybe that was what I needed. I didn't care for birds at all, but I sort of liked the idea of a rare monkey. Something different—not your run-of-the-mill dog or cat. *Maybe I ought to get a monkey,* I thought.

"If you're not going to ride that bike, do you think you could get off and let me have a turn?" a male voice said.

I gave him one of my aunt's *who the hell do you think you are?* looks and got off the bike. Jeff, the club manager, who never missed a trick, came rushing over to introduce us, but by then I had already decided that Anthony Shaw was a jerk.

"Didn't you say that your aunt is in Japan this month?" Jeff asked. "Anthony here has business interests in Japan."

"Wonderful," I said, and walked on into the dressing room to change. Unlike some of the people at the club, I didn't go there to expand my social life, I went there to work out. It did occur to me that Anthony might have asked Jeff to introduce us but I really wasn't in the mood to get excited about any guy I met right then.

As I anticipated, Anthony was waiting for me as I walked out of the dressing room. "How about dinner?" he asked.

"I've eaten."

"Well, dessert then."

"No, thank you."

"Your phone number?"

I rolled my eyes again and said, "Dream on." Whenever I'm rude to people that way, I pretend I'm Julia. And whatever she would say comes out of my mouth. I tossed my hair back in the manner of Julia and walked around Anthony and out the side door to the parking garage. I was a little disappointed he didn't follow me. He actually was sort of cute. He looked to be about forty, and there really isn't anything wrong with being extremely sure of yourself.

"Why on earth didn't you go out with him?" Crystal asked me the next day. This was while we were sitting on the school patio ostensibly writing out lesson plans. Mainly we were talking. "You didn't have a date all summer long, I can't believe you turned him down," Crystal said to me.

"I am not about to become one of those women who goes to her health club palpitating anxiously for some guy to look in her direction."

"Where else are you going to meet guys? The only new man on the faculty this year is T.J. Damron."

"Who is married and has four kids."

"I'm not surprised. How did you find out?"

"He's in Mrs. Harmon's old room. Next door to me. We talked. He's nice, Crystal. His wife's a teacher as well."

"Hunky-dory," she replied. Crystal had recently turned thirty-two and was so anxious for a husband that's about all she could talk about. She had already gone through the folders of all the kids in her homeroom to see if any of them were being raised by a single father. One of the women who taught in the art department had met the man she married this past summer just that way. Eloise called to tell Jimmy Earl's father about the fantastic artwork his son was doing and, lo and behold, Mr. Earl turned out to be a widower. He came to the art show to see the pottery and fell in love with Eloise. Poor Crystal. It didn't look like she was going to luck out that way.

"Maybe I should join your health club. Mine is about 90 percent women," she said. "The ad in the singles magazine isn't working out."

"Crystal, I read something in the paper not too long ago about a woman who met a serial killer that way," I said. "Or maybe it was something I saw on daytime TV this summer. I can't remember—my brain is gone. But I don't care if I end up an old maid like Aunt Kate. That's preferable to getting involved with some psycho."

"I've only gotten two replies, and the ad has been in the paper three weeks," she said. "I don't think I'm going to meet anyone at all, much less have to worry about whether or not he's a psycho."

"What were the two replies?"

"I thought you'd never ask," she said. "They're hysterical. Actually, they're hysterical in a pathetic sort of way. I'm not worried about either of these men being psychos or serial killers. These guys are more than likely too dumb to get away with boosting candy at a convenience store."

I had to agree with her. Neither one of them could spell or write more than a four-word sentence. One of them came right out and said he wanted to lick her pussy. "This is disgusting. I can't believe you are subjecting yourself to this." Then I had a horrible thought. Were these things coming to her house?

"Where are the envelopes?" I asked her. I was relieved to see that they were addressed to a post office box number. "At least you aren't giving out your home address," I said.

"I'm not stupid, Robin," she told me. "Just desperate."

"You are not desperate, Crystal. Relax, you've got plenty of time to get married."

"That's easy for you to say, you're not thirty yet."

I felt older than thirty though. The next night, at the club, when Anthony came up to me and said, "Let's start over," in a perfectly sincere voice, I smiled at him and said, "I'm Robin, sorry I was rude before." I thought I was doing it so I could introduce him to Crystal, but sometime over coffee I realized that I wasn't going to introduce Anthony to anyone, I was going to date him myself.

Anthony was perfectly honest with me. He told me from day one that, at age forty-five, he had no desire for kids. And he felt that as much travel as his business required, marriage was unrealistic for him. But—and this was the hook for me— he did want someone to travel with occasionally and to go out with when he was in Houston. "I'm more interested in travel than marriage myself," I said. I looked him straight in the eye and lied my head off. Never start a relationship off by lying, it will get you in trouble every time. I should have known that. I guess I did know it, but I didn't want to think about it right at that particular moment. It had been a very long, very boring summer.

JULIA

This past October was the first homecoming I had gone to since I was a senior. I hate homecoming. It is such a charade. But it was Danny's ten-year reunion and he harassed me for months about going. "Did you get a babysitter yet?" he asked me about once a day after Labor Day. Used to be Danny's mother would have come over and stayed with Robert. But she's dead now, she died before Gracie, who is named after her, was born. It was very sudden and unexpected. She was only fifty years old. To tell you the honest truth, if I'd known Mama Clark wasn't going to live any longer than she did, I'd have been a lot nicer to her.

Their house, which I can see from the kitchen window of my house during the winter when the oaks have no leaves, is as good as empty. Mr. Clark virtually lives in Galveston now, where he plays golf every single day. Danny doesn't even call his dad up every night with the farm and ranch report.

Usually Susie will keep the kids for me, or Mother will, but I hate to ask Mother. However, Susie and Butch always go to homecoming themselves so it had to be Mother or no one.

Not that I don't trust Mother, but she isn't good with kids. I know that from personal experience and I also am aware that she is partial to Gracie. One thing I hate is the way Mother plays favorites.

At the dinner after the game, I got into a conversation with Josh Winter, Danny's best friend from high school. Josh is a lawyer now and had just committed the colossal error of moving back out to Cypress Springs.

"Why on earth do you want to live out here in this little dipshit town?" I asked him.

"I could ask you the same question," he said.

Before I could answer, Danny interrupted us. "Don't let Julia get started on what is wrong with Cypress Springs," he said. He rolled his eyes at me as he said that—we were just talking, none of us was dead serious about this conversation. However, even though we were just talking back and forth, the truth is I've never really liked this town.

"I live in Cypress Springs for my children, Josh," I said. "Otherwise Danny and I would be out of here so fast it would make your head spin."

"You didn't have kids when you and Danny built that house," Josh said.

Josh had this challenging look in his eye. He and I had always liked sparring back and forth. If it wasn't that I imprinted with Danny at such an early age, Josh and I would have gotten together—at least for a fling of some sort. He has always liked me, I know that. But we probably would have fought a lot. We're more alike than Danny and I are. *Maybe it wasn't such a bad idea that he was back in town, after all,* I remember thinking. I grinned at Josh and he shook his head at me as if to say, *Julia, you're a mess.* Actually, I was just starting to have fun. The game had been a big waste of time.

Football is boring enough when the weather is good, but I've never understood why grown people will choose to sit outside all afternoon long in drizzling rain and watch little kids all padded and helmeted up run back and forth at each other trying to get their hands on a lopsided ball.

It was right at that point in the conversation that the school superintendent, Joe Powell, stood up and started tapping his spoon on his glass to get everyone to quit talking and listen to him. While people settled into seats I started making bets with myself about who was going to join us. I was sitting between Josh and Danny at one of the round tables for six. There were three empty seats at our table. I guessed someone like Pattie Lanell, who is divorced with two kids, would come twitching over acting like she wanted to say hi to me when all the time what she wanted to do was get Josh to notice her. I was wrong. Mrs. Singer and her husband and their retarded daughter, who graduated the year I did, pulled out the chairs and sat down. Mrs. Singer teaches Home Ec. Her husband drives the truck that delivers liquid petroleum gas. The daughter, as far as I know, sits in front of the TV. She's gotten huge in the nine years since we graduated. Every time I run into her in town with one or both of her parents I have to stop myself from shuddering where they can see it. That girl gives me the creeps. She is such a zero. She doesn't even try to do anything with her life. I mean, she could weave potholders or something, couldn't she? Danny and Josh immediately started making conversation with both Mr. and Mrs. Singer. Danny even managed to talk to the girl. I find it hard to talk to people when I don't want to see the person sitting in between them. I know that it is wrong to feel this way about Mrs. Singer's daughter, but I can't help it.

Butch and Susie were way across the room from us, sitting with some of Butch's classmates. Other than the two of them, I didn't see anyone in the entire elementary cafetorium I wanted to talk to. Yvonne and Peter had come, of course. I was glad her brother had stayed away. Mr. Powell made the usual lame little remarks that pass for jokes and then told us to enjoy the dinner and be sure and stay for the dance. They'd gotten (are you ready for this?) the high school brass band to play. "That's it, you've done it now, Danny," I said to my husband. "You'll never get me to one of these crapola functions again."

"Lighten up, Julia," Josh said to me. "You could at least pretend you're having a good time."

We glared back and forth at each other for a minute. Next thing I knew I was hearing this squeaking sound. My eyes, along with the rest of the eyes in the room, swiveled over toward the door. Maria Garcia was pushing Julie in her wheelchair into the room. *They should oil that chair,* I thought. And I felt grateful we had the Singers sitting at our table.

Conversation in the room stopped. I felt so sorry for Julie. Everyone was looking at her. She looked like, since the accident, she hadn't aged a day. Time stopped for her the year we were seniors, I guess. Her hair was still thick and dark and curling on her shoulders. Her skin, which is a dark rosy shade of brown, glowed like she was illuminated from the inside out. I don't remember what she wore or what her sister Maria looked like but I can vividly see Julie's eyes. Dark brown. The same brown as mine. We stared at each other as she rolled across the room.

"Hi."

"Hi."

"Sorry."

"Not your fault."

"Still, I blame myself." One of these days Julie and I will actually say these words to each other.

Marie pushed Julie up to a table and the squeaking stopped. Danny and Josh and I left before they brought around the trays of fruit cocktail cobblers, which the freshman girls in Home Ec class had prepared especially for the alums. As we drove away, the windows in Danny's Suburban were rolled down and we could hear the high school band tuning up. "Whatever happened to your friend Robin?" Josh asked me from the backseat.

"You know how it is with big city folks, Josh. If you don't, you are fixing to find out. Watch and see how fast your Dallas buddies drop you." It bothered me a lot that Robin and I didn't have anything in common any longer. And I never ever would have believed she'd have changed her phone number without letting me know the new one. I wondered about her Aunt Kate. Did she still serve roast beef every Sunday lunch and slice up the leftovers for next week's sandwiches for Robin to take to school with her? Was Robin married yet? I imagined myself calling her on the phone. *Hi, Robin, this is Julia,* I would say to her. But I didn't know what I'd say next.

ROBIN

Memory is such an elusive thing. I think about it sometimes, the things you remember, the ones you forget. And about how sometimes the strangest, most obscure memories stay with you. Take for example Halloween the year I was in the third grade. Why do I still remember that so well? Aunt Kate made me a clown suit with a pointed felt hat. I went trick-or-treating door-to-door with the two little girls who lived on our block. Kasey went as a skeleton in a glow-in-the-dark costume her mother purchased at Woolworth's. Linda wore a sheet with eyeholes cut into it. She used her mom's makeup to draw a face on the sheet and tied the ghost costume around the waist with the sash from her dad's bathrobe because the sheet was so long it kept tripping her up. I would have worn makeup myself, except Aunt Kate did not own any.

We traveled all around the block we lived on and one other one as well. All told, Kasey, Linda, and I rang the bells of thirty-two houses. We went alone. I came home swinging my plastic candy-filled pumpkin feeling responsible and adult.

Why do I recall that night so vividly? I can't think what I wore or did any other year on Halloween night. They've all blurred together. But the third-grade Halloween stands out. So does Halloween the year I turned thirty. Because that was the night I told Anthony that I was pregnant.

We'd been together over three years. Because of Anthony, I owned a wardrobe that could have hung in Julia's closet. My closet was crammed full of clothes I had purchased to wear to the places Anthony liked to go on the increasingly rare occasions he was actually in Houston.

Crystal, who had met and married Mr. Right several years earlier, was the only person at work to learn the true story of what had happened to me. I told Aunt Kate most of the entire story, minus a few of the less savory details, several days after my last encounter with Anthony.

"Damn it, Robin," Crystal said when I first told her. "I've been waking up every morning for the past twelve months cramming a basal thermometer into my mouth and you go and get pregnant the month you go off the pill. It isn't fair!"

It wasn't fair. It was a giant screwup on my part. I wanted to blame Anthony, but I had to be honest and admit I had gotten myself in this predicament. This is how it happened. Aunt Kate had had to undergo a hysterectomy four or five years before. Thereafter she kept after me to have regular Pap tests. So I got more reliable about going to the doctor, despite the fact I had several years' worth of pills on hand from the supply Crystal had given me the day she got her engagement ring.

And the year I turned thirty my gynecologist said to me, "Robin, you've been on the pill five years, you need to take at least a six-month break." I stopped taking the pills that day. Because I had actually been on the pills since I was a junior in college. Ten years.

On the first of July I flew to San Francisco to meet Anthony. I'd been there almost three days before I remembered the diaphragm I'd left at home in the medicine cabinet. After the first panicky thoughts came and went, I decided I didn't want to spoil my vacation worrying about something I couldn't do a thing about. To the best of my recollection, that is the last time I thought about it.

I suspected I was pregnant before I started back to school in mid-August, but I did my best not to think about it. Anthony was out of the country from the middle of August until late in October. During that time he called me exactly four times.

"Robin," Crystal said to me over and over. "Call Anthony yourself. You have to tell him."

I didn't call him. Every time I thought of what he was going to say when he learned the truth I decided I could wait a little bit longer before I broached the subject. I passed the point where I could have gotten an abortion. Not that I considered having one. But I deliberately chose not to inform Anthony of my pregnancy until after the time for terminating it had come and gone.

He called me at school on Halloween. "Dinner tonight," he said. "Meet me at six at the Warwick."

He no longer had a Houston apartment. He stayed at the Warwick whenever he was in Houston. While he was there, he treated the staff like they were on his exclusive payroll.

"Come over to my apartment, you bring dinner," I said. I'd made up little pumpkins with Halloween candies in them to give out to all the kids who lived around me, and I had no intention of letting Anthony spoil my plans for the evening. He could have called me at least twenty-four hours in advance to let me know he was coming into town.

I'd already given out half of the pumpkins when Anthony arrived with dinner. Between setting the table and fishing around in the pantry looking for the wine glasses and running back and forth to the door handing out candies to the ballerinas and Pac-men and whatever else the kids were coming as that year, I didn't have a minute to give Anthony the attention he expected.

"Turn off that outside light and sit down at the table," he said to me when I popped up to answer the door for the second time after we'd sat down to eat.

"Let me get the door, Anthony, I don't want to disappoint the children," I said. I wasn't intentionally sabotaging the evening, but of course I already knew that it was over between us.

"Well, I'll be damned if I want to eat my dinner cold," he said.

"Kids are more important than the occasional grilled tuna and wild rice dinner," I said.

"Not to me they are not, certainly not little urchins I don't know and have no intention of knowing."

He was sitting there, still in his three-piece suit, although in deference to the informality of the occasion (I wore a Halloween shirt, faded jeans, and was barefoot), he'd loosened, but not unknotted, his tie. Anthony never liked to completely undo his tie because of how long it took him to get the knot exactly right. His shoes were on his feet. I guess if you wear custom-made shoes, you'd don't feel the same urge to kick them off that people who wear standard size shoes do.

As I popped up for the third time to answer the door's summons, I said to Anthony, "Well, I hope you feel differently about a child that is your own. Because, come April, you are going to have one."

When I turned back around from the door he was standing beside the table. His cooling meal was forgotten. His tie had been snugged up around his neck.

"What are you saying?"

"I'm pregnant."

"How did that happen?"

"The regular way."

"You know what I mean."

"My doctor suggested I go off the pill. I forgot to bring my diaphragm to San Francisco. I got pregnant. I am thrilled. And I *am* having our baby."

The doorbell rang. Anthony walked over to the door carrying the tray of remaining pumpkins. He poured the entire trayful into the outstretched grocery bag of the little devil standing there. Then he shut the door and turned off the outside light.

"I will be fifty years old in seventeen months. I have no

desire to complicate my life with children. You *will* get an abortion."

"I will *not*."

We glared at each other one last time. After Anthony left I realized my hands were cupped protectively around my belly.

JULIA

It wasn't cold enough to freeze but still, for some reason, I woke up thinking I should get up out of bed and go outside to look at our electric water pump. We have to wrap it to keep it from freezing up sometimes during the winter. Danny and I built our house new, but the well has been here for over a hundred years and we don't have an underground pump for it. The pump we have, which is, I would guess, thirty years old itself, is aboveground. When it goes out, we'll replace it with one that doesn't need so much coddling, but until that time, why toss it out? It works.

The house that was here before ours, we tore down. Mostly what we had to do was have the debris hauled off. The house itself had burned at one time and the part that didn't burn down had mostly fallen in on top of itself and all that was required of us was to give it the final push. Mrs. Shrimpton came out with her husband to salvage nine carved mantels and the wood from the floors. She couldn't take it all—much of it was all buckled and warped.

"What on earth do you want that junk for?" I asked her.

"Julia, these mantels and the hardwood from the floors are valuable heirlooms," she said. She insisted on giving me a check for five hundred dollars. I thought she was nuts until I saw one of the mantels in her store with a price tag on it which read three hundred fifty dollars.

"Who would pay that for this old thing?" I asked her.

"I've already sold four of the mantels," she replied.

"Well, I wouldn't have them in my house," I told her.

THE REASON I was outside at three in the morning wasn't actually to check the well. It was because after I woke up thinking of the well this voice told me to go outside and see something. I think the voice belonged to the man who lived in the house that started falling down years ago. The house was a goner long before Danny and I came along. That night was the first time I'd heard his voice, but I had seen him outside our house on more than one occasion. The only thing that didn't fit about him being an old man who lived long ago was his khaki shirt and pants. I don't think they wore that sort of clothing one hundred years ago—or even fifty years ago, for that matter. But I could be wrong about that. I described him to both Danny and Mother. I didn't tell them I was describing a ghost. I said it was a man I'd seen up in town and thought I should have known.

"What kind of car does he drive?" Danny asked me.

"I didn't see one," I said.

"Well, he sounds like half the men in this county. Next time you see him take a look at his car."

"Did he have any jewelry on?" Mother wanted to know.

"I don't think so, at least I never noticed any," I was forced to reply.

His shirt was always buttoned clear up to his neck and his hands were generally stuffed in his pockets. All along I had wondered if he could be a descendant of the original owners of the house. Perhaps a son of theirs. The Clarks bought this property maybe fifty years ago. I don't think any of the Clark relatives ever lived in the house that stood where Danny and I built our house. I doubt my khaki man is a relative of my husband's.

"Julia, get up now and come on outside. There is something I want you to see." Those are the exact words I heard him say. I got up and walked outside and sat down on the front steps of our house, which stood exactly on the spot where Mr. Forester's house had once stood. A cold front had blown in sometime earlier. I'd heard it right after I'd gone to bed. The blustery wind had blown on through and left in its wake a cold, crisp winter night. I wore a granny gown and held on to the quilt I had wrapped around my shoulders. My feet were bare, so I tucked them up and folded my gown underneath me.

I might have known I wouldn't be alone for long. Danny keeps up with my whereabouts, and it wasn't ten minutes before he joined me. I sat on the front steps, my eyes on the road which runs past our house. At first I couldn't see a thing. Not even a cow moved in the pasture between our house and the farm-to-market road which runs past our place on into Cypress Springs. It wasn't as if the night was pitch black dark either. The stars were out and the moon was full. Because of the stillness of the night, I didn't feel all that cold wrapped in the quilt that my grandmother had made. Actually, I felt all revved up inside, pleasantly jangly and warm with anticipation. Nevertheless, the cup of coffee Danny handed me felt agreeably warm in my hands.

"What are you doing out here in the middle of the night?" he asked me.

"I couldn't sleep. Something is fixing to happen."

Danny put his arms around me and pulled me close to him. He'd brought out another quilt, one I kept draped over a chair in the den. It's the one I used to spread over the carpet every time Robert and Gracie wanted me to have a picnic with them in front of the television set so it smelled like Kool-aid and Play-Do. As Danny spread it over both of us, I inhaled its aroma. It was as if Danny had brought the entire family out with him. "Kids will be up any minute now if we're not quiet," I warned. At that time they both slept in the bedroom on the front part of the house.

"Not for another two or three hours, I checked on them," Danny whispered back to me. "What is it you're expecting to see?"

"Promise not to groan or roll your eyes?"

"Promise."

"Mr. Forester told me to look outside, something is fixing to happen."

"Who is Mr. Forester?"

"The ghost who lives with us."

"No shit," Danny replied. He didn't groan and I couldn't see his eyes.

"How long have you and Mr. Forester been acquainted?" he asked.

"About a year now. This is the first time he has actually said anything to me."

"Super."

Danny and I settled in together, he rested against the step above him, I rested against him. Gradually more and more of the pasture became visible. Eventually I could make out individual trees that lined the gravel road running up to our house. Through the trees came the gradual lifting of darkness which signals approaching dawn.

I saw movement before I heard anything. The darkness hadn't lifted well enough to see much more than movement as far away as the road. "Look, Danny! Through the trees." I was whispering and pushing closer to him at the same time. I felt glad that I wasn't alone. I suppose I must have been expecting some more members of the Forester family, although I can't remember that specifically. I know what I actually saw wasn't what I had been expecting to see. I do remember that for sure.

Whatever/whoever was coming down the road from town moved slowly and steadily. Sound travels in the night, but I was staring so hard that I saw them moving before I heard their birdlike voices. Their voices drifted across to me as careless little chirps. The sounds were muted, had I not been watching so intensely I wouldn't have known that I was actually hearing anything. There was the crunch of gravel underfoot. They traveled slowly. Quietly. Steadily.

"What the hell?" said my husband. His arm pulled me into his chest in a protective gesture.

"Shh! I want to see them. Don't frighten them away."

There is a break in the trees where the driveway meets the main road, where our fence stops for the cattle guard crossing. I stared at the road beyond the cattle guard, concentrating on keeping my eyes from blinking. I didn't want to miss seeing them.

Maria, who was pushing Julie, stepped off the paved road onto the gravel. Just for a step or two, but enough to make the gravel crunching sound I'd heard before. "What the hell?" said Danny again. But he was relaxing. His grip on me had loosened.

"I didn't think it would be Julie and her sister," I said. I felt disappointed.

Danny stood up. "Where are you going?" I asked him.

"To get the car. It is too cold for them, out here miles from town. I'll give them a lift home."

"They've been out on our road before. Spying on me." I was just starting to feel anger. "They'll be okay. Besides, Julie would never get in the car with you."

"Why not?" Danny asked me.

"Because you are married to me and Julie hates me."

THE NEXT MORNING after breakfast I bundled the kids into the car and went over to Butch and Susie's to tell Butch what was going on. "Julie and her sister have been spying on me, Butch. They were on my road last night at three o'clock in the morning."

Susie was in the kitchen, putting a pan of sweet rolls in the oven. Susie makes all her own bread. She's a great cook, which is probably why Butch is fifty pounds overweight. He was sitting at the table, drinking coffee and reading the paper, when I walked in the door with Robert and Gracie trailing along behind me.

"Come again?"

"Julie and Maria. Maria was pushing Julie in her wheelchair. No telling how often this has happened before. Likely as not they come right up to our windows and look in while we're asleep. You're going to have to do something about it, Butch."

I saw the look Butch and Susie exchanged and it made me furious. "If you don't believe me, you can ask Danny, he saw them the same as I did."

"What did you see?"

"Well, we were sitting on the porch and saw them go past, what did I just tell you?" Butch didn't ask how we came to be on the porch at that hour and I decided not to tell him about the ghost right then. It would have complicated matters.

"They came right up to the house? Inside the fence?"

"No, they didn't come across the cattle guard."

"So the two of them were simply taking a walk on a road which we all know is public property?"

"The road in front of our house is too far off the beaten path to be considered public. They were there to spy, you know that as well as I do. What other reason could there possibly be?"

"What's to spy?"

"Your guess is as good as mine. But I think you'd better talk to them, Butch. I don't like it. It gives me the creeps."

"I'll talk to Danny," he said.

"Talk to Julie," I advised him.

I felt a lot better once I'd told Butch. I was sure he'd do whatever needed to be done. I rounded up the kids and drove on into town. Since we were out I thought I might as well run on into the grocery store and get that chore over with. Because Susie was in the room with us the entire time we were having this conversation, I knew Butch hadn't wanted to get into the subject of people spying on us. I understood perfectly. I felt the same reticence around Danny.

AUNT KATE

I knew the minute I walked into the hospital room that something was dreadfully wrong. My niece was alone in the room, in tears, her two-day-old daughter nowhere to be seen. Rachel was not in the crib beside her mother's bed where I had last seen her, nor had the baby been in the nursery I had just walked past. My heart almost stopped. "What is wrong, my dear?" I asked Robin. I was holding my breath so hard that my chest actually began to hurt before I remembered I needed to breathe again.

It took Robin a good few minutes to stop crying and get words out. "Aunt Kate," she finally said. "Everything is such a mess and I don't know what on earth I am going to do." Her face was deathly pale except for the puffy red blotches she gets when she has been crying. "The doctors say they need a sample of Anthony's blood. Or at the very least they've got to have some information about his blood type. Rachel has an elevated bilirubin, whatever that is. The nurse says I shouldn't take on, it is almost for sure that this is just normal baby jaundice, but maybe not, maybe it is something serious. How does the nurse know? She isn't the one who went to medical school! The doctor also said it is because of something called the ABO reaction Rachel had. At least I think that's what he said. Aunt Kate, I'm so worried!" Robin's tears started all over again.

I simply stood there, my heart breaking. I didn't know what to do, I'm no good in situations like this, anyway, and I knew immediately that the blame for most of what Robin was going through could be laid directly at my door. This wasn't simply about the fact that Robin and Anthony Shaw had decided to go their separate ways. "Where is the baby?" I asked as I started breathing again. First things first, I reminded myself. We could cope with this.

"They took her away from me! They took my baby back to the nursery because I couldn't stop crying, I feel so rotten, what on earth have I done to her? I doubt they'll even let me have her back, I know they think I'm awful because I don't have a husband. Or a father and a mother!" At this point the words were tumbling out of my poor child so fast that I don't believe she had the vaguest notion of what it was that she was actually saying.

"I blame myself for this, it is my fault entirely," I said to her but I doubt that Robin heard me. I put down the books I'd brought in with me. Now was no time to read to Robin. I found a washcloth in the bathroom and ran cold water over it. "Put this on your face, dear, and try to stop crying. I'll go see about Rachel and we'll work this out. Everything is going to be just fine," I said. As soon as I saw that Robin was marginally calmer, I went off to the nurse's station. I needed to see Rachel with my own eyes and I wanted to talk to the nurse myself.

The calmer I acted, the more I actually began to feel that way. This news about the baby wasn't new information to me. Rachel had started turning yellow almost immediately after birth. I'd stopped at the library on the way home the previous evening, where I'd found three excellent chapters on babies who are born with jaundice. I was sure the child was going to be just fine. However, *Robin* looked awful. I was dreadfully worried about her.

"THE NURSE IS bathing Rachel right now, they'll bring her back within the hour, she is fine, trust me," I said to Robin when I returned to the room minutes later. She lay there in the middle of that hospital room and stared at me. I don't think I've ever seen a more helpless look on that child's face. It broke my heart, it truly did. If I could have gone back twenty-six years and made different decisions about what I was going to tell her as she grew up, I would have done so in a minute. I should never have let her grow up in ignorance about her family, I'd sensed that for years, but right then, watching her feel completely helpless because she couldn't produce a blood sample from her own baby's father, I was forced to confront the error of my own ways. I'd buried my head in the sand for too long, far too long. And by so doing I had taught my niece to do the same.

"I'm so sorry, my dear. You deserved better from me, I feel that I have failed you." But of course it was long years past the time when I could have done what I should have done back when Robin's mother died and left me to take charge of her young daughter. What I needed to do right at this particular time was to help Robin take care of her own child's needs. "I'm so sorry," I said to Robin. "I will speak to the doctor and assure him there is no history of liver disease in the family. And I will get the information regarding Anthony Shaw's blood type and family medical history this very day. What you've got to do is calm down. The nurse will be bringing Rachel back in here any minute and your baby needs you to quit all this crying and carrying on and take care of her. Remember, sweetheart, you are the grownup now. It is up to you to take care of little Rachel, you are her mother."

"I don't feel grown up, Aunt Kate," she said.

I was thankful to hear that her voice sounded normal again, even if her face still had huge red welts raised all over it. "I'll tell you a little secret, no one of us ever does feel completely grown up. The trick is to act like you do until you start believing it yourself."

I'll take care of the matter of Mr. Shaw first, I thought, *and then I'll deal with the issue of Robin's father.* Driving downtown, I promised myself that this time I wasn't going to let it slide. As soon as the current matter was settled, I was going to locate Robin's father for her. But of course the road to hell is paved with good intentions and soon is a relative term. And Robin's father proved difficult to locate.

This might take a while, I realized, as I drove into the parking garage of the Milam Building. I had a twelve-page medical history form with me that one of the nurses had provided. I had been profoundly thankful to see, as I rounded the corner leaving the nurse's station, Robin's friend Crystal stepping off the elevator clutching a stuffed animal and an overladen Foley's shopping bag. "You stay with Robin, I'm going to sort out this medical history snafu," I had said to Crystal. Crystal's at the hospital, I reminded myself. I was glad that Robin wasn't alone, I knew that Crystal would stay with her all day long, if necessary. Crystal really was a good friend to Robin. I must have reminded myself of that fact a dozen times during that long day.

With my medical form in hand, I walked into Anthony Shaw's office and informed the young lady guarding the outer office that I was the great-aunt of his newborn daughter and I would not be leaving until Mr. Shaw completed the documents I had brought with me. They were needed by the doctors at the hospital and, if necessary, I would get a court order to see that my niece had the information she needed to insure her child's medical needs were appropriately met.

The young woman took the forms from me and disappeared for approximately twenty minutes. She returned to her desk empty-handed. "Mr. Shaw is unavailable at the moment, but we will see that he gets your message," she said.

"I will wait here until I have the documents," I said to her. "They are wanted at the hospital."

Her eyes widened. For a brief space of time, she simply

stared at me. I don't suppose too many people stood up to her boss the way I was doing. I felt a surge of pride at my own temerity as the young woman backed away from me. This time it was ten minutes before I saw her again.

"Actually, Mr. Shaw isn't in the office this morning," she said. "But we will get in touch with him as quickly as possible."

"One of the advantages of being retired is I have all the time in the world. I can wait," I replied. I looked at my watch as I once again folded my hands in my lap. An entire hour had elapsed. Robin and Rachel are fine, I reminded myself.

The young lady did not return to her desk for almost another hour, although the door opened several times to permit her artfully tousled curls to peep out at me. "We are doing the best we can," she said. "You could go on home, I could messenger the medical history over," she rather hopefully gushed the first time she looked around the door over to the leather sofa on which I sat. The second time she was slightly more cordial. "There is coffee out in the lobby, help yourself," she said. The third time she popped her head out, nodded, and jerked her head back inside without a word. I suppose she was checking to see if I was still there.

She came out with the forms completed and sealed inside a manila envelope, walked breezily across the room to me and handed them over with a flourish. "This took some doing," she confided. "Mr. Shaw is in Amsterdam, his assistant has been on the phone with him for the last hour."

"I appreciate the alacrity with which you acted," I told her.

"You are very welcome. I hope your niece does okay, and the baby, too," she said. Whereupon she blushed and looked guiltily around the room as if wishing her employer's illegitimate child good health might not be in the best possible form.

GETTING A MEDICAL history from Anthony Shaw was the easy part of my amend-making efforts. Getting a medical history regarding Robin's father proved to be more difficult because of the firmness with which I had closed that door and the length of time which had elapsed since I had done so. However, after spending most of the next day on the telephone, I managed to locate the sister of an aunt. She took my telephone number and called me back within an hour. The woman gave me as much medical information as she had been able to gather. "This is all they know," she told me. "I don't think there are any diseases that run in that family," she added. "And I'd of heard. I've lived here all my life." Obviously she did not consider alcoholism a disease. But then Robin already had that on her mother's side. Because of course my mother, Robin's grandmother, drank like a fish.

I carefully preserved the woman's name, address, and telephone number in case Robin should ask for it at some future date. The one question I did not ask the sister of the aunt is, "Whatever did happen to the young man? After he was released from prison, I mean." The woman, Letha Wilson, did not volunteer that information either.

ROBIN

I never saw Anthony again after the Halloween night he left my apartment in such a huff. Rachel was born in April. He never darkened our door either at the hospital or once we'd gone on home to our apartment. What I am going to say may sound like bravado, but it isn't, it is the dead level truth. Except for some totally weird postpartum thing, which occurred while I was still in the hospital, I have never had the slightest desire to see or hear from Anthony again. Once my daughter was born, the only thing I needed or wanted from him was a basic medical history and information regarding his blood type, that was it. Aunt Kate was a saint. She marched over to his office and got the information I needed and came back in waving the sheaf of papers she had had him fill out like they were some victory banner. I wish I could have seen his face while Aunt Kate was standing over him demanding that he fill out page after page of medical information. I'll bet it was a stitch. He may even have sweated a little around the edges of that perfectly starched collar he is bound to have had on.

I wasn't the least bit sorry to have lost Anthony. Not for myself, that is. Because the truth is, my first impression had been right on the mark, he really was a jerk. It did bother me a little bit that Rachel wasn't going to have a father—the same way I had never had one. But the two of us had Aunt Kate, and I got to where I appreciated my aunt more and more every single day that passed.

I do want to be scrupulously honest. I did hear from Anthony after Rachel was born. The day I was to leave the hospital with my four-day-old baby, some well-dressed flunky from Anthony's office showed up clutching a manila envelope like it was a flotation ring and he was adrift in the deep blue sea. "From Mr. Shaw," he said to me and handed over the envelope.

There was a check inside as well as a typed letter. Anthony expected to cover all our hospital expenses. He would send me a set amount of money each year to care for my daughter.

While he did not wish to be involved in Rachel's upbringing himself, he had no desire for either of us to ever want for anything. The check enclosed was for an incredible amount of money. His letter stated that he would send a check just like that one every year on or about Rachel's birthday for the next twenty-one years. I was requested to sign the accompanying document. The letter and the document sounded like four or five lawyers had worked for days to compose them. The check was typed and signed with a scrawled, totally illegible signature. I didn't do more than glance at the accompanying document so I'm not sure exactly what I was expected to sign my name to. I tore both the letter and the document up, ripped the check into several pieces as well, and crammed the shreds back into the envelope and shoved the entire mess in the face of the anemic-looking kid from Anthony's office. "Tell Anthony Shaw he's a chickenshit and my daughter and I don't want a dime from him," I said. I believe that is the only time in my life I ever used the term "chickenshit." I frequently recall having heard Julia use it, so I am sure that is where that came from.

I had a great pregnancy, I loved every minute of it. My pregnancy I now characterize as the calm before the storm. After Rachel arrived my life began to rearrange itself at a dizzying pace. It wasn't enough I had a new baby. Within months of her arrival it seemed as if I had an entirely new life as well. And I'd thought I'd had the old one planned out so well. *Everything under control,* I recall saying right before she was born. Sure it was. Control is such an illusion.

When Rachel was two months old I took her to the pediatrician for a visit. We stopped by my school on the way home, ostensibly so I could pick up my check. Of course the main reason was so I could show Rachel off. I timed my visit for when I knew Crystal and most of the other teachers would be in the lounge getting ready to go out to lunch. This was the last day of school, the kids were gone and the teachers were busy finishing up for the year. I was surprised at the long faces. They were so glum, not a one of them even noticed Rachel.

Crystal took Rachel from me and said, "You'd better sit down, Robin."

I sat down at the big table in the middle of the lounge and looked from one doom-and-gloom countenance to another. Just when I thought I'd explode if someone didn't say something, T.J. winked at me. "It's not that awful, it's just that they've been redrawing the boundaries for the high schools. This is going to be a tech school next year."

"What does that mean?"

"It means the vast majority of us will be transferred to other schools."

"Which other schools?"

"No one knows. We'll all be receiving letters before July the first."

"That isn't fair! We've signed contracts for here," I said. But I knew even as I spoke that the standard contract teachers signed wasn't for any particular school, it was an agreement for employment within the district itself. "What are we going to do?"

"About all we can do is wait and see," said Mr. Healy. "I do suggest if you know any principal at a school where you'd like to be assigned, you call and put in a good word for yourself." Mr. Healy had taught in the Houston Independent School District for years and years, he probably did know people with some influence. I really didn't. Not more than to nod to.

Crystal ditched the faculty luncheon and she and I went over to the park and ate the last of a Whitman Sampler one of her students had given her. Rachel drank her bottle and lay on her blanket, looking around at the shadows made by the sun filtering through the leaves of the tree. "Shouldn't you get back to school? It is after one," I said to Crystal.

"What are they going to do, fire me?" she asked. I felt the same way. It is amazing how fast an institution can kill your loyalty.

I HAD MOVED from my first apartment about two years after Julia married. I moved to a new complex on down Fountain View where I could get a two-bedroom townhouse with a patio. Fortunately I hadn't moved into an adults-only section, so I hadn't had to move again when Rachel was born. All I had to do was convert my study into her nursery. Since I hadn't known what I was having, I'd painted the room a pale creamy yellow. Crystal and I spent days and days stenciling zoo animal borders on the walls. The white wicker furniture was new, the first brand-new furniture I'd ever bought. I paid an outrageous sum of money for it. Actually I started paying on it when I was five months pregnant and Aunt Kate insisted on paying it off when she learned what I was doing, so I should say I made the downpayment and Aunt Kate did the rest. If I'd never appreciated Aunt Kate before, watching her in action during the months before I had my baby would have led me to do so. She acted like the fact that her unwed thirty-year-old niece was having a baby was the culmination of the greatest dream of her life. Between her and Crystal, I could have sat in my living room for the entire pregnancy and done nothing but gestate. They both really went wild, shopping and getting ready for the coming event. Every childcare book they bought me they read first so they could highlight the salient parts. It really was a great time.

I loved my apartment and the fact that I had my own baby in it with me made it truly perfect. Then all that changed. I was thinking about where on earth I would be teaching when school started up in the fall as I parked my car in the garage. I put my purse over one shoulder, the baby bag over the other, unhooked the car seat and hoisted Rachel out. She woke up and looked around before she put her head on my shoulder and fell back asleep. I was upstairs, inside her bedroom, about to put her down in her crib when it hit me. The back door. The lock hadn't actually clicked open when I turned the key. The door had been pulled shut, however the lock hadn't been engaged. I always locked that door when I left the house. That was as routine with me as brushing my teeth before I hopped into bed. I *knew* that I'd locked the door. I'd put Rachel in the car and gone back and picked up the baby bag I'd left outside the door, locked the door, put the apartment keys in the baby bag, and gotten in my car and left.

I froze. I stood there clutching Rachel, not having the first idea what I should do. I replayed what I could remember of the downstairs part of the apartment I'd just walked through. I'd walked in the back door, which opens into the kitchen. The kitchen had looked normal, just the way I'd left it. The counters were clear, the dirty dishes out of sight in the dishwasher. I'd walked quickly through the dining room and living room and straight up the stairs, concentrating on moving as quietly as the proverbial mouse so Rachel would stay asleep. I had been hoping for a nap myself—put her in her bed and pile into my own, that had been my plan. I couldn't remember anything out of place in either of those rooms, but the living room was pretty cluttered and I hadn't looked around. I didn't know for sure that I would have noticed any additional clutter.

I reasoned with myself. There couldn't possibly have been anyone downstairs. Not unless that someone had hovered in the half bath under the stairs. The front door surely had been shut with the chain on. I thought I would have noticed had the door been ajar or the chain hanging free.

Which left the closet in Rachel's room, my bedroom and closet, and the upstairs bath. The bath, a long **L**-shaped room, had a door opening to it from the hall, as well as one from my bedroom. *If anyone has been in my apartment, they're long gone by now,* I told myself. The house seemed so quiet. I listened as hard as I could. And all the while I was doing that, I imagined someone on the other side of my daughter's bedroom wall listening back.

I made myself move over to Rachel's closet. Clutching her, I opened the door and turned on the light. The closet was empty. Turning back to her room, I eased her into her bed and walked out of her room. Still moving as silently as I could, I pulled her door to, locking it as I did so.

What I did next was totally uncalculated. I took off one of my shoes and threw it as hard as I could at the wall on the other side of the stairs. Then I threw the other shoe. Both of them made an amazing amount of noise. I stood still and listened. Nothing. Not even Rachel appeared to have heard me. I wanted to go into my room and pick up the phone beside the bed and call for help. But I was afraid to move. Suppose someone was in there. Suppose the telephone wires had been cut. I looked for something else to throw. There was a bath towel hanging on the railing, still damp from my morning shower, and a picture on the wall—that was it. I threw the picture. Rachel slept through the thud and the shattering glass. But I was sure if my next-door neighbor was home she'd have heard. And Mrs. Corley, a widow, rarely left her house. I stood still and listened and prayed that Mrs. Corley wouldn't let me down. When the phone began to ring, I ran into my bedroom, diving headlong onto the bed in order to reach the phone before the person I imagined lurked in the bathroom, out of sight behind the shower curtain, could head me off. "Call the police, someone is here in my apartment," I said into the receiver, without so much as pausing to hear who was on the other end of the line.

"What is going on?" Mrs. Corley said to me.

I had the phone pressed to my ear. "Someone's here," I said. "Call the police," I repeated. I hung on to the phone like it was a lifeline as I pushed myself back up off the bed and turned to face the room. I was deathly afraid to turn around and look— however, I had no choice. I wasn't alone here, it wasn't only my life at stake, I had a child to protect. Even once I had looked around the bedroom and established the fact that I was alone, I still felt frantic inside. I looked from where I stood, and saw Rachel's door, still closed. My closet door was standing wide open, I rarely closed it. As far inside it as I could see, there were only clothes and tumbled shoes. At least I was alone upstairs, I reasoned, but I didn't feel safe. In fact, I knew I wasn't safe. I still held the phone, it had been clutched to my chest, I realized. "Send help," I whispered into the phone one more time. "Please send someone to help me." I could hear Mrs. Corley clearing her voice. "Are you all right? What is going on?" she asked me. Before I could say another word, there was a third voice on the line.

"Hang up the phone," someone said. I knew the awful terrible voice could only be coming to me from the downstairs extension. Chills went through my body. Tears came to my eyes. I was too scared to do more than clutch the phone in my shaking hand. I couldn't have said another word if my life had depended on it. The roaring sound from inside my head grew so loud I barely heard Mrs. Corley's voice.

"I'll get the manager," she said. "And the police. And I'm on my way myself. It will not take me ten seconds. Whoever you are, *you get the hell out of there!*" She sounded steely and composed and as angry and ferocious as the very devil. Hearing her voice, no one would imagine her to be arthritis-crippled and eighty-seven years old.

I heard him leave because he left the phone in the kitchen off the hook. I heard a clunk as the phone hit the floor, followed by the sound of the kitchen door opening and closing. The roaring in my head didn't stop. It could be a trick. *Do something,* I told myself. I didn't move, though, from my spot at the head of the stairs, until I heard Mrs. Corley and the manager and official-sounding male voices moving around downstairs. And then all I was able to do was sink to my feet on the top stair and dissolve into tears.

AUNT KATE WAS in Thailand, not due back for another four days. But Crystal and her husband, Richard, came over the minute Mrs. Corley called them for me. That night I packed up the necessities for Rachel and me and moved over to Aunt Kate's house. I spent the next three days calling every school district within a fifty-mile radius of Houston. The day after Aunt Kate arrived home from Thailand, I had four interviews lined up. I took the first job offered to me—it was at an elementary school, but I wasn't about to complain. I only went back to my apartment to pack and help load the U-Haul truck. And then Aunt Kate and Crystal were with me every minute I was in the apartment.

DELL ADDISON

I knew the minute she came in the door who she was. This was a Saturday morning around 9:00 A.M. I always open up at 7:00. Seven to seven, seven days a week, I tell people. Makes it easy for them to remember that way. My house is right behind my store, The Market Basket, so people know in a genuine emergency they can knock on the door and I'll open up the shop and get them what they need. But I frown on frivolous emergencies. *I'm there half my life,* I say to folks. *That should be enough for anyone, so don't go calling me just as the ten o'clock news is coming on, telling me you have to make brownies for little Johnny's school party tomorrow and you're fresh out of eggs. You should have thought of that sooner.*

She had curly brown hair and big blue eyes and if I hadn't known for a fact she was thirty-one years old and the mother of a two-month-old little girl, I would have taken her for a college kid looking for directions into Houston. *Keep on Highway Ninety,* I tell people, *and it will take you right straight into downtown Stillwell. You can get on Interstate Ten there. Highway Ninety runs into Ten the other side of Stillwell. Seven miles down the road you're on and take a right. It's marked, you can't miss it. Or, if you're in a big hurry, you can turn right at the light up ahead, you can see it from here, there's only one traffic light in Cypress Springs so you can't miss it, and that street, which happens to be Second Street, will take you straight out to Interstate Ten. Exactly one and six-tenths of a mile from the light you'll run into the big road.*

Interstate Ten will take you straight into Houston. People always stop and ask just before they would have found where to go on their own. I'm practiced at giving directions. My store is about the last one open on Front Street. Since Interstate Ten came in, most people choose not to stay on Highway Ninety.

She picked up the *Cypress Springs News* and looked at the front page. "Can I have a copy of today's paper?" she asked me.

"That is today's paper, it will be today's paper for an entire week. Until next Thursday, as a matter of fact."

"Oh," she said.

She put her quarter on the counter and started looking through the paper. "Is there a tax?" she asked.

"No, no tax," I said to her. As I said, I had already figured out who she had to be, but I hadn't yet realized what she was looking for.

"There don't seem to be any ads for apartments," she said.

"There aren't any," I told her. I watched her blink those blue eyes back and forth, first at the paper, then at me.

"No apartments?" she asked.

It was obvious to me she'd lived in Houston too long. "Not a one. Houses. Those we have. And there are several garage apartments people have done up for one reason or another. But no one has been moved to build an apartment building in Cypress Springs."

"Where do people live if they don't have a house of their own?"

I was starting to worry about the third-graders whose education was dependent on this scared-looking young woman. "Might be they rent. There *are* some trailers in a trailer park over on the Stillwell Highway. But Mr. Addison mentioned over breakfast this morning that some ne'er-do-wells have moved into the trailer park. It isn't where I would like to see a young schoolteacher with a tiny baby living."

"How do you know who I am?"

"Who else could you be?" I said to her.

"Well, I don't see any for-rent section in this paper at all."

"Isn't any. People have a place they want to rent out, folks generally hear of it through what you might call word of mouth." Houston people get so used to things like rental sections they forget they can rely on their own common sense. Why pay for an ad to run in the paper if all you have to do is mention to Howard Barns over at the post office that the folks who rented your daddy's old house are moving out? If anyone is looking to move, he will be aware of it.

"Do *you* know of any place to rent? Someplace where you would like to see a schoolteacher and her baby?" she asked me.

"As a matter of fact, I just might. I was talking to my sister yesterday on the phone."

"Your sister has a place to rent?"

"No, my sister Elsa lives way out on the prairie, a good ten miles from town. The only house she has is her own. Which was built by her husband in the year 1940. However, I said to Elsa that I had been wondering about where the new teacher was fixing to live. Elsa thought you might be planning on living in Houston and driving back and forth, but I knew that wasn't practical. Not for one person, much less a young mother. We put our heads together and came up with Josh Winter's house. The one that belonged to his grandmother on his mother's side. He's been refurbishing that house for several years now, and it looks to me like someone should be living in it."

"I might know Josh Winter," she said to me. "Is he about my age? Tall. Dark hair."

"That's him," I told her. I wondered where she'd got to know Josh Winter, but I didn't think it was polite to ask. I gave her directions to his law office, which happens to be in the old Schroeder house across from the shopping center, and sent her on her way. Right before she walked out the door, I remembered Ruthie Suarez.

"Oh, honey, there is one more thing. Ruthie Suarez. I thought of her just this minute. She used to keep the Turner kids, but the last one is in the fifth grade, Ruthie has been home cooling her heels for over a year now. She and her husband live on the place next to my sister. Elsa has said to me on numerous occasions that Ruthie is about to go stir-crazy. She is not cut out to stay at home. What Ruthie likes is to take care of folks' children. You take this phone number and give her a call."

Robin Tilton gave me a dazed-looking smile and took the paper I'd written Ruthie's name and phone number on. I hoped once she got herself moved and settled in, she was going to have a little more on the ball. Otherwise, the third-graders were going to run rings around her.

JULIA

I first heard that the school board had hired a teacher for the third grade from out of Houston when I was in Millie's Beauty Shop getting my hair trimmed. "Isn't your Robert going into the third grade?" she asked me.

Millie knew good and well Robert was going into the third grade. It irritates me no end when people ask a question they know the answer to. It is a dumb way of getting around to saying whatever it is they are trying to say.

"No, he isn't, we're having Robert repeat second grade,"

I said. That served to draw Millie up short for a few seconds there.

"Oh, Julia, of course he is going into third, your Robert is smart as a whip," she said. "Have you heard that they hired a teacher from Houston? You know they've been desperate to find someone to replace Miss Myrtle. The school board met last night and voted to offer some woman from Houston a contract. I'm not sure they were all pleased with her, but she was the only applicant with a college degree."

Miss Myrtle retired. Not a minute too soon. She could barely put one foot in front of the other any longer. I was relieved Robert wasn't going to have to have her. She taught me in third grade. And I think she has a long memory.

"Oh," I said, which is all it takes to keep Millie going.

"Yes. Young girl. Your age. Robin something or other. With a baby. And no husband."

I knew the minute she said Robin it was going to be her.

"Holy shit! Robin Tilton! Is that who it is?"

"Julia," Millie fussed. "Look what you just went and made me do. I've cut a hunk out of your hair."

"It'll grow. Is the teacher Robin Tilton? Did she go to Texas Tech?"

"I have no idea," sniffed Millie.

She was so pissed at me you'd think it was her hair with the gaping hole in it. "Don't sweat it, Millie, you know how fast my hair grows. Hurry up, I've got to call my brother and see if they really hired Robin."

I LET ROBIN spend Saturday and Sunday getting her U-Haul unloaded into Josh's grandmother's house. Monday morning, bright and early, I went over with cheese biscuits and champagne. Robert and Gracie, who were eight and seven that year, I left at home watching the television. "There's nothing on," Gracie complained, because she wanted to go to town with me.

"Count your lucky stars you've got television," I admonished her. "In my day it hadn't been invented yet."

"Really, Mom? What did you do all summer long?" she asked me, her eyes big as saucers. She couldn't imagine there had been life without television.

"Gracie, Mommy is teasing you, she used to watch the Mickey Mouse Club, remember she told you that yesterday. You found her old ears in Gram's attic," Robert reminded his sister.

Robert was completely dressed, his shorts even looked as if he'd pressed them. That kid has always been Mr. Neatnik himself—he keeps his toys on the shelves in better order than most toy stores do. I have no idea where he gets it from.

Gracie, on the other hand, is a typical kid. She still had her pajamas on and I knew if I didn't remind her she'd go all day long without combing her hair or brushing her teeth. I make it a point not to get after her about stuff like that. I don't want to turn into a nag the way my mother always was.

It's funny, I treat my kids exactly alike. I read this somewhere, treat kids like they are adults. Let them know you respect them. I've always done that. So Robert turns out to be responsible enough for ten kids and Gracie would lose her head if it was detachable. Who can explain it?

Gracie kicked the chair and scowled at me. She doesn't like to be reminded of things, it makes her feel like a baby. "So, Mom, what about the Mickey Mouse ears?" she demanded.

"Well, that's all we had, just the one television show. The television was only on from four to five weekdays, the rest of the time it was a blank screen. Mornings in the summer there were no cartoon channels, I had to help my mother work around the house."

"I don't believe you," Gracie told me. "You're bullshitting me."

"Gracie, you better quit that cussing, you know your grandmother is gonna have a fit if you slip and say something nasty in front of her."

"You do it, Mom."

"That's exactly how come I know it is not advisable. From firsthand experience. Listen up, you guys. Uncle Butch is coming over later, you ask him about the television," I said. "And remind him about the papers on the desk Gramps left for him. I'm sure your daddy is apt to forget." I figured the thought of Butch coming over later would keep Gracie from getting too upset at me taking off without her. Summer vacation was almost over, thank God. My kids and I were beginning to get on each other's nerves.

Robert nodded and gave me a yes ma'am before he walked across the room to make sure the papers were where I'd said they were. Gracie, of course, wasn't through arguing with me. "What am I going to do while you're gone?" she whined.

"You could clean your room," I suggested.

"No," she said. "It's my room and I like it the way it is."

Sometimes I regret I ever made that rule about as long as the health department wasn't condemning us they could keep their rooms however they liked. I guess I never figured a kid of mine could stand to live in such squalor.

"Help Daddy paint," I suggested.

Her eyes lit up at that. I decided it was time I got out of there. Danny probably wouldn't be thrilled. Gracie and Robert are at the age where they like to help but sometimes they are more apt to get in the way. They'd be okay, though.

They were turning out fine. You can't coddle your kids too much. It isn't good for them. Danny, who was painting the trim on the house that day, promised to keep an eye on them as I drove off. Not that they were likely to get into any trouble. My kids rarely fight. They're as good friends as my brother and I always were. And Robert takes after Butch. He is extremely responsible, if a little obsessive about this neatness thing of his.

JOSH

It didn't come as a surprise to me when Robin Tilton finally walked in the door of my office saying she had been hired to teach at the elementary school and was wondering about renting my grandmother's house. My mother had called me a week earlier, just as I was about to walk out the door to run over to her house for dinner, to say that she couldn't imagine where the poor girl was going to live if I didn't rent out Grannie's house, had I finished replacing the upstairs plumbing yet?

"Mother, I was thinking maybe I'd live in the house myself," I said to her.

"That house is entirely too big for a single man," she said.

"Too big for a single man but fine for a single woman?" I asked. Mother didn't waste any time telling me that Robin was no longer a single woman, Robin Tilton had become a mother. *Too damn bad,* is the thought that came to mind. I vaguely remembered Robin from Danny and Julia's wedding years ago, and I recalled I'd thought she was sort of cute at the time. If there was a baby, doubtless there was a husband.

Mother did not let me flounder about in ignorance for long. "She isn't married," she said in a hushed voice. "The school board has gone and hired an unwed mother, Josh. Times have changed, your daddy and I were talking about this very thing today at lunch." I knew what that meant. Mother had talked for a good thirty minutes while Daddy nodded his head at her.

As soon as Mother hung up, I sat back down at my desk and picked up the phone to call out to Danny and Julia's. My thinking went something along the lines of *Julia will know what is what, she'll be able to tell me all about Robin.* This wasn't simply idle curiosity on my part. Because of the house situation, I really needed to know what was going on. Sitting there at my desk, my eyes went to the windows, where I could see straight across the street into the barbershop. The Methodist preacher was getting a haircut—it looked like he would be Frank's last customer of the day. The hardware store was already locked up for the night. However, Dr. Schmidt still had someone over inside his office. I didn't recognize the truck parked next to his Buick though. Tom's Grocery was still open, but there didn't seem to be anyone inside shopping. Since opening my law office in town several years earlier, I had gotten to where I seemed to know most of what people in town were up to. It wasn't that I went out looking for the information. It just seemed like my office, where it was located right across from the town square, was a natural vantage point. People coming and going went past and I looked out and saw them. Or else someone dropped in to talk. Or Mother phoned. I didn't mind knowing all of the town news, but I wasn't exactly enamored of it, either. I don't really care for gossip and it seems to me people, even those of us who live in little towns, have a right to keep our business private. Somehow it never seems to turn out that way, however.

No one answered the phone over at Julia and Danny's. That was okay with me. I hung up and hoped I wasn't turning into a gossip like everyone else in Cypress Springs seems to be. Sometimes I feared Julia had been right. Perhaps I should have stayed in Dallas. Although, for the most part, I liked Cypress Springs. *What the hell, it was home, I thought.* I didn't really want to live in Grannie's house, I could rent it out if necessary, I decided. At that time I was living in a little two-bedroom frame house that my parents had bought and fixed up for my sister before she moved to Houston. I could stay where I was. Fixing up Grannie's house had sort of become my hobby. I wasn't in any hurry to move in over there.

I locked my office door as I left. I was going to drive three blocks over to Mother's, eat dinner, and leave long before dark. My parents are always in bed by nine o'clock. Except on the nights when she has company coming, Mother has been known to serve dinner at 5:00 P.M. Farmer's hours, they call them out here.

I knew I wouldn't have to wait long to find out what Julia and Danny knew about Robin Tilton, because I was playing poker at Danny's house later on that night. I was right on the mark there, Julia knew more than I did. She knew all about the new teacher. "Robert is going to be in her class, can you believe it? My ex-roommate ends up my son's third-grade teacher? What a trip!"

"What led her to choose Cypress Springs?" I asked Julia.

"Beats me. I thought Robin had more smarts than that myself. I was figuring it up today, can you believe it has been nine years since I've seen Robin?"

"What happened? I thought the two of you were best buddies," I said.

Julia shrugged. "I have no earthly idea," she said to me. "I plan to talk to her about it the minute she moves into town. You are renting her your house, aren't you, Josh?" she asked.

"It seems as if everyone but Robin thinks so. I haven't heard the first word from her."

"You will. Hear from her, that is. If not, you really ought to give her a call. She's *got* to live in your grandmother's house, Josh. Otherwise it's that creepy little trailer park. I wouldn't want my dog to live out there. If I still knew Robin's number I'd call her up," Julia said.

"There is such a thing as information. Call and get her number," Danny said.

Julia glared at her husband. "I'll wait for her to get to town, thank you very much," she snapped. Next thing you know she had turned right around and smiled at me. "Did you hear Robin has a baby girl?" she asked. "I'm going in the attic tomorrow first thing to drag down all of Gracie's stuff. I guess all along Robin's baby is who I've been saving it for. I'm going to tell her she's got to have a boy next year so I can pass on Robert's baby clothes as well!" Julia stood up and stretched. She looked like a sleek cat. A dark reddish black jungle cat not domesticated beyond the surface. "No one who lived in our dorm would have predicted that of the two of us, it would have been Robin who had the nerve to have a kid all by herself! I myself didn't know she had it in her!" she said.

Danny was in the dining room, rummaging through a cabinet, looking for the poker chips. "Julia," he called.

"Look in the playroom, the kids were playing store this afternoon," she yelled back to him.

He finally found them in the garage in the wheelbarrow. No one even tried to figure out the how or why. Midway during the search, Julia pulled their wedding album out from under the middle of her bed. "Look at these pictures, Josh," she said. "I wonder if Robin has changed much."

I grimaced as I looked at the pictures. Robin might look exactly the same, but I hoped I didn't. "Why didn't I have the sense to try that monkey suit on before time to wear it up to the church?" I asked. "Look at my knobby ankles."

"It was kind of high water," Julia agreed. "Although I have to admit that this is the first time I've noticed the fact that your tux was too small, Josh. I barely remember the first thing about my wedding. Well, actually, I do recall the mother of all hangovers that I had."

Julia leaned back on the couch with her legs dangling over one side. Her hair was back in a ponytail, the same way she'd worn it off and on since first grade. She herself hadn't changed much since her wedding as far as I could tell. "I can't wait to see Robin," she said again. When the rest of the men arrived to play poker, Julia stood up and headed back for her bedroom, taking her wedding album with her. "I've got to be sure to stash this under the bed while I'm thinking about it," she said. "Because if Mother ever sees that Gracie has taken the markers to it, the shit is gonna hit the fan."

After she disappeared down the hall I happened to look at Danny. The smile on his face was just starting to fade. He's always thought Julia was the cat's meow. Obviously he still did.

ROBIN

Crystal's husband drove the U-Haul truck. His brother rode along with him to help him unload. Aunt Kate came out in her car. Crystal rode with me. She traveled in the backseat to look after Rachel, who slept the entire hour. Off and on Crystal leaned over the back of the front seat to say something to me. "Want me to stop so you can move up to the front?" I asked her several times.

"No, I'm okay," she replied. I could see her in the rearview mirror. Adjusting the blanket. Patting the little hands. I did the same thing myself when I was alone with Rachel. It was hard to get used to the wonder of her.

"What on earth?" Crystal said when I pulled up in front of the house I'd rented.

"It was this or a trailer park with the ne'er-do-wells," I reminded her.

"How can you afford it?" she asked.

"The rent is cheaper than I was paying on my apartment."

"Jeez, maybe Richard and I should move out here. You could rent us the top floor. This place is huge. You think we'd like it in Cypress Springs?"

"I'll let you know in a year," I said to her. It was hard for me to imagine her and Richard living in a little town. Crystal, particularly. She had a fit if her manicurist took a vacation that lasted over a week. I doubted seriously there was going to be a manicurist in Cypress Springs.

Now that I was in the middle of my own move, it was difficult to imagine myself living in a small town any more easily than I could see Crystal doing it. I don't make changes easily, and I had had cold feet over the prospect of moving out to Cypress Springs ever since I'd turned in my resignation to HISD. But as soon as I'd start to think something like, *Maybe I should have stayed put—Rachel hadn't had three months in the darling nursery Crystal and I had worked so long on,* I'd remember the sick voice on the downstairs extension that day, and my resolve would harden once again. I couldn't have stayed in my townhouse. And who knows where HISD would have assigned me. I might be, as Julia used to say, bored to death and buried alive in Cypress Springs, but I wouldn't be scared to come home nights. And now that I had a child, it wasn't as if I had only my own safety to consider.

Richard and his brother left about two to take the truck back to town. Crystal was upstairs hammering on something. Aunt Kate was in the kitchen, and I was in the living room looking around at all the emptiness when the doorbell rang. I think I must have jumped a foot. "Robin, get the door, I'm mired in contact paper," Aunt Kate called. She sounded completely normal. I was going to have to get used to answering the door myself again. Since the break-in I'd been staying at Aunt Kate's, and when the doorbell rang she was the one who went to see who it was.

I peeped out the window first. The woman standing there was tall and wiry. Her hair was short, gray, and permed. She wore a skirt and blouse and dangled a large black pocketbook from her arm. In her hands rested a plate of cookies. She didn't look dangerous by any stretch of the imagination, but I wasn't back to trusting my own instincts right then. After all, I'd waltzed straight into an apartment that had been broken into and never noticed the first thing amiss. Probably at some point I'd walked so close to the intruder he could have reached out and tapped me on the shoulder. The entire time I had failed to sense the least whiff of danger.

"Who is it?" I called out.

"Ruthie Suarez, come to see the new teacher and her baby."

I recognized her name as the one I had been given, first by the woman at The Market Basket, and later by Josh Winter when I spoke with him about renting his house. But I had not called Ruthie Suarez and asked her about babysitting. Yet here she was. Completely unsummoned. If she *was* who she said she was.

I opened the door against my better judgment, uncomfortably aware of the fact that Ruthie Suarez, like Josh's house, most likely was the only game in town.

She walked right in. "Ruthie Suarez," she said to me. "I hope you haven't got someone else in mind for your help, because I heard from my neighbor that you've got the cutest little baby. And I do love to take care of people's kids."

"How does your neighbor know what my daughter looks like?"

"Dell Addison is her sister."

I couldn't recall showing the lady at The Market Basket a picture of Rachel, but maybe I had done so. "I don't see your car."

"We only have the one, Ed dropped me off. He'll be back to check on me at five—I told him you never know what to expect on moving day."

It was 2:00 P.M. I couldn't imagine why she thought applying for a job should take three hours. "I haven't even gotten us moved in yet, I'm not ready to think about sitters."

"I can help with the unpacking and settling in, I'll need to know where things are anyway once you start to teaching and I'm looking after the little one."

I should have sent her packing. Her appearance was entirely too convenient. I was very suspicious of someone who showed up at my door and announced she was here to look after my daughter. Just as I was thinking of ways to ease Ruthie Suarez out the door, Crystal called from the top of the stairs. "I need you, Robin, we've got to figure out where to put the mobile."

Aunt Kate appeared at the kitchen door. "You go on up there and help her, she won't rest until she has that nursery set up," she said. "I'm Robin's aunt Kate," she said, introducing herself to Ruthie. "Come on in the kitchen and look at what we've got to get done. M-m, cookies, did you bake them?"

By the time I came back downstairs carrying Rachel, Aunt Kate and Ruthie were talking together like they were old pals. "You know, Mrs. Suarez, I'm not sure that I'm ready to make a decision today," I began. I'd been rehearsing my words and had a paragraph all set to go.

"Call me Ruthie, no one calls me anything but Ruthie."

I started over. Aunt Kate was holding the stepladder Ruthie was on top of, so it was hard to talk to her. All I could see was her back. She was cleaning off the top of the cabinets using a wet rag and wearing rubber gloves she must have brought with her. I certainly had never seen them before. "Ruthie, it is sweet of you to offer to help, but I can't possibly afford a housekeeper."

"I wouldn't call myself a housekeeper. I take care of the baby and the house, I'm what you call the help. Help in Cypress Springs is a sight different from housekeeper in Houston. Young mother like you, you have no business worrying about money. What is it you had planned to pay the lady in Houston?" I wondered just *what* Ruthie and Aunt Kate had been talking about. Becoming a mom appeared to be pushing me back into a shell of timidity. Aunt Kate, however, as a new great-aunt, seemed to have busted out of her normal reticence with a vengeance.

"I couldn't have afforded someone to come in. Rachel would have gone to day care near my townhouse." I went ahead and mentioned the sum that the day care had been going to charge me. I wished more than anything right at that moment that Julia and I were still friends so I could phone her up and ask her did she know this Ruthie? And was it safe to hire her to look after my daughter?

"My word in heaven! That is more than a gracious plenty for me. Mrs. Turner paid me less than that to look after her kids. And she had four at home at one time. I wouldn't expect near that much."

Aunt Kate nodded her head at me as if to say, *See there, I told you this would work out.* I, in turn, nodded a weak acquiescence to Ruthie's back, feeling as if once again my life was slipping out from under my control. At least I still had two weeks before I faced the trauma of going off to work and leaving my little girl at home to fend for herself. Two weeks can last a very long time.

AFTER AUNT KATE and Crystal departed late Sunday afternoon, I sat down to a bowl of the soup Aunt Kate had left bubbling on the stove. She'd also filled my pantry with groceries she had purchased from Tom's Grocery, which I had learned from Ruthie was one of only two grocery stores in town. Things cost more out here, Aunt Kate commented as she unpacked her grocery sacks and loaded my pantry shelves. That didn't seem to have stopped her from buying enough to feed a family of four for a month, however. She and Crystal also hung curtains and unpacked every single box before they left. The house still looked bare, because I had nowhere near the amount of possessions it was designed to hold.

Crystal left carrying measurements for Rachel's room she had taken in order to have an idea of how much stenciling she had in store for her. She also had a list of things she was going to bring out to me the following weekend. "Crystal, I don't want you to do all that," I said.

"Don't worry, I'm not going to spend any money, I'm going over to my aunt's!" Crystal's aunt is the exact opposite of Aunt

Kate. She never throws a thing away. Their entire family has gotten in the habit of taking things to her. She's the family repository for possessions, Crystal says. Their aunt has furnished no telling how many start-up apartments for her nieces and nephews.

While Aunt Kate and Crystal had been bustling about, I seemed to have spent my first weekend in Cypress Springs following either Aunt Kate or Crystal around from room to room, carrying Rachel if she was awake, wondering to myself where the two of them got their energy. And worrying about when I'd get mine back.

Even Ruthie got into the act. She insisted on working until past dark Saturday night and all day Sunday. By the time Aunt Kate and Crystal pulled out of the driveway Sunday night, Ruthie was hugging them and waving bye like she'd known them as long as I had.

Ruthie was at my house at seven o'clock Monday morning. "If you're going to lock this back door, you'd better give me a key," she said. "Otherwise, I'll be standing out here waiting for you to run downstairs and let me in for half my life. I need to be able to get inside and get breakfast going. Once school starts you'll want to be leaving the house before eight o'clock in the morning." I opened my mouth to tell her she didn't need to start coming to work until I did, which wouldn't be for another two weeks. But I'd had a hard night. I'd slept in Rachel's room, on a single bed that was designated as the bed I'd sleep on when she was sick. The door didn't have a lock so I'd pushed the rocker in front of it and wedged the back of it under the doorknob. The thought of Ruthie arriving every morning at seven was, I must admit, a welcome one. "What time does school start?" I asked her.

"Children riding in on the bus arrive about eight-fifteen. The others come in at assorted times. But the pledge of allegiance gets recited every morning at eight-thirty-two. You'll want to be there at least by eight—most of the women get there at seven-thirty. But none of them have babies." Looking backwards, I can point to this conversation as the first indication of my eventual acclimation to small town life. I didn't think twice about the fact that my newly hired housekeeper was telling me what time I would be expected to arrive at work.

JULIA SHOWED UP at about nine with a case of champagne.

"What on earth?" I asked her.

"Don't panic, I'll help you drink it," she said.

"Holy shit, that is exactly what I am afraid of," I said to her. And then we fell into each other's arms, both of us crying and laughing all at once.

Ruthie was there at the kitchen sink, watching us. I noticed she had a nice smile on her face. "Looks like you two could use a good visit," she said. "If you'll just hand me the keys to your car, I'll run your wash up to the laundromat."

Julia's hands went to her hips. "I cannot believe my ears. Wait until I get ahold of Josh Winter. The very idea! He's too cheap to put you a washer and dryer in here. We'll fix his little red wagon. What happened to the ones out in the garage, I'd like to know."

"Gave out. I called him up and asked him that very question myself Saturday night," said Ruthie. "But he's got some new ones on order, Sam over at the hardware says they should be here in a week, ten days at the outside."

For a minute there I had the weirdest feeling. I felt like I was watching a play and had somehow wandered onto the stage instead of staying put in the audience where I belonged. Then Julia looked at me and the feeling went away. It really was great to see her again.

"You have definitely changed," she informed me. "You're talking as bad as I do. What's this *holy shit* business? And you've gone and had a kid. Let me see her. Then we've got to get all the baby crap I brought you out of my station wagon. By that time the champagne should have chilled sufficiently."

JOSH

One thing Julia Salwell and I have in common is the two of us hate the idea that half the town might be able to predict what we are going to do before we do it. Because I knew people, starting with my mother, were holding their breaths, waiting to see if Robin and I would hit it off, I didn't so much as darken my new tenant's door until she'd been living in Grannie's house for over a week. Even then, it was only because I needed to install the new washer and dryer in the garage that I went over. "You didn't have to do this," she said. "It's nice enough of you to let me live here. I'm used to taking my wash to the laundromat."

"House needs a washer and dryer," I said to her. "Folks in town would never let me hear the end of it if they saw you uptown washing your baby's diapers."

"This *is* a little place, isn't it?" she said. "But Rachel wears disposables. It's an extravagance, I know, but . . ." She shrugged.

Robin was sitting there, her hair was pulled up out of her eyes, which were so blue they put the sky to shame, holding Rachel, who was about three months old and probably the sweetest baby I'd ever laid eyes on. Actually, she was probably the first baby I'd ever really looked at. Normally babies don't hold much interest for me. Robin sat in an old wicker chair that had been in the garage forever. It looked like it was made for her to sit in. "Next time I'm at my mother's I'm going to get the rest of the furniture to that set out of her garage—spray paint it and put it back on the porch. Unless you mind?"

"No, I like wicker furniture on porches," she said. "Would you like for me to buy it from you?"

"Goes with the house," I told her.

"Sure it does," she said. "Like the washer and dryer. Otherwise people might talk." We both smiled right about then. Maybe because we were both so close to Julia it didn't take us long to get comfortable with each other.

"One thing you need to know, people *will* talk. So don't be surprised at anything," I warned her. "Of course, I wouldn't want to go stepping on anyone's toes," I said. I looked first at Rachel and then back into Robin's eyes, so there would be no doubting what question I was asking her.

"He's long gone," she said to me. That was all the go-ahead I needed to hear.

JULIA

Robin and I hadn't even finished up her Welcome to Cypress Springs champagne before she had to start to work. "It's a crying shame you've got that job," I said to her. "Otherwise, once my kids get back in school we could really have some fun."

"If I didn't have this job, I'd be in big trouble," she said. "I've got to earn a living."

We were sitting in her living room listening to the rain pound down onto the tin roof. Ruthie, for the first time in two weeks, wasn't there when I drove up. "Where's your help?" I asked Robin.

"Since school starts Monday she thought she'd stay at her house today, cook up some food for Ed. The way she's been carrying on it's like she's getting prepared for some siege."

"Don't you hate having her underfoot all the time?" I asked.

"No, I like it." Robin said. "I am getting spoiled, however. Before I even think of something that I should do, Ruthie's up and done it."

Robin did look good. The first time I'd seen her after she moved in she'd had shadows a foot long under her eyes. Those were long gone now. Obviously, having Ruthie around didn't bother her. *To each his own*, I thought. I'd never felt the need of any help in my house. "Having someone working in my kitchen, even someone as nice as Ruthie Suarez, would be too much like living with my mother for me," I said. Immediately I wished I hadn't brought up Verona. I didn't want to think about her, much less talk about her. The day before we'd had a real knock-down-drag-out. The first one in years. The first one ever in front of my kids. All over whether I was or was not an unfit mother.

I'd walked in not five minutes past noon carrying DQ burgers and fries to find her standing at my kitchen stove stirring a pot of spaghetti she'd mixed up for the kids to eat. Both of the little traitors were sitting there scarfing down noodles and meatballs like they were starving—as was my husband, who was sitting at the table with them, shoveling it in as well.

"Well, excuse me!" I said. "This *is* my house, Mother, would you kindly tell me what you are doing?"

"I am cooking a decent meal for these poor children. Which, if you were any kind of mother, you'd be home doing yourself instead of spending every day up at Robin Tilton's guzzling down champagne!"

"Where I spend my time is none of your damn business, Mother," I told her. She made me so mad I couldn't think straight. To come in and run me down in my own house in front of my own kids. At the same time I was telling her to get the hell out of there if all she was there for was to criticize me, I was picking up the plates they were eating off of and throwing them in the sink, where unfortunately two of them shattered. As soon as I heard the sound of the breaking dishes, I really lost it.

"Now you've gone and made me bust up my dishes," I said, and then I picked up the pot of spaghetti sauce and tossed it straight out the back door onto the porch, which is painted white. It really wasn't a pretty sight.

"Verona, you run on home, we'll take care of this," Danny said and walked her past me toward the door. I wouldn't have hit her even though I felt like it. The kids hadn't moved.

"You haven't heard the last of this, young lady," Mother said to me as she left.

"Neither have you. I'll tell Daddy and Butch, see if I don't," I said right back to Mother. The thing I have learned with her is never, never let her intimidate you.

That night, for the first time in a long time, I woke up hysterical from a nightmare. Danny says I said to him, "She's going to tell on them, I know good and well she is. And they'll have to go jail." I don't remember it at all. The last thing I remember is going to bed and thinking I was still so upset I'd never sleep, and next thing I knew I was out like a light.

ROBIN

I think that the outline of a life amounts to nothing more than a series of ups and downs. However, I hate that expression—*Life has these ups and downs.* Sure it does. I could draw you a diagram of my life. It would look like an electrocardiogram of a very average person. *Bop-bop-bebop-bebop,* and on and on and on . . .

I guess the year I lost my parents and came to live with my aunt might have been the first one to distinguish itself on the graph paper. Probably it looked like I was scared at first, and then sort of numb thereafter until I got back to normal rhythm again. My line probably had lots of pep the four years I was in college—I felt so much more alive after I met Julia. I think I didn't worry as much as I had in the past because she showed me how not to. After college, maybe I sort of slowed down a little. Leaving college and going to work was sobering. Julia's wedding signaled the start of a hibernation period similar to the one I experienced when I was four, and it was back to *bop-bop-bebop* time. Up until I had my daughter. Then the highs and lows returned with a vengeance. Worry shoots the heart rate up the same way exhilaration and hilarity will.

After Rachel was born, I worried about Sudden Infant Death Syndrome. I'd never even heard of it before I got to that chapter in one of the small mountain of baby books I read. I can still recite to you—verbatim—the line that haunted me: "Sudden Infant Death Syndrome is an infrequent occurrence, but it is a rare mother who does not breathe a sigh of relief on her child's first birthday, since it is an unexplained but generally accepted medical fact that SIDS rarely occurs after a child turns one year of age."

It wasn't only SIDS. I worried about what she was eating. I measured the formula she drank and recorded every ounce that went down that child for the first year of her life. I kept the records on the refrigerator. When Ruthie fed Rachel while I was at work, she was instructed to be equally meticulous in her record keeping. One day, I actually tried to scoop the spit-up back into the bottle Rachel had finished, so I'd know how much to subtract from that feeding's total.

Was she sleeping enough? Was she sleeping too much? Would I know the difference? When I became a mom I discovered that your normal twenty-four-hour day isn't long enough for all the things I could come up with to worry about. Fortunately, it wasn't just me and Rachel and Aunt Kate all alone any longer.

Moving to Cypress Springs turned out to be fortuitous for me and my daughter. Between Ruthie's matter-of-fact approach to child care and Julia's flippant, carefree way of raising her kids, Rachel lucked out. By the time she was a year old, I wasn't worrying so much, which meant I was a better mom. And, of course, Josh and I sort of linked up right after I moved into his grandmother's house. It might be that he'd been there, in the back of my mind, all the years since I'd first met him at Julia's wedding. Much as I liked his company, though, once he started talking about marriage I started worrying all over again. I am essentially a very conservative person, and the thought of any change, even a good one, makes me nervous.

Rachel doesn't take after me, probably because her formative years have been spent in Julia's presence. I know that she copies her Aunt Julia the same way I used to try to do. Rachel isn't afraid of a thing, and she isn't shy about letting me know what she wants, either. When she first learned to talk, one of the questions she asked that shot fear through me was, "Why don't I have a daddy, Mommy?" Later, she wanted to know if she could have a baby sister for Christmas. She repeatedly asked why Aunt Julia didn't teach school the way I did. One day she announced that, even if

Josh wasn't her daddy, she was going to call him **Daddy** anyway, since everyone had a daddy except her. "I don't," I said to her. "Mommy doesn't have a daddy, either. Some people do, some people don't. You and I don't, Rachel."

"My . . . Want . . . A . . . Daddy," she used to say back to me, articulating it so that if I hadn't understood her the first few times, I would perhaps now get her meaning. She also emphatically wanted a baby. "Rachel need a baby too! My need one," she told me. What could I say to that?

SATURDAY MORNINGS RACHEL watched the cartoons for one hour. While she sat in the living room, mesmerized, her Cheerios scattered around her, Josh and I sat at the kitchen table drinking coffee and eating whatever homemade delicacy his mother had sent over with him. Evelyn should have run a bakery. She spends most of her time in the kitchen turning out these really fantastic cakes and cookies and the rest of the time giving them away because her husband "isn't a sweets eater" and she "wouldn't be able to get in and out of her own kitchen door" if she ate all that fattening stuff up herself.

That particular morning it was freshly baked apple strudel. "If your mother doesn't stop this, I'm going to get fat," I said as I helped myself to the second piece.

"She's hoping you'll marry me. Variation on a theme. The way to win a daughter-in-law is through her stomach."

I laughed uneasily. Josh had decided we should get married too. He agreed with Rachel—she needed a daddy and he thought he was the one she ought to have. I thought Josh and I should continue sleeping together as discreetly as we had been doing for the first two years I lived in Cypress Springs. Eventually things came to a crisis.

"It's almost three years now," Josh reminded me. "I want us to get married," he said.

"What is married, anyway?" Rachel wanted to know.

I had thought she was still mesmerized by the television, otherwise I never would have let Josh get started talking about us getting married.

"Married is what some people do and some people don't do," I said to her.

"Married is what a man and a woman do when they love each other and always want to be together," Josh clarified.

"Huh," Rachel said and turned and walked back toward the living room. She has always been a smart child.

IT WASN'T JUST that I was being stubborn. I've never been one of those people who makes changes easily. Moving to Cypress Springs was a big step for me. Once I got used to my life here, I liked it a lot—I liked the town, I liked my job, I liked the friends I had made. Truthfully, I had never been happier in my life. I'd have been a fool to rush into changing all that.

Even though I'd feared I'd hate Josh's grandmother's house because it was so big I'd never feel safe in it, it is a wonderful house. I can't imagine anything bad ever happening here. It's ironic, though: as I was growing more and more to enjoy the feeling of the large, spacious, and essentially empty rooms, Josh's mother (aided and abetted by my aunt) was working to furnish them. Nature abhors a vacuum, and Evelyn Winter doesn't tolerate one much better.

Between the living room and the kitchen is a hall. The kitchen opens into it. A back door we never use opens into it. The dining room opens into it. The living room opens into it.

As if that weren't enough, the stairs from the second floor end in the hall. Fortunately, the hall is a big room so the doors don't bounce off each other, but there isn't much wall space in the hall for furniture. At first, all I had in there was a round braided rug Aunt Kate bought for me. Now I have the rug and Josh's family heirloom hall tree. Evelyn just up and sent it over one day. One morning I answered the door and saw Raul, who works for Josh's dad, standing outside on the back porch. "Mrs. Winter sent me," he said.

"What for?" I asked.

"To bring the thing to you. The thing for your hall."

From where I stood I couldn't see the bed of his pickup and I had no idea what it was Evelyn had sent over. "Well, bring it inside, I guess," I said. I picked up the phone to dial Evelyn and find out what was going on. "Let me call and see what this is all about," I said.

"Mrs. Winter is on her way over," Raul said. I hung the phone up without dialing.

Maybe having Evelyn for a mother is why Josh decided to be a lawyer. You can't reason with Evelyn. You have to plead your case—if (and this is a big if) you can get her attention. I did try to talk her out of putting the hall tree back in the house. "Evelyn," I said, "I agree that the hall tree looks gorgeous in your mother's house. I'm not disputing that fact. But I don't feel comfortable borrowing it from you."

"It belongs right there in the back hall," she said. "It has never looked right anywhere I've tried it in my house. I woke up this morning and said to Pete, 'Pete, I won't rest easy until the hall tree is back where it belongs.'" All the time she was saying this she was pulling things out of the front closet and draping them on the hall tree. Evelyn talks in paragraphs. "Perfect! Don't you agree?" she asked me.

I guess I just stared at her. I am sure I didn't nod unless my head was bobbing around in confusion.

"I remember that hall tree from when I was a little girl," Evelyn continued. "We never took our coats down from one season to the next. Sometimes when the weather turned cold, I'd rush inside and grab the first coat or sweater that looked familiar to me and find I'd outgrown it. Whereupon I knew I was to throw it in the laundry hamper and remind my mother to wash it and send it to the poor. Since I was the youngest child in our family, when I finished wearing something it went into the poor box that was kept up at our church. If it still had enough life in it, that is. My mother could tell by washing a garment and holding it up to the light and scrutinizing it closely whether or not it had enough life in it."

"Evelyn, really and truly, I don't feel comfortable using your family's hall tree," I said.

"Nonsense," she replied. She left as quickly as she had arrived. "I left raspberry pound cakes baking in the oven," she said on her way out the back door, "I've got to get on back home." She didn't even turn back around to admire the hall tree in his rightful place once more as she left.

I picked up the phone and called Josh at work. "Your mother brought the hall tree that has been in her family for three generations over here," I said to him.

He laughed. "Mother thinks if she gets your possessions and ours in a big enough tangle you'll be forced to marry me!"

"Josh, this isn't funny. What I am trying to say is, as lovely a piece of furniture as your family hall tree is, I do not relish the responsibility of having it here."

"Where did she put it?"

"In the hall. *Where it belongs.*" Unconsciously I mimicked her. Josh, recognizing what I was doing, laughed.

"If it will make you feel better, you and I can move it out to the garage tonight."

"The garage has a dirt floor!"

"Robin, I don't feel like arguing with Mother, and it'll take a small war to get her to accept that monstrosity back into her house. How about you keep it at Grannie's for now, and I'll tell Mother she is under no circumstances to show up at your door with any more furniture unless she clears it with you first. How about that?"

"How about that," I said.

Julia noticed it immediately. She also picked up its implications. "You and Josh must be getting married soon. Evelyn's sending over the family heirlooms, I see."

THERE IS WORRY and then there is The Big Worry. It isn't as if I spent day after day worrying. Or even wondering. Robin Tilton has no parents. That's a given. But sometimes it came on me like summer lightning—heat lightning, some people call it. There will be blistering days, one right after another. Hot and dry. Hot and humid. Hot and breezy. Hot and still. Then, from nowhere, comes the summer storm. Dark clouds. Bolts of lightning. You gear up for action but there is none to take. The storm moves on of its own accord, leaving you to attend to the aftermath, which may be nothing more than water in your car, which poured in through the windows you left rolled down thinking it wasn't really going to rain. Or maybe there actually was no rain at all. And maybe, rain or not, the wind caused havoc that left half of an oak tree on top of your car. There's no gauging in advance the impact of the sudden summer storm.

said, "I told her at the latest we'd be back tomorrow, and that I'd call her this afternoon one way or the other."

"Robin, if you persist in telling all you know, you'll continue to rob your life of any semblance of mystery."

I laughed at her. With Julia, even hard times have places where you absolutely have to stop and laugh. She won't have it any other way. Curiously, once we started out that morning I wasn't all that nervous. I was pretty calm and not particularly worried. *Let's get on with this,* I think I said as we drove out of Cypress Springs.

"JOSH TOLD DANNY who told me that the two of you are getting married soon."

"Oh, he did?" I was surprised to hear Josh had said anything to Danny. I'd said maybe. *Maybe, Josh, I will marry you—if I don't find out anything too awful about myself next week. And IF I concur that us getting married will be a good thing for Rachel.* I don't know why I said that. I already knew it would be good for Rachel. She and Josh acted like father and daughter. And it wasn't just a father that Rachel would be getting. Evelyn had acted as if Rachel were her bona fide granddaughter almost from the day we met her. Josh was wonderful—his parents couldn't be nicer. It was me who was weird. Some days I couldn't believe myself, the way I had kept on and on dragging my feet when the subject of marriage came up. I'm lucky Josh and his entire family didn't say *what the hell,* and give up on me entirely.

For some reason, every time I'd catch myself starting to think I really should go ahead and marry Josh, I'd see this big question mark hovering right in front of my face. Father . . . question mark . . . Father . . . question mark . . . and on and on and on, until that's *all* I could see. Josh wanted to adopt Rachel and we were going to have to get the papers signed by Anthony in order for that to happen. I wasn't relishing the prospect, but I was going to do what needed to be done. I sort of told Julia all of this. "I *am* going to marry Josh, but I don't think I've exactly told him so yet," I said.

Julia didn't bat an eye. "About time," she said. Even if she had been surprised, she wouldn't have let on. Julia likes to be the one who does the surprising. "Evelyn has already reserved the church and the fellowship hall for the tenth of August," she told me.

"What? You have got to be kidding me!"

Julia laughed with delight. "I figured you didn't know that!" she said. "The only reassuring thing I can think of to say to you is Evelyn can be a pain in the butt but she is nowhere near as hard to take as Verona is. So you can be thankful for that."

"She reserved the church?"

"She called up there to talk to Brother Simpson and said there was going to be a summer wedding and she knew it might be getting tight. You know how every Methodist and his dog has started having summer family reunions in the fellowship hall. So Brother Simpson pulled out the calendar and penciled you and Josh in for the first available Saturday after the Fourth of July. Brother Simpson is to call Evelyn first before he lets the date get away."

"How do you know this?"

"Millie at the beauty shop. Who else? I'm sure she got it straight from the horse's mouth, Evelyn herself."

"I wonder if Josh has heard," I said. I did think that August tenth really wouldn't be a bad date if I went ahead and married Josh. That would give us time for a honeymoon before I had to go back to school. We could go somewhere special. New Orleans. Or the Caribbean. *If I went ahead and married Josh.*

The thought occurred to me that it would be nice if I could simply forget my diaphragm one night and wake up married the next day. Failing that, perhaps Josh and I could just have a vacation. Last year we'd gone to Yellowstone together. Evelyn had told everyone in town that we camped out all the way up there and back in separate tents. I have no idea where she got that from, but I certainly didn't run around behind her back contradicting her.

Benavides turned out to be a very dusty, lost-looking little town. It's not really on the road to anywhere so it is easy to understand how it seems to have this adrift-in-a-time-warp aura to it. Julia and I stopped for gas at one of the three gas stations on the town's main street. Looking back in the direction we'd come from, I caught myself watching for the next vehicle to arrive. As an old car came driving in, slowly, kicking up a cloud of dust despite the fact that the road was paved, I imagined that I was seeing a movie: the opening credits were beginning to roll. This was going to be a movie of ominous import because the credits appeared on the screen in total and complete silence. There was no music. No theme song. Just a car traveling down a dusty road into a forgotten town.

I pulled out the piece of paper Aunt Kate had given me. *Letha Wilson, great-aunt of Robin's father, Benavides, Tx, 555-7786,* it read. The phone number no longer worked. I'd gotten up the nerve to dial it about two days ago, after having the paper in my possession for almost six months. "I'm sorry, Robin, this was all I was able to find out. I tried my hardest after you had Rachel but it was too late by then. I blame myself. I should have taken care of getting the information together when you were a baby but I didn't. I *am* sorry." Aunt Kate had a hard time meeting my eyes.

Benavides didn't look like a friendly little town, it looked suspicious and hostile to me. If I'd have been alone, I think I might have been tempted to fill up the car with gas and turn around and head right straight back home. Only, with Julia accompanying me, I had too much pride to turn around without asking the questions I'd come to ask.

"Can you give me directions to Letha Wilson's house?" I leaned over toward the window on the driver's side of the car and asked the man who pumped the gas and wiped off the windshield. I insisted on paying for the gas even though we were in Julia's car. We were always in Julia's car. If she's going, she's going to drive, that is one of her things.

"Two blocks up this road, keep going in the same direction you were heading. Past the junior high, stay on this same street. There is a playground and her house is not the house past it but the next one. Blue with darker blue trim. Starting to peel, her son should have painted it last year, wouldn't have had to scrape it then. Cactus and concrete statues in the yard. Front door is always open. Letha has her ways. She has to see out. Get out of your car and walk up to the screen door and knock hard. She'll hear you but it may take a minute for her to get to the door. She's slower than she used to be. I'm not talking out of school. She'll tell you the same thing herself. Who did you say you are?"

"Thanks ever so," Julia said and drove off. I didn't look back, but I could feel him staring at us until we'd rounded the curve and disappeared from his sight.

Julia stopped the car in front of a house with cactus and concrete statues and a hard-packed dirt yard and turned off the engine. "I hope you know what you are doing," she said. "I'm going in with you. Just in case this woman's son turns out to be a weird hairy Hell's Angel or worse." Her eyes widened and I knew the same thought was whistling through both our heads. Was the son my father? The one who hadn't painted the house when it would have been timely to do so? Aunt Kate had said, "This woman knew your father. She was an aunt of his, I think."

LETHA WILSON WAS a poor lonely old woman, that is the best that I can come up with to say in her defense. I don't think, even in Benavides where she had lived her entire life and was presumably one of the townsfolks, that most people, having visited her once, would be likely to return quickly. After she let us in the door, Julia and I sank into the sofa in the living room. The sofa emitted a cloud of dust, which caused me to start sneezing. Wordlessly, Julia reached into her purse and handed me a tissue. Letha's chair, across from where we sat, had a large square footstool in front of it, situated about five feet from the television screen. There was a path leading to the television set that made a square that ran from the kitchen to the living room chair and on to the hall. Undoubtedly the hall led to her bedroom and bathroom. You could chart the routine of Letha's life from the well-worn indentations in her carpet. She was old and lonely and she turned off the television and sat down across from us hoping we'd stay all afternoon.

"Of course I know something about him, I know everyone ever lived in this town. That'll be the one who married the girl from McAllen. He's the one you're asking about? I might know about that. Let me think. Did you say you drove in from there? No. From Cypress Springs. Wherever in the world. Near Houston? Well, I'll swan. I never heard of that place. But then," she chuckled, "there's more than a few ain't heard of Benavides, I'll swear to that. Except I don't. Swear. Wasn't raised to, don't find the need to," she chuckled again. "Let me get you something from the kitchen. Hot day. What would that be? Lemonade." She stood up and walked out of the room without ever looking in our direction.

"Mrs. Wilson, we don't need anything to drink," I called to her disappearing back. She didn't appear to have heard me. Julia and I exchanged a look.

"No lemons. Water will have to do. My son, Jackson, he's a good boy. But I guess he didn't notice I put lemons on my list," she said, handing each of us a glass. I gulped the water down like it was Alka-Seltzer. In one long series of swallows. I was holding my breath so I wouldn't have to smell it going down. It had taken me forever to get used to Cypress Springs water, but, since I had, I hated the taste of water from other places.

"Want more?" she asked. "Looks like you must have been thirsty."

"No, no, this was plenty. About your nephew, Mrs. Wilson. Kyle Connors. He was my father. I want to get in touch with him. You did have a nephew named Kyle Connors." We'd established that fact earlier, but the conversation kept veering off.

"Kyle. I remember Kyle. Cute little thing, he was. Blond hair, big blue eyes. Like all the young folks, didn't want to stay here in Benavides. Can't blame them. But it does take the life out. Go to church with me Sunday. Any Sunday. You'll see in a minute what I am referring to. No one there under sixty these days. Grown and gone. That's what folks say about their kids. They're grown and gone."

"Where did he go?"

"He had a hard life. His father, Juan Connors, just as soon take a strap to that child as to look at him. The mother didn't like it, but she wasn't one to say boo to a goose. Nothing she could do except wring her hands. Can't blame the child if he took off the first time the going got good."

Julia looked over at me and back at Mrs. Wilson. She didn't raise her eyebrows or shrug but I knew what she was thinking. We were wasting our time.

"You see Main Street? Like to nothing still open. We got the grocery store, the five-and-dime. That's about it. Post office and the cafe. What else? You notice anything else?"

"Three gas stations," Julia said.

"What for? Ask yourself? For folks to get the gas in their cars they need to up and get away from here." She smiled at us. I really didn't like her smile. "If I was a bit younger I can't say I wouldn't be gadding off myself."

"What happened to Kyle Connors? Do you know?"

"Why did you say you were asking?"

"I'm his daughter. I want to find him."

"I did hear he married. But I swear, I wouldn't have been able to put a name to *who* he married. Who was your mother?"

"Sandra Tilton."

"Not from around here, I'll venture. Doesn't ring a bell. Oh, that's right, you said from McAllen. Now it does seem to me I might have heard that."

"Do you have any idea where he went after he married?"

"I might if I had the time to think. Young people in such a hurry. Too rushed to think. Can't even think, you go so fast. Television is responsible for that. Minister preached on it Sunday last."

"He and my mother were in a motorcycle accident the year I was four. That was 1955. My mother was killed. He was hurt. I want to find out what happened to him after that."

"Motorcycles, you say? *Dangerous* motorcycles, I say. When young Kyle bought himself a motorcycle he signed his own death certificate if you ask me."

"Did he die?" I asked.

"All of us have got to some time or other. That's a fact. His mother, my younger sister, she's been gone close to twenty years now."

"Aunt Kate, who raised me, doesn't know what happened to him. It's like he just vanished," I said. To my own ears, my voice sounded younger than my three-year-old daughter's.

"That could have been it," Letha agreed.

JULIA AND I drove out of town the same way we had driven in, with the credits rolling. This movie was also silent, a black-and-white production—1920s, maybe 1930s. The only thing of any significance that I had learned from Letha Wilson during the two hours Julia and I sat perched on her dusty sofa was that there might be a sister to my father, Sassy Connors, living in Detroit. Or Denver. One of those big cities the name of which started with a *D*. Only if she had married, which was likely, pretty as she was, her name might not be Connors any longer. At first I'd thought the flitting cagey look on Letha Wilson's face reflected some knowledge she was loath to part with. Gradually, during the two hours I sat in her front room trying to talk with her, it became apparent that her cagey look was nothing more than a reflection of her desire to hold Julia and me captive for as long a time as possible.

Julia stopped the car at the last gas station on the way out of Benavides. "What are you doing?" I asked her. The gas tank was still full.

"I'm not leaving here empty-handed," she said.

When she returned she was carrying a telephone book that looked like it had been used primarily as a coaster and contained at the most twenty-five pages. "Did you swipe it?" I asked her.

"No, I paid ten dollars for it. The guy was thrilled. When we get home, you're going to call up every person in this book. Someone is bound to tell you more than Letha Wilson was willing to!"

"Perhaps Letha told me what I needed to know, Julia."

She raised an eyebrow at me.

"Think about it. He was a cute kid who had a rotten childhood and left town. After my mom died, he kept on going. Even if I find out all sorts of additional details, that isn't going to give me back a father!"

"So you're ready to let sleeping dogs lie, are you? Evelyn is going to be so pleased." Julia grinned one of her big grins at me. "Have you got your wedding all planned out or are you going to let Evelyn run yours the way Verona did mine?" she asked.

PART V

JULIA

The last time I saw my father I was standing in my front yard. I remember waving and thinking that he hadn't looked better in years. His color was great. He'd lost weight, but actually that was all to the good. Daddy was always a little portly if he didn't watch himself. I particularly noticed the twinkle in his eyes. "Stay for dinner," I said to him as we walked outside. "We're cooking hamburgers out by the pool." He'd been at my house all day. Ostensibly Daddy was supervising the two men who were landscaping our backyard around the new pool. Actually, every time I looked out my kitchen window, Daddy was either lifting something heavy or digging holes and planting bushes himself. He spent the entire day working harder than any of the hired help. "What do you pay them for if you do all the work yourself?" I asked him. "You never work harder than when you work for yourself," he replied. Outdoor work always did agree with him, the same way fishing did. I think if he was out in the fresh air he never considered what he was doing work.

"Come on, there's plenty to eat," I urged him, trying to get him to stay longer once he'd announced it was time to call it a day and head for home. Probably some sixth sense was nudging me there.

"Can't. Your mother is at home cooking up something wonderful for me to eat."

"All the more reason for you to stay right here, Daddy. Tell you what, I'll make the supreme sacrifice, I'll call Mother up and ask her over as well."

Daddy laughed as he shifted his truck into gear. "Since when does your mother wait for an invitation?" And then he was gone.

I felt sorry for him, driving home to Mother and the new French cookbook she'd ordered from some chef show on television. The television was what Mother had replaced AA with when she started drinking again.

WE NEVER GET phone calls in the middle of the night, so when it rang I knew immediately it was bad news. I was prepared for something bad, but not for the worst. All my life, when I realized I had to get ready for something serious, I'd worry that it was Daddy or Butch the bad news was going to be about. But the night Butch called to say that Daddy was dead in his bed at home what I thought of when the phone rang was Mr. Forester. Maybe because he'd been hanging around. Or maybe because Daddy had already joined him. I'm not sure how long it takes from a person's time of death to when they're a mobile spirit; it probably varies with the circumstances. But that night when the phone rang, as Danny was reaching over to answer it, the thought which came to me was, *This is going to be Mr. Forester with a message for me.* I tried to get myself to wake up enough so I'd understand what it was he was saying.

MOTHER INSISTED ON having the funeral two days later. She said there wasn't any reason to wait. I wanted to put if off for another day, but Danny said another day wasn't going to make it any easier, better if we go ahead and had the funeral when Mother wanted to have it. "What difference does a funeral make?" I said to Susie. "Dead is dead and a funeral isn't going to change it." The only reason I'd suggested waiting in the first place was I was hoping Daddy would have contacted me and let me know he was okay so I wouldn't have to sit through the funeral not knowing. Unfortunately, in some circumstances it takes a long time for spirits to get through. I know that it is true sometimes they go on and don't so much as look back. However, I have always been sure that my daddy would never do something so cruel to me. It was a matter of time. And timing. Time is the most difficult thing to comprehend. People who are in body wear watches and look at calendars and make appointments, which they may or may not keep. Not spirits. So while I knew it had been one day and then two and then on into a number of weeks, to Daddy the time elapsed might have been no more than the blip of time. Time is different for spirits. I've learned that fact from no telling how many different sources.

DANNY

After Tom's funeral, I expected that Julia would gradually start to get back to herself. I knew it would be hard for her—if ever there was a Daddy's girl, Julia was it—so I was aware it might take some time for her to get over Tom's death. But I never thought she'd go off the deep end the way she did.

At the funeral, she was as composed as a statue. Verona cried and carried on, Butch shed some tears, and there were several places where I caught myself blinking hard. Tom Salwell had been a good man. Not perfect. But a good man.

I kept my arm around Julia for the entire service. It felt like I was trying to hold onto a lamppost. That's how stiff she felt. It seems to me that she paid close attention to what was going on around her. It wasn't like she was lost in a fog. Julia stood. She sat. She spoke. She shook hands. She said, "Thank you, Daddy would have liked that," over and over to everyone who so much as nodded at her. I did not see her eyes blink once.

"Did the doctor give Julia something? She acts like she's drugged," Robin whispered to me at the funeral home the night before.

"As far as I am aware the doctor hasn't been consulted," I whispered back. I was watching Julia very carefully. So were Butch and Susie. She appeared calm and composed to all three of us. *Julia is holding up.* Words people are always saying. In her case it was true. Julia held herself together until her daddy was buried.

Tom was buried on a Thursday. On Friday, I left to go off to get some work done. "I'll be home about eleven, will you be all right here by yourself?" I asked Julia.

She was still in bed. I could tell she was awake, although she didn't pull her head out from under the covers to look at me.

"Do you want me to stop in town and pick up anything? I'll be at the Rollins place this morning so I can easily run through town on my way home. Milk? Eggs? We need anything?" Julia hated to go to town for one or two things—she never missed a chance to get me to pick up something for her.

"No. I don't need anything," she said. She sounded normal.

"Susie said she'd be home all day, call her if you need anything."

I waited a bit and when she didn't say anything I said good-bye one more time and walked down the hall. The kids were at the kitchen table. I drove them to school. As usual,

they'd cooked breakfast for the three of us. Nothing out of the ordinary about the morning as long as you were willing to overlook the fact that they'd buried their grandfather the day before.

"Are you sure you're ready to go back to school?" I asked them. Gracie had her piano lesson on Friday and she didn't want to miss that, she said. When Robert said he'd rather go to school than stay home, I couldn't blame him. There is just so much sitting around a person can do.

When I came in for lunch the house felt the way I imagine a crime scene waiting to be discovered feels. Still. Forbidding. The kitchen looked exactly the way it had looked hours earlier. So did the rest of the house. So did Julia.

"Julia, shouldn't you get up?" It was hot as the devil in our bedroom. She'd turned the heat on; she'd switched off the central air and had the heat going full blast. The temperature outside was close to ninety. Inside our house it felt even hotter. Julia had not only a sheet, but several blankets piled on top of her. "Are you okay?" I asked.

"I'm trying to sleep," she said.

"I'll get my own lunch, can I fix you something?"

"I want to sleep, go away."

Julia has never been one of those people who sleep until noon, even when she's sick. There wasn't anything I *had* to do that afternoon. I decided to stick around. The new paint for the barn had been sitting there in the cans for a good six months, I could get started on that. Once the kids came in on the school bus, they could help me.

AFTER A WHILE, we hired a woman named Lupe to live in. "Julia," I said, "Leonard has a cousin who needs a job, a woman just over from Mexico who doesn't speak English yet. I thought maybe we could use her to help out here, until you get back on your feet, that is." I was hoping to light a fire under Julia. Months ago, if I'd have told her that I was considering hiring a housekeeper she'd have let me have it. Now she didn't so much as bat an eye. She sighed and said, "Suit yourself, it doesn't matter to me." I really did start to worry about Julia after Lupe came to work for us.

Lupe was nice enough. The kids and I didn't have much trouble communicating with her, the three of us know enough Spanish to carry on a basic conversation. Julia, who doesn't speak the first word of Spanish, looked through Lupe like she wasn't in the house.

"Mom, Lupe wants you to make a grocery list," I heard Gracie say to Julia.

"You tell her what you feel like eating, honey, Mommy isn't hungry."

Robert wanted Julia to help him with his science project. Something to do with a model showing body systems. Usually she was so good at that kind of thing. "Call Aunt Susie," Julia said to Robert. "Aunt Susie can probably find out what you need. She used to teach school."

"That's Aunt Robin, she taught school until she had Jeremy and Justin," Gracie reminded Julia.

"Oh," she replied. "Well, call her."

"Julia, the kids need you, you've got to pull yourself together. I know you miss your father, but he's gone, we're still here." I tried on several occasions to talk to her after the second month and then the third month passed with her the way she was. She was going through the motions but that was all she was doing.

"I am trying, Danny. But I miss my daddy. You know how he was always there for me. It's like I can't concentrate on anything until I see him again." I had the sense she was waiting for Tom to come back. The way she said, *I miss my daddy*. Like he was gone on a trip rather than cold in the ground.

We were doing everything we knew to do. Butch worried the least. Julia will come around, he said, give her time. In the end that's what we did. Once we ran out of ideas for other things to try, there didn't seem to be any alternative.

Then Verona and Butch and Susie came over for hamburgers one Sunday night. I was cooking them on the grill out by the fire. "Labor Day is next week, the kids will be back in school the day after, can you believe this is Thomas's last year?" Susie said.

She looked over at the pool where both of her kids were swimming. Thomas was almost six feet tall, his younger brother, Eugene, was even taller than that. My two, Robert and Gracie, were swimming around their cousins looking like slippery eels. Since they'd spent the summer in the pool, their color was that of copper pennies shimmering in the pool lights. Eugene and Thomas, who had been working with Butch, had farmer's tans. From the neck up and on three-quarters of their arms, they were brown and leathery. The rest of their bodies were white and sickly looking.

Julia had joined us. Actually, she had a bathing suit on for the first time since her father died.

I noticed her watching the kids. "First summer in my life I didn't get a tan," she said. I felt optimistic the minute I heard her words. "I don't know why I ever cared about whether my skin was white or tanned," she went on to say. "What difference does it make in the long run any-way? Daddy certainly doesn't care if I have a tan this year or not."

"Where's Lupe?" asked Verona. "Julia, you don't know how lucky you are to have a live-in. I should have been so fortunate when you and Butch were small."

Julia narrowed her eyes at her mother in the way that used to mean she was fixing to let Verona have it. Normally I would have geared up to referee. Or duck. But this time I leaned forward in anticipation—Julia throwing a fit right about then would have been a wonderful sight to see.

She didn't follow through, though. She looked at Verona with thoughtful eyes for a minute, then she leaned back in her lawn chair and closed her eyes.

Butch changed the subject when he pulled a paper out of his pocket. "Is this what you wanted me to look at, Mother?" he asked. *Try another subject,* I could feel him thinking. Lately we were all getting good at that.

He had a drawing of Verona's most recent proposed renovation to her house. Since Tom's death Verona had busied herself with renovation to the house plans and projects. She'd been over with no telling how many house decorating books trying to get Julia to help her decide about paints and new linens and whether she ought to stick with her Scandinavian motif or try something different. Julia never bothered to so much as look at the books and fabric swatches when her mother put them down in front of her.

"Well, now, Mother, this isn't a bad plan, but I think you might want to rethink the added room, seems to me you're going to knock out the back half of the house just to enlarge your bathrooms and get yourself a sewing room," Butch said.

"You're going to end up spending a pile of money you won't see again."

"What's money? You can't take it with you," Verona said.

"You can say that again," Julia said.

"I have to have bigger bathrooms, Butch. So I can put in those new square bathtubs they've come out with. Have you seen the kind with the whirlpool jets? I had Ed Schultz out and he said the only way to get those tubs in was to knock out the entire back wall of the bedroom wing and enlarge the bathrooms. And while we were doing that, since I'd have to have a new roof in the process, I might as well add a sewing room off my bedroom. Square off the entire back of the house. I like this idea. You know that I'd just as soon get rid of that patio, I've never liked it."

I felt Julia's interest. She leaned forward in her chair to get a look at the drawing Butch held. I looked over his shoulder as well. *Better and better,* I thought. Verona could build three-story bathrooms onto her house, for all I cared. The first I realized there was something unusual going on was when I heard this low-pitched growl right beside me. It was coming out of my wife's mouth.

"What the hell?" I said as I looked up and saw Julia standing up glowering for all she was worth at Verona. I got up so fast my own lawn chair fell over. Butch and Susie both stood up as well. Fortunately, the kids were all in the pool and not paying any attention to the grownups.

"Over my dead body you'll go tearing into that house," Julia said. "It doesn't surprise me in the least to hear you've never liked that patio, but as far as I am concerned you are stuck with it. Do you hear me, Mother? You are *stuck* with that damn patio." Her words came out quiet and deadly.

"It's my house, I'll remodel whatever I feel like," Verona

said. She was the only one not looking at Julia. Maybe she didn't realize how angry her daughter had become, or maybe Verona liked to flirt with danger, because you didn't have to look at Julia to feel the difference in the atmosphere.

Julia snatched the paper away from Butch and ripped it to pieces.

Verona looked over at Julia with as much expression on her face as if Julia had said to her, *Nice day, isn't it, Mother?* "I will make any changes I have a mind to make," Verona said, but she didn't seem to be putting much force behind the words. "You say the bathrooms wouldn't work, Butch?" she asked. She was carrying on as if Julia hadn't just threatened her.

"If you're just trying to fit in bigger bathtubs, then take out the closet in between the bathrooms. That will give you plenty of room for the tubs."

"But I need a sewing room."

"There are three bedrooms you aren't using."

"Well, let me think about this, I didn't really want to have to go to the trouble of a new roof, all that hammering overhead," Verona said.

Julia watched the two of them like a hawk during this conversation. When Verona finished speaking, Julia nodded her head in satisfaction. The next day she fired Lupe. She sent her over to Verona's to work. This meant Verona had to refurbish the maid's room off her garage. While she was at it, she added a cedar closet out there, and took out the closet inside the house so she could accommodate two bathtubs, the combined size of which is almost that of our swimming pool.

"Mother has never taken a bath since I've known her. Her skin's too dry. She always takes showers," Julia said after she'd been over to look at the new bathtubs. "But then, I always knew she was nuts."

ROBIN

Generally speaking, the fact that Julia had an abortion her senior year in high school was a taboo subject, but I suspected the memory still bothered her. I vividly remembered when she came to the hospital to visit me after I had my third child, Justin. Julia-fashion, she appeared with a bottle of chilled champagne, a gorgeous lace-trimmed peignoir set, and gift certificates for "the works" at Millie's Beauty Shop. "For you," she said, dumping the packages in my lap as she pulled a corkscrew and crystal champagne glasses out of her purse. "Let's drink a toast to the new arrival. Cute kid," she said, nodding at Justin, who was asleep in the little rolling cart from the nursery, "but I think it's high time you got off this breeding kick, Robin," she continued. "Enough's enough. Three kids, two of them in diapers, it's going to take all the fun out of life if you're not careful!"

I laughed, so did Aunt Kate after her initial gasp of surprise. Actually, I believe being around Julia is what has caused Aunt Kate to loosen up the way she's done in recent years. The three of us drank champagne and joked and talked for about thirty minutes. One of the nurses unbent enough to take a minuscule sip of the wine Julia poured into my water glass and pressed on her. After Aunt Kate left, Justin woke up. Julia picked him up and put him on her shoulder, where he snuggled in and fell back asleep before I could get a nipple on the bottle I was fixing for him. "You know, I'd have three myself if I hadn't had that abortion," she said. Her eyes, when she looked at me, were brimming with tears.

I didn't know what to say as I stared into her eyes. I felt lost in them. Usually, when I've been stuck dumb floundering around for the right words, I'll mull over the situation for days if necessary until I come up with the right I-should-have-said-this-or-that statement. But to this day I'm not sure what I should have said to Julia at that particular moment.

JULIA WALKED IN my kitchen carrying the Ouija board we used to fool around with in college. "Remember this? I'd forgotten all about it. It was stuck up in Mother's attic with some boxes I'd shoved up there back when I moved out of my Houston apartment."

"Yes, I remember that thing," I said. I thought maybe she was bringing it over so Rachel could play with it.

"So come on, let's go in the living room, I want to see if it still works," she said.

"I can't, Julia. I was just leaving to take Justin to the doctor. He gets his six-month checkup today."

"And shots!" Jeremy added.

"And shots," I responded, thankful Justin was still too little to know what was in store for him. At the same time I felt relieved that I had an excuse for not sitting down at the Ouija board with Julia. For some reason the idea no longer appealed to me.

"Listen, Robin, I'm going to try to contact my father, maybe we can find yours as well," she said to me.

"Julia, you don't think that thing really works, do you?" I asked her.

"It used to, don't you remember?"

"I remember us carrying on like it was talking to us, Julia. But now it seems like something we invented to give ourselves a thrill. A kid's game."

"Don't you want to know more about your father?" she asked me. I thought of the Benavides telephone book, which was lying in my desk drawer. I'd had it three years now without making the first phone call. I'd run across it last week when I had to find Rachel's birth certificate to order her a Social Security card. I did open it to the C section. Why, I couldn't tell you. Of course I knew that Kyle Connors's name wasn't going to have materialized in there since the last time I had looked. There were still only two Connorses in there. And four other Wilsons. "Julia, I don't really want to know anything about my father any longer," I said. "I've given up on all of that."

A COUPLE OF weeks later I was out at Julia's one morning. Her kids were in school, so was Rachel. My boys were home with Ruthie. I'd gone out to help Julia with the Halloween costumes we were making. Actually, the two us at the sewing machine was a case of the blind leading the blind. Neither one of us knew what we were doing. However, Julia was determined we weren't going to ask her mother or anyone else for help. We were going to make the damned things ourselves if it killed us. I wasn't that concerned, my kids were too little to worry about what their clown suits looked like. But Julia's kids were older. Gracie, in particular, was likely to refuse to put on her cheerleader uniform if it didn't shape up any better than it presently looked.

"Let's do the Ouija board," Julia said. "I'll finish ripping out that seam later."

"Don't you think we ought to finish these today?" I asked her.

"No, Gracie's already said she wants to wear my old cheerleading uniform, which is in Verona's new cedar closet. And Robert said not to worry, he'd as soon be a scarecrow again this year, so all I have to do is sew patches on his jeans and shirt and stuff some straw around him. I'm sick of sewing. I can't think why I ever let you talk me into this!"

"*Me* talk *you* into it! Who was it convinced me not to buy the costumes when we were in Houston last week. 'Oh, Robin, don't buy those tacky things for your kids to wear, you and I can make them so much cuter and cheaper.' Who said that, I'd like to know?"

Julia flashed an unrepentant smile at me. "I guess maybe it was me. But look, Robin, your kids' costumes are as done as they're going to get and they do look better than the ones you were all set to buy. At least, they probably will at nighttime, which is the only time the kids wear them anyway. I mean, it's not like you're going to put the costumes on Rachel, Jeremy, and Justin and send them to church dressed up as clowns, are you? So let's talk to Ouija."

"We ought to at least clean up this mess."

"I'll do it later. Come on back in my room, I've got Ouija there."

"Have you been doing this lately?"

"I tried several times with Danny but he's a skeptic. Ouija won't talk to nonbelievers. You remember that, don't you?"

"I remember hearing you saying it to the other girls in the dorm. That's what I remember."

"So let's get on with it." She'd turned off the lights and lit candles in the room. I felt a flutter of excitement. What difference did it make, it wouldn't do any harm for us to pretend a little.

JULIA

The year after Daddy died it was like Mother and I couldn't be hateful enough to each other. I think she blamed me for his death, because he *had* been working out in the hot sun all day at my house before he went to bed and had the stroke or heart attack or whatever it was that killed him. I blamed myself too. I couldn't look out my patio doors and see the swimming pool shimmering at me without thinking, *Julia, if you hadn't had to have a pool and have it landscaped all green around the sides, your daddy would be here today.*

"We should fill the pool in, I hate it," I said to Mr. Forester. *It won't bring your daddy back,* he said to me. All along I wondered why it was Mr. Forester I saw and never Daddy. I asked him, "Have you seen my daddy?" He never would give me an answer. Ouija said my daddy was fine, but busy, and sent me his love although I suspected Robin engineered that message because she thought it was what I needed to hear. When we asked for news of Robin's daddy, Ouija said he didn't have any news of him, that not even Ouija had infinite knowledge. That is what made me suspicious. The word *infinite.* It sounded a lot more like Robin talking than Ouija to me.

Mother brought me some things from her attic. Now that she had Lupe living in she was busy thinking up things to keep her busy. Mother didn't want to lose Lupe, because she liked having someone there at the house with her. But it galled her to pay Lupe and not see her working a good eight-hour day. They got the attic so cleaned out you could eat off the floors up there. Mother brought me this big box with all my old school papers in it. "What for?" I asked her.

"I've stored them for you long enough, it's your turn now," she said.

"Mother, I don't have room for these things, I don't have a floored attic," I reminded her.

"Well, make room or throw them out, it's up to you. I've taken care of your possessions all I care to."

"What did you do with Butch's papers and report cards?" I asked her.

"That is none of your business," she said.

"So you're keeping his but not mine," I said. She didn't bother to answer me, which let me know that I was right.

That night I did something stupid. But I'm not sorry. It was about 2:00 A.M. We had a full moon, the night was bright as day outside. I walked outside because I couldn't sleep and there was the shed. Our shed is a big building, big enough where if you wanted to you could park four cars in it easy. It is as tall as a two-story house. Danny originally built it for a combination workshop and equipment storage building. However, it had so little inside it that walking in you were stuck by how empty and hollow it felt. Danny had just painted all of it, the tin roof included, a dark forest green. I walked all the way around the shed. Before I knew what I was doing, I found myself pulling the ladder over to the side of the building that faces the road. I gathered up a can of white paint and a four-inch paintbrush and went to work. Scaling up and down the ladder, I made the letters as wide and tall as I possibly could. I wrote YOU NEVER LOVED ME on the side of our shed, where it was plainly visible to cars passing by. I painted it for all the world to see. Then I took the box of papers Mother had left inside my garage out to the barrel where we burn trash and put a lighted match to it. I waited until the fire was going good before I pulled the ladder back into the shed and put the paint away. The brush I dropped into the can of turpentine where Danny had left his paintbrushes soaking. And then, because I still couldn't sleep, I sat out on our front steps and watched over by the well for Daddy and Mr. Forester to appear.

ROBIN

I could still see Julia standing in the hospital room, holding Justin, her eyes frozen with old tears one Saturday morning—years later—as we talked about birth control pills for Julia's thirteen-year-old daughter. I felt soft toward Julia—protective. "Julia, Gracie is a baby herself. I don't think she should be taking BC pills. Have you mentioned this to Danny? I'll bet you a million bucks he doesn't know what you're thinking. How are you going to explain it to him?"

"Maybe I won't explain anything, why should I? Gracie can take the pills and keep her mouth shut. Or what about this? Suppose I grind them up and put them in her juice every morning? Then she'll be perfectly safe and never know the difference."

"Julia, that's—," I stopped, not wanting to say the words I was thinking. Devious. Immoral. The kind of thing she accused her mother of doing. "It isn't right, Julia," I said.

"So? You think I care about right or wrong? I don't want Gracie coming to me in a year or two pregnant. She's going out for cheerleader. I'm being practical."

"Just talk to Gracie, Julia," I advised. I have no idea what she did or didn't do about the pills. She's never mentioned them again and I've never asked. Gracie made cheerleader. Somehow I doubt very seriously Julia had her on birth control pills. Gracie, hardheaded as she was, wasn't a foolish kid. And I think Julia knew it. Also, Gracie, unlike her mother, never went steady. She's had lots of friends, male and female, but seldom the same boyfriend two months running. And if, to this day, Gracie has gotten serious about one of them, that fact is probably the only well-kept secret in Cypress Springs.

Aunt Kate got to hear the story about Julia painting a message on the shed behind their house for the entire town to cackle over. "I'm only sorry Danny is painting over my masterpiece so fast," Julia was saying when Aunt Kate came downstairs that Saturday morning. "I wanted the words to stay there on our shed until they were so weathered everyone in town had come to accept them as part of the landscape."

"What words, Julia?" Aunt Kate asked. She had her gardening gloves in her hands and was ready to step out the door, but she couldn't resist Julia's conversational gambits. I often think Julia plans how to word her statements to achieve the maximum dramatic effect.

"A while back, in the middle of the night, I painted a message to my mother on the side of our implement shed. I wrote, 'You never loved me,' in the biggest letters I could make. I wanted the whole town to see it. The only thing that makes an impression on Verona is something everyone in town is talking about."

"Oh," said Aunt Kate, frowning. She couldn't decide if Julia was serious or not. "Is this some new fad? Perhaps an idea she got from a movie?" Aunt Kate asked me after Julia had gone home.

"No, I don't think she got the idea from a movie," I said. It concerned me that Julia had opened herself up to public scrutiny the way she had.

Everyone probably was talking about it. "What did your mother say when she saw it?" I myself had asked Julia.

"Nothing. The same way she always clams up when she doesn't want to see the handwriting on the wall. 'Do you get the message, Mother?' I asked her. "'Julia, I have never understood your particular brand of humor,' she said back to me."

I had to laugh at Julia's scowl. It is the truth, her mother has never understood Julia's humor. Perhaps because, as far as I can tell, Verona doesn't have an ounce of humor herself. At least not where her daughter is concerned.

IT WAS NOT too long after my three kids went through a bout with strep that I brought up family history with Aunt Kate again. What I thought of as my history would lie there dormant like a volcano and as good as dead for years on end until, for no discernable reason, the pressure of a lifetime of unasked and unanswered questions would once again begin to make me uneasy and irritable. "Rachel, I don't have to tell you why you can't go to town on your bicycle, you just can't go and that is that!" I hate it when I start snapping at the kids. It didn't help that Aunt Kate was there in the kitchen with me trying to keep a calm, neutral expression on her face. She never ever snapped at me. I don't know how in the world she kept from it, and I'm not about to ask her, either.

I was sitting in the kitchen trying to fill out the forms for Justin's official entrance into the public school system. Judging from all the questions they wanted answered, you'd think they were going to do brain surgery on him instead of simply enroll him in kindergarten. "You know I get so tired of putting down 'I don't know' when a form I am filling out starts asking about what diseases my parents and grandparents had. I'm going to go to McAllen and at the least look up my mother and grandmother's medical records. And then I just may have another go at the people who knew my father."

Aunt Kate nodded calmly at me. I had the feeling, probably erroneous, that she had been waiting for me to say exactly those words. "I'll go with you," she said. "Otherwise you won't have the first idea where to look."

"How hard could it be? How many hospitals were there in McAllen back then? And how many doctors?"

"I have no idea," Aunt Kate said. "But, Robin, the truth is you weren't actually *born* in McAllen. You were born near there, however. Whereas your mother and I were born in Mission, Texas. Born and raised there—I swore I'd never go back. So did Sandra the last time I saw her. But that just goes to show the truth of the old saying, never ever say you won't do something. Because sure as anything you'll end up doing it. Sandra was buried in Mission. Not me, however."

As always when Aunt Kate brought up her funeral arrangements I found myself scrutinizing her carefully. Was her color good? Bad? Different in any way? How about the circles under her eyes? And her weight? Had it fluctuated? Moles? Any changes? I'd read the seven warning signs for cancer so carefully for so long that I sometimes found myself dreaming of them. I could also recite the symptoms of depression and impending suicide equally facilely.

"You're not wanting to give any of your possessions away, Aunt Kate, are you?" I asked, watching her eyes as I spoke.

"Not that I know of," she said, looking if anything a little surprised at the question. "Why, Robin, sweetheart, is there something of mine you would like to have?"

WE ARRIVED IN Mission late in the afternoon. The first thing we did was check into the Vali-Ho Motel located on U.S. Highway 83, the road which, had we kept on traveling on it, would have taken us up beside the Rio Grande River all the way to Laredo. Since there were six of us—me, Josh, Aunt Kate, and the three kids—we took two of the combination room/kitchenettes. One for me and Josh and the boys, one which Aunt Kate and Rachel shared. The following morning Josh and the kids left to drive to Brownsville to go to the zoo, Aunt Kate and I set out to exhume the past.

"What exactly is it you hope to discover, Robin?" she asked. "We can visit the cemetery and look at the grave. We can go by the house where your mother and I were raised. We can see what has happened to the records of the family doctor. Or there is the nursing home where Mother spent her last years. It just depends on what you are hoping to learn."

"Since we're here, let's do it all," I said. I had my camera with me. I was determined to find out what there was to know about my mother and leave Mission with as much solid information as it was possible for me to obtain.

Once you get to a cemetery there isn't actually much to do other than stand there. Her grave was marked by a granite stone engraved with her name and dates. It lacked so much as a simple Bible verse or a "Beloved wife of . . ." below her name.

"My mother died a long time ago," I commented.

"Yes, she did."

"But the name on the stone isn't my father's name."

"Your mother kept her name."

I had a flash of insight. "She and my father weren't married, were they?"

Aunt Kate smiled apologetically. "I don't think so, Robin."

"It doesn't matter, Aunt Kate," I heard myself reassuring her. Who was I to worry about legitimacy? I hadn't been married to Rachel's father either.

"Of course it doesn't," she assured me.

My grandmother had five or more husbands; neither of her daughters had one. But the second daughter, my mother, had me. I supposed I ought to be thankful to be alive instead of worried about what diseases my ancestors might have carried. Standing there in the hot Texas sun, I did feel grateful. Something about the cemetery. All those headstones pointing to the final resting places of what used to be people. What did it matter who my parents had been? "So what if I didn't have a traditional childhood, I had good one," I said to Aunt Kate. "That's what is important."

"Thank you for saying that, my dear," she said. Not another person in the world says "my dear" to me the way she does. I like hearing it.

I took several pictures of the grave and several more of the entrance to the cemetery as we left. I knew I'd develop the film, but I doubted I'd ever look at the pictures. As cemeteries go, this one was not particularly picturesque and I hadn't felt any connection at all to the headstones there. I was driving the car we'd rented, so I stopped just outside the gates. "What about going to her house next, Aunt Kate? Can you remember how to get there?"

"Oh, yes, I remember where the house is. Follow the railroad tracks. That way."

I turned down the street expecting to see some small cottage similar to the one Aunt Kate and I had lived in in Houston; I drove carefully, following my aunt's directions and wondering what it would have felt like to have grown up here, to have been driving along seeing these streets as familiar rather than foreign. The house my aunt directed me to stop the car in front of caused me to gasp in surprise. "Here?" I asked. I'd thought perhaps Mission was going to look similar to Benavides, but if Benavides had houses like the mansion my aunt was pointing out, Julia and I had missed them completely when we'd driven out there to see Letha Wilson years ago.

"This is it. Of course, no one lives here now. And it certainly didn't look like this back when my mother was alive."

There, in the middle of town, sat a three-story stone house, which rose grandly up in the middle of a lot as big as some city blocks, a lot which was landscaped into gardens highlighted with meandering rock paths and well-tended flower beds. The entire house and grounds were surrounded by a white wrought-iron fence. Beside the gate, which appeared to be locked as well as latched shut, rested a heavy metal and stone sign informing us that we were parked in front of the Museum of the City of Mission.

"Mother bought the house with some insurance money she got when her first husband died. It wasn't stone as you see it now, it was a large clapboard boarding house. The entire back wing and garage section was added on after Mother sold the house. While we lived there, she took in boarders. None that stayed too long, as I recall. The house was drafty and cold and Mother never found the money to keep it painted. Nor was she much of a housekeeper. The kitchen was down a separate flight of stairs on the ground floor and the dining room was up above it on the second floor, so most of the time we ate in the kitchen. Frequently, during the times we had no boarders, she and I ate standing up at the stove. Mother hated cooking. I'm sure if she had realized that microwaves and instant meals were soon to make their appearance she'd have hung on a few years longer than she did. Simply for the pleasure she'd have taken from obtaining a three-course meal from such minimal effort."

Aunt Kate was staring up at the house as she spoke. We'd gradually started walking, our feet moving slowly down the sidewalk that extended outside the fence. "Where was your room?" I asked my aunt.

"The bedrooms are all located on the second and third stories. I had one on the back side of the house, on the second floor. There are two bedrooms as well as a living and dining room on the second floor. Upstairs were four more bedrooms, sometimes those were let out." She frowned at the memory. "For years, the only bathroom inside the house was off the kitchen. Two flights of stairs down and through the entire house to get there. I was ten before Mother had one of the third-floor bedrooms converted to a bath. Big old houses aren't all they're cracked up to be, Robin." But I *like* the one Josh and I live in, I started to say.

The strangest thing happened to me. I mentally stripped away the fence and the elaborate gardens and began to visualize the house as a smaller white wooden one. I began to see a strong similarity between the house Josh and I lived in, the one which had been his grandmother's, and the one I had just learned had once belonged to my grandmother. Our house was smaller by half. However, it too was several stories high, with big windows and high-ceilinged rooms, and had deep porches which ran around the entire house. Our house had old oak rockers on the front porch which Rachel and I bought at a yard sale the first year I lived in the house. My rockers looked to be very similar to those sitting out on the porch of the house Aunt Kate and I were slowly walking around. "When did it become a museum?" I asked.

"The people who bought it from Mother's estate fixed it up to look like an English country place and then, after several years, decided to move on. Mission had a way of doing that to outsiders, encouraging them to go elsewhere. When the couple, their name was, I believe, Cooke with an *e*, went for several years unable to find a buyer, they donated the building to the city for a museum. It is also used as a library these days, I understand."

"Did you and Mother help run the boarding house?"

Aunt Kate actually shuddered. "Sandra wasn't anything more than a child when I left home, Robin. I can't tell you what her life was like in this house. I know I disliked living here. And no, we didn't help run the house. No one ran the house. Which is why it wasn't a rousing success, I would suppose."

"Were you poor?" I asked. "What did you do for money?"

"Mother had her ways. I might have gone without new school shoes some years, but there was always food on the table." Aunt Kate sighed heavily. "Robin, your grandmother Aurora Jane Jamison simply was not a conventional person. She'd go out to buy me school clothes and come home with a rabbit jacket despite the fact that the temperature rarely dropped below fifty degrees in the valley and there would be some winters no one would ever put on more than a sweater. We might run out of milk or eggs time after time, but she was never unable to scare up the ingredients for a martini cocktail."

"Is that why you don't drink, Aunt Kate?" I asked. "Did your mother drink?"

"Yes. She drank."

Closed on Tuesdays, read the sign on the fence. Unfortunately this was a Tuesday. I was so anxious to see inside that I briefly considered scaling the fence so I could peer in the windows. "I'd like to see it," I said.

"You and Josh can come visit tomorrow morning before we start back. I'll stay with the boys and Rachel while you take the tour. They can swim in the motel pool," Aunt Kate suggested.

AUNT KATE LISTENED to me rhapsodize about the house she'd been raised in over dinner. Her arms were folded against her chest and she frowned at me several times as I was talking to Josh. Finally, she spoke up. "All old white two- and three-story houses look more or less the same," she said. "It truly isn't remarkable that there are some similarities, Robin. The house you live in is nothing like the old boarding house, nothing like it!"

For some reason I'd been elated to learn that my grandmother had raised her two kids in a house which was now an elegant museum. I couldn't wait to get inside and look around. My grandmother, who'd been such an embarrassment to my aunt, didn't sound all that awful to me. One thing I have noticed is that the farther removed some relative is, the less likely you are to be embarrassed by the unconventional way in which he or she lived. Otherwise, why would the people in Australia consider it a social asset to be able to trace their ancestry all the way back to one of the prison ships?

Aunt Kate continued to look uncomfortable. Aurora Jane wasn't far enough removed for her. "Robin, you really won't find out anything about your past there. The museum doesn't have anything to do with our family. I hate to see you getting so excited about this."

"But it's an adventure," I said to her. "You've never been in the museum, surely there is some mention of Grandmother in the house's history."

"Have it your way," Aunt Kate responded with a sigh.

Josh and I did go look at the house the next day, and I'm glad I went, even though Aunt Kate had been right. The house had changed. In the basement were some black-and-white "before and after" pictures, meant to show both the house's transition and its remarkable comeback. I could understand why Aunt Kate wouldn't have had fond memories of it. During the years she had lived there, the house had looked as derelict and disreputable as any flophouse in any Western movie I'd ever seen. "But I'm glad I know that," I said to her as we drove back to Cypress Springs. "It doesn't pay to romanticize the past."

BUTCH

Susie was the one who talked to Mother. She was hanging up the phone as I walked in the back door. "Your daddy's dog died sometime today, Verona wants you to come over the minute you walk in the door. Hot as it is, old Dog is attracting flies and smelling up a storm." Mother's never been an animal lover, so her words shouldn't have surprised us. Still, Susie and I exchanged a look acknowledging that those words were callous even for Verona.

"I don't doubt Dog grieved himself to death," Susie said. "We could have brought Dog over here to live with us after your father died. I don't know *why* that thought never occurred to me before now."

Poor old Dog. Since Daddy died I doubted he'd had much more than a food pan shoved at him once a day. I found myself agreeing with Susie, we should have taken him in. Too late for that now, however. Much as I wanted to, I didn't take the time to sit down at our kitchen table for a beer. "I'd better get a move on and get this over with," I said to Susie.

"You want to take a nice cold Coke with you?" she asked.

I wanted a beer. One thing I look forward to all afternoon long is that first cold beer after work. "I guess you still don't hold with drinking and driving," I said to my wife. I knew she hadn't made any radical shift regarding her thoughts on the subject of her husband walking out the door with his truck keys in one hand and a beer can in his other hand. Susie's a great wife, I don't mind that she has her ways. She doesn't approve of drinking, but she keeps beer in the house for me, whiskey as well. However, it's against the law to drink and drive and if you don't know it, then just pull up in our driveway and hop out of your pickup with an opened beer in your hand. Susie will be more than happy to remind you.

"Have a beer before you go, I could live with that," she offered.

That's what I mean. She's real tolerant. I got lucky when I married Susie. "I better not sit down. Mother will be calling again in ten minutes. Don't hold supper for me, Susie."

"I'll study till you get back, I hate eating alone," she said. Susie's in law school. With both the kids out of the house she decided she wanted something to do. This is her last year. She's planning on working for Legal Aid after she graduates, although no one but me knows that yet.

I've told her that if and when Legal Aid sets up an office out here in Cypress Springs we'll never hear the end of it. People in Cypress Springs think the federal government is for keeping up the roads and running the armed forces. They don't mind paying their taxes, which they regard as the responsibility of good citizens. However, Cypress Springs people are real serious about the general populace pulling their own weight. You want a service, then you damned well ought to be ready to pay for it. Those were my dead daddy's exact words. As a rule, folks around here don't hold with welfare.

I'm gearing up for the day when Verona learns that my wife is going to be offering free legal advice to poor people. Verona thinks Social Security is the scourge of this country. To hear Verona tell it, Social Security cost her two good maids. Never mind the fact that both of the women were past sixty-five and ready to retire.

All it will take to set Verona off on one of her tizzies will be to learn that Susie is going around making sure that people such as the migrant workers who are regulars here year after year are aware of the benefits to which they are entitled. Susie is committed to the idea that migrant workers deserve better than they are getting, and she is ready to Do Something. "Go for it," I've said to her.

Ever since I read some of these articles Susie has brought home, I've felt thankful that we personally don't employ migrants any longer. That part of Salwell Farm and Ranch, Inc., ended back when I was in high school. One winter Daddy up and went out and bought the first mechanical cotton picker this county had seen. It turned out to be a lemon. He spent more time tinkering with it than running it. After several years of that he said to hell with it, and quit the cotton business altogether. I was in college at that time and I wasn't consulted. Neither was Mother. Not that I'd have suggested any different; still, I remember the shock I felt when I came home for some holiday my senior year at A&M and learned we were out of the cotton business.

Mother still carries on about Daddy giving up our cotton allotment. The way these programs are, you give up your space in them likely as not you won't get it back. As far as I can see, between rice, which we still grow, and cattle, which granted has its ups and downs the same as any other business you might name, we're doing okay. Cotton's long gone as far as the Salwell family is concerned. Thank goodness. It might prove to be embarrassing if we still employed migrants once Susie starts representing them.

I'm all for her doing what she proposes to do. But I've tried to warn her to prepare herself for some flack. People in this town have long memories. Verona isn't the only one around here who can tell you blow for blow about the time over ten years ago when Fred Siddons's son and his wife moved out to Fred's farm. Fred told people Freddy was finally coming to his senses and was going to work for his old man. "Freddy's back home to learn the business from the ground up," Fred said. Fred has a farm where he runs cattle, he also owns the town's only insurance agency. Freddy was purposing to become the cattleman in the family.

Next thing I heard, Freddy and his wife had started having these big arguments in the middle of the City Cafe. Apparently she was a screamer and young Freddy didn't mind screaming right back at her. Then Freddy took in this hippie couple with a baby without even mentioning it to his father. All five of them were living out in the old farmhouse on Fred's land. The woman nursed the kid in public and took a job at the truckstop waitressing. The man, who had hair down to the middle of his back and wore love beads, never so much as applied for, much less found, a job. The worst moment for poor old Fred came when the food stamps the hippie couple had applied for arrived in his business mailbox at the post office. Of course, no one opens anybody's mail. However, the postmaster can't help but notice return addresses. And he isn't hesitant to comment on what he sees.

Fred's wife, Doris, who ran the insurance office, came back

to their place of business holding the envelope from the Welfare Department, Food Stamps Division, out in front of her like it was a live snapping turtle she was carrying by the back of the shell. "This is it, Fred, you are going to have to do something. We're never going to be able to hold our heads up in this town if you don't." Evelyn Winter, who was in the office with Fred when Doris walked in, says she tried to tell both Fred and Doris that what some friend of their son's did was no reflection on Fred and Doris. But of course that wasn't the way they took the fact that food stamps were being delivered to their business post office box. Fred and Doris took that very personal. Freddy and his wife and their hippie friends left Cypress Springs in a matter of days. I never heard any details concerning the circumstances.

Lupe was in the kitchen when I arrived at Mother's. "Donde está Mama?" I asked her.

Lupe raised her eyes to the ceiling and informed me Mother had taken to bed with a sickness caused by the dead dog—specifically, the sight of the dead dog coupled with the smell of the dead dog and the flies which the dead dog was attracting. If I didn't remove the dog she didn't know what the Señora might do.

"Don't waste your sympathy. Mother will bear up," I said.

"Sí, sí," responded Lupe. I was reasonably sure Lupe hadn't understood a word of my response, which had been in English. If I'd thought Lupe understood English all that well yet, I wouldn't have been so blunt.

Dog was laying on the patio. I could see that he hadn't been dead all that long—his body was barely beginning to stiffen. He was attracting flies, although the smell was mostly in Verona's head. I'd brought a tarp around to the patio with me. I wrapped the dog's body in it and carried it out to my truck. He didn't weigh much at all. Lupe watched me from the kitchen window. Mother was standing behind the curtains at a bedroom window. She was like a kid, standing off to one side, thinking she was invisible, unaware that I could tell she was standing where she was by the pale, well-manicured hand which held the curtain out from the window. I resisted an urge to holler, "Bye, Mother, I know good and well you are watching," and got in my truck and drove over to Julia's.

Danny was the only one home. Their kids, who are in high school and have their own car now, were off somewhere; Julia had gone to a baby shower with Robin.

Danny and I are much better friends than we were when he and Julia first married. I guess the years have mellowed all of us. "Tell me again why we can't just bury the dog without Julia being informed," he said to me. Used to be he most often had this angry note in his voice when he talked to me. Not so much in recent years, however. I think we understand each other. Heaven knows we've been through some things together. You don't get to be Julia's husband for over fifteen years without encountering some trials and tribulations along the way.

"She will want to run the show, trust me on this one. Every goldfish she killed when she was a kid, we had to have a funeral. Since this was Daddy's dog, I figure it would be a good idea at the least to tell Julia he's dead before I bury him."

Danny looked at me and smiled. "Julia as a child, she must have been something," he said.

"You have no idea," I replied.

We'd finished off a six-pack and started on the second as well as polished off two cans of peanuts before I heard Julia's car pull around behind the house. She came in the back door, smiling and looking all happy. It had just been in the last few months Julia had gotten back to where she was acting like herself again. Losing Daddy was real hard on Julia. I hated that I was going to have to tell her Dog was gone now too. I never could predict how something like this was going to affect her.

"Julia, sit down, I've got something to tell you," I said to her. I'd been waiting there for well over an hour and I was ready to get this over with.

"I knew it, the minute I walked in the door and saw that long look on your face, I knew good and well something had happened. It's Mother, isn't it? Something has happened to Mother."

"No, no, nothing like that," Danny said.

Julia shot him a look. "Let Butch tell me," she said to her husband. That's the kind of thing which used to royally piss Danny off. Not that I could say I blamed him. I don't like the idea of Julia depending on me and Daddy the way she's always done, either. It isn't completely healthy. But she got in the habit of doing it long before Danny appeared on the scene and there doesn't seem to have been a whole lot any of us could do to change her. Julia always has had a mind of her own.

"Not one of the kids?" she gasped, clasping both of her hands to her heart. Julia sort of folded herself into a kitchen chair and stared at me all wide-eyed. "Tell me, Butch," she said. "Before I pass out. You know how I hate suspense." I had the oddest flicker of a memory right then. For some reason I found myself thinking of the movie *King Kong,* which used to come on the late show once or twice a year. As a kid Julia had a positive fascination with that damn show. When she knew it was coming on, she'd watch the news with us, then beg me and Daddy to stay up with her so she could see

King Kong. "Stay up and watch it yourself, we have to get up in the morning," Mother used to say to her.

"I can't watch it by myself, I'll be scared," she'd reply.

"Then go to bed like the rest of us," Mother's response would fly right back at her.

"But I *want* to see it!" Julia always said. Nine times out of ten I ended up sitting in Daddy's recliner watching that movie with her. She always sat on the ottoman about three feet from the television until the scary part came on. Then she'd push her ottoman back beside the chair I sat in and hide behind it. I never could understand the fascination that movie had for her.

"Dog's dead, I'm sorry, honey," I said to her.

"Daddy's dog," she said, and her eyes filled with tears. "It's not enough I lose my daddy, now his dog has gone with him," she said to the room at large. Danny and I both nodded sympathetically. "Poor old Dog, I know exactly how he felt. With Daddy gone, he just lost his will to live. I understand, I truly do."

I let out the breath I'd been holding. Julia was going to be okay. She was getting into the theatrics of the occasion.

"How did it happen?" she asked.

"Peacefully, he went in his sleep. It is better this way, Julia," I replied. Despite the fact that it had been years since we'd last conducted a pet funeral, I fell into my role with ease.

"Just like Daddy. Butch, Danny, do you realize that? Dog was completely and totally loyal to Daddy. Dog died the exact same way Daddy did."

We nodded our agreement. Danny reached over and patted Julia's hands, which were clasped in her lap, in a supportive way.

"We'll have to have a funeral," Julia said.

"Of course we'll have a funeral," I agreed, mentally congratulating myself. "I was waiting for you to arrive before I took Dog out to the animal graveyard," I said. "Danny and I can go on out and dig the grave. You don't have to come along just yet, Julia." This had been a dry year—I knew that hacking away in the hard earth would take some time.

We have this plot of land, back in some trees behind the house Julia and I grew up in. For some reason or other, that is where we have always buried the family pets. We've got graves from back before Julia was born, as well as some more recent ones which come from my kids' pets. Julia's two kids, I just that moment realized with a little shock of amazement, hadn't ever had any pets in the first place. That seemed odd to me, Julia grew up with dogs and cats, so did Danny. It seemed a little strange to realize that, so far as I could remember, Robert and Gracie hadn't had so much as a pet rabbit.

Not that the animal graveyard lacked for graves. In addition to the numerous pets from her childhood, Julia had also officiated at several funerals for young calves. These calves happened to have come to Julia's attention before they could be hauled off and disposed of in the way in which most dead farm animals meet their end. Julia has always been sort of a fanatic about the necessity of decent funerals for dead animals.

"You know, Butch, Dog ought to be next to Daddy, that's where Daddy would want him. I think we ought to bury Dog in the real cemetery," she said. "Daddy always said old Dog was more human than most people. And he was Daddy's best friend. Dog *should* be next to Daddy. I'm sure of it."

"The hell you say, Julia. You can't bury a dog in the Methodist Cemetery, it's against the law. You know better than to even suggest something so outlandish." I shouldn't have been so quick to speak. One way to get Julia all bent out of shape in a hurry is to tell her she ought to know better than to do something she's got in mind to do.

"Which law are you referring to?" Julia said, her chin thrust out at me. "Just because your wife is in law school, Butch, that doesn't make you some legal expert. There is no law that says Dog can't be buried next to Daddy and you know it."

Danny was watching us with interested eyes and a little smile he probably didn't know he had on his face. I could have used some support right about then.

"Julia, the First Methodist Cemetery is for people. Not pets. Nobody puts their dogs out there. Think about what you are suggesting, would you just stop and do that? You wouldn't want to be buried next to a dog would you?"

"I'd a sight rather be buried next to a dog than some people I know," she replied. "You're not going to talk me out of this, Butch. If I have to, I'll dig the grave myself. Or call up High Sullivan from the funeral home and get him to do it for me. He's got a special little tractor he uses."

I cringed at the idea of the talk which would get around town if Julia called High and engaged him to do Dog's funeral. If I knew High, he'd fall right in with her. Anything for a dollar. Next thing I knew, she'd be turning up her nose at the tarp I had Dog wrapped in and deciding to buy him a casket.

I made one last attempt to reason with her. "Look, Danny, tell Julia she is way off base here," I said.

Danny gave Julia exactly the same kind of smile Daddy always gave her when she was wheedling him. "Well, Butch, I don't know that it will do any great harm if the First Methodist Cemetery is where Julia wants to bury her daddy's dog," he said. Danny talks real slow as it is—when he's had a couple of beers he really draws the words out. By the time he'd said, "Well, Butch," I'd figured out he wasn't going to give me a damn bit of support.

"Well, hell, let's get a move on, worst that's going to happen is we'll bury the dog and someone will come along and make us move him," I said as I caved in. I don't know why I ever expected any different. There isn't a person alive in the world who can argue with my sister successfully. Danny doesn't even try. Whatever fool idea she comes up with appears to be just fine with him. "Nobody ever got sent to jail for burying a dog, not as far as I ever heard," I said.

By this time it was almost seven in the evening. If we were lucky we'd be able to get in and out of the cemetery without attracting any attention. And as long as we buried Dog in the Salwell family section we'd probably get away with it. Maybe, if we were very, very lucky, we could bury the dog and no one would even learn what we had done.

"I bought some azaleas last week," Julia said. "I'm going to bring them, too. I want to plant them around the fence on the south side."

"Well, get them out, I'll put them in the truck," I said. Danny found some shovels and a water hose, which he tossed in the back of the truck as well.

In the end we also carted out there and planted two live oaks she'd bought for the area right on top of Daddy's headstone as well as the azaleas and of course there was the dog, which I hate to admit we buried right next to Daddy. My only hope is that Mother hangs on long enough to where, when they go to dig her grave, Dog's bones will have decomposed and no one will realize that he got to her spot before she did.

Driving home I said to Julia, "Now don't go telling Mother where Dog is buried. She'll assume he's in the animal graveyard if you don't tell her any different."

"I don't talk to Mother any more than I have to, Butch. I know how she is," Julia assured me.

I didn't say anything back to her. I am sure Julia believed the words she spoke about not talking to Mother any more than she had to. But there is "has to talk to" and then there is "has to talk to." Julia sure "has to talk to" more often than is necessary.

Julia was sitting in the truck between me and Danny. She leaned back in the seat and stretched her legs out across Danny's lap. "That was a great funeral, don't you think, honey?" she asked. "I'm sure Daddy was right there with us, watching and approving. Didn't you feel him there?"

"Well," Danny said, giving her this smile he saves for Julia and only for Julia. "I'm sure if you felt your daddy there, he was there."

"His spirit was there, I'm sure of it," she said.

First thing I said to Susie when I walked in the door was, "Julia is damn lucky, Danny indulges her worse than Daddy did. Not every man would put up with his wife burying her daddy's dog in her mother's spot."

Susie laughed when I told her what we had done. By then I was able to laugh at it too. What the hell, as long as Verona didn't find out about Dog's final resting place, what difference did it make?

ROBIN

Small towns seem to have an inordinate number of funerals. I said that to Aunt Kate this morning on the phone. Usually, if she's in town, Aunt Kate comes out on Saturday and spends the weekend with us. But this weekend, partially because she was just back from her latest trip, but mainly because we had a funeral to go to, she'd decided to stay in Houston. "Seems like one funeral a month lately. Why do you think that is, Aunt Kate?"

"Everyone knows everyone in a small town," she ventured. "When someone dies, everyone goes to the funeral." Aunt Kate was barely back from a three-week African safari. Before Aunt Kate dies she plans to see every single place she's ever been intrigued by. I think she's still got dozens of places on her list. That's good. Once you retire, a purpose for living is critical.

Some funerals are easier than others. I am thinking of old people's funerals. All of us attend wearing somber clothes to pay our respects. "Well it had to be, he or she had a good life, let's be grateful for that," we comment as we move among ourselves. The words ring true.

But when someone young dies, then it is hard. If it was unexpected there is the shock as well. Susan Carson, one of the elementary teachers up at the school, died in a car crash this past week, leaving a husband and three children only barely grown. The oldest was pregnant with what was to have been Susan's first grandchild. Susan's funeral was hard. I don't expect a woman recently turned forty, a woman I sat in faculty meetings with for three years, one with everything to live for, to perish in a car crash.

Julia and Danny stopped by our house on their way home from the church. Neither they nor Josh and I went out to the cemetery. "Ruthie may want to leave. We need to get home," was the excuse I offered for Josh and me. Ruthie, who normally has the weekends off, had volunteered to come on Saturday so Josh and I could both attend the funeral. "Stay as long as you need to," is what Ruthie had said to us as we left. But I was looking for an excuse not to go to the cemetery. I just didn't know what I could say to Susan's family.

"I don't think I ever went to a funeral in my life until I moved out here," I said to the people assembled on our kitchen porch. Besides Julia and Danny and Josh, Ruthie had pulled up a chair and joined us. My kids were running in and out of the sprinkler under the big oak trees. Gracie, who is in high school now, had gone upstairs to pull out a pair of my shorts and one of my T-shirts so she could join them. She's the sweetest kid—looks exactly like Julia except for the fact that she's still much shorter than her mother. She's every bit as natural as Julia always has been as well. If she feels like running around barefoot in our yard with the kids she'll hop right up and do it.

"I can't remember the first funeral I ever attended," Julia said. "Heavens, I grew up going to funerals. I used to love to go out to the cemetery with Mother and our maid. They'd weed and prune around the graves and I'd wander from one headstone to the other making up stories about the people who had died. There's one grave there, the girl was only fourteen years old when she died. The family had a picture of her put in a frame carved into the granite. She had long blond curls and big blue eyes, I asked everyone I knew what she had died of, but I never found anyone who even knew the family. It was the saddest thing."

"I suppose my mother's grave is like that—I doubt people going to the cemetery in Mission know who she was. There wasn't ever much of a family there to speak of, and certainly since my aunt and I left there hasn't been anyone. My mother was only twenty-two when she died."

Ever since our trip to Mission I'd found myself talking

about my mother and grandmother as if I'd actually made contact with them. Somehow or another, seeing where they had lived seemed to have made them more real to me. But I still couldn't close my eyes and call up any real memories. When I tried to, all I got were images of photos I had seen.

"Cemeteries are peaceful places. I was just out there yesterday, watering the trees and shrubs we planted in the Salwell section," Julia said.

"Won't be peaceful long if Verona's poking around in the family plot today," Danny said as he gave Julia a quick little kiss on the top of the head. "You thought of that?"

"Mother's not interested in cemeteries anymore. She hasn't been for years. She'll go to the graveside service for poor Susan for the least amount of time she can before she heads straight for home. Besides, what do I care if she finds out? We had a nice service for Dog and that is what is important," Julia said. Julia has told everyone who'll listen about the nice funeral she provided for her father's pet. It is only a matter of time before someone mentions it to her mother. That is a small town for you. People complain about it, but I personally believe they like it this way. I know I do. There's a safety that comes from all this common knowledge. I'm glad my children are growing up here.

AFTER JULIA AND Danny and Gracie left, Josh went out in the backyard and put the tent up for the kids. They've got a new one, which their grandparents Evelyn and Pete found at the Army Surplus Store. It is big enough for at least a dozen kids. Evelyn said the price was the same for any size tent in the store, so she and Pete went through them all to find the biggest one there. Josh says he wishes they hadn't gone to all that trouble. This tent is the kind the entire platoon gets together to assemble. Josh finally had to get me and Ruthie both to come out and help him get it up. It was that complicated. One side would go up and the other would collapse— that sort of thing. And there were a million or so of the stakes to hammer into the ground.

"We're not taking this down until they outgrow it," Josh said when we finally got the thing up. That was fine with me. This is another great thing about little towns. You don't bring everything inside at night for fear it will walk off.

After supper the kids had their baths and took their sleeping bags out to the tent to spend the night. Josh and I sat on the kitchen porch in the rockers sipping iced tea and talking. I could hear Rachel's voice starting in on the ghost stories. From experience we knew all three kids were within thirty minutes of heading toward the back door screaming hysterically. About the time it got good and dark they'd hear a sound and they'd be out of the tent and inside the house like a shot.

"Rachel ought not tell those stories," I said to Josh.

"No fun if you're not scared," Josh replied. "Didn't you ever sleep out in the backyard?"

"No, the first time I ever slept in a tent was the time you and Rachel and I went camping in Yellowstone," I reminded him.

I SUPPOSE IT is human nature to compare the childhood your children are experiencing with the one that you had. All day long I'd kept coming back to the fact that Justin, our youngest, who is four now, was the same age I'd been when I'd gone to live with my aunt. Rachel talks about the trip to Disney World we took the year she turned three. Justin can tell you about things we did last year without hesitation. It seemed to me as if I ought to have some memories of, at the least, my third year.

"What's the first memory you have?" I asked Josh.

"I remember when my big sister threw a golf ball and hit me in the head. I had to get stitches."

"How old were you?"

Josh frowned while he thought. "I have no idea—two, two and a half. Why?"

"It seems to me as if I ought to remember something of my life before my parents died," I said.

"Is that bothering you again, Robin?" he asked me.

"I guess maybe it is," I replied. "I'm going to phone Aunt Kate. It has occurred to me to ask her something."

AUNT KATE AND I weren't on the phone but maybe ten minutes. Afterwards I went back outside and sat on the porch beside Josh. It was your typical peaceful Saturday evening. The kids were still in the tent and the sun had completely dropped out of the night sky. Our kitchen porch faces the town of Cypress Springs. Although I'd never thought of this before, the house Josh and I lived in, the one which had been built by his grandparents, was technically the last house in town. Past our house there were several fields belonging to Josh's dad and then his family's rice dryer. After which you were out of the city limits.

Our kitchen porch faced the south side of town. Sitting on it, we could see the lights go on in his mother's kitchen. Beyond that, dotted here and there all across town, the lights in the houses were being turned on. Between the front porch lights and the moonlight, Cypress Springs managed without streetlights quite nicely.

292 • EXCUSE ME FOR ASKING

"It's sad that kids growing up in the city don't get to see the stars come out," I said.

"But they have a choice of four or five movies on the weekend. There are compensations," Josh responded.

His words surprised me. I'd always assumed Josh felt exactly the same way about small towns that I had come to feel. "Aunt Kate says it drove her nuts that there wasn't a decent library within fifty miles of where she grew up. Much as she likes to visit us, she'd never live anywhere but Houston," I said.

"I'm sure there are lots of people who feel that way," Josh said.

"Do you sometimes wish you'd stayed in Dallas?" I asked him. I hadn't known Josh at all during the years he lived in Dallas. I really couldn't picture him there, even as a tourist.

"No, I like it here, I just don't think it's perfect. Some of the things a large city has I wouldn't mind having here. I simply don't want them enough to live in a city. Libraries are one thing I do miss. Movies are another."

"You're right, of course. Mission, which is a lot bigger than Cypress Springs, wasn't perfect either."

"Did your aunt tell you what you wanted to know?" Josh asked me.

"Yes, she did," I said.

IT WAS THE thing about funerals. As soon as I had mentioned that the first funeral I'd ever attended had been in Cypress Springs I'd started asking myself this question: surely I went to my mother's funeral, didn't I? Aunt Kate had just confirmed that fact for me on the phone. She and I both went to Mother's funeral. It had been a small service held, not in a church, but at a funeral home. There were at the most fifty people in attendance. No music except the funeral parlor's tape player playing appropriate recorded funeral songs through their speakers. The casket had been closed.

Aunt Kate said the main memory she had was of those awful scratchy tapes. If she'd listened to them ahead of time she'd have said "No, thank you" to the music part of the service. There wasn't a graveside service. Aunt Kate had seen no need to prolong something that wasn't going to improve itself with extended ceremony. The entire time she was telling me this I'd had my eyes shut, trying as hard as I could to see what she was talking about. But I didn't have a single memory of my mother's funeral.

"What about my grandmother's funeral?" I had asked her. That is when I learned there hadn't been a funeral at all for Aurora. Per her written instructions her body was cremated and her ashes strewn over the state of Texas by a pilot she had commissioned to do the job before she entered the nursing home. "She had it all written down," Aunt Kate said. "Every arrangement made, everything paid for in advance. When she wanted to use it, her mind was clear as a bell."

"What about my father's funeral," I had asked Aunt Kate on the phone. Before she could say a word it came back to me— he didn't die when my mother did. I kept forgetting I knew that. Still, I continued to think of him as dead, the same as my mother.

There was another thing about my father. Along with the mental photo images of Mother, Aunt Kate, and Grandmother, I'd started seeing photo images of my father. Only, as far as I knew, I'd never seen pictures of him. So either my mind was making up a picture to fit what I'd heard of him, and one to go along with the pictures I had seen, or else I was actually remembering my father.

"Did he have a blond flattop and wear glasses?" I had asked my aunt earlier that evening on the telephone. "And were he and my mother almost exactly the same height?"

"Yes, that description more or less fits, Robin," she'd said to me.

"I think I can remember him, Aunt Kate." As soon as I said that to her I felt a tremendous wave of sadness sweep over me. I'd read an article lately, one of those exposé kind of things. In this one, it was suggested as fact that John F. Kennedy didn't die in Dallas. The author argued that the Camelot President was still alive but trapped inside a deep coma, his whereabouts, his actual existence, the occasion of a giant hoax perpetuated for the good of the country. That article may have been where this vision came from:

There is a hospital bed and a blond, flattopped man attached to tubes and wires. He is thin under the sheets, almost emaciated. However, he is breathing on his own—I can see the slight rise and fall of the sheet over his chest. The tubes are for food, the wires, blood pressure monitors. He is alive but in a deep, deep coma. On the table beside the bed sits a pitcher filled with cool water. I can see the moist beads of dampness collecting on the outside of the clear glass. Sunlight comes into the room and reflects off the lenses of his black plastic–framed glasses, which rest on the bedside table beside his water glass and box of tissues.

"Is my father still alive in a nursing home?" I had asked Aunt Kate.

"Whatever gave you that idea?" she asked.

"It just occurred to me to think that."

Aunt Kate was silent for a minute. No, she told me, my father, to the best of her knowledge, remained in the prison hospital only briefly. His injuries were a broken leg, cuts and abrasions, nothing life-threatening.

"Prison?" I asked. Why wasn't I surprised at the word? Surely my aunt had never revealed this fact to me before this time.

"It was so stupid. The two of them tried to hold up a liquor store. Your father didn't have a weapon. Apparently when the store owner reached under the counter for the gun he kept there Kyle panicked and threw a bottle of vodka at him. Besides some broken bottles and a cut on the poor man's head, there was no damage to speak of. Had not your mother been killed as they fled from the scene I'm sure your father would have gotten off with some kind of probation. As it happened, however, the judge threw the book at him. He was sentenced to six years in Huntsville."

"He got out when I was ten."

"And disappeared, Robin," Aunt Kate had said. She went on to admit to me that the year Rachel was born she hired a private detective to try to find my father, all because of how distraught I was that I didn't have any information about my parents. She says she has a file three inches thick to document that the detective looked. "He left no stone unturned, Robin," she had said. The detective's best surmise was that Kyle Connors changed his name when he left prison. That would have made sense, I suppose. How else could he have started over? It would also explain why neither my aunt nor I nor the family he had in Benavides ever heard from him again.

"Why didn't you tell me this earlier?" I had asked my aunt.

"I just couldn't bring myself to," she told me. "I knew that I shouldn't have kept it from you, Robin. I just never could seem to find the right time to tell you."

As I hung up the phone, I'd felt tired. I always knew this, I told myself. I always knew my father went to prison. Otherwise I would have felt surprised at hearing the news tonight. Before going back out on the porch to join my husband, I had closed my eyes and tried to see my father again. I could see him young, like my mother. When I mentally put him back in the hospital bed I'd seen him in as Aunt Kate started talking, I realized that that image also was of a very young man. I'd been right all along. My father had died for me at the same time my mother had.

"DO YOU THINK Aunt Kate should have told me about my father years ago?" I asked Josh.

"Would knowing about your father have made a big difference, changed your life in any way?" Josh asked me.

"I guess not," I replied.

"I think your Aunt Kate did the best she could, Robin. You couldn't ask for any more than that."

"Should I tell the kids?" I asked.

"About your father?" Josh asked me. I could hear in his voice that he was surprised at my question.

"I don't want them to grow up with question marks the same way I did. When you don't know the truth, you assume it is something too awful to be spoken of."

"Not necessarily," he said. "Tell them whatever you feel like, but don't be surprised if they aren't all that interested. They're kids, Robin. The fact that you lost your parents when you were four isn't relevant to them."

"I'm going to tell Julia," I decided. I needed to tell someone.

PART VI

VERONA

In the years since Tom passed on, I have done my best to keep myself busy. Most of the advice I've been given from well-meaning friends has been to do that very thing. "Keep yourself busy, Verona, it will get easier," they have said to me. "The passage of time will help, and you will find that your grief won't always be as sharp and piercing as it is today." When people start talking like that I just nod my head and change the subject. Nothing so boring as a woman harping on her own troubles.

I don't like to think of death or funerals or who is going to be resting where. Used to be I was faithful to a fault about keeping up the Salwell family cemetery plot, but these days I don't care if I never lay eyes on that place again. Let someone else tend to the clipping and mowing and watering through the long hot summers, for some reason the cemetery has gotten to where it makes me feel uncomfortable. Julia can look after the family plot; Julia and Susie and Butch can all three of them take care of it. They're younger than I am. I've done my time.

I'll never get over the shock of my own husband's demise. "It's a blessing Tom went without warning, that he didn't linger and die a wasting death the way Claude did," Millie at the beauty shop said. Claude was Millie's younger brother. Claude did not die of cancer the way they gave out. He died of a socially unacceptable disease, which was the direct result of the way he lived his life. I don't think it is polite to dwell on this, but if Claude in his youth hadn't been known to frequent the house of ill repute which used to be located back off Highway 90 right outside of Stillwell, he would be alive today. I also know that Claude and several others I could name had the habit of going to Reynosa on Saturdays and not returning home until late in the day on Sunday. Sometimes it was as late as Monday morning before they would roll back into town. They said they were going to the horse races over in Mexico, but we all knew different. Not to speak ill of the dead, but your chickens do have a way of coming home to roost. I was always thankful my own husband wasn't the type to get involved in such shenanigans. Tom was a good Christian man, I couldn't have asked for a better husband.

I never thought it would be me being referred to as the wife of the deceased. Death comes to us all, of course I know that. But when all is said and done, I didn't expect it would be my own husband laid out for viewing at the funeral parlor. I don't think that I'll ever get used to being a widow. I can't go down the hall to my bedroom without looking around to see what article of clothing Tom has left scattered about. It would be such a relief to stumble over his shoes left right in the doorway where I couldn't miss stepping on them. Or to have to pick up the smelly socks he took off and left on the floor right beside his recliner in the den.

I can't cook for one person. At the least I cook enough for a family of four—leftovers Lupe can eat or take home with her when she goes to visit her relatives on the weekends. I threw out the *Better Homes and Gardens Cooking for One Cookbook* that Sandy Paben gave me. "This book has been so helpful to me," she said, "so I went out and bought one for you, Verona." The minute she left the house I put the book straight into the garbage can. I am not cooking for one and that is all there is to it.

Since Tom passed, I have been going up to the church several mornings a week to help out in the office. Fridays I usually end up staying most of the day because it is generally Friday afternoon before I can type and run off seventy-five copies of Sunday's bulletin. That's too many, but we are ever hopeful. When I go, I usually take something I've baked along with me for Brother Simpson to carry home with him. I subscribe to the *Southern Living* cookbook series. Their dessert books have some wonderful recipes, which I've been trying out.

Brother Simpson is the skinniest man I think I have seen. I've been telling him that I am going to fatten him up if it is the last thing I do. He's got a wife, but I don't know what the Methodist Church is coming to—she is as skinny as he is and drives into Houston every day to go to work, leaving him out here to fend for himself. Their daughter, who is in high school now, is every bit as skinny as her parents. I just don't think that family eats enough.

I had no idea the extent to which people impose upon the men of the ministry. You would not believe the people in this town, the vast majority of them women, who show up at the church regularly to hold forth about their woes. Some of them have appointments scheduled the way you'd call up and make an appointment to see your doctor.

"You should send them packing," I've said to Brother Simpson. "They are wasting your time." No wonder it is Friday afternoon before he can get the information together for Sunday's bulletin. There have been times when I've come close to pulling out the hymnal and choosing the hymns myself, he is so far behind. Brother Simpson always says pastoral counseling is a big part of his job and I shouldn't worry about him, he enjoys what he does. "Maybe counseling is part of your job, but you should remember that a little advice-giving goes a long way," I said. I've yet to be convinced that he knows the point at which counseling stops and being imposed upon begins.

When I got the news that Wiley Sutton had died (it was a car wreck right in the middle of Front Street), I could have used some counseling myself, but I have more pride than to run up to the church at all hours of the day and night spilling my guts. I didn't say a word to anyone although Wiley's passing did hit me hard. When you have only had intimate relationships with two men in your life and suddenly both of them are dead, it can cause a person to stop and think. Not that Wiley and I were ever close, but we did have this shared history. It hurts knowing he isn't still here with us in the land of the living. Somedays I get so despondent I just don't know what I am going to do. I don't let on, though, I've always been one to keep a stiff upper lip and you won't catch me changing my ways in my old age. Not that I feel old yet. I don't like to think of age, much less talk about it, but it never hurts to prepare yourself. When I think of all that I have had put on me in my lifetime, I don't suppose it should come as any surprise to me that I am still having to struggle to maintain my equilibrium. At least, thank the good Lord, I've managed to hang on to my pride.

ROBIN

"You know Carol Slater?" I said. "Her husband told her when she got pregnant with Cindy and the twins weren't yet a year old he didn't want her to have it! Can you imagine? His own kid! Then when they did amnio and discovered she was carrying another girl he got drunk and stayed that way for two days. Even Verona said it was a disgrace, she never felt so sorry for any woman in her life."

"Julia's been here today, I take it," Josh said to me as he walked in the back door. He says I always greet him at the door quoting the latest gossip when I've been spending time with Julia. He is right and I suppose I ought to watch it, but actually I kind of like hearing this kind of news. It isn't as if the things Julia and I talk about hurt anyone. I am not going around gossiping all over town. Josh is the only person I repeat these things to. Well, I do talk about them with Ruthie, but she is right here in the first place so I am not telling her anything she doesn't already know.

"It wasn't just Julia who heard that thing about Carol's husband, Josh," I said. "Ruthie heard the exact same thing. You know Carol and Dave Slater live out near Ruthie." Carol and Dave Slater's newest baby wasn't the only subject we had talked about, either. "Did you hear about this fruitcake up in Corsicana?" I asked Josh. "Verona Salwell can't hold a candle to this woman. Some psychic told her when she finished building her house she was going to die. She decided the only safe thing was not to ever finish building on it. She had carpenters at work permanently, building on first one addition and then another. Some parts of the house you can't get to from others because the whole thing got so complicated. The woman ended up with over a hundred rooms in her house before she died. It was some twenty years under construction. Julia says the woman was quoted as saying she got to where she couldn't fall asleep at night unless she could hear the sounds of hammering and sawing all around her. She had workmen at her house twenty-four hours a day. Year after year after year."

"You two are making that up!" Josh said.

"No, I swear we are not! Julia read it in the Austin paper. She hopes Verona doesn't run into the same psychic. You know how Verona is always wanting to redecorate."

"I didn't know Verona was in the habit of seeing psychics."

"Actually, I'm not sure that Verona does. At least if she does, Julia hasn't ever mentioned it to me. But Julia has. She wants me to go up to Austin next Wednesday, she's got us both appointments with this woman who reads the cards. Julia heard she's fantastic."

"Robin, you don't believe in this stuff. Tell me you don't believe in it."

"Well, Josh, I don't totally believe it. But, on the other hand . . ."

"Oh, shit," he groaned at me, but he gave me a big smile so I knew it didn't really bother him.

Actually, I think that there are times when you can learn a lot from a psychic. I told Julia that since I know all I really need to know about my parents, it would be fun to see this woman. I could ask her about my father without worrying about what the answer was going to be. I mean, since I've learned he was healthy when he got out of prison and that he knew where I was all along, I no longer worried that he might have been searching for me all these years or anything like that. So if she said, say, that he lived in Arizona and was married again with four kids and grandkids even, I could say, "Oh, how interesting." Her answer wouldn't really matter to me one way or the other. Well, it might matter, like, I *would* be interested. But it wouldn't make any difference in the way I go about my daily life. That's what I mean.

The thing I don't believe in doing is to ask a psychic to predict the future for me. Well, not other than perhaps in very, very broad terms. The future can take care of itself as far as I am concerned. If there is good news, it'll be good when I get it. And why hear bad news before you have to? In this particular instance I echo my aunt's sentiments exactly.

Julia wanted to find out if she should go to law school like Susie was doing. And she said she wanted to know how much longer her mother was going to live.

I raised my eyebrows at that.

"Why?" I asked her. Verona looks to be in perfect health. She and Julia were getting along pretty well too. Besides, I do think it seems a trifle macabre to go asking a psychic how much longer your mother is going to be alive.

"It's no accident that Susie has become a lawyer," Julia said to me. "We may need more than one in the family."

"What?" I asked her. Sometimes, when I was talking to Julia, I'd start smiling before she even said anything for me to smile at. We'd been friends so long, I had gotten to where I knew before she opened her mouth when she was going to say something that would make me laugh.

"You heard me, Robin. You think your family is the only one with a checkered past. There are things I could tell you. You have no idea the trouble it would cause if what my father once did got out."

"You already told me about the woman at the coast that he had the affair with," I reminded her. Julia used to talk about this woman who lived down on the coast, had ratted hair and too much jewelry and makeup, and wore polyester pantsuits. She only saw her once, but that was enough for Julia. Julia thinks it was a slap in Verona's face, of course, but she says there were times when she didn't blame her father a bit. "Did I tell you I asked Butch did he call and tell Marla Daddy was dead before or after the funeral?" she said.

Technically this wasn't any of my business, but Julia and I are really close and I was very interested. If that makes this gossip, well then, people have to talk about something, don't they? "When *did* Butch call Marla?" I had asked. Our conversation made me think of some movie I'd seen, one where the woman spent her entire life in love with some man married to another woman. And, in the end, when both the man and his wife died, his kids, who were still little, went to find the mistress. I couldn't remember the details well enough to recall how that happened, but I could see in my head the little boy and his little sister walking up to that cottage. I pictured them as a little Butch and a little Julia.

"He called her before the funeral. Marla told Butch she and my father had agreed years ago she wouldn't come to the funeral out of respect for Mother."

"You're kidding," I said.

"No. Butch went down to the coast after everything was said and done with to see her. He had a letter Daddy left with him to take to her. Daddy asked Butch to mail it if he couldn't go in person, but Butch said he thought it was the least he could do. That is the way Daddy would have wanted it to happen, he said."

"You and Butch are so lucky your mother never found out about Marla," I said. Verona isn't dead yet and if she ever learns about Marla, much less that Butch went to visit her, there is no telling what she'll do.

"Don't we know it! The shit would hit the fan all over town. Only it wasn't Marla I was talking about, Robin. There are things I could tell you, things you wouldn't believe." Julia sounded as dramatic as she ever gets when she said that.

"I'll bet," I said, and left it at that. I sort of thought she was talking about something real at that point, but I didn't want to act overly curious. Julia would tell me more when she wanted to.

Julia has always been fascinated by mysterious stories—hers, mine, anybody's. For instance, she has said she wants to see the museum that used to be my grandmother's boarding house. I told her that the museum itself is nothing special, just a fixed-up old house, actually—with antiques, of course. Frankly, these kinds of museums are sort of common in little towns all around Texas. Inside the house, in the basement, they have photos of what the house was like when the Cooke family bought it from my grandmother. Aunt Kate was not far off the mark when she called the old house a wretched hovel. I'm surprised they didn't simply tear it down and start over rather than have someone come along and fix it up into a showplace. But Julia has decided that the fact that my mother was raised in a house which is now a museum is something that needs more looking into. It is hard to convince her that, as far as I'm concerned, there isn't a reason in the world to go back down to Mission, Texas. That house has no more connection to me than does any other old historical building I've ever been in.

The next day was Tuesday. And then came Wednesday, the day we went to the psychic.

We were on the outskirts of Austin when I noticed Julia staring at the woman driving the car next to us. "Do you know her?" I asked.

"No, but it's weird. This happens to me all the time lately. I see someone, like a flash of them out of the corner of my eye, and I think 'Oh my gosh, that's so and so,' and I turn my head and look again all set to say, 'Well hi, what on earth are you doing here?' and it's some person I've never seen before in my life. I think maybe I'm going crazy. Or perhaps I need glasses."

"The very same thing happens to me sometimes. I think if there's a person who's been on your mind, it can be sort of normal to think it might be them."

Julia rolled her eyes at me. "Does the woman driving that tan Toyota look like my cousin Kaye or doesn't she?" she asked. She sounded angry.

I looked again at the woman in the car next to us. Truthfully, she didn't look like Julia's cousin to me. But I hated to say that. "It's probably her eyes, or the eyebrows. That's it—see how that lady's eyebrows run straight across her face? Kaye has eyebrows like that. And her hair is almost the same color as Kaye's. I've seen Kaye wear the identical hairstyle. I can see how she could make you think of your cousin Kaye."

"When you first looked at her, did you think, 'Oh, there's Julia's cousin Kaye?'"

"Actually, no, but your cousin hasn't been on my mind. Maybe she's been on yours."

"I never think of Kaye. It has been months since she has even crossed my mind. You know, even if we are second or third cousins, I barely know her. And I most definitely don't think about her!"

By then the woman had realized she was under scrutiny and had started giving us nervous little looks. I don't even want to speculate on what she thought about us and what we were up to. What Julia did next didn't improve matters as far as that poor lady was concerned.

"Hi, Kaye," Julia yelled and she began to wave her hand excitedly. "Imagine running into you over here in the middle of Austin. We don't see each other for months on end when we both live in the same two-bit little town and here we go running into each other in the middle of Austin! Small world, isn't it?" Since both cars had their windows rolled up, and Julia at least had her air conditioning going full blast, it was unlikely the woman, whatever her name was, understood Julia's words. I don't know if that was good or not.

The poor woman kept looking at us and then looking away. I imagined she was praying for the light to turn green so she could drive on to wherever she was headed before Julia got any more agitated. Just then the light changed and the driver of the car behind us didn't wait a split second before he laid on his horn. The lady in the car next to us didn't hesitate either, she got her car into gear and peeled out of there. Julia waved one more time before she put her foot down on the gas pedal.

"Maybe it was Kaye's half sister she never knew she had," she said. "The same way that if Marla and my dad had children I'd have some half siblings I know nothing about."

"Good Lord, Julia," I said.

"I think I'm going to ask Doris about that, too," she said.

"Who?"

"Doris. The lady we're going to see," she said.

I don't think I had heard her name before. I had expected a psychic to have a name slightly more exotic than Doris Jones. "She charges sixty dollars for a half-hour appointment, one hundred dollars for an entire hour. Are we sure we want to do this?" I asked.

"Of course we do. It's too late to cancel now, anyway. She's exactly like the dentist. Unless you give her twenty-four hours' notice you have to pay whether you come or not."

JULIA WENT BACK into the kitchen with Doris first. I sat in the living room of the little house, leafing through a *Family Circle* magazine and listening to traffic sounds. Doris had all the blinds pulled down and she had heavy drapes over the windows as well. However, outside noises intruded regardless of the window coverings. That was probably just as well. Otherwise I might have been able to hear what Doris and Julia were saying to each other.

Doris lived on one of those streets that was residential years ago but had become a four-lane thoroughfare in recent times. She was about fifty or sixty years old and had pictures of her children and grandchildren lining the mantel across from the chair I'd chosen to sit down to wait in. The front part of her house was dusty, smelling almost as if it had only recently been opened up after an extended vacant period. I could smell some kind of stew aroma coming from the back of the house, and I surmised Doris had her dinner bubbling away in a Crock-Pot as she worked.

When it was my turn to walk back into the kitchen, I discovered I had been right about the smell. Doris had an avocado green Crock-Pot plugged in on her kitchen counter. I'd have bet money she was cooking a beef stew in it. She also had a combination television-radio on the counter with aluminum foil balls balanced on the antenna ears. This room wasn't dusty. The windows, with the blinds pulled up and the curtains tied back, looked out onto a nice backyard. I felt a lot better about Doris once I settled into one of the chairs at her kitchen table and got a chance to look around. Her kitchen looked nice and homey.

Doris told Julia she should most decidedly pursue advanced studies. However, she noticed that Julia herself is gifted with extremely well-developed psychic abilities. Doris saw Julia in a profession less conventional than the legal field. Even if Julia should go to law school, she said, it would be important that she stay open to options which will be appearing to her. She predicted Julia's family would see several major changes within the next year but couldn't say if that meant Verona was going to die. Julia told me she's had the feeling that her mother isn't long for this world for some time now. "Verona's started acting old," she said. "I can't put my finger on what it is, but she's passed some invisible line regarding proximity to death. I know it." Julia also asked Doris if the crime her father committed (which I assumed meant the adultery) would ever come to light.

"Not in the way in which you are afraid it will happen," Doris told her. Julia said that was enormously reassuring for her to hear.

We were halfway back home to Cypress Springs when Julia said, "I'm going to take the bull by the horns. I've avoided it long enough. I'm going to do what needs to be done about the patio at my parents' house." Then she paused for several minutes as she lit a cigarette. Finally she added, "Doris said that I ought to be sure to tie up loose ends of my past before I embark on the next chapter of my life. You know, I need a clean beginning."

I didn't ask what the patio at her parents' house had to do with Julia starting law school, because I was busy thinking over the things Doris had told me, which hadn't made a whole lot of sense. At least I wasn't able to make much sense out of them at the time. Doris had said I was going to have several more children, which I sincerely doubted. The doctors tied my tubes at the same time they delivered Justin. When I said as much to Doris she frowned at me like I wouldn't know that particular fact about myself. "The cards don't lie," she informed me. I found myself hoping my doctor hadn't lied. I had specifically chosen not to have Justin at a Catholic hospital because they won't let the doctors do tubal ligations there. Josh and I really didn't want any more kids.

Doris also suggested that I pay attention to the number five and that I eat more bananas. I don't particularly care for bananas and I've heard all I care to hear about the number five as well as most of the other numbers. The boys listen to "Sesame Street" regularly. I thought it was kind of cute when Rachel watched it, but "Sesame Street" has gotten very, very old the third time around. Julia and I might have had a better time shopping in Austin that day. At least I'd have come home with something concrete to show for my one hundred dollars. When I asked Doris about my father, she said that for some unknown but significant reason, my father did not wish to contact me at this time.

"Does that mean he is dead?" I asked her.

"I assumed that he was. Either dead or wishes to be," Doris replied. I can remember her words exactly.

Now, to be perfectly honest, I think that Doris must have some psychic abilities or she never would have said that the way she did. Because it fits what I know about my father perfectly. I was careful about the way I phrased the question. What I said was, "I haven't heard from my parents in some time. Could you give me any information on my father?" I do think the subject of my parents is a dead issue now. I'm not going to ask any more questions. I know all there is to know.

Julia says that she thinks going to consult Doris was one of her more inspired ideas, that Doris was just what she needed to get herself pointed in the right direction.

IT WASN'T TOO long after the first trip to Austin that Julia quit smoking. As far as I could tell she just up and quit. She threw out all the cigarettes in the house and told Danny he was quitting as well—they had kids to set an example for, and she wasn't having cigarettes in her house. Danny keeps some cigarettes out in his truck glovebox, but he's cut way down as well. That's good, I guess, because Doris told Julia it was imperative he give them up entirely to avert some health disaster. She didn't say cancer but, as Julia says, what else could it be?

We've been back to Austin to see Doris several times. I don't know—somehow or another I don't see this as doing either one of us all that much good. Although, as I've told Josh and Danny, if they were to see Doris for themselves they'd see she is nothing more than a very ordinary housewife. Julia says the same thing. Doris simply uses her abilities the way all of us could if we troubled ourselves to learn how to do what she does.

Julia and I had our first and last garage sale recently. It turned into more work than we bargained for, and I never plan to have another one. We spent four days hauling things outside and pricing them and all day Saturday selling them. The kids had a ball, but I can think of better ways to earn money in the future. Unfortunately Julia got her mother all upset right at the end.

Julia let the cat out of the bag when she said, "I'll buy that, I know just the place for it," about this little cast-iron dog doorstop that Evelyn had brought over and marked one dollar. Verona was standing there. Julia said she hadn't seen her mother, but the truth is she knew she was there.

"Where are you going to put that tacky little thing?" asked Verona.

"On Daddy's grave, to keep him and Dog company," Julia said.

Verona's eyes widened. "What do you mean, Daddy and

Dog?" She closed her eyes and then opened them again and glared at Julia. "You didn't!" she said, sort of sucking the words in as she said them.

"Sure did. Ask Butch. Or Danny. They were both there. Don't worry, Mother, we had a nice little service. We'd have let you know, but it was one of those spur-of-the-minute things."

Verona turned on her heel and stalked off. Driving away, she passed Julie Garcia, pushed by her sister Maria, coming to the sale. She was so angry she didn't stop and say *how are you* to the girls, much less *remember me to your mother and be sure and call if there's anything I can do for you.* Verona always makes a big deal out of speaking to them, so it is noticeable when she does not. I watched her drive away in such a huff that she covered the poor girls with dust and probably scared them half to death in the process. I saw Maria push Julie almost into the ditch because she wasn't sure Verona wasn't fixing to run them down with her car.

I've had it with garage sales and psychics.

JULIA

I think it was an excellent idea to consult Doris that first time. I've been back to see her a total of four times since my first visit. Robin has always gone with me, but she doesn't consult Doris herself every time. Robin says she doesn't have any burning questions she wants answered right now, but I think that she is simply avoiding what is staring her in the face. She does have a father out there somewhere. At least there is a chance she does.

Doris has been extremely helpful to me. I can't imagine what I would have done had I not had her to fall back on during the past year. To say that my life has not been easy this past year is a gross understatement. I thought the year Daddy died was the worst I'd ever feel, but I've come to realize that all through that period of time I was avoiding dealing with reality. Sort of along the lines of the way an animal hibernates through the winter. Not that I was wrong. I did what I had to do for my own survival. But my father is dead now, and the time has arrived for me to come into my own. This is how Doris expresses it. I have to say that it has not been easy. My family, in particular my mother, has given me grief every step of the way.

Danny and the children didn't really understand what I was after, but they at least refrained from criticizing me up one side and down the other. I did spend a significant amount of time away from the house, most of it at Mother's, although certainly that was not because I was enjoying being over there. I explained all that to Danny. "I have to take care of some very important business and I have to do it now," I said to him. "Life is fleeting. You can't put things off until tomorrow forever. Eventually you get to where you don't have a tomorrow." That is what happened to my daddy, you know. He certainly didn't plan to die and leave unfinished business behind the way he did. If you don't work things out while you are in body, you will be doomed to hang around after your death trying to resolve them. And of course it is harder to accomplish anything when you don't have your body. All Danny had do to was look at Mr. Forester and he should have been able to see that.

Butch and Susie both tried to convince me that if I was determined to take up the patio, I ought to at least hire someone to help me with all the heavy work. "Look, Butch, it is to save your skin, not to mention your soul, that I am doing it this way," I said to him. You wouldn't think I would have had to draw him a picture like that. He suggested Lupe's cousin could come over and help me with the digging and carting off. "Just because Alfredo doesn't speak English doesn't mean he doesn't *talk*, Butch," I said.

"I give up. Suit yourself, Julia. Do things the hard way if that is what you want. When has anyone ever been able to talk sense to you anyway?" It really hurt my feelings when Butch said that to me. After all, what I was doing was mainly for his own protection. But, as I said, at least I had Doris on my side. She made a tremendous difference.

I was so sure of what I had to do. I was going to find those bodies and give them a decent burial. Send them to God. What caused me problems was exactly how to go about it. I didn't want to expose my father's memory to public horror. And I certainly don't want to get any of the rest of us in trouble with the law. That wouldn't have brought those poor migrants back to life.

I still don't know what their names were. I worried that when I did find the bodies I was going to have a hard time commending them to God since I wasn't sure of what to call them. Have you ever attended a funeral where there weren't any names for the deceased? Everywhere I turned I ran into obstacles. For the want of a better solution I called them Juan and Juanita Doe because I did know that they were Hispanic.

Although Daddy fired the gun and he and Butch buried the bodies and laid the brick patio on top of them, it had always been Mother I blamed. If only she hadn't screamed. That is what scared Daddy so bad that the gun went off. If she hadn't screamed, then Daddy wouldn't have shot them. All along it seemed to me that Mother is the one who should have shouldered the lion's share of the guilt. For years, in my mind, the reason for the two deaths had more to do with Mother's mouth than my father's finger on the trigger of his shotgun.

One of the things I've come to see in recent days is that I was wrong to blame Mother to the extent that I did. Doris says that Mother's reaction was fright, the same as Daddy's, and that if she'd had the gun she'd have shot and he'd have screamed. I confess I had never thought of it that way before.

THE PATIO, WHICH Daddy and Butch laid over thirty years ago, wasn't hard to remove. The concrete mortar between the bricks had gone dry and crumbly, and it was simply a matter of loading up the wheelbarrow time after time and taking the bricks back to behind the horse shed where Butch and I kept our horses when we were kids. There weren't any horses there any longer. The shed had been empty for years and years. It was in such poor repair that I suggested we go ahead and pull it down. Mother said for heaven's sake, she didn't want to get involved with the horse shed—a good wind would knock it over and then she'd burn the rubble. The older Mother has gotten the less she has wanted to listen to reason. It scared me to see this, because if Mother had died and left me with all these questions unanswered, it would have been all that much harder for me to get everything sorted out. Doris and I both realized that I couldn't get on with my real life purpose until I had taken care of the unfinished business my parents created.

"Mother, I'm taking the patio out," I said to her when she asked what on earth I thought I was up to the morning I started work. "Don't give me that aggrieved look, you've said it needed to be carted off for years. All the patio is is weeds and broken bricks. I'm doing you a favor."

We were both thinking of the bodies buried underneath the bricks, but we had never mentioned them out loud before and we didn't start doing it then. It took forever, but I got the entire area cleared.

I FINALLY GAVE it up as fruitless. It took me days and days to arrive at this point, and my hands did look horrible. I should have used gloves. However, I hadn't wanted to stop even long enough to mess with gloves. I had wanted to get the job over and done with. I think that is normal—once you finally tackle something you've put off for most of your life, you don't want to be messing around looking for gardening gloves. You want to go ahead and get what needs to be done, done.

"What are you going to do now?" Mother asked me. "You're not going to leave that dirt pile in the middle of my backyard. This is just like you, Julia. You start some big project without thinking it through. At least when the bricks and weeds were still there I didn't have the prospect of a muddy pit staring me in the face. What do you think that area is going to look like once a good rainstorm comes along? People will be tracking in dirt and filth right and left."

I sat back and let her rant and rave. No one ever goes in and out the doors to the patio. When I first started work out there, I had to almost get a crowbar to open the doors the first time. I swear to you they'd rusted shut.

I didn't rush the job. It took me a good two weeks but I went over every inch of the area. Doris said three feet, at the most four feet should be deep enough. She saw Juan and Juanita clearly and their graves were very, very shallow. It wasn't easy to do. Some of that dirt was as solid as cement. In most places I sifted through the earth a good five feet down. I finally arrived at the conclusion that there weren't any bodies under the bricks.

That is the point at which I called Doris and made an appointment to drive back up to Austin for her to consult the cards for me. Mother suggested that I call Millie and get myself a manicure before I went anywhere. "Have you looked at yourself in the mirror lately?" she asked me. That is typical Verona, concerned about externals when I was doing my dead level best to get her out of a mess she and she alone created.

It seemed to Doris that she could hear running water near their graves. I felt the sickest sensation when she said that to me. The only place that could possibly refer to is the pet cemetery, which is near the river. Surely they didn't bury them there, I thought. I decided I was going to have to ask Butch. I didn't have anyone else to turn to. And I certainly couldn't excavate the entire pet cemetery. It is a huge place, bigger than a football field.

Driving back from Austin a thought occurred to me. I get some of my best ideas when I am driving. That is why I always like to drive myself if it is possible. There was one other thing I could try. This was definitely the last ace up my sleeve. I really wanted to take care of Juan and Juanita myself. Sort of like this would be my last gift to my father, who died doing for me. I knew that I had depended on other people entirely too much in my life and I was ready to break that cycle.

I spoke to Doris on the phone and she agreed it was worth a try. I hadn't smoked dope since I was in college and then I only tried it a few times. Back then I never cared for marijuana cigarettes, but I did get some really neat highs from marijuana brownies. Doris says she never recommends this sort of thing to her clients. However, she has seen it work. The heightened awareness can lead you to recall things you've forgotten you know. We both agreed that of course I knew exactly where the bodies were buried. I am bound to have known this since the night the accident occurred. I was eight years old then. That is almost thirty years ago now. Juan and Juanita had been in limbo for thirty years. Enough was enough.

"I wouldn't have the first idea where to get any dope," I said to Doris. The last time I bought any I was living in a dorm in Lubbock, Texas.

Doris didn't know anyone who smoked dope either, but she called one of her friends who was able to put her hands on some. I decided to try it one time and then if that didn't work I'd have to go to Butch.

When I went over to Mother's I noticed Mr. Claywell's truck parked at our house. Mother was having the patio sodded. I'm sure she thought she was covering up the graves before the rains came and exposed the bodies. Little did she know. She didn't ask and I didn't tell her. They weren't there. They never had been.

It was while I was waiting for the dope to arrive in the mail (Doris packed it in foil and put it in a fruitcake tin to make it look like she was mailing me cookies) that I noticed I had started getting a headache every time I looked at the patio for some reason. All I had to do was look out the bathroom window at the patio and my head started to throb. I think maybe this had been happening to me forever and I had just then begun to notice it. Doris says this type of thing is very common. As my perceptive abilities develop I'll become more and more aware over all, she thinks. As

Doris says, perceptivity is not always a blessing. Many times it is a burden.

She's giving a course in how to read the cards to a select few people next month. I definitely plan to take it even if it does mean driving two hours up and two hours back from Austin one night a week for six weeks. It will be worth it. The first time I went to Doris she said she saw me taking advanced courses but not in the legal field. This proves she was right. Because of course I have no interest whatsoever in the law any longer.

"DAMN, DAMN, DOUBLE damn!" I said. "Mine, Mother, they are mine. You may not have any of my brownies." Shit. What a mess. That was all I needed, Mother getting stoned on me. I had decided I ought to do the brownies at Mother's and sleep the night in my old bedroom. To set the stage and maximize the possibilities of insight is the way I reasoned it out. I thought Mother had gone to bed, but apparently she smelled them cooking. At least she says the smell of the chocolate was all over the house. In the end I had to let her have one to shut her up. She sniffed at me that she didn't know why I was carrying on so, that they had a burned taste and I'd better leave the cooking to her and Lupe in the future. "Fine with me, Mother," I said, hoping she'd go on back to bed before the dope took effect on her. It used to take me at least ten minutes. I took the pan of brownies with me to my room and locked the door behind me. "Good night, Mother," I said to her.

The next morning Mother said she had weird dreams during the night. She attributed it to what she ate and told me she ought to have known better than to go to bed on a full stomach.

"Did you dream anything specific?" I asked her. I'd eaten

almost half a pan of brownies myself and I still didn't know where they put the bodies.

"Of course I dreamed something specific, Julia! What do you think? What is a dream if not specific?"

"Well, go ahead, tell me," I said to her.

"It was a dream about someone I used to know. Such a stupid thing I won't dignify it by talking about it."

I didn't press her because it was obvious she wasn't talking about Juan and Juanita. I left to go up to town to visit Robin. "Stay out of my room," I told Lupe before I left. I didn't want her in there poking around. I left the pan of brownies under the bed because I thought maybe I might take one more stab at it before I gave up.

I wasn't able to get back over to Mother's that night. It was Danny's and my turn to chaperone the dance after the football game and Danny wasn't about to let me off the hook. I can't tell you how much I hate the idea that I have been chaperoning high school dances. If it weren't for the fact that I have two kids in high school now, they'd never get me up there. The place gives me the creeps. It hasn't changed one iota since I was in high school. The last thing I ever expected was that I'd return to the high school some day as a chaperone. It's ludicrous, that's what it is. The chaperones were always such old fogies. I'm not like that in the least. Neither is Danny. So what were Danny and I doing standing around watching the teenagers pair off and acting as if we are there to supervise their behavior? What the hell do we care what the teenagers are doing?

I DON'T BELIEVE in putting off what needs to be done and I know that I need to get this issue of Juan and Juanita resolved. Doris says that she thinks a funeral isn't what is needed—if it were, they'd have been where I thought they were when I went looking. She thinks an intercession would do. But how on earth can I arrange an intercession? I don't know their names, I don't even know where their bodies are. When it comes right down to it, I don't know the first thing about them other than the fact that they were young—I'd say probably teenagers, early twenties at the very latest—and both of them had huge dark eyes. They were crouched together on the ground, holding onto each other for all they were worth, when I looked out the patio doors and saw them, so I can't say if they were tall or short, fat or slim.

"Wouldn't someone have missed them?" Doris asked me. "Perhaps if you check the newspapers for that time period you could come up with their names. There was surely some kind of a search when two people didn't come home one night. Even if they weren't from Cypress Springs, someone had to have missed them."

"Doris, they were migrants. Migrant workers who had come in huge trucks with other workers to pick cotton for my dad. No one looked for them. That is how he got away with it."

"Tell me again how he shot them," she said to me. Doris and I were both puzzled, we'd been so sure that if Juan and Juanita weren't under the patio, I'd be able to see where they were when I meditated after eating the brownies. But I hadn't come up with a thing. Nothing. Zip. Nada. It didn't make sense.

"He didn't mean to. Daddy got up and went to the den doors because I'd gone in the bathroom in the middle of the night and heard someone outside. I woke my parents up and told them someone was trying to break in, so Daddy took his gun when he went to look. At the same time he pulled back the drapes to look out, Mother flipped on the outside lights. It all happened so fast. The screech of the drapes on the drapery rod, the flash of the floodlights, Mother's scream, which lasted forever. She was holding on to me by the shoulders, saying, 'Julia, this imagination of yours is going to be the ruination of you, there is no one out there, now you take a good look,' just as she flipped on the light. Then she screamed and her fingers dug into my shoulders so deep I think she left bruises. Daddy was so surprised he pulled the trigger. That is how it happened."

"What happened next?" Doris asked me.

"You're not ever going to tell anyone this?" I asked her. All of a sudden it occurred to me to worry that she'd turn us in.

"Of course not. There is such a thing as the confidentiality issue here," she reminded me.

Of course I remembered that. If I ever started reading cards for people I'd be doing the same thing. What I learned from my clients I would regard as a sacred trust. "Mother and I went to bed. Butch helped Daddy bury the bodies. I didn't actually see them do it, but I've always known that is what they did."

Doris picked up her cards and started dealing them out in a pattern I hadn't seen before. "Don't say a word, Julia," she cautioned me. "Something is coming through."

"Julia," she said, "this is very strange."

I could see that myself.

PART VII

ROBIN

Aunt Kate is slowing down. I have recently begun to notice that she hesitates as she goes up and down the stairs. This past weekend wasn't the first time that I saw her stop midway up and hold on to the railing while she took a deep breath. She has been doing that for some time now. I simply haven't wanted to see it. "Have you noticed Aunt Kate has been slowing down?" I asked Josh.

Josh admitted that he had observed Aunt Kate doing exactly the same things I had noticed.

I really was worried about my aunt, which made me impatient with Julia. Julia's a great friend, but sometimes she is so oblivious. She's enrolled in graduate school at University of Houston. She's getting a degree in psychology, specializing in dreams. Josh and I both were a little puzzled when we first heard this.

"Dreams? You are studying dreams? What can you do with a degree in dreams?" Josh asked her.

I don't believe she answered his question. If Julia doesn't have an answer to a question, she simply acts as if she never heard it. I don't think she has any earthly idea what she will do with a degree in dreams, if there is such a thing in the first place. I've never heard of one myself. However, Aunt Kate says that there is a degree in anything imaginable, so she is sure that it is possible for Julia to get one in dreams.

Danny really is super. He told Julia that he and the kids would keep the home fires burning while she went back to college if that is what she wants to do. Not many men would be so understanding. Josh and I had them all over to dinner one night. At the last minute Julia couldn't come, she had to study. I believe, between one thing and another, this has been happening a lot lately. Julia has been so preoccupied. I told Josh I thought maybe this all began back when she and I started seeing Doris. Josh said, "Nothing doing. Julia has been this way her entire life. She can't lay it off on some woman up in Austin who cooks beef stew in her Crock-Pot while she gazes into her crystal ball." I must have told Josh a dozen times that Doris doesn't even own a crystal ball, but he's talked about her crystal ball so much he almost has me believing in its existence.

IN MY OPINION, Julia became too obsessive about graduate school. She took fifteen hours the first semester and made a four-point, which she was determined she was going to maintain. I warned her that she ought to slow down, that she was going to get sick of it long before graduation. I reminded her that Robert was in his senior year and she was missing out on times with her kids she won't get back. Julia said that seeing her kids in high school gave her the heebie-jeebies, and she wasn't ever going to regret not attending every little function the fools that run the school have up there. I asked Josh how someone who was voted runner-up for homecoming queen as well as Most Beautiful her senior year could have such horrible memories of her own high school years. He said that Julia is probably remembering someone else's high school career. The one she talks about doesn't sound like the one she had to him either.

BECAUSE OF THE tension we both were under, Julia and I had a big fight. I cried after she left because I had never in my life had a fight with anyone like that. Even when I was a kid I never got into screaming matches like the one Julia and I got into. I called Aunt Kate on the telephone and asked her these questions. "When I was little and played with other children did I fight with them?" I asked her.

"I don't recall any fights, Robin, but I am sure that you were involved in the occasional altercation."

"Did I scream 'I hate you' at anyone?"

"Not that I recall."

"Did I tell anyone she was too stupid to breathe?"

"Heavens, no, what are you talking about?"

"Aunt Kate, I just said those things to Julia, I feel so awful," I said. Then I had to hang up because I was crying so hard.

That was not at all like me.

JULIA

It was just one of those weeks. Every person on earth has them sometimes. I wish Robin hadn't taken what I said the way she did. Hell, I can't even remember what it was I did say to her.

She was right, I couldn't maintain the pace at which I started grad school. Second semester, I dropped three of my courses after the first week of classes. I only took two courses that semester. I was getting too stressed out driving back and forth every single day of the week. That way, I only had to go to Houston on Tuesdays and Thursdays. One class was at nine in the morning, the second one was at two-thirty in the afternoon. The first week or two after classes started I drove over to Gulfgate and had lunch and shopped for several hours, but then it occurred to me that if I'd study in the library instead, I wouldn't have much homework to do the rest of the time. It worked out fine that way.

I am still glad that I decided to further my education. I can't tell you all the things I learned. Take the subconscious, for example. Of course I always had one, everyone does, but I went for years not knowing it was there. You wouldn't believe what I now know about the significance of dreams, either. One I had a few nights ago is a classic example of the way your dreams send you signals from your subconscious.

First off, I sat up in bed crying and didn't even know I was doing it until Danny shook me awake. In this particular dream I was a young girl at a big carnival, the Texas State Fair kind of carnival, although I don't think that is what it was. I had on a red-and-green checked taffeta dress with a white lace collar. It had a dropped waist and a pleated skirt. I remember that dress so well, it was my favorite party dress one year when I was in junior high school. Around my neck I wore pearls, which belonged to my mother. My hair was pulled back in a ponytail tied with a bright bow that matched my dress.

As I walked into the fair I carried two children, a boy and a girl. That's the last I saw of me in this particular dream. The next thing I saw was a woman's arms wrapped around the children. The arms put the little boy down somewhere—on a bench, I think. I can't recall that part for sure. There weren't any words in this dream, but the boy knew that if he stayed still and sat quiet as a mouse where he was, she'd come back for him. The arms were tanned and covered with fine white hairs. At the ends of the arms were beautifully manicured hands. That is how I knew this dream was not about me. The arms ended in manicured hands with the nails painted blood red and I've never used any nail polish other than a clear glaze in my entire life.

The little girl was tied to a waterwheel, one of those decorative ones that works. It goes round and round. At first the child smiled, thinking she was on a Ferris wheel. She wasn't scared, she thought it was a game. The wheel came up, up, and over. The up in the air part lasted a long time. She thought at first she'd be at the top forever, but then the circle started down, and it kept going until the part of the wheel where she was tied dipped under the water. When the wheel came back around, the little girl was dripping water from all over her clothes. Her hair was soaked. Her mouth was open and she looked like she was wailing and crying, however, I couldn't hear any sounds she was making. The wheel kept on going round and now the little girl kept her eyes shut tight because by this time she knew that she wouldn't be at the top forever.

What goes around, comes around. I always like to give my dreams a title. I had to turn on the bedside light in order to write that dream down. Sometimes I have to wake up two or three times a night to write down my dreams. Everyone has several dreams an evening. We dream constantly. Most of us, however, have been conditioned not to remember our dreams. It wasn't until I had almost the entire dream down on paper that it hit me, that little girl on the wheel, she was wearing the exact same dress I had on in the first part of the dream.

In some cultures people discuss their dreams. Instead of the morning news they discuss what they dreamed the night before as they eat their breakfast.

No one in my family appears to remember their dreams. There is a method which works every time. When you go to bed you set the alarm to go off every two hours. Generally, you'll catch yourself in the middle of some dreams and be able to write them down. This will work until you get yourself in the habit of waking up at the end of dreams, which is the best time, of course. Otherwise, it is like you are missing out on part of your own movies.

Robin is one of those people who doesn't remember her dreams as a rule. I used to be the same way, I have to admit. She's getting better at it, despite the fact that she can't use the alarm clock which can be set for three subsequent times in the same evening that I gave her for her birthday. Josh claims to have a hard time getting back to sleep if the alarm goes off over and over. That's just resistance, I told her. Josh doesn't want to remember his dreams. People are afraid of their dreams, I've been surprised to learn.

When Robin and I had a fight, it was one of those things that came out of left field. I certainly didn't see it coming. She was talking about this dream she had remembered and I pointed out that it looked to me like she was still searching for her lost parents, particularly her father, whom she never did even have a picture of.

"That's crap, Julia," she said.

I pointed out to her that her extreme irritation was proof certain that I had hit on a valid point. One thing led to another, and pretty soon we were slinging insults back and forth the way Mother and I still do sometimes. I never knew old Robin had it in her, to tell you the truth. I'm going to wait a few days and then call her up. I'll act like nothing happened and see what she says.

I REALLY COULDN'T believe that I had made it into my second year of graduate school. Back when I was in college for the first time no one would have taken me for the studious type. I got to wondering what kind of a psychologist I would turn out to be after Butch asked me what I was planning to do with a master's degree in psychology. That's the first I really thought beyond the courses I was taking.

Susie has her own law office; it is located in one room of the house Josh Winter renovated for his law office. She leases space from Josh and has office hours three and one-half days a week. I thought somewhat along the same lines myself. Although, of course, I wouldn't have rented space from Josh Winter. Actually, I did have a building in mind. It was one that Daddy owns—owned, I guess I should say. I am sure it must be in Mother's name now. It is an old two-bedroom house located in the block behind the shopping center that Millie and her husband built on the street where she had her beauty shop and he had his auto repair business. Millie and Harold tore down both those buildings and put in a strip center, which fills up one entire side of the main street, going from Ave. A to Ave. B. They put in space for five retail businesses. Millie's beauty shop is in the middle. On one side of her there is the Merle Norman place, on the other is a tanning parlor. The two outside stores aren't actually open yet, but one is going to be an antique shop and the other will probably become a new dress shop.

Cypress Springs is really growing. It seems to me that this town has certainly gotten to be big enough to support a psychologist. Heaven knows I could name a dozen or more people who need some good therapy. And that was just reeling off the names that came to me without half trying. Of course, I wouldn't be able to get started until I passed the state licensing exam, and if I didn't go on to get my Ph.D. I'd have to find someone to supervise me. If I am not mistaken, Dr. Schmidt ought to be able to supervise a psychologist. Since he is still the town's only medical doctor, I have no doubt he'd be sending me people to talk to once I opened up my office. You have no idea what percentage of the medical profession's time is wasted by people whose only problem is in their heads.

Verona, for one, is a perfect example. She's always running up to Dr. Schmidt for a new prescription of Valium to get her through some trial or another. Not long ago, I went to pick her up to drive her to a funeral. "Are you going to be okay?" I asked her. Her eyes were red and she was twisting one of those lace hankies that she buys by the gross. She likes to flap them around as if she was Miss Scarlett getting set to see Rhett off.

"Yes, I'll be fine," she said. "I took half a Valium this morning. And I have the other half in my purse if I need it." All this for a man she barely knew. She was only going to the funeral because his wife taught both Butch and me when we were in elementary school and she thought it would be rude not to go.

I told Butch I wanted to fix up the house on Terrell Street for an office. He said I'd have to talk to Mother, since she owns the house. "Talk to her for me, Butch," I said to him. She listens to Butch. Mother has a hard time taking me seriously. It is the result of her upbringing. She was never brought up to respect women. You should have heard the way she carried on about Susie becoming a lawyer. Susie is lucky she didn't need Verona's permission to open an office, otherwise she'd be operating out of her kitchen.

I'M NOT GIVING up on becoming a psychologist, but I can tell it may take longer than I originally thought. I woke up this morning and realized that I had overslept and that I didn't care if I was missing school or not. I decided to take the next semester off entirely. The sun was already so high in the sky my bedroom was like an oven. Danny had left some juice on the table for me along with the paper, which he brings home from town about nine or ten o'clock every morning. I called Robin before I remembered we were mad at each other.

"I'm sorry, I can't remember exactly what I said to you, but I am sorry," I said to her.

"Oh, Julia, I was going to call you. I never should have said you were too stupid to breathe. I can't believe I said that to you."

She was so down on herself that I laughed at her. Robin doesn't slough off things the same way as I do. I couldn't even recall her saying I was too stupid to breathe to me, which shows you how little effect her words had on me.

We were sitting by the pool when Gracie came home from school. It wasn't yet one o'clock, but she has arranged her schedule where she doesn't go a full day. Back when I was in high school, they'd have stuck me in study hall before they'd have let me hop in my car and drive home, but things are different now. "Mom, you're home today!" Gracie shouted when she walked out the back door.

"Yeah, I've decided one college student in the family is enough. I'm quitting." For the time being. I probably should have said *for the time being*. It still doesn't seem to me as if I could have a son who is a freshman at A&M. Gracie will be off to college in not all that long, either. Not that I'm going to go all Susie Homemaker, but it will be nice to spend more time with my daughter before she too goes off into the wild wild world.

"You're quitting school now? In the middle of the semester? Can you do that, Mom?"

"I can if I want to," I said. Robin got this knowing look on her face. Like she'd been expecting me to drop out of school ever since I started. But of course she couldn't have known that, I didn't know I was going to do it myself up until today.

That's the way it is with me, sometimes I don't have the first idea what I am going to do until I hear myself telling someone about the plans I have made. As soon as I hear myself say the words out loud, I know I've made the right choice. Sitting by the pool, I picked up Gracie's *Seventeen* magazine and started leafing through it. "You can't imagine how sick I've gotten of textbooks. It'll be fun to read a magazine and not feel guilty that I'm not studying," I said to Robin. Actually, I think I've learned about all I needed to learn. I'm bored with dreams and the last thing I want to do is spend three and one-half days a week sitting in some house up on Terrell Street listening to people like Mother yammer on and on about their problems.

Robin laughed when I said I'd learned my lesson with her, I was out of the analytical business for good. This is weird, but I think I am finally getting domestic. Or mellow. Or something. Lately, I've found myself thinking about stuff like planting new plants in the flower beds and that I need to get the inside of the house painted—things I haven't paid attention to in years. I even might like to take my daughter shopping. I used to swear I'd never drag a kid of mine shopping and force her to try on cutesy little costumes.

I reminded myself that I needed to spray the roses that grow on trellises along one entire side of my house. Mother doesn't have a rose bush in her entire yard. "Plant the first rose bush, it's an open invitation to bugs," she has always said. I'm glad I don't listen to her when she starts telling me what to do. I love the way the roses look cascading all along the side of the house. It hasn't been hard to keep the bugs at bay. I spray regularly and never let them get a toehold.

Mother drove up in the driveway about the time I was congratulating myself on not listening to her about what to plant in my yard. She has this sixth sense, I swear she does. Just when I'm telling myself I don't need her, she'll appear. She is totally perverse that way. Gracie was inside the house making cookies, but Robin and I were still out by the pool sunning. Rather, I was sunning. Robin, as usual, was coated with sunscreen and under the umbrella to boot. She's positively phobic about getting burned.

"I drove past the cemetery on my way out here. Maria was pushing Julie out of there. I didn't realize they had anyone buried in our cemetery," Mother said.

"I haven't inventoried the graves, so I couldn't tell you who they have buried where," I said to Mother. She was being snobby, implying that Mexicans don't get buried with the Methodists.

"But they are Catholics, aren't they?"

"How would I know, Mother? Why didn't you stop and ask them?"

"Julia! The very idea, that would be rude."

Robin was staring off into space. Whenever Robin is around and Mother acts like a jerk, Robin goes deaf and dumb. I decided now was the time to ask Mother something that had bothered me for a long time. "Mother, why did you act so mean when Daddy gave them that house?"

"I don't know what you are talking about, Julia."

"Yes, you do, Mother. After Julie's accident, when the Garcias needed a house to live in because the one they'd always lived in before burned to the ground, you pitched a fit that Daddy gave them the old house in town."

"I most certainly did not."

"Yes, you did. You told Daddy they should pay rent, that people who are given things don't appreciate them."

"I said house payments, Julia. I said the Garcias could pay on the house and then when they'd paid it off it would mean that much more to them."

"I'm glad Daddy didn't listen to you. Julie's family deserved that house!"

"Why, pray tell, did they deserve the house?"

"Because they worked for our family for years and years and they didn't even have any retirement. That is what Butch says, Mother. He said it was like Mr. Garcia's retirement to give him that house."

"Julia, your father, rest his soul, wasn't always perfect. If he and everyone else in town would have quit coddling that girl, she'd have gotten up out of that chair years ago and walked on her own two feet."

"Mother! Julie is paralyzed, she can't walk!"

"Little do you know! The doctors said there is nothing wrong with her, she just doesn't want to walk."

"That is not true, Daddy went down to Rosewood Hospital in Houston with Mrs. Garcia and talked to the doctors. You weren't there, you don't know what they said."

"I don't recall that you were there either, young lady."

"Daddy told me the doctors said that nothing appeared on the X rays, but that didn't mean that she didn't have some spinal cord injury that didn't show up on the film. Nerves are very minute things, Mother. Even X rays can't prove when they're hurt and when they are not. They said they had done all they could for Julie and she might as well come home. That is what the doctors told her, Mother. Why would Julie spend her life in a wheelchair if she didn't have to, Mother? Answer me that question."

"Why indeed?"

Robin stood up and stretched and yawned loudly. I think she'd ignored us for as long as she could stand to sit still. "Hot day, isn't it?" she asked. Robin isn't too good at things like changing the subject. She doesn't know how to be subtle.

"Yes, it is," Mother said. "That sun is so bright, it was a day just like this when Wiley Sutton was killed. That's the worst car wreck we've had to happen in this town since they put in the stoplight. Do you realize that? Poor Wiley, he was driving into the sun and plain didn't see the other car. At least, that is all anyone could ever figure out."

"Who are you talking about?" I asked.

"Wiley Sutton. Julia, surely you remember Wiley Sutton? The Suttons lived on the farm about four miles from the one my father owned. There were four Sutton children, Wiley was the youngest boy. He married some nondescript woman from over in Hempwell, they had three little girls. All of them younger than you, and none of them looked the first thing like you, either."

"Mother why on earth are you talking about Wiley Sutton? That poor man was killed over a year ago. For heaven's sake, Mother!" At first, I had no idea who it was she was talking about. She started in talking about that wreck like it had just happened. I've sort of suspected either she's hitting the bottle too much again or it's the Valium. Heaven help us if it is Alzheimer's. Butch and I won't be able to pay Lupe enough to keep her in the house with Mother if it is Alzheimer's. "Have you been drinking?" I asked Mother. Actually, it might be better if it is alcohol, at least we could keep that away from her.

"Julia, the very idea! It is not yet five in the afternoon. Of course I haven't had anything to drink. But I do feel fine today for some reason. So I think I will have something. Can I bring you anything?"

Mother acts like my kitchen is her kitchen. It used to irritate me when she'd walk in my house and take over, but what the hell, I can't change her and I've wasted my energy long enough trying. "No, thanks," I said to her.

"How about you, Robin? Can I get something for you?" she asked. Always the grande dame. I don't think Mother realizes everybody and their dog sees clear through her when she goes into her Southern gentlewoman charade.

"No, ma'am, thank you," Robin replied. "I ought to be getting on home," she said. "Ruthie is going to be wondering what on earth has happened to me. I never stay gone all day long." She didn't make a move to leave, though. As soon as Mother walked inside the house, Robin leaned back down on the chaise she'd been sitting on. We both sat there, enjoying the sunshine. I could hear Mother in the kitchen talking to Gracie. Mother says that cooking is genetic, Gracie got the gene from her, it apparently skipped me, however. They do both like to cook, although I am thankful Gracie is nothing like my mother otherwise.

When I finally had to go inside to go to the bathroom I am sure it was fate that prompted me to step into the kitchen at the exact minute I did. I heard Mother on the phone talking to someone about selling some land. I wish just once she'd consult me on this type of thing. Since Daddy has been gone, she'll call Butch and ask him before she makes the least little decision, but she has yet to ask me a single question.

"Mother, who are you talking to?" I asked her. It was after all my phone she was talking on.

"Clarence White, if you must know," she said.

"I didn't hear the phone ring."

Gracie answered me, "It didn't ring, Mom, Gram called him. She's going to sell him the back part of her property. Maybe. She is going to consider it."

I will admit that pissed me off. First of all, because if Mother doesn't have the decency to consult me on her business decisions you'd think she'd at least inform me what she is doing before she goes talking to my sixteen-year-old daughter. I said as much to her.

"It just came up, Julia," Mother said, "and I had no idea you would be interested. You don't care anything at all about the farm. If it weren't for Butch I'd have had to sell the entire place years ago. You have no idea how hard it has been on me, a woman alone, trying to run a business all by myself. It has been so difficult since your father passed on."

I hate the expression "passed on." Daddy didn't pass on. He died. And the stuff about her having to run the farm. What a crock. Mother never has known one end of a cow from the other. Butch has run the farm for them since he finished college. Daddy himself used to say if it hadn't been for Butch, he'd have sold out long ago. Daddy never wanted to be a farmer, he wanted to be a doctor. But he was the only son and he didn't have a choice. He told both me and Butch he never ever wanted us to feel tied to the family business. We were to choose what to do with our lives based solely on what it was we wanted to do. However, once Butch came home from college with a degree in

Ag and started working with Daddy and it was obvious he loved doing it, Daddy was glad to get out from under the entire farm and ranch operation. "It's all yours, son," he told Butch. Daddy often told me Butch was a better rancher than he'd ever been. "You love it or you don't, Julia," Daddy said. "There's no faking passion for your work." He meant what he said. After Daddy more or less retired, it was Butch doing the day-to-day scut work, nine times out of ten Daddy wasn't even there. He was off fishing. It just goes to show that Mother didn't know the first thing about her own husband, otherwise she'd have never said that about it being hard on her since Daddy died.

There is no point in mincing words with Mother. I said to her, "I think you ought to have your head examined, you can't sell off part of the farm. Have you even talked to Butch?"

"Clarence just called me this morning, Julia. I haven't talked to anyone at all yet. Of course I will consult your brother before I agree to sell any land."

I had known before I asked the question that she hadn't consulted Butch, otherwise he'd have told her that she couldn't sell the back part of her property. The pet cemetery is located there.

I wasn't sure if Mother knew the bodies were there or not. My guess was, not. I knew I was going to have to talk to Butch. I could see that. Otherwise Mother might have rushed out and signed something and gotten us all into no telling what kind of mess.

SUSIE

Julia came flying into my office this afternoon. She had a T-shirt on over her wet bathing suit and her hair was billowing out around her like it was electrified. *Déjà vu*, I thought. Will

Julia ever get too old to run into the room without her shoes on, demanding that I find Butch for her right this minute? "Julia," I said, "I really don't know where Butch is, have you tried the house?"

"No, I came straight up here to see you, Susie. You're a lawyer now, and heaven knows I think we are going to need one."

"What are you talking about, Julia?" I asked. From years of experience with Julia's emergencies, I knew when she was blowing things out of proportion. "Did you get a ticket for driving your car barefoot?" I teased her.

"No, I did not. Susie, this is serious business we've got to get settled. I overheard Mother on the telephone talking to Clarence White. That old letch, everyone in the Methodist Church knows not to let him near you when he offers you his arm to usher you to a seat in the church, he'll pinch your boob without thinking twice about it."

I started laughing the minute I heard what she said because, although I'd never had it happen to me, the minute Julia said what she did I recognized the truth of her words. They fit. I never have been comfortable around Clarence White, although I couldn't have told you what it was about him that bothered me.

"Susie, this is no laughing matter. Clarence wants to buy part of the farm, the back part along the river where we have the pet cemetery. If you could have heard Mother sucking up to him, giggling and acting all fluttery, you'd know that Butch and I have to stop her. We've got to stop her fast. Mother doesn't care that he's a letch, all she knows is that he's rich and his wife died years ago. Poor woman, probably head-to-toe bruises before she went." Julia shuddered. "Can you imagine being married to that creep?" she asked me. As usual, she didn't slow down and wait for an answer. "Susie, we haven't got a minute to waste," she rushed on. "Mother will end up giving the land to him if we're not careful."

"Calm down, Julia," I said. "I'll tell Butch tonight, Julia. Land sales take time. You don't have to worry, Verona isn't going to sell anything immediately." It *is* Verona's land. If she wants to sell it, technically that is her business. Of course I didn't say this to Julia.

"Look, Susie, I don't know what the word for it is, but I want you to go ahead and draw up the papers so that we can have Mother declared too nuts to sign anything. We'll nip this thing in the bud. Otherwise, I don't know, it could be awful." Julia gave me one of her dark tragic looks and shuddered again.

That might have been the end of it except Butch and Danny happened to be driving past and saw our cars parked out front. They decided to come in and see if Julia and I wanted to go out to dinner. Julia started right in. "Butch, we've got trouble. Big trouble. Clarence White wants to buy the part of the farm that's back beside the river. The pet cemetery."

"I heard that, Julia. He ran me down at the truck stop, said he'd called Verona, apparently she said it was okay with her if it was okay with me."

This was all Julia needed to hear. "You see what I mean, Susie?" she asked. "You better sit down right this minute and get started on those papers, we don't have a bit of time to waste."

"What papers?" Butch asked.

Julia gave me and Danny one of her mysterious looks. Uh-oh, I thought, here it comes. Sure enough, she turned to Butch and said, "Maybe we should talk in private, Susie and Danny don't need to hear all this."

Poor Butch. Actually, both he and Danny both looked sort

of dazed. "Julia wants Verona declared legally incompetent," I went ahead and spoke up. I thought I might as well let Butch see what he was up against.

"What?" Butch asked. "What is it you want, Julia?"

"Butch, don't make me draw you a picture, the part of the land Clarence wants to buy is the pet cemetery. Doesn't that seem a little, well, if not suspicious, highly risky, to you?"

The look Butch gave Julia was haunted. There isn't any other way to describe it. "Clarence said he wants some land back along the river because he'd like to have access out to the highway from the south side of his property. He wants a strip about five acres wide by about fourteen or so acres long. Nothing we would miss."

"But what will he do with our pet cemetery? Just stop a minute and think about that, Butch Salwell." Julia's hands were on her hips and her eyes were flashing. She'd have made a hell of a trial lawyer, I thought, if she could have managed to keep herself on one subject long enough to argue a case. Even as I realized that not a word she was saying was making sense, I found myself hanging onto her words with bated breath. I guess Butch and Danny were probably doing the same thing.

"The pet cemetery?" Butch asked.

"Yes, Butch, the pet cemetery! Now watch what you say, don't go blurting anything out," she cautioned him.

"Julia, none of us even have any pets any longer. Mother doesn't, you and Danny don't, Susie and I don't. I think we can safely say our pet cemetery days are over." Butch smiled at her. Julia did not smile back. When she's intense, that is all she is.

"Suppose Clarence goes digging back there?" she asked.

"Why would Clarence go digging, he doesn't have any interest in pet cemeteries. It's a road out to the highway he wants, Julia," Butch said.

"Butch, I don't know exactly why Clarence might get to digging around, I just know that the possibility exists that it might happen. We can't risk it." Julia scowled at Butch, who doggedly returned her look.

"Come on now, Julia," he said. He sounded like his father, I realized. I took a good look at Butch and noticed how much he'd grown to look like his father. He was probably as tired of these histrionics as Tom got to be. They are only humorous in retrospect. Julia was still holding forth. "Butch, I've seen them build roads. First thing that happens is they go in with bulldozers and dig. I'll bet you'd forgotten all about that, hadn't you? They'll have to dig back there to put a road in." Julia gave Butch a triumphant look as if to say she had proved her point.

"Okay, sure, I'll talk to Clarence, explain that's where we buried the pets, ask him to make sure the graves don't get disturbed. Thing is, Julia, when was the last time you were back there? It's been so long, I'm not sure we can even tell where the graves are any longer."

Julia should have been calming down, instead she was looking more and more upset. Butch could see it, so could Danny. None of us understood what she was so upset about.

"All right, I'll have to go ahead and say it. Don't blame me, you're the one who pushed it to this point. Ask your wife if you don't believe me. She's a lawyer now. Susie will tell you. There is no statute of limitations on murder, Butch."

Danny, who had been lounging against the wall over by the door stood straight up. Butch looked like someone had knocked the wind out of him. Me, what was I doing? I pulled a yellow legal pad over to me and picked up a pencil as if I was going to start taking notes.

"You heard what I just said, Butch, don't act like you didn't," Julia said. She'd forgotten that there was anyone else in the room, all her energy was focused on Butch. She started striding back and forth in front of him. "You helped him bury the bodies, you're guilty of something, you know. Don't think simply because Daddy is dead that all the danger of this coming out is past."

Butch blinked several times and wiped his hand across his eyes. He was concentrating so hard at this point that he had this intense frown on his face. I realized that I'd been holding my breath and slowly started letting the air escape. *Who knows? Who the hell knows what is going on in her mind?* I thought.

Butch nodded his head so vehemently that it looked like his head had fallen clear down to his chest. He didn't give up, though. "They were only pets, Julia," he said. "A couple of dogs, who knows how many goldfish, the Easter bunny, that cat without a tail you found on the highway."

"Butch, don't think you can skate out of this by acting dumb. Juan and Juanita are there. You know good and well that's where they are. They weren't under the patio. The pet cemetery is the only place they could be. I can't believe you could have forgotten that. Either you show me where they are and we'll get out there first thing in the morning and move the bodies, or that land stays in the family."

Butch was totally confused, but Danny stood over by the door there looking calm and unflustered. If anything, the look on his face was one of pleasant expectation. Actually, I don't think he knew what was going on either, but he'd gotten real relaxed about Julia over the years. I suppose it was that or fritz out the way Butch looked like he might be doing right about then.

"I don't remember any dogs or cats named Juan and Juanita," Butch said to her.

"Butch, don't be dense, the migrants, I am referring to the migrants." Julia looked over at me and said, "Remember, Susie, you are our lawyer so what you are hearing is confidential."

"Right," I said.

Neither Danny nor I tried to interject anything into the conversation. When Julia gets on a tear, everyone sort of takes a backseat and lets Butch deal with it. When she's like this, she won't talk to anyone else, anyway. Besides, Danny and I certainly didn't know anything about Julia's childhood pets. What could we have said at that point?

"Are you talking about migrant pets?" Butch asked.

"I am talking about the boy and girl Daddy shot! The prowlers! The ones you helped him bury! You can't have forgotten them, Butch. Don't try to act like you have."

Surely they didn't shoot some of the dogs and cats, I thought.

"That's what this is about?" Butch said. He nodded his head as if he'd finally gotten something sorted out. "Daddy didn't shoot them, Julia, he shot *at* them."

Julia didn't listen to all of what Butch said. She kept on talking, "I heard him shoot them, Butch, and I won't lie on the witness stand either. So you'd better stop Verona because if those graves come to light then it's your neck on the chopping block."

"Julia, hush a minute and listen to me. Daddy shot *at* the kids who were in our yard that time. That's who you're talking about, aren't you? That night those kids from the migrant worker camp were looking in our windows and Daddy shot through the door at them. The whole incident scared Daddy so bad that he got rid of his gun, wouldn't have one in the house after that."

"He got rid of his gun because it was a murder weapon,

Butch," Julia said. Her jaw was squared like she was getting ready to do battle. *She really could have been a lawyer,* I thought for the second time that afternoon. "Daddy got rid of the gun so it couldn't be traced to him when the bodies came to light."

Butch gave Julia a sad, sweet smile. "No, sweetheart. Daddy got rid of the gun because he couldn't stand to have it around anymore. He said he'd been lucky, he wasn't going to chance Lady Luck a second time. The night his shotgun went off he blew out most of the glass panes in the French doors; he said he learned his lesson right then and there. No more guns."

Julia didn't look quite so sure of herself any longer. Her eyes were flickering back and forth uncertainly. As always, once the fire and furor died down, I caught myself feeling sorry for her. "Mother screamed her head off, Butch. You know she did."

"Yeah, she did. So did you, Julia. You two screaming like banshees along with the sight of two people right outside the door to our house is what startled Daddy so bad he came to pull the trigger. He told me later he never had a worse scare in his entire life. He'd been through Pearl Harbor, shot and been shot at, got wounded, but nothing compared to the way he felt when his gun went off and he saw those two poor scared-looking kids standing there looking right at him."

"They were dead on the ground, Butch," Julia said. Her voice came out whisperlike. "Don't you go lying to me about that." Then her shoulders slumped. I noticed she'd quit tossing her hair back out of her face. You could barely see her eyes for the curtain her hair made across them.

Butch was out of his chair, reaching out for her. "They weren't dead on the ground, Julia. The poor kids were so scared they probably wet all over themselves, but neither one of them was hurt. They stood there staring at him until Daddy shooed them out of there. 'Get back on home,' he told them. And they got."

"Butch, Daddy took you outside with him to bury the bodies."

"We fixed the hole in the door, Julia. It had been raining all that week, the rain was coming in. We taped it up. Daddy had me take the gun out to the truck and lock it in the lockbox. The next day, he carried it over to a gun dealer's and sold it. Didn't want it in the house."

"I saw blood."

"No, you didn't, honey. You must have imagined that part."

"No, I didn't, I don't imagine things!" Julia said. Then she burst into tears.

Butch's arms were still reaching toward her. He stood motionless, I don't think he realized what he was doing. First his eyes moved as he watched his sister cry. I could tell he was blinking back tears himself. I don't think he realized when his head began to move sadly, back and forth. We all of us stood there for what felt like forever.

It was Danny who finally walked over to Julia and put his arms around her. As soon as he did that I started breathing again. For a minute or two, Julia sobbed quietly into Danny's shoulder. At first we were all too dazed to think. Finally I moved, too. I walked around my desk to where Butch stood. He put his arms around my shoulders and pulled me up against him. Butch started talking, speaking softly. "I hadn't thought of that night in years, Julia. It really was pretty awful. We'd had lightning and thunder off and on for hours. And then that mess. Afterwards, Daddy and I taped cardboard over the entire door opening. The whole time we were working, his hands were shaking something awful."

I could tell the exact minute Julia started to recover. She straightened up and scowled at Butch. "Why didn't you tell me Juan and Juanita weren't dead? You should have told me the truth, Butch," Julia said.

"Aw, honey, I never knew you thought they *were* dead."

"All these years, Butch! It isn't as if I didn't have better things to do with my time!"

Julia isn't the only person to come out of that family who defies belief—that's what I thought when I heard Butch apologizing to Julia for not telling her her father hadn't actually murdered two people and he and Tom hadn't actually dragged the bodies down to the pet cemetery and buried them.

"That's okay," she said. Her voice was magnanimous as she forgave him. "It wasn't really your fault, Butch. I was right all along to blame Mother. She *said* it was my fault those poor kids were dead on the ground, that if I'd stayed in bed where I should have been, none of that would have happened."

Butch wiped his hand across his face again. I know that gesture. It's what he does when he wants to make sure the tears he is feeling don't show. "Oh, shit, Julia, you ought to know you can't take what Verona says literal. Especially when she's upset. She was upset that night. I remember her carrying on about the mess in the den, her good door all busted to smithereens."

"I don't exactly recall going to bed, Butch. I remember getting up and getting you and Daddy because I was scared. I remember the noise the gun made and the sound of the breaking glass. The next thing I remember is Mother screaming and telling me to get myself back down the hall, I was to blame for whatever had happened and if I knew what was good for me I'd get myself back to bed and let you and Daddy clean up the mess I had made. Mother said all the three of you ever did was clean up the messes I made." I don't think Julia had any idea that there were tears running down her cheeks again.

EPILOGUE

BUTCH

My Lord, I never knew that Julia thought we'd buried two kids in the pet cemetery. I said to Susie that it boggles my mind to think Julia could have ever in her wildest dreams thought Daddy and me capable of doing such a thing. I'm sure it was one of those times she got an idea in her head she didn't think through, otherwise she'd have seen right off how ridiculous she was being. It is her imagination. Julia has always had this imagination that sometimes runs away with her.

Julia's off to Paris now, and it's not the same with her gone. After all was said and done, we didn't sell Clarence the land he wanted. Not that Julia getting upset was the deciding factor. However, the more I thought about what she said, the more it seemed to me she was right. Her reasoning was wrong, but I got to where I agreed with her conclusion. We don't need the land for any practical purpose, but it is part of our family history. Sure, we haven't got pets right this minute, but that's not to say we won't someday. Both my boys are married, I imagine I'll be a grandfather before too much longer. Grandkids are likely to want little puppies and little kitties. And there are Julia's two as well. Who's to say at this point what they'll be wanting. Why go selling off land for no good reason? Someday we may need a pet cemetery. Or a pretty spot along the river.

That back fifty-odd acres, even if it is too marshy for cows, is a pretty spot. Daddy and I taught Julia how to fish back there along that river. Daddy'd bring some fish back from the coast and we'd slip them on her hook when she wasn't looking, back when she was little enough to where we could get away with a stunt like that. She'd give the cutest little squeal and jump for joy every time she pulled her fishing line out of the water and saw a big fish dangling in front of her. Once we even built a campfire and cooked the fish for her right there on the spot. I don't know if Julia remembers all of that, but I do. I went back there to the cemetery with Susie after Julia told me the crazy thing she'd been thinking all these years.

"It's pretty here, it's like it isn't part of the farm at all. Just look at all these gorgeous trees with moss hanging down from the limbs," Susie said.

"You've seen this place before," I said to Susie.

"Never," she replied.

That surprised me, to realize I'd never thought to bring my wife back to the river. The boys and I had gone back there to bury some of their pets, but my kids had never had to have funerals the way Julia always had to have them. I suppose, with one thing and another, Susie never got back there with us. I wished I had thought to bring her before.

"This is a nice place for a picnic," I said to Susie. "Julia always loved picnics when she was a kid. Maybe you and I can start picnicking."

SUSIE

Butch thinks he's changed. The more he changes the more he stays the same. First thing he asks me when he comes in every day is, "Did you get the mail? Anything from Julia?"

He and Verona are just alike. Verona's on the phone the

minute the mail gets to her house. "Nothing from Julia, have you heard from her?" You'd think Julia had been gone three years instead of three weeks.

ROBIN

Julia called from New York. "I'll be home tomorrow," she said.

"Did you have a good time?"

"The most wonderful time you can imagine. Robin, you aren't going to believe this but . . ."

Right about then we got disconnected. I can't wait for her to get home to tell me what it is I'm not going to believe.

JULIA

I don't plan to make a big deal out of this, but I think I must have been French in my last lifetime. I felt so at home the entire time we were in Paris. When people talked French, even though I don't understand a word of that language, it was like I comprehended every single thing they were saying. The whole time we were there I kept saying to Danny, "This place fits me! This is where I belong." I am sure I must have been French in my last lifetime. It makes sense to me. I've got a call in to Doris up in Austin. I remember she told me about this lady she knows who can help you get in touch with past lifetimes. Robin says she's not the remotest bit interested in going with me, but I know Robin. When all is said and done, she'll go along.